Frances Paige was born in Scotland and is married to a psychiatrist whose thinking, she admits, has greatly influenced her approach to characterisation in her novels. A prolific writer under her own name, *Three Girls* is her first novel under the pseudonym of Frances Paige. She and her husband live in Lancashire and travel regularly to south-west France, her second love.

Three Girls
Frances Paige

CORGI BOOKS

THREE GIRLS

A CORGI BOOK 0 552 12503 2
Originally published in Great Britain by Souvenir Press Ltd.

PRINTING HISTORY
Souvenir Press edition published 1983
Corgi edition published 1985

This book is set in 10/11 Cheltenham

Corgi Books are published by Transworld Publishers Ltd.,
Century House, 61-63 Uxbridge Road, Ealing, London W5 5SA,
in Australia by Transworld Publishers (Aust.) Pty. Ltd.,
26 Harley Crescent, Condell Park, NSW 2200, and in New
Zealand by Transworld Publishers (N.Z.) Ltd., Cnr. Moselle
and Waipareira Avenues, Henderson, Auckland.

Made and printed in Great Britain by
Hunt Barnard Printing Ltd., Aylesbury, Bucks.

Three Girls

PROLOGUE
May, 1968

'NOW that they've closed the Sorbonne, I'm beginning to worry. Do you think we should still go?' Tricia was ready underneath her candlewick dressing-gown. ('Easy to wash, dear,' her mother had said. She believed in cutting chores to the minimum.)

'Our café is certainly in the same *quartier* as Gay Lussac.' Crystel, whose beauty was a matter of curves, warm brown hair gilded where it waved back from her brow, teeth rounded where they met the pink gums which matched the pink lips, beauty enhanced by artifice. And a pale mauve chiffon negligée. Her mother, Tricia thought, is a peasant in south-west France and mine is a well-educated Englishwoman full of good works. There is no justice.

'Jan. What do you think?' When the three of them had arrived at the Language School in Boulevard Raspail last September, it was her rich accessories as much as her American accent which had appealed to Tricia. 'Momma bought all this junk for me . . .', junk including the Vuitton vanity case in which she was now rummaging. 'She's got French ancestry, Leroy was her name, from *Le roi*, she says. I didn't say "no" to a year in Paris.' Nor had Tricia, with time to wait for her University place and parents who didn't want her hanging about.

'Think?' Jan used her hands like a French girl. 'It's not a question of *think*. It's Crystel's birthday! She'll never be nineteen again, I *am* nineteen, you've *still* to be nineteen!' her voice rose in a wail.

'But . . . barriers at Gay Lussac, cobblestones wrenched up, old cars, anything they can lay their hands on.' Tricia had read out the news to them this morning. The student unrest

7

hadn't escaped them even in the Boulevard Raspail where the pupils were a comparatively sedate bunch, not to be compared with the dash of those at the Sorbonne.

Crystel had shed her negligée while they were talking. She stood, a mini-skirted vision, white-booted, *sac* over her shoulder. 'I am ready. General de Gaulle has said that violence cannot be tolerated in the streets. Besides,' her smile was ravishing, 'he will know it is my *anniversaire*.' Her accent had a huskiness, the vowel-flatness of the Midi. She had come to have it ironed out, to make her career in Paris.

'That settles it,' Tricia said.

* * *

Their friendship had started when the three girls were allocated to the same attic bedroom high above the Boulevard Raspail. Perhaps it was their very differences which had drawn them together. We complement each other, Tricia had thought, to whom the other two were at first like strange birds of paradise.

She had only known Latham and conformity, small-town conformity. Paris was liberation, a stretching of the spirit. Jan and Crystel had backgrounds she was never tired of hearing about, and the friendship which grew between them was based on a mutual liking and curiosity about each other. Crystel she recognised as a true-born sophisticate in spite of her rural upbringing, Jan as a romantic, unsure of herself, moody, but given to wild bursts of enthusiasm. It took Crystel to point out that they were all small-town girls.

Sometimes as they went about their haunts in Montparnasse, window-shopped in the *Vaugirard boutiques*, sat in the cheap little cafés around Place St Sulpice, strolled on fine Sundays in the Luxembourg, joined in the crowds thronging the Boulevard St Germain, (Jan and Crystel hoped to meet the Sorbonne students there), Tricia would have the feeling that something was being nurtured in the three girls which would become important to all of them later. She said this once and Jan looked surprised.

8

'You could be right. Anyhow it's what I dreamt of back in Johnstown, to be on my own, the fun . . .'

Crystel's golden-brown eyes held Tricia's. 'You are perceptive. For me too it has meaning, even more so than learning to speak with a Parisian accent. It is like the construction of a house in our village. I have watched them at work, the slow shaping of the limestone, the tiling laid so carefully. A good house takes care and time.' She burst into laughter at their serious faces. 'So does a *cassoulet!*' Then she was saying in a peasant woman's raucous voice, *'J'aime bien manger.'* Vowels flat.

Those talks were a revelation to Tricia. She was an only child and she'd never had close girl-friends. Her mother was too busy with voluntary work to keep open house, her father did his entertaining for the Bank outside. Her life from the time she went to Grammar School had been directed towards examinations, and the year in Paris was by way of being a reward for her success. She also had a suspicion her parents were worried at the sudden upsurge of teenage parties, and the young men who'd appeared on the scene. (Although she'd overheard her father saying he wouldn't mind if she married well.) A feather in his banking cap, she'd thought.

'What do you think of Paris?' They'd gone up one day to Sacre Coeur to get the view, and were sitting on the steps. 'I mean, really think. What has it done for you?'

'Paris is Paris, no more, no less.' Crystel shrugged. 'My heart is elsewhere.'

'It's funny you should think like that and look like how you do. You're so smart.'

'*Chérie,* beneath every smart suit in Paris there is someone who longs to touch the earth. Who dreams of his place in the country.'

'I guess Paris is an escape for me,' Jan said. 'So far nothing but *nothing* has gone right in my life. I know you think that's crazy, Tricia.' She was more French than the French the way she used her hands. 'I've never pleased my mother. Poppa's okay, but she thought working in a Playgroup was just the end although I loved the kids. Paris is my last hope. Where I'm going to find myself. Maybe *her* last hope.'

'Paris,' Tricia said slowly, 'is for me the three of us setting

9

out, not knowing where we're going. I don't think we'll ever forget it . . .'

*   *   *

The café was crowded, and they had difficulty in finding a table. Crystel fired the *ripostes* as they squeezed into the only vacant one at the window. It wasn't the French Tricia's mother had hoped the School would impart, but it was greeted with respectful admiration. Crystel bowed, her short skirt flicking as she sat down. 'I can be *bien-levée* where necessary.' She smiled at the girls as she lifted the menu. '*Les grenouilles,*' she announced. 'That will be my treat for the *anniversaire.*'

With the frogs' legs they had champagne, Tricia's treat, and then the *ragoût* which was Jan's, a concoction whose origins were masked by an aromatic battery of spices. From time to time the *patron* appeared behind the bar to shout at his wife who was serving. He spoke sharply to a young man who'd spilled a carafe of wine. Jan looked apprehensive, her hands fluttering over her plate. 'He's jumpy tonight. Ask the girl next to you if she's heard anything, Crystel. I've got a feeling there's going to be some kind of a bust-up.'

'Sure, kid.' Crystel liked to give an international flavour to her conversation. She bent forward and whispered to her neighbour, barely knife-and-fork distance away.

'I'm psychic tonight.' Jan smiled apologetically at Tricia. 'And this is, sure as hell, horse.' She pushed her plate away. Tricia tried to look non-committal. When slang took the place of Jan's Baltimore accent, it was a sign she was upset.

Crystel was back with them. 'Mademoiselle here says nothing has happened yet with the police. She's not worried. She's staying here.'

'Good, I'm starving. *J'ai la dale.*' Tricia also liked to give flavour to her conversation. Her voice was drowned in a sudden shouting and screaming in the street, of people running.

'Oh, come on!' Jan said, jumping up, white-faced. The window beside them burst with a dull heavy sound, a stone flew through it and struck her a glancing blow on the forehead, then smashed against a mirror. 'Oh, my God!' she said, sitting down again. 'Oh, my God!' Blood was streaming down her face.

There was silence for a second before the excited babble of French voices broke it. Tricia began to struggle out of her seat . . . sympathisers drew their tables out of the way . . . but Crystel was already bandaging Jan's head with a chiffon scarf she'd been wearing.

'I think it only grazed you, Jan.' Tricia had reached her. She saw the shock in the girl's face and tried to speak calmly. 'Could you get up, do you think? We'll get a taxi to the doctor.'

'Oh, yes, get me out of here!' She rose, swaying, and, supporting her on either side, they pushed their way to the door. Some of the other diners had decided to get out too, others who'd remained at their tables looked up as they passed, whispering to each other. The *patron* was going mad in the background, waving a towel like a referee in the ring.

'An innocent young lady! And my window broken by those imbeciles! This place doesn't pay as it is and now everyone goes . . .'

'*Quel idiot!*' Crystel muttered. She left them and went to the bar, came back looking even more indignant. 'In Maurac they'd have given us that on the house!'

Outside, the narrow street was blocked with people pushing against each other, some in the direction of the Luxembourg, others towards Rue du Four. A student on a chair, (where had he got the chair?), shouting, 'The old order has grown old!', was causing the crowd to swirl and eddy round him. Tricia saw the chair wobble precariously, and then he disappeared as if he'd slid down a manhole.

'Don't worry, Jan,' she said, 'we'll soon get a taxi.' She saw Crystel shake her head. Not a hope. 'D'you feel better?' She was falsely cheerful.

'I think so. My goodness, what a thing to happen.' She was still pale. One side of her black hair swung stiffly with dried blood.

The crowd was a tightly-packed entity, a frightening swaying beast. 'What's the hold-up?' she asked Crystel.

11

'*Les barricades.*' Flat-vowelled, cryptic. She could see the worried frown.

And then it was like a film in which they had bit parts. Black-clothed visored police were suddenly there as if they'd erupted from the sewers, laying about them with batons, faceless behind riot shields, breaking up the tightly-packed crowd into people who fell, struggled to their feet again, screamed, groaned, swore. The girls, still locked together, were swept along with a troop of students and pushed into a police van with them. Through her shock Tricia heard the wailing of the sirens as they went speeding through the streets, and all around her the excited talking of the students, much of it unintelligible. She put an arm round Jan who was leaning against her, met Crystel's eyes. The beautiful face was calm. The shoulders shrugged. A Gallic shrug.

*   *   *

They were shaken out of the *saladier*, as she heard Crystel call the police van, and herded through the main office of a Police Station into a room which had '*Salle D'Attente*' in an illuminated box above its door. It was locked behind them. Tricia, keeping her arm round Jan who was speechless with fright, saw Crystel in another part of the room. She was talking earnestly with a group of students. She's okay, she thought, she can take care of herself. Jan's different. She needs someone. And me? I'm frightened to death, and yet, strangely, I'm excited. I'm being tested . . .

'They won't have room in the cells for us.' She turned to the dark young man who had spoken. 'It's a small station.'

'What do you think they'll do?'

'Rustle up some staff and keep us here. March you girls off if they can find somewhere else, for facilities, you know . . .' He looked at her. 'Are you scared?'

'Worried,' she said, trying to smile. Her face felt stiff. She could feel Jan trembling against her. 'My friend got hurt . . . in a café.'

12

'Poor thing. It happens. To the innocent as well. I should not worry, though. We are unimportant. Any moment now they will be storming the barricades. Do you realise that?' His voice rose. 'Any moment!'

'Who'll win?' she asked, which struck her, even in her dazed state, as a very English remark.

'The students, of course! *Mon Dieu*, to think I'm missing it!' He clutched his forehead.

'You're safer here.' She thought she should point that out.

'What is safety? Safety!' His black eyes were scornful. 'That is the word for cowards. Freedom is what matters. Perhaps mademoiselle, freedom for the individual will mean more to you now that you've been swept up from the streets like rubbish and brought here. Locked up like a criminal against your will. *D'accord?*'

'*D'accord.*' It was beginning to make sense. A police officer in an important-looking uniform came in and addressed them sternly. Several people said, '*oui, monsieur.*' A girl began to weep. He went out again, locking the door behind him. It was beginning to make even more sense.

'He issues warnings,' the young man said, 'threats. Our day will come. Student movements are international, a reflection of the state of society. Don't believe people when they tell you we demonstrate in a spirit of adventurism. Or only for the sake of student reform.' His voice changed. 'You're English, aren't you?'

'Yes.'

'I thought so. You have that look. But magnificent eyes.' He narrowed his own. '*Voyez*, our solidarity with the oppressed wherever they are cannot be over-emphasised.' He shook his finger at her, said in apocalyptic tones, 'You, my dear mademoiselle, are caught tonight in the trap of naked truth. This is your last chance . . .'

'*Attention!*' Stentorian voices interrupted the young man's flow. A policeman and policewoman had come into the room. They talked so fast, one following the other, that Tricia only caught snatches of what they were saying, 'separation,' 'miscreants,' 'punishment . . .'

Fear filled her, bowel-loosening fear. She tightened her arm

13

round Jan for her own comfort also. Crystel had joined them now. She heard with relief the laconic voice translating. 'The men and women are to be split up as soon as they can find accommodation. Toilet facilities are available, but the authorities must be approached, and each person will be conducted singly to the appropriate place. Failure to obey rules will result in punishment.'

'I'd be too scared to go,' Tricia said, deciding to forget about her need.

'They don't know what's hit them,' the young man said. 'It's only a branch station. The central ones are full up.' And, looking admiringly at Crystel, 'my name's Jean Paul, by the way.'

*   *   *

Fear and tiredness reduced the volume of talk but it still went on quietly. Tricia became fanciful through lack of sleep, and thought of herself as being like L'Île St Louis, the steady, whispering flow washing against her like the Seine. Jan sat up occasionally, pale but calmer, and joined in. Her hands fluttered.

Waves of talk, swelling then dying again at the commands of *'Silence!'* from the policeman and policewoman stationed in the room. 'Arrangements are being made . . .' Their words came to her from far away. She was in a daze, still seeing herself as L'Île St Louis, and that the Seine, that quiet but persistent flow of talk, was wearing away, bit by bit, her smooth ramparts, her preconceived attitudes.

She pondered on what the students were saying, and felt under her skin for the first time in her life, the tragedy of Vietnam, the poverty of the Third World, the misery of badly-paid workers. She whispered once to Crystel. 'As a Bank manager's daughter, I've led a very sheltered life.'

'That's it! That's what it's all about, don't you see?' Jan's fear had gone, temporarily. 'We *needed* this. It *had* to happen to us . . .'

14

Crystel shrugged. 'Every Frenchman is a politician.'

'Well, of course,' Jean Paul said, 'the English and the American mademoiselles have nothing to worry about. One word from their Embassies and they'll be released.'

'What about me?' Crystel asked.

His mouth turned down in a smile. 'With looks like yours, *chérie*, who needs Embassies?'

* * *

In the early morning something happened. There was shouting, cheering in the streets, which was taken up by those inside. The girls found themselves on their feet with the others, singing The Internationale, being kissed by many unshaven faces, embraced by tired-eyed girls.

'We've won! It is victory at the barricades!' Jean Paul said.

'How do you know?'

'Didn't you hear the cheering? Good news travels fast.' He was catatonic with excitement. 'Freedom for the individual! Everyone is with us. You've lived through history tonight! You've seen the Established Order collapse!'

* * *

The two sentries had summoned help at the outburst. Once again Authority was in the room, in its important uniform, quelling the talk with an upraised hand. *'Silence!* Decorum if you please! You will follow my subordinates quietly . . .' Fear showed on everyone's face. The three girls stayed close together.

'Where are they taking us?' Jan's temporary excitement had gone. Her eyes were dark with terror. To the guillotine, Tricia thought wildly. She had been deluding herself that they were going to get off lightly.

'They may have found separate cells for us,' Crystel said. 'Just follow and don't cause trouble.' You'd think, Tricia said

15

to herself, that she was in the habit of being swept off the streets 'like rubbish', every night of the week . . . the cold early morning air struck their faces. They were going down steps.

'Is it to a dungeon?' Jan said, her voice shaking.

'No, we're in the street! We're free!' Crystel was jubilant. 'They've decided to let us go! Empty us out the way they emptied us into the *saladier*. Come on!'

They linked arms and began the long walk back to Boulevard Raspail. They were on the opposite side of the river, but Tricia had a good sense of direction and Crystel seemed to have cat's eyes. The streets were quiet except for small groups of people who were hurrying as they were hurrying.

They walked quickly, forgetting their tiredness, the relief of being outside making them light-footed. 'Free!' they said to each other. 'You have to be imprisoned to understand what it is to be free!' There was a seed of joy buried somewhere in Tricia's tiredness, Crystel's eyes were bright, and Jan, the scarf off now, showed her blood-caked bruise like a badge.

*   *   *

That night drew them closer together. Previously their conversation had been mostly personal. Now they talked about what life meant and why things were the way they were and why some people had so much and others so little. And that it might be necessary to examine their conscience and decide what they stood for.

Long afterwards, when Tricia was to think of those days, her clearest image, apart from the traumatic experience in the police station, was of night-time in the bedroom high above Boulevard Raspail, Jan's hands fluttering as she talked, Crystel's robe like a mauve mist round her, the emanation of her beauty which was as tangible as the French texts on Tricia's knees. She was the only one who worked in bed.

For, of course, they remained true to type. As the examinations grew closer Tricia studied more diligently, while Crystel and Jan did the minimum. 'You are foolish not to come with us,'

Crystel would say, 'you have *chic*, even if you are a little reserved. But those eyes . . . they'd go mad at the Sorbonne for those eyes.'

Crystel and Jan had profited in more ways than one from their incarceration that night. There was a constant stream of invitations to parties in other attic rooms in Montparnasse. Sometimes, as they came creeping in with the dawn, Tricia, turning over on her pillow, would reflect that being the star pupil for the year was small consolation.

Jan became dreamy and dark-eyed because she had fallen in love with a law student. 'It's the real thing, I guess . . .' Crystel was besieged by admirers but took it lightly, even allowing the girls to laugh over her *billet-doux*. But she didn't let herself be monopolised. Didn't she have her career in Paris to think of?

* * *

It was she who suggested they should go to Rue Vaugirard and buy souvenirs. 'We are friends for life now,' she said. 'That terrible night made it so. It was the . . . come on whizz kid, what was it?' She appealed to Tricia.

'The cement?' She remembered Crystel's house analogy.

'That's it. The bond. *Regardez*, before, we were like new-born kittens. We have many at home because my mother can't bear to drown them. Eyes closed against the world. Now our eyes are open.'

'Gee, that's so *true*,' Jan said, touching her bruise or what had been her bruise. At one stage she'd hoped it would leave a permanent mark on her forehead like the German students with their ritual sword slashes.

'We have a kind of . . . Sisterhood now,' Tricia said, feeling shy as she said it. 'Let's make a pact to live our own lives . . .'

'And not follow the pattern set down by our parents,' Jan put in.

'My parents don't set down any patterns,' Crystel said.

'You know what I mean, clever French cat. We grew up

17

that night. Our eyes were opened, just as you said. Our souvenirs will stand for that.'

'Remember Jean Paul?' Tricia smiled and raised her hand in the air. 'Freedom for the individual!'

They bought keyrings with a clover-leaf medallion in silver. As she pointed out, 'They're trefoil in design, which is symbolic. Three girls, three nationalities, three words, Liberté, Egalité, Fraternité. She laughed. 'And I'm being pedantic.' She'd begun to criticise herself more since 'that night'. Anyhow, they're bound to come in useful, and it's better than cutting our wrists and writing our names in blood.'

*   *   *

They parted with many promises, and tears from Jan; many tears. Tricia was going back to Latham, soon to start University, Jan to Johnstown in Maryland . . . she was lukewarm about that . . . Crystel to spend the summer with her parents. She would apply for jobs from there, although she agreed that no letter could adequately convey her new-found Parisian accent. 'But you see, I have to be back in my village for a time. The longing is deep and strong. Can you understand?'

Tricia didn't feel like that about Latham. It was home, certainly, but simply a stepping-off place. And after University, London would be her goal.

CHAPTER ONE
December, 1968

TRICIA Baker that was, Mrs Roger Newton for the past four months, stood with her champagne glass in her hand and felt the baby move inside her, an eerie sensation as if her body had split into two living parts. Roger had told her to remain seated, as had his mother who took an overly-sentimental interest in 'Roger's baby', but at nineteen it seemed ridiculous to join old Mr Deakin wheezily filling the arm-chair in the corner. Now well over eighty, he was the astute bank manager who had financed the Latham Development Trust at its inception.

Howard Newton, Roger's father, was paying tribute to old Malcolm at this moment, standing in a strategic place in front of the Rococo fireplace . . . Tricia had pleased him when she'd first visited the house with Roger by identifying it as Louis Quinze, and hadn't added, 'fake'. In Paris last year she'd seen its original in Madame Pompadour's apartments in Versailles. She listened to the assured voice,' . . . great honour, Malcolm, to have you here today in our humble abode,' felt her attention wander again.

The furniture of the room, in odd contrast to the fireplace, was mostly Victorian, its shining surfaces a source of pride and joy to Mary, her mother-in-law, who thought the fireplace 'too fancy for Latham', perhaps because its intricate shell motifs and curlicues prevented it from being easily polished. 'Our dining-table has a bloom like a damson plum compared to the one at The Crescent,' Tricia had said to Roger. Already she found house-keeping tedious, resorted to synthetic spray-on polishes as a quick aid to the problem. 'Mother only uses vinegar and water,' he'd said so seriously that she'd laughed and then kissed him when she saw the surprise on his face . . .

'Of course we're all sad that the Old Man isn't here to

celebrate with us today, but no doubt he's looking down on us from above.' Quick quirky smile, precursor of a joke. 'I've no doubt he'll be kept busy up there building illustrious mansions at competitive prices, if I know Jolyon Roger.' He was referring to his father, the founder of the Trust.

Everyone laughed, especially the younger members of the office staff who had also been invited. Howard believed in making them feel part of the firm. Each applicant for a post was interviewed in the board room under the portrait of the great Jolyon Roger. One young girl let out a high pitched giggle, and Tricia saw Miss Baines, the supervisor of the typing pool, give her a sharp-elbowed nudge.

'But at least we have his old and valued friend here, the man who supported and believed in him in those early days at the end of the First World War, the man who occasionally applied the brakes but supplied the cash.' The emphasis at the beginning of the two words brought another laugh. 'The first transaction my father made, and Mr Deakin will bear me out in this, was to buy a row of terrace houses at one hundred pounds each and sell them for ten pounds more!' There was an unbelieving titter. 'Small profits and quick returns, that was the way of it, eh, Malcolm?' Howard flashed his handsome regular-toothed smile. Tricia had never found out if they were his own. 'Sleight of hand on the dentist's part if they are,' Roger had said when she asked him. He always looked a little surprised at her direct questions.

Old Mr Deakin rumbled, moved in his seat, hemmed and hawed. His voice was surprisingly soft coming from such a big frame, a barely audible whisper. Maybe years of speaking confidentially to his clients had made it reflect his discretion.

Not like my father, Tricia thought. James Baker was Malcolm Deakin's successor. He's the jolly keep-in-the-cupboard type. When Roger had proposed to her he'd said, 'I'd jump at the chance if I were you. We're LDT bankers, always have been, it couldn't be more suitable. Never mind your University place. Yes, I know you had plans for a career, but that can come later.' Her mother had said little in comparison. Perhaps she was too busy giving advice at all her committees, perhaps it was because Tricia had never asked for it.

Her mind had been fixed on marrying Roger with all the single-mindedness of an eighteen-and-a-half year old Catholic girl who felt she couldn't go to bed with a man she wanted without the blessing of the Church. And then, while she was uncertain, knowing she wasn't in her right mind, or her usual logical mind, Howard Newton had swung the balance. The two families had been dining together one evening and he'd taken her aside.

'I know you'd be giving up a lot, Tricia, a bright girl like you, but I want to say this. Roger needs you. You're like me, strong . . .' She'd thought of David, her brother who'd died and how he'd needed her, and it had put an element of sacrifice into marrying Roger, made her bury the knowledge that her feeling for him was mostly lustful, compared with his passionate adoration. And now there was the baby coming, 'our first intentional mistake', she'd called it . . . she came back to Mr Deakin who was wheezily eulogising Roger's grandfather.

'Jolly Roger, he liked to call himself, you know. Had a quick mind, liked a joke. Put adverts in the papers under that name . . .' His voice died away as if he'd used up the air in the room.

'And can you remember any of those adverts, Malcolm?' Howard looked round smilingly like a 'feed' on a stage. 'What about the Trust's emblem?'

'Ah yes, the flag . . . that evolved, don't you know.' The old man's voice was like squeaky chalk, 'Jolly Roger, the Pirate. Those adverts . . . ' he shook his head, puzzling, 'let me see . . .' His face cleared. "Let Jolly Roger . . . sell your house for you." That's it. "Make your dreams come true." ' Everybody laughed and he said with the petulance of the old, 'I ain't finished.' A fresh intake of breath, like bellows working. "the nail them . . " it came with a wheezing rush, ' "to the Jolly Roger Mast!" ' Everybody let themselves go this time, even Miss Baines who took off her severe spectacles and wiped her eyes.

'What a showman he was,' Howard said, standing up. He sat down again because the old man was wagging his finger pettishly at him.

'Everybody's in such a hurry these days, hurry you into your

21

grave, they would . . . I was going to say, young Howard, that's how the idea of the flag emblem, er, evolved. He always insisted on it being printed alongside his adverts, drew the original himself, nothing he couldn't do. And later when he gave up being a house agent and became the founder of the Latham Development Trust, thanks to the Bank, of course, he, er, *incorporated* the initials "LDT" in the centre of the flag. Like it is today on every piece of notepaper, envelope . . . '

'Even on the Trust tie,' Howard put in.

'I was going to say that. Little flags.' He nodded several times, looking around, rumbling like a spent volcano, 'That's the way it was.'

'And that's the way it is,' Howard said, seizing his chance and getting to his feet. 'A proud emblem which the public recognises as representing security. Thank you, Mr Deakin.' There were still a few subterranean rumblings but he cut across them. 'And now to the reason for our little celebration here today.' He spread his feet apart, settled himself comfortably on the Bokhari rug. 'The good news.' The whole works now, Tricia thought, feeling a soft kick against her lower left rib. 'Will he never get to the point?' Roger muttered in her ear. 'All right, darling?' She nodded, smiling, not looking at him.

'Shouldn't we have the bad news first Howard?' a loud voice asked. It belonged to Richard Forsyth, the Company solicitor. Tricia had gone out with his son, Nick, before she went to Paris. He had presumed she might travel lighter if she lost her virginity to him. She hadn't. But it was at a party he'd taken her to that she'd met Roger. His approach had been different, shy, appealing. 'Don't go to Paris, I've fallen in love with you . . . '

'Spoken like a legal man, Richard. But there *isn't* any . . . ' The love in Roger's eyes had stayed with her, restraining her. No, that's nonsense, she thought, and why am I harping on about Paris today? Is it this kicking baby which is reminding me that my freedom's over before it begun! All those fine ideals . . . I've lived in a dream-like gratification of the senses those last few months, a kind of organic state. She looked up at her father-in-law, erect, chest out, handsome, rich-suited, the smooth features dominated by the high-bridged Newton nose. I

22

was willingly manoeuvred . . .

'A piece of nostalgia first.' He smiled round indulgently. 'Sit down, Tricia,' Roger murmured, 'he'll go on for ever.' She shook her head impatiently, she enjoyed standing, feeling the baby move inside her. 'The Kingsley Heath Estate was bought by me when I was twenty-two years of age in 1942 . . . ' Howard's eyes sought out his son's . . . 'three years before you were born, Roger. I was home on leave. A real snip. Father was always a bit of a buccaneer, liked to see it in me. He let me put in an offer to the Government which was accepted. There was a great deal of farm land and an airfield which the RAF held at a nominal rate. Twenty years later when it was closed down the land reverted to the Trust.' He waved a hand. 'Are you still with me?' There was an amused murmur.

'We let the hangars for factories and such like and decided on our great project for the rest, the building of a Garden City to be called Kingsley Heath.' He spoke softly, forefinger raised. 'But along came the dragon. A by-pass was planned by the County Council which would cut right through the middle of our land.' He looked in the direction of the two grey-haired men standing near Tricia. 'How long have we fought that legal battle, chaps? Come on, Bob?'

'A decade, Howard. Ten years to a day.' Tricia remembered Mr Pritchard, the Trust's accountant, at her wedding, and his dull-looking wife. Why is it forceful men always have dull wives? Look at Roger's mother . . . she still found it difficult to call her 'mother-in-law', felt too young to call her 'Mary'. She seemed only to come to life when Roger was there, dwindled in the presence of her husband. She liked showing Tricia photographs of her son which she kept in a carefully-annotated album, 'a small secretive boy, my Roger'. Her father-in-law was neither small nor secretive, standing there booming confidently at his captive audience.

'Right. A decade of legal hassle which you all here have coped with efficiently and with little or no friction, a difficult matter when you're dealing with any local council.' He might have singled out Roger, Tricia thought. He's sat through that interminable Enquiry practically every day since we've been married, and years before. He's worn out, drained . . .

23

His father's quick smile flashed out, seeming to bring together the people in the darker corners of the large drawing-room. There was an expectant hush. 'I said I had good news.' Tricia saw he had a letter in his hand. He waved it above his head like the Jolly Roger flag. 'We have received formal approval of our project, the Kingsley Heath Garden City!'

There was a burst of clapping, raised glasses, a murmur of talk. Few in the room, she thought, with the exception of the junior staff, could have been surprised. Roger had told her a week ago. Still, you had to be generous. She joined in the clapping, bending forward to speak to Roger. 'He's terribly pleased. No wonder.'

'There's more to come.' Roger looked pale. She'd noticed it before, a kind of general fatigue, a lack of stamina. Maybe his father sucked his strength. She'd wanted sometimes to tell him not to be browbeaten, but it was less tangible than that, and besides she was too young, too unsure as yet of her position in his family.

Howard was holding up a hand. Quirk to the handsome mouth. Joke coming. 'Pray silence for the bearer of even better news!' He waited for and got the expected laughter. 'This decision couldn't have come at a better time. You all know the huge Research Complex which is being built on part of the Estate? The hush-hush Government place? It's now completed, and when it's fully staffed it will employ over two thousand people! Now where do you think they're going to find houses?' His eyes caught those of the young girl whom Tricia had noticed. 'Miss Farquharson, Gillian, isn't it? Another glass of champagne if you can tell us the answer.'

The girl blushed, Tricia saw her being nudged by Miss Baines, and then she stammered, 'Kingsley Heath, Mr Newton.'

'She's hit the nail on the head. Fill up her glass, Roger. If she's off work with a hangover tomorrow, you'll forgive her, won't you, Miss Baines?'

'I'll see what I can do, Mr Newton,' Miss Baines said, looking prim, and yet her eyes weren't, there was a momentary flicker, a familiarity. Did he call her by her first name in private, Tricia wondered. She believed it was Stella. Roger said she'd always doted on his father. Maybe they'd been

24

lovers. Stella made her sound . . . different. And with her hair loose and her glasses off . . . oh, stop it, she laughed at herself.

'Of course we've a lot of work still to do,' her father-in law was saying. 'We need a special diversion for Kingsley Heath and we've to obtain site approval for those factories which will be affected by the road diversion. But I know I have a staff of surveyors, architects and planning officers ready and willing to meet this challenge. We'll employ further specialist help as the project proceeds . . . so it's all hands to the plough now. This firm, started by Jolyon Roger Newton in 1920 . . . there's his picture behind me, same nose . . . ' he tapped his own and there was ready laughter, 'has been founded on initiative and drive, on the understanding of the man in the street and his problems. In our own humble way we've been responsible for maintaining a high level of stable employment in this area, and in a larger context we've been partly responsible for a major social change in the outlook of many people in that we've helped them to own their own homes.'

'Hear, hear!' Mr Deakin rumbled. 'Couldn't have done it without the help of the Bank, though.' He lifted a warning forefinger.

'Right, Malcolm, but benefits on either side, eh? Where did the money come from for those fine premises of yours in Market Street?' Tricia saw her father half-rise from his chair, his arm up, like the best boy in the class.

'From satisfied customers.' He let out a loud guffaw. Latham was proud of its Bank on the corner of Market Street and Royal Street. Tricia as a schoolgirl had boasted about her father working there. The palatial structure had given her early a sense of his importance. It had certainly given him a sense of his own. 'Well, James, I'm sure at last one of those fine Corinthian pillars belongs to the Trust!' The light touch again. Roger, she thought, all his life has had to be like those people here, an admiring audience. 'What was it my father said? "Nail your dreams to the Jolly Roger mast." Now it looks as if they're going to come true. Kingsley Heath will be no bungaloid land, that I promise, no dull rows of houses like peas in a pod. Kingsley House, the original mansion of the Estate will become

25

our focal point. You know it well as a Natural History Museum . . . ' his voice went booming on.

It came back to her. The interior of the mansion with its chequered hall, the showcases with their stuffed birds and beasts, their dried flowers and ferns. David, her brother, had loved it. She remembered how his feet drummed with excitement on the step of the go-chair . . . they didn't call them that now . . . as they went between the stone pillars and up the rhododendron-lined drive.

'Show me Cock Robin, Tricia. Hurry!' She remembered the wasted face lighting up when she stopped at the showcase with the small world inside, the nursery rhyme in artefacts. He'd been feather-light in her arms, unplanned child, she suddenly thought, as if her own pregnancy had told her this. His constant ailing had saddened their home. Part of the jingle came back to her. 'I said the dove, I'll mourn for my love . . . ' Sadness gripped her, nostalgia for her own girlhood, remorse for things not done.

Had that been why she'd always tried to please her parents, an attempt to make up to them for their sadness? She'd worked hard at school. In Paris she'd been too studious. Paris . . . with the name came remembered sensations, smells, and how she'd thought her first Pernod was the most decadent thing she'd ever tasted . . . was it because of David that she'd wanted a baby?

Behind her day-dreaming there was still the steady booming of her father-in-law's voice, like the rhythm of the sea. '. . . built round a village green, little courtyards, pleasure parks for children . . . ' and the picture he drew had the same kind of dream-like substance as the world behind the showcase in Kingsley House. Both were creative concepts, the nursery rhyme world had been expressed in moss, stone and bracken, Kingsley Heath was still in Howard's mind. It would be marvellous to be involved in it . . . something was happening. The voice which had been a background to her thoughts had faded, stopped.

'What's wrong?' she whispered to Roger. And then the person who'd blocked her view had moved and she could see Howard holding himself straight, almost too straight.

'It's a dream I've carried in my mind for a long time. We

26

hope to have the first show-house completed by . . . ' the voice faded again, ' . . . and the first family move . . . ' She saw the ruddiness drain out of his face as if a tap had been turned off, the glass he was holding fall and roll on the carpet.

'Get him to sit down!' a man's voice called behind her. As if he'd been challenged Howard pulled himself straight, lifted his chin to speak again, then his body crumpled in a boneless kind of way on the floor.

The roomful of people acted as if they'd been stirred with a stick; people were talking, others hushing people from talking, others again giving advice. She found herself with Roger, kneeling on the carpet beside her father-in-law. His eyes were open. The expression was more of disbelief than pain.

'Don't worry, Father. Take it easy.' Roger's voice was shaking. Tricia, stroking Howard's cheek, turned to see her mother-in-law behind her, hand held to her mouth.

'Howard, what is it? What's happened?' She went down on her knees, lifted one of his hands ineffectually and began to rub it. 'Oh, Roger, what is it?' She was whimpering. Howard turned his head away impatiently.

'Get a rug and cushions, Mother. Hurry, hurry!' Roger was distraught. A lank piece of hair had fallen over his brow. They looked alike.

Trica helped the weeping woman to her feet. 'Yes, do that, Mrs Newton. He'll be all right.' Mrs Pritchard was there, sensible in her navy-blue dress with its white pique collar and revers.

'Come along, Mary.' She put an arm round her. 'I'll help you to find them.'

Tricia bent down to Howard. She thought he looked less grey. 'Roger will stay with you. I'll go and phone the doctor.'

'Good girl.' He nodded. 'Too much damned fussing around here . . .' he closed his eyes.

She pushed through the confused crowds in the hall towards the telephone. She knew Dr Chapman's number. Mrs Newton had recommended him for the baby 'because he was always so good with Roger'.

Mrs Chapman was brisk once she had separated true from false. 'I'm not sure if the doctor's in . . . oh, it's Tricia *Newton*!'

'I'm at my father-in-law's house. He's just had some kind of a turn.'

And then, the grey voice like the man himself. 'Don't worry. I'll be right over. Told him to let up a little.'

CHAPTER TWO
April, 1969

WHEN Tricia was in the nursing-home after the birth of Emma, she had a letter from Jan Sirica stamped in Paris which surprised her.

> *'I came across my clover-leaf keyring the other day, and I thought, I must write to you and Crystel. You were the one with the big words, tripartite and all that jazz, but we had something going for us, always will have . . .'*

Oh, God, yes, she'd been prune-mouthed. And prudish. The flower-decked room, the smell of Roger's pink roses mixed with talcum powder and disinfectant, swam away to be replaced by that top-floor bedroom in Boulevard Raspail. What had *it* smelled of? Girls and beeswax, deodorant? and no clinical neatness, no envelope-cornered bed. Clothes everywhere, shoes, bottles, pots of cream, books.

She remembered Jan's laugh, her blue-white, slightly prominent teeth. 'My teacher at Johnstown High School used to warn us against small town mores. Have you never heard the corny old joke about Columbus? That's another no-place.' Those waving hands. 'They say America has still to discover Columbus . . .'

She lifted Jan's letter, glancing at Emma, the rounded skull with the soft fuzz of hair, Roger's nose, the Newton nose . . .

> *'You'll remember George Cook and how I couldn't see anything else for him. He was Paris for me. You didn't go to any of those parties. I bet you're a real egg-head by this time. I bet too you didn't jump into bed with a man as quickly as we did. With me it was just George. Or maybe you didn't tell us . . . sometimes I thought you were putting us on, those great eyes of yours . . .*
>
> *'You knew my background, rich kid, parents no time for*

29

blacks. Sometimes I think Momma sent me to Paris to get away from them. They were all around us in Johnstown. Momma is really of the old school, Ettie, short for Etienne . . . I guess I must have told you that. I was always going on about her. George is proud of being black. Black and bright. His father was killed in 1960 in the Detroit race riots, a steel worker. That made a lot of difference to George. He wanted to be accepted for what he was, not turned down because of his colour. He got to study in Paris because of a scholarship he won. He was mad to see France.

'I didn't sleep with him to spite my mother. Can you believe I never thought of George as black after the first night? Crystel knew how I felt. There's not much racial prejudice with the French. What I didn't tell either of you when you left was that I wasn't going back to Johnstown. I lied at first, wrote and told Momma the Course had been extended. Well, I stayed here with George and I had a baby last December, George Clayton Cook, I kind of knew it was coming when I wrote home. I was terrified. Clay's four months old, coffee-coloured with black astrakhan hair like his Poppa's and I think he's just cute . . .'

Tricia lent back against her lace-trimmed pillows, her shoulders shaking with weak laughter. Jan, with a black baby four months older than Emma, had pipped her at the post. She'd been going to write too, give them a surprise.

'I guess this is my confessional day. I'm going to write and tell Crystel as well. I was ill for a time and couldn't . . .and then there was all kinds of trouble with my parents. They were so bitter . . . I suppose you couldn't blame them, the irony of fate and all that. I don't want to remember those letters from mother . . .

'But today I felt happy. I had a letter from her asking me to send a picture of Clay. I cried and cried. I didn't tell you. George and I aren't married. He's got some funny ideas, and with me being ill and everything, I guess we never got round to it. We've just gone on living and loving together and it doesn't seem to matter here in Paris. In Johnstown that would be something else.

'Funny, I said this was my confessional day and yet I'm not a

30

Catholic like you and Crystel. Crystel once said English Catholics were more religious than French ones. The ritual was there for her when she needed it but she didn't feel somehow that she was sinning if she went against the Church's teaching, morally, I mean . . .

Nor should I, now, Tricia thought, lifting her eyes. She'd grown wary of the conventional Catholicism she'd known at home, brought out like a 'device' in times of stress, when David had died, or as a moral contraceptive to prevent her from sleeping with Roger without the blessing of the Church. I'd be different, in Paris . . .

'We have a little apartment in St Denis, and the people around are kind. It's laughable to think we all came to perfectionner le français, except Crystel, of course, who wanted to get rid of that adorable Midi accent, and here am I bargaining at the market with the other French housewives. I keep my eyes open for Jean Paul. Didn't we talk after that night with him in the police station, discovering ourselves, discovering the world . . .

'All I've discovered is that I'm a small town girl. I've not been very clever but I love George and I adore Clay. Crystel, I bet, is leading a life of luxury in the Rue St Honoré . . . I see her as directrice of a perfume company . . . while you, well, you were the whizz kid. You'll be a don now . . . isn't that what they call them in England? With letters after your name, or shaping that way, anyhow if I know you, you'll be the toast of old Academe.

'Write and tell me all about it for the sake of our Sisterhood . . . how we laughed going into that shop but felt solemn at the same time . . . and tell me if you ever see that man, Roger something, whom you said had fallen for you before you came to Paris . . .'

She looked up as the door opened. Roger was smiling at her, the same quirky smile as his father without his self-confidence. He came eagerly towards her, bent down and kissed her, then caressed her face with his hands. 'Pansy-eyes.' He'd called her that on their honeymoon. 'You look beautiful. I love you very much.' He sat down on the bed, put his hands on her shoulders and drew her towards him.

31

'Careful. I'm tender there.'

'Oh, I'm sorry.' He reacted too quickly to mild reproofs. 'But you're feeling all right?'

'Marvellous. Are you eating the food I left? You look thin.'

He laughed. 'There's enough in the freezer to feed a family of five for a month. Mother's always adding to it. And your mother pops in from time to time.'

'"Pops" being the operative word?'

'Yes. She's been elected president of the Golf Club now. And there's Parky blundering around and making cups of tea all over the place. Poor soul, she's harried to death with her husband and the kids, especially Minnie, and God knows what else. I'm harried too.'

'In the office?' He nodded, gave a long-suffering sigh.

'How's your father?'

'He's pretty good. Organising everybody. You know father. He's always . . .'

'. . . on your back?'

'One step ahead of me even when he's supposed to be taking it easy. But, honestly, Tricia, now he's talking about bringing in another man.' His face darkened. 'I'm not good enough, I suppose.' I shouldn't have started this, she thought. 'His dream town's rapidly becoming my nightmare. Those spine roads . . . the chartered surveyor he's put in over-rides all my decisions. It's infuriating.'

'Let him get on with it. You've got to learn to delegate too.'

'That's all very well but father expects me to know every detail so I *have* to get involved.'

The conversation had a familiar ring. She always seemed to be bolstering him up. Although she hadn't any experience of business she often felt she could have handled the problems better than he did. She recognised it was difficult being the boss' son, especially someone like Howard, but you had to assert yourself. Roger's complaint was that people found him easier to get on with than his father because he saw everyone's point of view. She'd never like to tell him that it was because he so rarely had one of his own.

'Then I'm getting endless complaints from the factories which have to move. I can see their point of view . . .' there it is, she thought. 'This man, Caldwell, he's just got his business going after a hard struggle, and he says he can't afford the loss of time in shifting his machinery. I suppose I shouldn't be sympathetic.' He smiled wistfully at her. 'You know me, Tricia. I've never been able to bulldoze people. I'd have been happier without that bloody LDT flat fluttering above my head. I'm sorry, I've brought the Trust along with me.'

'Never mind. You've got to get it off your chest. Do you realise you haven't looked at your little daughter?'

'I didn't want to disturb her.' He went round the foot of the bed and stood at the cot looking down on the sleeping baby. He touched her face gently. 'She's lovely, the bits that aren't like me.'

'You're very handsome and you're fishing. All the Latham girls were mortified when I married the most eligible bachelor in town, you know that. You just want me to say it.' She smiled at him.

He came back and sat on the bed again. 'The luck of it,' he said softly, looking into her eyes. 'Sometimes I can't believe my luck. The agonies of jealousy I suffered over Nick Pritchard, and then you hopping off to Paris for a year. I was crazy about you.' He bent forward and kissed her gently, his hand finding her breasts, a gossamer touch. Fondling was important to him. 'Miss you darling, in bed,' he murmured in her ear, 'it seems so long.'

She felt the sexual tug, the same sensation as when Emma was feeding. She pushed him gently away. 'D'you know who this letter's from?' She lifted it.

'Another of your admirers?'

'I thought I'd only one. It's from Jan Sirica, one of the girls I met in Paris. She had a black boy friend, American too, and she's had his baby, last December.'

'Good God, are they married?'

'No, they haven't bothered.' She saw the coolness in his face. 'And her parents are racist.'

'Bit of a blow for them.' His distaste was evident.

'You sound shocked.'

'What nonsense.' He blustered a little. 'People can have any colour of babies they want, in and out of wedlock. I'm just

33

seeing it from the parents' point of view.'

She laughed, exasperated. 'Why not see it from Jan's? She met this man, fell in love with him, and through carelessness or design, she had his baby. It happened to us.' She was conscious of a smugness about her own position, safely married, with a white baby, wife of the son of the town's most influential citizen. A copybook rightness.

But underneath the smugness there was envy of Jan, of her courage to fly in the face of convention. Freedom for the individual . . . *her* parents pushed her into it, she thought, as mine did. And as Roger's father did. I'll never influence my children like that. Her eyes met Roger's, and she felt ashamed of the love in them. 'Oh, don't look so solemn, small secretive boy.' His mother's words came into her head.

'I was watching your face. Are you really happy?'

'I'm very happy. I've got you and a lovely baby. And I'm coming home tomorrow to look after you. You're fading away.'

'They want you to stay in for a day or so more. I had a chat with the gynaecologist. The baby was a month early, don't forget.'

'How the Latham tongues wagged at that!' She didn't feel so prudish. She turned her mouth to his, and as she lifted her arms she felt a dragging ache. She held her breath.

'What's wrong?'

'I don't know.' She tried to laugh. 'Something down below, as Parky says. Poor Parky . . .' She remembered the doleful gynaecological details she liked to fill their coffee break with.

'You've gone white.'

'Have I? Well, I'd better ring for the nurse. You trot off home.'

'No, I'll wait.' He sat up and slid off the bed to stand anxiously looking down at her.

'Don't get all hot and bothered.' She felt frustrated and miserable and there was a sickening aftermath to the ache now. The nurse came bustling in.

'What's this husband of yours been up to?' she said, dimpling, and then her expression changed. 'Something wrong, ducky?'

'Nothing much. Go outside, Roger. Have a coffee or something at the canteen.' She said as he shut the door reluctantly behind him. 'Husbands are the end, aren't they?'

'Mr Newton didn't look any too happy when you were having the baby. Some of our husbands quite enjoy it. But he was whiter than you . . . now let's see what's going on . . .'

I don't like this lark at all, she thought, child-bearing. I could have been strolling about the University without a care in the world, in old Academe with the dons . . .

CHAPTER THREE
December, 1969

SHE scarcely knew where the time had gone since Emma's birth, and here she was, having a family dinner party, a week before Christmas.

For the first three months after the baby's arrival she'd been debilitated, the result of what Dr Chapman called a slight toxaemia of pregnancy. Sometimes she wondered if it was the result of a slight degree of resentment at finding herself married with a child before she was twenty when she'd meant to do so much with her life.

She'd lost weight, and her face took on an angularity which it was never entirely to lose. She didn't realise that the thinner lines gave her eyes an added beauty. She hated herself in the mirror, was sometimes shrewish with Roger, and thought of Emma as a kind of rubber stamp on their marriage. All those high ideals in Paris, she'd think. I'd do it differently again . . .

But then new life rushed into her. She'd gone to bed one night feeling miserable and wakened a new person. 'Look at that laburnum against the blue sky!' she said, sitting up in bed. The glory of their house, if it had any, was in its setting of trees. Emma became the most beautiful baby in the world and she adored caring for her. (Emma was naturally all sweetness and light at this turn of affairs.) She even enjoyed the routine of housekeeping although she had sense enough to know that wouldn't last.

Roger was in the seventh heaven at the change in her. He'd always taken his temperamental colouring from her, and his fearful nature had been even more cast down while she'd been unwell. 'I'm taking you away for a holiday,' he declared. 'We deserve it. Don't laugh. Mother will take care of Emma and

36

we'll get in a nurse to help her. Father can like it or lump it.'
He was as near being masterful as it was possible for him to
be.

In fact, Howard was just as enthusiastic. Since his own
illness there had been a bond between he and Tricia, and he'd
called often to see her.

'You're the only one who knows I'm going through an
identity crisis,' she'd said to him once.

'Maybe so. We need you, Tricia. Besides you're like me,
you'll snap out of it when you're ready. You'd offend your own
idea of yourself if you didn't.'

She and Roger went to Corfu in June and spent two glorious
weeks there. She noticed almost for the first time in six months
she had a body, and while it was a bit skinny, that she could
enjoy using it again. They swam, walked, danced, soaked up
the sun. Roger said she would wear herself out.

He'd been without her far too long, and they had a second
honeymoon which proved to be a good deal more sophisticated
than the first. There were new skills and pleasures to learn.
Their bodies, tanned, fit and deprived, were eager pupils.
Sometimes she thought she was more eager than he was. They'd
leave the pool in the middle of the afternoon to go up to the
shuttered bedroom and make love. It was their 'blue period',
she said, blue sea and blue sky. She didn't want it to end.

*   *   *

And now she was pregnant again. She blamed the second one
on a slight attack of guilt after that holiday in Corfu. She
hadn't as yet told the family. Her mother would say, 'How
nice,' hiding her surprise, and her father would make his usual
joke about another customer for the Bank.

Everything had gone wrong on this day of days. Mrs Parkin-
son, 'Parky', her help, hadn't turned up, but had sent word
with one of her brood that she would come as soon as she
could. The youngest had been 'taken bad.' Tricia had set to
herself, wishing she hadn't waited for the promised assistance in

37

the first place. The house was large and difficult to run, and had been bought for them by Roger's father as a valuable piece of property rather than as a suitable home. 'Live in it for a year or two till you look round,' he'd said. 'We shan't lose money on it. You never lose money on a house if it's in the right location.'

Help was impossible to find in Latham. The factories on the periphery employed most of the female labour, and now that the new scientific complex at Kingsley Heath was operating, the remainder had been mopped up. Only born losers like Parky were left.

She didn't think a great deal of the dinner she was preparing, conditioned by this time to the foreign dishes which the young marrieds liked to put on . . . 'We discovered this way of doing Vichyssoise in a little place in France.' She laughed at their foibles but conformed. Howard, however, liked plain fare with no fancy sauces. The turkey was sizzling away happily in the oven, but she was engaged in stuffing green peppers with force-meat, and keeping an eye on a piquant sauce. 'There are other people besides your father,' she had said firmly to Roger.

'Everything has to centre round Grandad,' she said to Emma, who was banging on the apron of her chair with a spoon. 'And you know you've bested me, you little so-and-so. As soon as I've finished this, off you go to bed.' She looked at the dark eyes raised to her, the irises circled in a soft purple which merged into the brown, thick dark lashes. 'Your eyes,' Roger said. She'd never been vain, perhaps because the emphasis had been placed on attainment at home.

The only really beautiful girl she'd known was Crystel Romaine. I suppose I had a crush on her, she thought, tasting the sauce from the wooden spoon. But not a sexual one, otherwise I should have been jealous of Jan . . . the telephone rang and she wiped her fingers free of forcemeat and went running along the dim hall.

That was another thing she disliked about this house, its lack of light. The ceilings were high, but the rooms were lit by a single tall window. There was none in the hall.

She lifted the receiver. 'Hello,' she said.

'Tricia,' she heard the deep, pleasant voice, 'it's your favourite

38

father-in-law. Am I interrupting your preparations?'

'No, I've nearly finished. Hey, don't tell me you're going to call off tonight?'

'Far from it. Mary and I are looking forward to it tremendously.' It was as if the mention of his wife's name made him more formal. 'I'm phoning to ask you a favour. I've got a man here, the new Planning and Sales Manager for the Heath. I was interviewing today.'

'Yes, Roger told me about it. Do you really need someone at this stage?' she said, greatly daring.

'Yes, I do, Mrs Roger.' He'd said more than once that she was a straight talker. 'Things aren't moving nearly fast enough for me. We need someone to integrate the next move.' He spoke as if Roger didn't exist.

'Roger's done all the groundwork.'

'I know he has. But he's got himself bogged down with the rehousing of the factories. He's a detail man, Roger.'

'But details take a lot of time. I think he was quite looking forward to the next stage.' And he'll think I've been swigging the cooking sherry. 'He really works terribly hard.'

'Only a tenth as hard as I did at his age, or one-twentieth as hard as Jolyon Roger. I know him, Tricia, through and through. Too much on his plate hassles him.' He laughed as if he'd said too much. 'Besides he's got a beautiful wife to come home to. I don't want to deprive him of that pleasure. About this man. Would it be all right to bring him along with us? I've asked him to stay overnight at The Crescent. He's from London.'

'Of course. I've got a mammoth turkey.'

'Fine. His name's John Russell, commonly known as Jake, he tells me. I'm winning him from a Property Development outfit in the south.'

'Stealing him, more likely.' She heard him laugh. 'We'll be delighted to meet him. Must go now, father-in-law. Emma's still up. Good-bye.' She hung up feeling glad about the stuffed peppers but sorry for Roger. It was tactless of his father to bring his new protégé, or at least she knew Roger was bound to see it that way.

Parky was in the kitchen playing with Emma. She was a big shapeless woman who looked about fifty years of age but was

39

actually thirty-six. Her features were lost in fat, but when you looked you saw the unlined skin, the fine eyes, the girl she'd been. She was a bad organiser, her children were always ailing, and the whole family seemed to have worn a path to the doctor's surgery. But her good-nature was boundless, and the smile she turned on Tricia was warm.

'Oh, Parky, you're here! Good. I've got nearly everything done. Would you put the vegetables on, except the stuffed peppers, that's those things on the baking sheet.' Parky's catering didn't stretch to stuffed peppers. 'And would you fill the water jug and put it on the table. Put some ice in it. Mrs Newton only takes water. Oh, and give the serving spoons a bit of a polish. They looked dull when I laid them out, but remember to wash them afterwards.' Once there had been a metallic taste permeating the lasagne she'd prepared with great care for a young marrieds' dinner party. She lifted Emma and made for the door.

'My youngest had a fit before I come out,' Parky said. 'That's what held me up. I sent Betsy to tell you I'd be along when I could.'

'Yes, she told me. I'm sorry.' She'd stayed to play with Emma which had been another hindrance.

'I don't like to say to the others it's a fit, leastways not to Betsy. She's delicate. I told the eldest and he kept saying, "Throw me a fit, go on." She always wets herself, you see, and it's clean knickers and *he* was late, "betting shop" I said to him but he just laughed and asked what there was for tea, men . . .'

'I'm sorry, Parky.' She realised she was waylaid. 'I mean about Minnie. Can't the doctor do anything about her fits?'

'Well, they're not coming so often now she's got those good pills. He says she wouldn't have any at all if I gave her them regular but you can't be everywhere at once, can you? *He* takes nothing to do with it, say's it's none of his bloody business though I'll admit he's good with her when he's there, but I say neither is betting mine, but you keep me short on account of it . . .'

Tricia felt the familiar guilt when she was regaled with what went on 'back there', as Parky called her home, guilt at her impatience, and an even deeper sense of guilt at being so fortunate when poor Parky was so deprived.

'Don't stay more than an hour,' she said, 'just do what I asked you then scarper. I really wanted you to wash up, but you shouldn't have come at all, leaving little Minnie.'

'Oh, she was out of it before I came away and Royston,' this was her husband's unlikely name, 'can look after her. To tell you the truth, Mrs Newton, lovey, it's a treat to come to a nice house like this and leave him to get on with it back there. Does me a power of good.'

Tricia felt guilty again at disliking her 'nice house'. 'If you do decide to stay, of course I'll pay you double.' She shut the door behind her on what was fast becoming a problem as much as a benefit. Perhaps I'll take to social work like mother, she thought, if my conscience is going to give me so much trouble.

She went into the nursery and put Emma into her cot, tucked her up firmly, bent and kissed her, full of maternal love for a second. The child's dark eyes seemed to rest speculatively on her. 'I bet you're as clever as your Grandad when you grow up.' She turned on the nightlight and went quietly out of the room.

'Was you saying something, Mrs Newton, lovey?' Parky was at the foot of the staircase, a pan clutched in one hand, her other resting coquettishly on a fat hip. Tricia groaned.

'No, I was just talking to the baby.'

'I never had time to talk to mine. Maybe I should have. But then he sings to them. He's got a fine voice, deep, you can feel it if you put your hand on his chest. Sometimes he sings to me after . . .'

'I'm going to have a quick bath. Listen for the door, will you?' She escaped.

James and Enid, her parents, were first to arrive. Her mother was dressed in her usual neat fashion. The colour and material of her dresses changed but the style never, what Tricia thought of as 'tarted up WVS.' Both of them were well-groomed, ageless. They'd looked like that for as long as she could remember, as if they were posing for 'Banker and Wife at Home'. Enid didn't ask if she could go up and see Emma, but sat down in an armchair at the fire, accepting a gin and tonic from Roger.

'Just what I need,' she said, sighing, and touched her dark sleek hair, rolled at the nape of her neck. That, too, had never altered. 'What a day I've had. Committee meeting at the WVS in the morning, bread and cheese lunch for Oxfam at the Town Hall, bridge at the Mastertons in the afternoon for the Save the Children Fund . . . then another committee meeting at the Golf Club. I've been flying about all day.'

'Roger's just in,' Tricia said. He'd come rushing into the bedroom when she was dressing, a whisky in his hand. 'I've put out the drinks. God, what a day.' She noticed he gulped down the whisky before he tore off his shirt.

'Howard working you as hard as ever, is he?' James asked, beaming over his glass at Roger as if he was a healthy Deposit Account. 'Stands over you with a whip? He's a chip off the old block and no mistake.' He's developed a real bank manager's face, Tricia thought, smooth with a twinkle.

'Not quite, James.' Roger was holding a full glass again. The only time Tricia had seen him relaxed was when they'd been at Corfu in June. 'But being in charge of the Kingsley Heath project is no joke.' She hated to tell him, smiled to soften the blow.

'Your father's bringing along the new man tonight, Roger. He phoned before you came in.' She saw the muscles tighten at the side of his mouth.

'Is he? So he's picked one.' He drank his whisky at a gulp and went over to the drinks table. He replenished his glass and came back to stand in front of the fire.

'Mr Newton's a perfectionist,' Tricia said to her father. 'There's a terrible amount of work to be done. Roger is run off his feet.'

He was genial but impartial. 'Ah, well, hard work never killed anyone and I'm making no complaints about the Latham Development Trust. It provides the jam for my bread.' He raised his glass.

'You've made this room nice, Tricia,' her mother said. 'I don't know how you manage it all.'

'Do you like it?' She was grateful to her for her tact. 'It's best at night. During the day it's a gloomy room.'

'It's because it's long and narrow.'

42

'Those old houses were planned by men, that's evident.'

'Do you think you could do better?' Roger's remark had an edge to it. He couldn't take much drink.

'I didn't say that.' She smiled again at him. 'But houses of character as they're called were usually designed with two maids and a char in mind.'

'Houses don't matter in the long run,' her mother said, 'I just leave mine to rot. Give it a good clean on a Sunday. James helps.' He looked at her, discomfited. 'Cleans windows, Hoovers the carpets.'

'Do you, Daddy?' She hadn't known that.

'Since you left, occasionally, yes. Don't mind being a Mrs Mop occasionally.' He sipped his whisky. 'We lost Mrs Green a year ago, can't replace her.'

'It's more difficult for you with Emma, of course.' Her mother looked bored with houses.

'I'm having another baby.'

'Are you?' Her face showed surprise. 'You're probably better to get it over and done with. Maybe you'll get one of the Kingsley Heath houses when they go up instead of this old place. I never approved of it . . .' her husband interrupted her.

'Congratulations, congratulations! You'll be hoping for a boy this time?'

'We don't mind,' Roger said, 'but I daresay father would like another Jolyon Roger.' There was a ring at the door bell. 'Talk about the devil,' he said. Tricia watched him walk too swiftly to the door, then fumble with the china knob. Her mother said when he was in the hall and the voices covered her own.

'Knocking it back a little, isn't he?'

'For goodness sake,' James said sharply. 'The boy's tired. Surely he's entitled to a drink in his own house.'

*　　*　　*

The dinner had gone well, the turkey had been succulent, the vegetables tender and the chiffon pie light. Parky had stayed to clear up, and even to serve, her face brightening with each course.

'Royston'll have his hands full tonight, lovey. Serve him right. I don't get much pleasure these days. It's a treat to see all those nice people, and your father-in-law, kindness itself. Slipped me a pound note when nobody was looking, a real gent.'

'Did he?' She'd been telling them about Parky and her domestic problems more as a topic of conversation than anything else. 'Married a West Indian who came off the boats at Liverpool. He spends most of his time in the betting-shop but he's good with the children. She has a hard time . . .'

All through the evening she'd felt gauche and younger than her years. The very efficiency of the meal seemed to make this worse, like a new bride who was showing-off before her in-laws. Jake Russell, the man whom Howard had brought with him, had been like a looming presence. And yet he was charming when he did speak, or perhaps polite would be nearer the truth, she thought at one stage, watching him as he listened to her father.

He was darkly handsome with deeply-set eyes under heavy eyebrows, but it was a face which needed to be illuminated by a smile, or at least stimulated by an exchange of ideas. Most of the time he'd been punctilious and withdrawn. He ought to sing for his supper a little since he's been thrust on us at the last moment. She didn't know why she was so critical of him, or so susceptible to his behaviour.

'We're hoping Jake will bring plenty of good ideas with him,' her father-in-law said at one point. Maybe he too thought that his protégé should shine more brightly in company.

'When do you start?' Roger asked abruptly. He'd been drinking too much throughout the meal. He wasn't drunk, just unpredictable, and she knew she'd been talking too much in an effort to cover up for him.

'It will take six months before I'm free of my commitments,' Jake Russell said.

Roger looked at his father through half-closed eyes, his head back. 'That's a long time. I thought you were in a tearing hurry to get going.'

'Jake's worth waiting for.' His father was bland.

'Have you planned a housing estate before?' Tricia met the deep-set eyes of her guest. Was there a glimpse of amusement there? Did he think her unbearably provincial?

'In my time.' He sipped his wine, looked at it contemplatively, twirled the stem. It's like throwing a line to a fish that won't bite, she thought irritably. 'What do you think of this house, Mr Russell?'

He raised his eyebrows, looked at the ceiling, swept his eyes to the iron mantelpiece which she'd painted white. 'It's itself. You never get that in a new house.'

'They grow up in time, and there's the joy of having everything fresh and new . . .'

'And putting up with its growing pains.'

'I know which I'd rather have.' She knew she was being tactless to her father-in-law. 'It's not that I can't look after this one standing on my head, but it's the amount of useless energy that goes on housekeeping when there's been no forethought in the design.'

'What would you do with all that useless energy?' His voice was mocking.

'I don't know. Maybe if I'd gone to University I should have found out, but I married Roger instead . . .' Oh, God, she thought what will I say next? She glared at this man who was upsetting her, turned it into what she hoped was a carefree smile. 'Don't think I regret it for one minute. Roger and I are very happy. We've one baby, and since the truth will out, another on the way.' She lowered her head and dug her fork into a piece of turkey. Her cheeks blazed with annoyance at herself. She heard Mary Newton twittering with delight.

'Your mother told me earlier, dear, and I whispered to Howard. We're so pleased.' She turned a loving look on her son. 'So pleased and proud, Roger.' A special accolade. Tricia raised her head slowly, hoping the colour would drain from her cheeks.

'Thanks, Mary.' She stumbled over the name, felt she had to make an attempt as a prospective mother of two. And since that man, Russell, was sitting there . . .

'Congratulations are in order, then,' Howard said, raising his glass to her. His look was quizzical. He knows I know I've made a gaffe.

'Thanks,' she said again, miserably.

Roger got up and went round the table with the wine. When he came to Tricia he bent over and kissed her cheek. His mouth felt wet, he smelled of drink. 'The prettiest young mother-to-be in Latham.'

'I'll second that,' Jake Russell said. His eyes were on her, speculatively, as if he was estimating her age, or indeed her prettiness.

'The idea is to get the family over before I'm twenty-one,' she assumed lightness.

'And *then* what will you do?' Saturnine, she thought, his looks are saturnine. And that long upper lip, cynical.

'She'll look after them and me, that's what she'll do.' Roger sat down heavily on his seat. 'We don't want any career women around here. *I*'ve got a career, a bloody demanding career. One of us is enough.' He wagged a loose forefinger at Jake Russell. 'I tell you, Russell, this is not a relaxing firm to be with, not relaxing at all. It's all go here from morning to night. Kingsley Heath is my father's baby . . . since we're on the subject.' He giggled, sobered quickly. 'He's determined to see it grow up to be big, healthy and strong, the pride of Latham, isn't that so Dad?' He veered round to Howard who looked wary. He wasn't used to being called 'Dad.'

Tricia looked across the table and caught her mother's eye. She had her usual air of deliberate non-involvement which she seemed to keep for sorties into Newton territory.

'What Roger says is perfectly true, Jake.' If Howard thought he was being needled he wasn't going to show it. 'I told you today how I acquired Kingsley Heath. But it's far from being my sole preoccupation. Houses are no use unless their owners can be gainfully employed within a reasonable distance . . .'

'Reasonable distance,' Roger said, nodding his head in agreement.

'I'm encouraging industries to buy land and build factories, and fortunately we've plenty of land to sell to them . . .'

'Foresight or just damned good luck?' Jake Russell was listening but unimpressed.

'A mixture of both, I daresay. Then there's the scientific complex the Government have built. Already the rental income we plough back is giving the Trust more per year than the whole cost of the Kingsley Estate when I bought it.' He took a sip from his wine and looked round the table. 'No, Roger,' Roger, who was filling his own glass from the decanter conveniently in front of him looked up apprehensively, 'I see Kingsley Heath as more than my baby. I see it as a stout prop for the Latham Development Trust and that's why I need stout men to run it.'

There was a pause. Tricia looked at Roger. His face seemed grey. Why does his father deflate him so much, she thought, feeling the familiar mixture of pity and love and something less audible. 'Shall we have coffee in the sitting-room?' she said, getting up. 'Take your time. I'll go and organise it. Excuse me.' She had to stop herself from running from the room.

Parky was sitting at the table drinking a cup of tea. 'I've done all the dishes, Mrs Newton, lovey, just having a cuppa. And the water's on for the coffee.'

'You're a treasure, Parky. Any squeaks from Emma?'

'Not one. Sleeping like an angel. I've been up to have a look at her.' She beamed broadly with wonder. 'That room, all to herself with those curtains with bears on them, like that great big one propped up in the corner. Good thing our youngest didn't see that. *She* would like a bear with wellies. And a hat.'

'Take it,' she wanted to say, except that it had been a gift from her mother-in-law, although so far Emma had shown complete disinterest in its presence. 'Come on, then, I'll run you home.'

'Oh, no, lovey, you're far too busy.'

'It's only ten minutes away. The two Grannies will keep things going for me.' It pleased her to make a gesture like this, show the supercilious Mr Russell that she wasn't dancing attendance on him. Besides Roger wasn't fit to drive. She flung on the anorak she kept at the back of the kitchen door. 'They won't even miss me. Ready?'

Parky lived in a tumbledown row of terrace houses near the railway. It was the red light district of Latham, she'd told Tricia once, and she'd looked out with interest for any tell-tale signs. The railway line depleted the value of the property. Was she beginning to think like her father-in-law? Still, if anyone bought up the row for a mere song, they'd probably find it had doubled or trebled its value in twenty years. One only needed a little capital and confidence. Property, if looked after, always escalated. Terrace houses in London fetched astronomical prices, and Parky's had a Georgian door and windows and could become a 'bijou residence' . . . yes, she was definitely thinking like a house-agent.

She said good-bye and more thanks to a happy Parky. 'I'll tell Royston all about it,' she said, heaving her bulk out of the car. She looked upstairs where a light was burning in a bedroom window. 'He's waiting for me. He has his points, I'll say that about him.' Her cackle had a sexual quality which didn't escape Tricia.

Didn't they say coloured men were virile in bed, she thought, guiding the car carefully out of the cul-de-sac? She remembered the Corfu holiday when she'd discovered that in spite of Roger's enthusiasm she was more insatiable than he was. His love-making was usually brief because of his excitement, and sometimes she felt he liked better the aftermath, the caressings, the fondlings, when her body craved for something less gentle.

He's more interested in belonging to someone, she thought. It was nice being out late like this alone, feeling like a truant from school, from her life, imagining the people she'd left behind in that narrow cell of a house; Emma sleeping upstairs in her cot, the long narrow staircase, the long narrow hall, tiled (and so cold just now in spite of the rugs), the long narrow rooms downstairs . . . what were they doing, saying? Were they wondering where she'd got to?

She thought of Jake Russell's eyes. Deep-socketed eyes could be disconcerting. She thought of his taciturnity. It's not what he says, it's rather what he doesn't say. I wonder what age he is? He'd managed to give nothing away about his background, his family or even his interests. Was he intriguing, or merely boorish? She remembered the occasional gleam of humour, she remembered her gaffe. What on earth had made her blurt out in front of him that she was pregnant? In the dark car she felt her cheeks go hot.

Her mother-in-law was sitting beside him when she took in the coffee tray, and she looked eagerly towards Tricia as if she was glad of the interruption. 'How quick you've been, Tricia!'

'I've taken Parky home. Do you want coffee?'

'No, dear. You know it doesn't agree with me. Silly me.' Her hands waved ineffectually.

'Mr Russell?'

'Yes, please. Black.' She poured the coffee and handed it to him.

'Sugar?' He shook his head.

'Now, dear,' Mary said getting up, 'I'll attend to that for you. You've done enough.'

'There's no need.'

'Do what your mother-in-law says,' Jake Russell said. She sat down and watched in silence as Mary poured out the coffee and bore the tray to the other side of the room, her chiffon sleeves flying. She heard him say. 'She wants to cherish you.'

'I know. She's a dear.' And then suddenly she was saying, 'I should never have blurted out about being pregnant. You'll think I'm a real small-town girl.' That's what they'd said to each other in Paris . . . 'It must have been embarrassing for you?'

'Why should it have been?' There was the mocking tone again. Now I've made another gaffe . . .

'It's a family affair. Boring for outsiders.'

He shrugged, sipping his coffee, as if he agreed. If it kills me, she thought, I'm going to give a reasonable impression of a capable young woman. She didn't know why she was so fierce about it.

'Are you married, Mr Russell?'

'Call me Jake. No, I'm not. I haven't any intention of getting married before I'm thirty, if at all.'

'Are you a woman hater?'

'No, just highly selective.' He expanded a little. 'Up-to-date I've been immersed in my work.'

'No outside interests?'

He smiled at her this time, and she saw the difference. His face came to life, was charming, she believed there was laughter lines under his eyes. 'This is like another interview.'

'I'm just trying to make polite conversation.'

'The gracious hostess?'

'Yes, I went to classes.' She had meant it as a joke but she sounded peevish to herself. She gave up, looked across the room where Roger was talking to her father, Howard to her mother and his wife. She must shift her concentration. How different the two women were. Mary had a faded prettiness with her rouged, cupid's bow mouth, so different from her own mother who looked impervious to fading. She's the strong one, she thought, and it came as a revelation to her. Father is just the front man.

She suddenly felt so tired that she could have wept. She had been working at high pressure since early morning, and the thought of another hour or two of this made her sway a little in her seat. She watched Roger cross the room to them.

'What would you like with your coffee, Russell? Brandy, Benedictine, we've got the lot, even some dreadful stuff we brought back from Corfu.'

'Ouzo? No, thanks. I'll have a spot of brandy, if I may.'

'Brandy, then, coming up.' Roger turned on his heel. He looked tired, too, Tricia thought, and pale. His Corfu tan had long since gone. Her mind was for a second full of impressions of the Island, the blue sea and the sky, the flowering shrubs, the rocks, the smell of heat coming from them. Sometimes they'd sat and watched the lizards darting in and out of their crevices.

'I tend to stick to Europe because I like exploring by car,' Jake Russell said.

'Do you?' Fatigue was breaking over her in waves. All she wanted was to go upstairs, to crawl under the bedclothes and sleep, Roger came back with a balloon glass of brandy.

'Tricia doesn't like liqueurs, but I can recommend this one. Apricot, Hungarian.' He had a book on wines and spirits. 'Rather special, I think. I'm having some too.'

'Remember you've to be up early tomorrow, darling,' she said as he turned away. Too late she realised she should have made her voice light.

'Now I've two tyrants.' She glimpsed the brightness in his eyes, the too bright smile. I'm so tired, tired, she thought, and

50

he'll be restless and wide-awake and he won't be able to make proper love because he's drunk too much and it's all too much . . . she found tears coming into her eyes and turned her head away, blinking, furious with herself.

'I'm going to France this year, I hope,' Jake Russell said. 'I worked for two years on the hydro-electric scheme in the Dordogne. Aquitaine. Aqua . . . water. Lots of rivers . . .' she listened in a dream to this man's voice. '. . . lots of history. That's my interest if you want to put it down in your questionnaire.'

'I thought it was buying and selling houses.'

'No, that's my passion. History's my pleasure.'

'I have a friend in the south-west.' She felt as if she was speaking in a dream. 'I met her in Paris. There were three of us. American, French and English. Tripartite, I said. The other two laughed at me. Something happened which . . . illuminated life for us. We made promises.' She sighed. 'That was when I was young.'

'What are you now?' She turned to look at him and he was smiling. They *were* laughter lines. They turned downwards in tiny corners under his eyes. The smile broadened his face, made it look different.

'An old married woman.' She had to smile back. 'I used to think Crystel, that's the French one, was the most beautiful girl I'd ever seen. Have you ever met anyone like that, where you get immense pleasure just from looking at them? Sometimes I get it with Emma, that's my little daughter. She has beautiful eyes. But it's the miniature perfection in her case. Isn't it strange? I'm not a motherly person. I don't see myself as some kind of earth mother going on having babies like some girls I know. I want to . . . extend myself, to work at something which interests me and excites me.' I'm drunk with tiredness, she thought. 'I don't know why I'm talking to you like this. It's not that I've been drinking . . .' Perhaps he'd take that as a criticism of Roger.

'It wouldn't matter.' He drained his glass and stood up. 'You look tired. I followed your father-in-law in my own car. Don't disturb them. I'll go now. Thank you. It was kind of you to include me in your family.'

51

'It was nothing. Anyhow, my father-in-law's wish is my command.'

He left her, shook hands briefly with the others, and was gone, waving aside Roger's effusive offer to show him out.

In their bedroom later it was as she'd thought. She half-slept while Roger panted on top of her with a weary kind of desperation, and sighed with relief when at last he rolled off her. She took him in her arms. 'It doesn't matter. We've got all our lives. You're tired . . .'

'I've drunk too much. And it was a bloody evening. Sorry, sorry, sorry.' He lay quietly, and his mind found another frustration. 'That chap Russell was the end. God knows what father sees in him.'

'Yes, I found him hard going.' She wanted to agree with everything he said so that she could get to sleep. Her body craved sleep as strongly as Roger had craved her.

'Of course it's bloody typical of father that he should appoint him over my head. It puts me in an invidious position to say the least of it.'

'I wouldn't put it like that, lovey.' Echoes of Parky. But Roger wasn't like Royston who had his points . . . 'He's putting in Jake Russell to help you.'

'As long as he's not putting him in to lord it over me. He was pretty high-handed, I thought, as if he had it all sewn up.' She turned a slow sigh into a deep breath. 'And I didn't like the way he looked at you.'

She laughed, swallowed it up in an outsize yawn. 'He looked right through me! He thought I was a provincial, ignorant, young-married fool hardly worth speaking to.' She was blushing again in the darkness. 'There's another baby on the way . . .' Oh, to be thirty and soignée! 'Don't give him another thought. He won't be here for another six months. He might never come at all.'

'I wouldn't put it past him.' She could hear the hope in his voice. 'His type like to see how the land lies. Cold fish, I thought.' He's tired, she thought, and disappointed in himself. His failure in bed with her typified for him his failure with his father. How different the real Roger was from the charming young man who'd wanted to marry her so much. He needed me, she thought. His instinct told him he needed me. Howard had seen it. 'Is he married?'

'No, I asked him. He likes travelling. He said he'd worked in France, in the Dordogne. Crystel lives there.'

'Who's Crystel?' His voice was slurred with sleep.

'Crystel Romaine, the French girl I met in Paris. She lives in a little town called Maurac. She was so lovely. I should have written to her. That time when I had the letter from Jan I thought I would, then I was ill, then I had to get better, then there was Corfu, and running the house, and looking after Emma. Where has all the time gone to, Roger?' But he was asleep, his head on her breast.

CHAPTER FOUR
December, 1969

CRYSTEL liked the flat she'd found in Maurac. It had been sad leaving her parents in their cottage at St Henri, Maman especially, but she would visit them on Sundays and perhaps go with them occasionally to see the cousins at La Mothe Fenelon who were her only relatives. Angelique and Justine adored Papa, and cooked all the dishes he liked best, *Tripes aux Cahors*, rabbit with prunes, and the flakiest of cherry tarts. They were both old maids and thought cousin Dominique so fortunate to have such a fine upstanding husband and such a beautiful daughter as Crystel.

Monsieur Derain, her boss, had given her a day off to move in although they were busy in his store with the Christmas rush. She was grateful to him, because she had been able to set the flat in order and now she was sitting on her patio in a sheltered spot beneath the mulberry tree, where she had a fine vantage point over the town. It was more like late September than December, she thought, as she stretched out on the flowered *chaise longue*.

The flat was tucked under the hill of the *château*, perched, in fact, on top of the garage of the house underneath. To get to it she had to climb the steep slope of the Rue du Château then turn into a little lane and from there go up the zig-zag flight of steps cut into the rock. If she used her moped Monsieur Rambeau underneath permitted her to run it into his garage beside his Fiat. Monsieur Rambeau had no ulterior motive. He was said to prefer young men if at all, which was convenient for her in the long run.

She sighed contentedly. It was a perfect *pied-a-terre*, she had told René. René Baron was her lover. His parents owned the

54

best hotel in Maurac, a fine place with a golden limestone front, flat-windowed, a big plane tree, and white tables and chairs on the terrace. It had badges of the various tourist organisations to which it belonged on the stout Renaissance door.

All the Barons were inordinately proud of their hotel, including René. Even when making love to her, which had been mostly in the forest near St Henri, or in his big Citroen, he had thought about the hotel.

'Wouldn't it be dreadful if some of our clients could see us?' he had said once after it was all over and he was picking bits of bracken from his hair. He got it cut at Monsieur Raoul's. Crystel sometimes thought they spent more time on men's hair than on girls', but the result was to their credit, brushed back to show René's widow's peak, and waved softly round his ears.

'They aren't likely to come along at this minute, René,' she had assured him. Considering he had pestered her ever since she had come back from Paris to sleep with him, she thought it was rather unfair of him to be worried now.

She wondered if she should have told him quite so much about the gay time she'd had in Paris. Especially about the party at the Sorbonne where she and Jan, the American girl, had gone wild and Jan had fallen for the buck nigger, George Cook. (She'd heard a weedy English student call him that.) Certainly he had stirred Crystel with his flashing smile and his raunchiness, but she liked a certain chic in her men. Now she was beginning to think it was only René's hotel training which gave him his showy good manners and his smart way of dressing. The boys were so nice, she'd said in a burst of confidence, that it was difficult to say no.

René had laughed at this, and squeezed her hard, but the next time he saw her he said Maman had been saying that Crystel had a certain reputation in Maurac since she had returned from Paris. She saw it had been a mistake confiding in him, especially as that evening, making love to her in the Citroen, he had been rough, demanding and rather *déchainé*. She was glad she hadn't told him about the letter from Jan saying she had a black baby. He would have had something to say about that.

She watched Mademoiselle Coco who ran the antique shop

in Rue Boniface putting out her plaster models. It was delightful having a bird's eye view. In winter, she only displayed them on fine days or when there was a market on. Today was ideal. The stalls were doing a brisk business because of the sunshine. She could see the man who sold the leather belts. He wore a large sombrero and had a Zapata moustache. She had bought a belt from him last week, a Spanish affair in tooled leather, and they had chatted in Spanish. He had complimented her on her facility for languages. 'It's my only facility,' she'd said, and he'd laughed and said he didn't believe that for one single minute. *No lo creo.*

That memory made her smile. Men were always making remarks like that to her. It was sometimes a nuisance, but most of the time she liked it. She liked men in general and at the moment René in particular, if it hadn't been for that reservation in her mind about *his* mind. But he had a lovely skin, and his legs were shaped beautifully, like a girl's.

She watched Mademoiselle Coco making her *arrangement*, completely oblivious of the people in the street around her. First of all she carried out the school-boy in his smock and short trousers, *accroupi*, bent back and knees so that she could push him under the school desk. She must have got the desk from one of the village schools which had been closed down. It had been scored by pen-knives, and there was an ink-well and a groove for laying pencils. The lid lifted up for keeping school books, and inside there was a rude word carved. Mademoiselle Coco didn't like customers to lift the lid.

She bustled in and out again, this time carrying the grandmother who wore lace mittens and a mutch. There were two grandmothers but the other one had a broken nose and she usually covered *her* face with a black veil to hide the disfigurement. Crystel watched Mademoiselle Coco putting the figure in a bending position by pushing the head forward.

It's the cradle, she thought, and sure enough the woman bustled in and out again, this time carrying a wooden cradle. Was it Sophie? She craned her neck to see which doll was inside, and saw the blur of yellow. Yes, it *was* Sophie, with a baby's cap on top of her too-yellow hair and her sophisticated face.

56

Mademoiselle Coco had once invited Crystel upstairs to her apartment to see her collection of dolls. She had told Crystel she put them to bed each night. 'They're my children, you see.' Crystel had agreed, pretending to admire the twins, a fearsome-looking pair with ugly peasant faces. 'How could I put them in boxes?'

The story went that she'd had a child herself which had died after she'd been put out by her parents. Crystel didn't have this all-consuming wish to have children. The American girl had it. She'd talked a lot about the Play-Group 'back home', and the 'kids', those long thin hands waving about. Intense and loving. All she herself wanted was a man to love *her*. Perhaps she was superficial, gay, like Mademoiselle Coco's young lady dolls dressed in frills and furbelows and large hats with flowers and fruit on them and feather boas.

She watched Mademoiselle Coco standing back to admire her *mise en scène*. The schoolboy was busy doing his sums, the grandmother had one hand out as if to rock the cradle. 'In the Nursery', Crystel thought. Sometimes it was 'A Day at Longchamps', or 'Le Four O'Clock', when the young lady dolls were used and, grand *pièce de resistance*, 'The Picnic', when she pushed out a little fiacre with a high-stepping plaster pony between the shafts.

Now Mademoiselle had come out with a rocking horse, a creature of flaring nostrils and an expression fierce enough to frighten any child. She looked around proudly, seemingly not at all discomfited that everyone was occupied at the stalls, propped up her placard in front of the rocking-horse and retired into her shop.

Crystel smiled. A window on the world, she thought, although it was only Maurac. She had once asked René if he had anything to do with Mademoiselle Coco and he had looked scornful. The only shops he knew were the grocers and the bakers and the hardware shops where he had to buy food and equipment. Only the best was good enough for *L'Hôtel de la Poste*, he'd said. Crystel often wondered if *she* would be good enough for *L'Hôtel de la Poste*, quite apart from René, whom she thought she would dearly like to marry.

The idea of finding work in Paris had faded into insignificance when she'd met him last Christmas. She liked the idea of being in the Reception Desk of the hotel, for instance. She was sure she could entice men to come and spend their time in the English Bar and the Renaissance Lounge. She had hinted at this to René and he'd looked disdainful. 'The only things which must entice men to our hotel,' he said, 'are good food, good wine and good beds.'

Maman and Papa had been understanding about her taking the flat in Maurac. In winter the journey on her Moped between St Henri and Maurac could be tiresome and, although they depended upon her, being their only daughter, (her brother was married and lived in Montauban), Maman had said she should try it out at least for the winter. She'd also said that if it meant Crystel found a good husband, it was for the best. Maman was still pretty, and perhaps she had been like Crystel when she was young, a target for men. On the other hand she had married Papa, not a great catch, but a hard-working *menuisier*, and they were very happy. Crystel felt she could be very happy with René in *L'Hôtel de la Poste*.

She saw René's head as he got out of his car in the steep Rue du Château, and then it came bobbing along between the hedge of the narrow lane before he was in full view as he ran up the steps cut into the rock and on to the patio. She got up from the *chaise longue* and flung her arms around his neck.

'Isn't this absolutely adorable, René? And don't you love this *chaise longue?*' She turned, one arm round his neck. 'Monsieur Derain sent it as a house-warming gift. Do try it.'

'No thanks.' He took his arms away from her waist and sat down on a wooden bench flaked with age which had been there when Crystel took over the flat. 'Do you think you should accept a gift like that from your boss? It looks strange . . .'

'But you know he sells them! It's probably one that has been marked down at the end of the season. He often gives us opportunities to buy goods to save them being stored. I got a barbecue for Maman and Papa at the last sale. They had never heard of such a thing.'

'We don't deal with him,' René said. 'We go to Perigueux for our requirements for the kitchen. There's a place there that deals solely with the hotel trade. They know what a hotel of good standing likes.'

'Well, that's a different matter.' She shivered slightly. The sun had left the patio and it was December again. 'Come indoors and see my little apartment, *chéri*. It's truly remarkable and so cheap.' She took him by the hand and led him inside. 'See,' they stood together, and she hoped he would put his arm round her waist. He didn't. 'A big salon, and off it there's the bedroom. Don't by shy. I know you haven't been in a bedroom with me, just in the forest, and the Citroen.'

She thought he shuddered. He must be cold. He followed her into the bedroom and looked around. 'It's very nice. No wash-hand basin, of course. Every bedroom in our hotel has a basin, a douche and a bidet. It is *de rigueur* for the best hotels. They tell me the flats on the hill haven't good drains. Is that so?'

'I haven't noticed. There's a *douche* in my *salle de bain*, and I poured a bottle of disinfectant down the *toilette* when I moved in. I should think that would make everything all right.' She looked at the bed, her *pièce de resistance*, she thought remembering Mademoiselle Coco, with its duvet cover of sprigged cotton to match the curtains and the walls. Monsieur Derain had again given her a considerable reduction, wall-paper included, otherwise it would have been impossible to have furnished in such a recherché style. 'I thought the bed was pretty. Try it.' She led him towards it and they sat down together on the edge. She wouldn't tell him that she'd got the duvet at a discount, as well as the sheets and pillows. Any mention of Monsieur Derain seemed to annoy him.

He turned towards her. 'You're looking prettier than ever today, Crystel, far too pretty. I . . . ' He turned away again, surprisingly. Usually when he looked at her he wanted to touch her. She had a flash of inspiration. It was the bed which was putting him off. She'd read a novel recently in which a certain couple had been quite unable to make love once they were safely married because they'd been in the habit of using his car for that purpose. They'd been forced to drive out to the country all that winter and park in chilly country roads. Eventually the girl had become pregnant, and lovemaking either in a car or in bed became impossible when the baby was due.

However, the baby cured him of his phobia. It cried a lot

during the night and the wife pushed him out to attend to it, making him absolutely desperate to get back to his nice warm bed. She liked novels which made her laugh, not the dreary soul-searching ones which were so popular just now.

Lovemaking should be fun. It was something to be enjoyed, and then how good it was to have a shower and a drink perhaps and laugh a lot because of the intimacy between them. She slipped off the edge of the bed and lay down on the white fur rug which had also been a sales bargain from Monsieur Derain. 'René,' she said.

He slipped down too, and lay half across her. 'You are an enchantress,' he said. 'You shouldn't do this to me. You make me mad for you and I find it impossible to resist you.' He was busy undressing as he spoke, doing the same for her. Practice in the confines of the Citroen had made him adept at this. There was a draught coming from the old floor boards, probably blowing all the way down from the *château*, but René's pleasure came first.

And he was such a good lover. His silken body, the hairs which she could feel growing down his spine, the strong, demanding curve of him. It was twilight already, and when she looked at his face she saw for the first time that his mouth was in a straight line across his face. Was it only now or had it been like that all the time?

And then she was lost in the pleasure of the whole thing. Nothing could be wrong which was so utterly pleasurable as this, so cleansing, so thrustful . . . she sighed and sighed again with pleasure although the hard floor through the fur rug hurt her back. She hoped René would get used to the idea of a bed.

Later they sat at the window with the supper she had prepared and a bottle of wine between them. The street was quiet now after the small evening rush of cars.

'I'm so happy,' she said. 'I feel . . . *libre*. That's what we used to talk about in Paris, after we'd been locked up in that police station. I told you, René . . .'

'Yes, and you told me about those parties you used to go to with the American.' When she looked at him she saw again the straight line of his mouth, and this time it seemed familiar to her. Yes, or course, Madame Baron, his mother . . . it was her mouth also. Perhaps it was a family trait and didn't mean much. Why should I not talk as I feel, she thought. I'm my own person, now that I live alone.

'I liked very much those two girls,' she said. 'It was as if we had known each other all our lives. Once Tricia relaxed she amused me greatly. She had the English sense of humour, and I saw in her a strength of character. Not so much in Jan, perhaps because she'd been repressed at home. She was crazy about this student she met. I can see her dancing with him, her black hair flying, her arms and hands snaking like so.' She held up her own arms, feeling the new negligée slip sleekly into her armpits. 'They were such expressive hands, nervous, as if they had two little lives of their own.'

She looked at René. His face was impassive. Why didn't he want to talk as she did? Lovemaking released you to talk, to discover each other. She wished very much to stir some response in him. After all, hadn't he been writhing and moaning on the fur rug with her only half-an-hour ago? 'I have had a letter from Jan,' she said. 'I didn't tell you about it. We always vowed we'd write to each other, but we didn't. I imagined they would be too busy and I didn't want to be the first. I am rather shy. Perhaps you don't think so, René?' She saw him raise his eyebrows, shrug. 'So, in this letter Jan told me she'd had a baby and was still in Paris.'

'What would you have expected?' He seemed to speak rather bitterly, she thought. And his eyes were fixed on the opposite side of the street. There was a light in Mademoiselle Coco's apartment. Would she be putting her dolls to bed now? She hadn't a black one.

'It's a black one,' she said, 'the baby.'

'Really?' He was still bitter. 'Does she know who the father is?'

Crystel blushed. She felt the heat spread into the cleft between her breasts and run down to her stomach. She was glad she was wearing her negligée to hide it. She blushed for her friend who had been truly in love, as George Cook had been with her. She remembered his brown eyes on Jan as they danced, how they never left her as he moved, and how he smiled, a rich white smile, only for her . . .

61

'It is her lover's baby, George Cook. He's a clever lawyer. Very well-educated, and extremely charming, always.' She loved George Cook at this moment. 'They are still living in Paris because I imagine her parents won't be too happy about the baby, but perhaps they'll come round to it in time. It is their grandchild, after all.'

'Can you blame them?' René said.

'I beg your pardon?' She lifted her glass and took a sip of wine.

'Can you blame them if they aren't happy about the baby? Their daughter goes to Paris to learn the language. No doubt they paid a lot of money for this privilege. She writes, I presume after a long time, and tells them she has a black baby by a nigger.' He used a rude word. 'Can you blame them?'

'I don't blame anyone.' She put down her glass because her hand was trembling. Her stomach was churning as if the blush had upset it in some peculiar way. 'There's no question of blame. She has a baby. It's a fact. It's also a fact that it is black, but if she is happy and she and George love each other, *c'est tout*. Everyone must live their own life . . .'

'That's it. That's it exactly.' René suddenly got up, turned his back to the window to face her. 'This is difficult, *chérie*.' His voice was firm. 'I shouldn't have made love to you tonight. For quite some time I have thought you and I aren't suited.' He held up his hand although Crystel hadn't spoken. 'Yes, I know we're suited in bed,' they hadn't been in bed, she thought, 'but that's not the whole story. I had a long talk with Maman . . .' he stopped again as if wishing to be interrupted.

'Go on.' She was surprised at the quietness of her voice.

'Someone of my station has to be careful in his choice of a wife. The Barons hold a prominent position in the town, and I as a son of the owner of the premier hotel have to bear that in mind. It is important that when I choose a wife it is someone who is . . .'

'Suitable?' The soreness had left her stomach now. It was in her throat, making it difficult to speak.

'In a way. Perhaps . . . a little dull, even someone . . .' the words came with a rush, 'who won't be talked about.' His voice suddenly changed. 'To tell you the truth, Crystel, you're

62

too seductive. I wouldn't have a moment's peace with you. They'd all be sniffing around the hotel, the wrong sort of people. It is not what Maman . . .'

'Wants?'

'No, no, I mean, it wouldn't do. After all, you did say you would entice men . . .'

'I didn't mean it in that fashion. I meant to be pleasant, solicitous, to build up your business.'

'I know, I know, *chérie*, but Maman thinks . . .'

'And what does your Papa think? Or is he not allowed to think? Oh, I know all about your Papa. Because he has a limp, and is much older than your Maman he is sent to the garden to grow the vegetables. And to come in at the back door with them so that he isn't seen . . . ' She got up. Her legs were trembling. 'You are loathsome,' she said, 'you are a mother's boy, you are everything I detest. I am not wicked, the way you say I am, or your Maman. Didn't you tell her how you kept pestering me to make love with you, waiting at the store every evening? Didn't she know that, or had you told her you were doing the shopping for your wonderful hotel? All I want is to be loving to one man, to give him everything, to look after him, to care for him. It's what I need, don't you see, just as Jan needed her baby, just as Tricia needed what she needed . . . I don't think she knew. My need is to love, but I will tell you this, René Baron, I am sorry, I will always be sorry I wasted my love on someone like you. What are you standing there for? Why don't you run home to Maman? Go on, get out of here!' She felt her bosom heaving. It was a pity the negligée was so low as to give him any pleasure at the sight.

But he wasn't looking. He was staring at the table. He muttered something about being sorry, he had put it badly, he would try to explain properly another time . . . and he was gone.

The salon was very quiet, except for the echo of her voice, and then even that died away. She sat at the table by the window, saw the lights of his car light up the narrow slope of the Rue du Château, heard the squeak of his brakes as he stopped before entering Rue Boniface. Mademoiselle Coco's light was still on. When it went out she would go to bed. She sat for a long time, dry-eyed, her knees trembling, and with the pain still in her throat.

CHAPTER FIVE

CRYSTEL spent Christmas with her parents at St Henri. Since René had left her she had felt some kind of malaise, nothing tangible, a slight loss of appetite and a disinclination to exert herself. She refused the invitations from the assistants in Monsieur Derain's store, and only wished to have the day end and return to her flat in the evening.

Sometimes she went to bed early, not bothering to cook. Other times she would sit at the window and watch the traffic going along the Rue Boniface. It was busier now because everyone was engaged in Christmas shopping, and Mademoiselle Coco had put up a string of coloured lights in her shop window although she had set out no more *arrangements*. The weather was too cold for people to stop and stare.

On this cold day, then, the day before Christmas, she turned off the main road at the farm where Monseiur Gautier kept his silky-haired goats. Each winter Maman wondered if it would be his last, but so far, when the first celandines appeared in the little copse, he would be back outside again on his little stool. He had driven a train in Paris before his *retraite*.

She whizzed past the cemetery with its circle of spruces, stopped at the *carrefour*, and then drove slowly through the village until she reached her parents' cottage. The door opened off the street, but at the back there was a fine view of the sloping fields belonging to the farmer. Maman always said she would never give up her view, even for the best house in Maurac. She ran the Moped round the back, took off her helmet and pushed the door open. As always she had a deep sense of peace.

And now she was in the living-room, and in Maman's arms, who was laughing and talking at the same time, and Papa was behind her beaming and saying, 'Don't I get in on this? After all, she's my daughter too.' Their love was uncomplicated and didn't stifle.

For the rest of the day she was happy working with Maman in the big kitchen, stuffing the goose with chestnuts and minced pork, scraping the potatoes for baking, and preparing the vegetables. She piped the chocolate icing on the *Bûche de Noel* while Papa cut wood in the back garden and Maman bustled about getting out the best china from the black armoire which had belonged to Crystel's grandmother, now lying in the village churchyard.

Maman and Crystel were going to the midnight service, but Papa would only drive them there and come back for them. Most of the men in the village did the same and, although Maman was not deeply religious, this was one service she never missed.

'It gives you a chance to sit and look back over the year,' she said. Crystel had told her she was no longer seeing René. She couldn't bring herself to say that he had given her up because his mother didn't approve of her. She didn't see any point in upsetting Maman who would have stormed against that stuck-up cow, Madame Baron, for daring to slight her beautiful daughter.

'We didn't see eye to eye, Maman,' she said. It had been a saying of Tricia's.

'I never liked the Barons in any case,' Maman had comforted her, 'and you know that any wife of René's would have to work her fingers to the bone. She wouldn't be marrying René. She would be marrying *L'Hôtel de la Poste*.'

It had made Crystel feel well again, or perhaps it was the peace of St Henri. Why bother about René Baron? She wasn't twenty-one yet. There was still plenty of time to find a man to love. Meantime she would attend classes in typewriting and shorthand in the evening school at Maurac, and try and work her way up the firm. Considering there was only herself and the old book-keeper in the office, the spinster aunt of Monsieur Derain, it would be difficult to work her way up very far, but at least she could take a greater interest in the running of the firm. It would please Mademoiselle Derain with her bird-nest of hair and the black pencil sticking out of it like a twig.

But her new feeling of well-being was quite shattered when her brother and his wife arrived on Christmas day from Montauban. She loved Robert, but she had never taken to Renate who had been known in the village as a bitch beyond endurance. They had never managed to have any family, and she kept an enormous *poupée* lying on their bed whom she called Babette. Crystel thought she was bizarre, and wondered why Robert had ever fallen in love with her.

She supposed it might have been because of Renate's magnolia skin. Perhaps she and Robert shared this liking for skins. This was what she missed most about René, the smooth silken feeling of his back and his limbs when she ran her hand over them, the way his body slid against hers in passion.

'I suppose you're living it up in Maurac,' Renate said after Papa had carved the goose, Maman had served the vegetables and sauces, and they were busily eating. 'I never thought it was a good idea to let her go and live in Maurac on her own, Maman.'

'Didn't you?' Crystel admired Maman. She never lost her temper with Renate. It was because she loved Robert, she had explained to Crystel, and she didn't want to make it difficult for him.

'I expect you're entertaining Monsieur René Baron most of the time, dinners *à deux* and so on.' Renate turned her attention again to Crystel.

'Renate,' Robert said, smiling unhappily, 'that's enough. Eat your goose.'

'It's only light-hearted chatter, Robert. Surely sisters should be able to tease each other.'

'I don't mind, Robert,' Crystel said, trying to copy Maman. 'I understand Renate's ways. As a matter of fact,' she turned to Renate, 'I don't see René Baron any more. He's given me up.'

'You mean you've thrown him over,' Papa said. He didn't often interfere. 'You've put it the wrong way.'

'No, Papa, it's best to be truthful.' She thanked him with her eyes. 'He gave me up because his mother didn't approve of me. That's the long and short of it.'

'See, what did I tell you, Maman?' Renate said, waving her fork, 'you've brought up Crystel wrongly. You allowed her to go to Paris on her own when other girls in the village didn't get the opportunity, and now you've permitted her to live by herself in a flat in Maurac. That's the way girls get a bad reputation and no husbands. No doubt Madame Baron decided it wouldn't do her hotel any good having her son know someone whose name was bandied about.'

'Tell me,' Papa said, his face red, 'where do you get all this know-how about bringing up children when you haven't had any yourself? Tell me that, eh, eh?'

'Quiet,' Maman said, 'it's Christmas. Renate is only teasing and we all think highly of Crystel. She was the best pupil at Maurac of her year, and it was the headmaster himself who recommended the year in Paris. He thought Crystel was the right material for an important job there, given time. I know for a fact she worked very hard in Paris. Her nose was to the grindstone all the time. And the way she talks now with that chic accent makes us all sound like peasants. No', she said, smiling at Crystel across the table, 'Papa and I have high hopes of our daughter.'

Crystel felt ashamed, remembering the parties in Paris and how little she had really worked.

* * *

She went back to Maurac after the Christmas holiday determined to work hard at evening school and eventually return to Paris. Her reputation was spoiled now. Renate was right. René would tell his friends in the Social Club that she was easy. She was quite out of love with him now, and she no longer felt depressed each morning when she awoke.

But her plans went wrong. Mademoiselle Derain became ill and it was doubtful if she would be back for some time. Monsieur Derain came into the little office to tell Crystel.

"A general debility, poor soul, perhaps her time of life. She

68

liked being here . . . she worked for my father . . . and she hadn't much of a life elsewhere. Now she may have to go to hospital. I don't want to fill her place. Do you think, Crystel, you could carry on for the time being? I'll get a junior to help with the typing.'

He looked so worried that she promised to do what she could. She knew his wife nagged, and that one of his children had been born disabled. He always looked so uncared for. She was sure he washed his own shirts, and the cuffs were often frayed.

'I'll do my best, Monsieur Derain,' she said, and they shook hands on it. His eyes were like those of a spaniel who had been patted on the head. All the same, it was with a feeling of panic that she tackled the neat ledgers which had been kept by his aunt.

Happily the task proved not to be beyond her. Her father had always given her the job of sending out his accounts, and she had no fear of figures. She liked arranging them, putting them into their place in neat rows, and she rarely used the calculator which Guy . . . Monsieur Derain . . . had bought for her. She had a quiet young girl to help her with the typing and, during the short winter days, she found herself too busy to think about anything but her work.

She grew to like the routine and the freedom of having her flat to go to at the end of the day. She would run the Moped beside Monsieur Rambeau's Fiat, sometimes stopping to have a chat with him if they arrived at the same time. He liked to air his political views and thought highly of Raymond Barre. He spoke as if the Elysée was an open door to him. Eventually she would say, *'Bon appetit,'* and climb the steps cut out of the rock and go into her flat. She had once or twice asked him to join her but he said he was a strict vegetarian and never dined away from home. Sometimes she saw the slim figure of a young man going into Monsieur Rambeau's flat and was glad for him, although a little envious.

She had made additions and alterations to her own flat, velvet curtains which Guy had offered her for nothing because they'd been made for a client who had changed his mind, a revolving bookcase which she had bought from Mademoiselle

Coco, and one or two pictures from the artist who had an *atelier* near the *château*. She also had long talks with him and he advised her always to buy original work. 'One must educate one's taste,' he said, 'even at the risk of making mistakes.'

She went home each Sunday for lunch and once a week went to her classes in Maurac. This necessitated some homework on other evenings, and that, with the occasional guest for dinner, generally one or other of the girls from the store, seemed to fill up her week. On the whole her time was spent with people older than herself. She told Maman she was getting as set in her ways as Mademoiselle Derain. It was found that she, poor soul, had cancer and she had gone to a private home in the country run by nuns.

But she didn't change her mind about René. He rang her at the office one day and asked if he might call at the flat to see her, saying that perhaps he'd been too hasty. 'Certainly not,' she said. 'Everything is finished between us. There is no place in my life now for you.'

She wept bitterly in bed that night. Perhaps she *had* got over her affair with him, but there was something missing in her life and she didn't have to wonder what it was. She turned her body over and pressed it hard into the mattress, clutching the pillow, her cheek against it. Maman had been quite right when she said she was not cut out to be an old maid.

CHAPTER SIX
1971

ON a hot August day, Crystel had a visit from Tricia's friend, Monsieur Jake Russell. Chantal, one of the front salon assistants, said he was waiting in the bedding department. She went quickly through the main salon which was full of occasional tables, flower-strewn wastepaper buckets and newspaper racks in shiny *papier mâché* which Crystel privately thought were enough to drive customers away. If her year in Paris had done anything for her it was to give her a sense of style which Maurac, or Guy, for that matter didn't possess.

A tall, dark-haired man was standing looking faintly embarrassed beside a king-sized bed topped by a plump duvet sprinkled with cabbage roses which were tied with blue ribbons. She sympathised with him *'Bon jour,'* she said, holding out her hand, 'I'm Crystel Romaine.'

'Bon jour.' His French was passable, abrupt, he spoke in short sharp sentences, and she got the impression he would have spoken in the same manner in his own tongue. 'I'm Jake Russell. A friend of Mrs Newton's.' He must have seen her blank look. 'Tricia Baker. She's married.'

'Married! How that surprises me! But I'm delighted, naturally. Do you know her well?'

'Quite well, I'm employed in her father-in-law's firm. She said if I was ever in this area I was to be sure to call on you. I knew you wouldn't be at home at this time.'

'No, I work all day.'

'You couldn't get some time off just now, could you? I'm afraid I'm just passing through. I thought we might have a coffee, or a drink.'

'I'd love to.' She was enchanted by the idea. 'But I'd have

71

to ask Monsieur Derain.' This man seemed to have none of
the gentleness of Guy, nor indeed the sexual charm of René,
but his abrupt manner had a certain fascination, *très anglais*, she
told herself, *très snob*. She saw Guy appear at the end of the
bedding salon, wend his way between the terrible twin beds
with brass trellis tops and bottoms shaped like miniature Gothic
arches. Who would ever want to sleep in twin beds for that
matter?

'Oh, there you are, *mam'selle*,' he said as he reached them.
He looked diffidently at this Jake Russell. 'I beg your pardon.
I see you're busy.'

'He's not a customer, *monsieur*,' she said, 'he's a friend of
my English friend. He's called to see me. He was just . . . '

'May I speak to you in private, *mam'selle* . . . ' he retreated
a few steps and she followed him, getting wedged between
another hideous pair of beds. She saw he was pale, his brow
furrowed. 'I've had a telephone call from the house, Crystel.'
He spoke hurriedly, lowering his voice. 'Michel is having a
little *crise de nerfs*. Madeleine says I must come home at once. I
was going to ask you to take over for me.'

'Well . . .'

'Of course if it isn't convenient . . .'

It wasn't his pallor so much as the washed-out collar of his
shirt with its frayed edges which decided her. 'Yes, certainly
it's convenient. Don't hurry back.'

'You're so reliable,' he said, 'it isn't fair . . .'

'Not at all. I'm pleased to do anything to help.' She went
back to Tricia's friend who was looking around with a disdainful
expression. Maurac gets the taste it deserves, she thought. 'I'm
sorry I had to leave you monsieur . . .'

'Russell. Jake Russell.'

'A little *contretemps*. My boss. He relies on me completely,
you understand.'

'Quite,' he said, looking more disdainful, more English if
possible. 'Well, can you come out?'

'I regret, no.' She had an idea. 'But if you like to come to
my flat at half past five, we might have a little talk. I'd love to
hear about Tricia.'

'It isn't possible, I'm sorry. I have to be in Albi for dinner with a friend. I got held up coming here. It was just a thought . . . didn't want to pass through Maurac without calling. Tricia . . .'

'Come into my office at least and my secretary will bring us tea.' She liked the sound of herself saying that.

Their tête-a-tête wasn't a success. The telephone kept ringing, and Janine kept interrupting her . . . Guy was right about people being afraid of responsibility . . . and she saw the frown deepen between this man's deep-set eyes. He was handsome without a doubt, but impatient because things hadn't gone the way he'd planned.

'Tricia has two children now,' he told her. 'I don't see much of her. She's very busy, I imagine, the typical young Mum.'

'Young Mum?' she repeated. 'Somehow I don't see Tricia as that. I was so sure she would have had a wonderful career.'

'I imagine meeting Roger put a stop to that,' he said.

'He is *aimable?*'

'*Aimable?*' His thick eyebrows went up. 'Yes, you could say that. As different as chalk from cheese . . . ' the telephone rang. She sighed. Just when it was getting interesting.

'Yes, yes,' she sighed even more deeply into the mouthpiece, 'yes, Madame Recamé.' Madame Recamé who always spoke for ever and could never make up her mind about anything except to keep on changing it. 'Yes, I'll go to the Furnishings Department and find out, madame. Yes, I'm quite sure they know to make up *six* pairs with a twelve foot drop, yes, I'll go right away, no, they won't have cut them wrongly . . .' when she looked up Jake Russell was on his feet and pacing about her small office like a caged tiger. I know what's upset him, she thought, he's autocratic, his career must come first and no one else's. This situation disturbs his ego. She was pleased to understand this smart friend of Tricia's at the first meeting. 'Yes, madame, no, madame, certainly, madame,' she said, 'good afternoon.' And looking up when she replaced the receiver, 'I'm afraid your valuable time is being used up.'

'Not at all. I feel I'm in *your* way. I can't abide anyone getting in my hair when I'm working. I should never have come to your place of business.'

'Not at all.' She remembered a word of Tricia's. He was

73

getting himself into a tizzy. 'You could not even spare the time to walk around our little town so that you'd be able to tell Tricia about it?' She smiled at him. 'I expect you know, Jan, Tricia and I studied together in Paris. I tried to make them see Maurac but I don't know if I was successful. Johnstown I could imagine. That's where Jan lived, in Maryland, USA. Her parents wanted too much for her. Mine just wanted me to be happy.' She smiled again at him and he gave her a quick charming smile in return.

'That's the main thing, isn't it? To be happy.' His smile died. 'I must push on . . . this appointment in Albi . . . but I'll have a quick look round so that I can give Tricia a thumb-nail sketch.' His deep-set eyes were suddenly blue.

'Next time, please give me more warning. My employer . . .' she had been going to say, 'is usually very understanding.'

'Unfortunately I shall be abroad quite a lot, in the States and Scandinavia. We want to see how other countries plan their . . .' The door opened. It was Janine, a worried look on her bespectacled face. Next time I shall tell her I didn't hear her knocking, Crystel thought, 'deportment,' I shall say . . .

'There's a representative from Brive here, Crystel . . .' and not to call me Crystel in front of strangers. 'He wanted to see Monsieur Derain, but he's told me you'll take care of everything.'

'Thank you, Janine. Shut the door quietly, if you please.' She turned to Jake Russell, 'You were saying, monsieur?'

'I'm afraid I shan't be in France much in the future. I'm sorry this has been an . . . abortive call.' She didn't know what that meant. He was on his feet, however, 'Goodbye.' His hand-clasp was firm. It left her with a feeling of sadness.

* * *

Mademoiselle Derain died peacefully that Christmas, although ravaged by cancer. Crystel went with Guy Derain to her funeral to represent the firm. The cemetery was bleak and cheerless. Cemeteries should be in sunny hollows, like St Henri, where one's bones could lie and soak up the sunshine.

She still didn't go regularly to church, but occasionally, as now, she thought of death and felt comforted that the priest would take care of everything when her time came. Guy said his aunt had been a staunch believer, and when the last rites had been performed had smiled and said, 'I go in peace.' She was quite bald on her death bed, he said, the bird-nest had been a wig, and she weighed only seventy pounds.

Madame Derain had been unable to come, and he and Crystel stood together in the searching wind, blowing, it seemed, all the way fom the Pyrenees, and listened to the priest saying what a good servant of the Lord Clothilde Derain had been. Crystel regretted they hadn't talked together more often, but no doubt she'd regarded her as young and flighty. I've changed, she thought.

Afterwards she and Guy got into his car, and when she saw his pale worried face she asked him on impulse to come to her flat. 'We'll have a cognac before we go back to the store,' she said, 'it'll warm you up.'

'Thank you,' he said without hesitation but not eagerly, 'I'd like that. I feel sad about my aunt, and today about life in general.'

'Cemeteries make one feel like that,' she comforted him, 'when I walk through ours at St Henri I feel . . . transient, one's problems fall into place.' I'm speaking as if my youth had gone, she thought. I should get away from Maurac, from its small-town atmosphere. I should go to Paris before it's too late.

In the flat he cheered up after a cognac and some black coffee, and talked about himself. 'Madeleine finds running the home and looking after Michel, our broken one, extremely difficult. He's a spastic, and she won't part with him, although the doctor has advised it for her sake as well as the other two children. She neglects them, almost seems to resent them being fit and healthy. I do my best.' You look neglected also, she thought, seeing the creases in his shirt collar. 'The worst thing for her is when I go on my business trips. Stock has to be bought and replenished, as you know. Sometimes it means Paris, sometimes Toulouse. I feel I don't give enough time to choosing. I mean to read books and periodicals which are sent to me, but at home there are so many demands.'

'There is no doubt styles change,' she said. 'When I was in Paris I saw the difference. My friends and I used to window-shop in the little boutiques around our Boulevard. I still have a memento.' She lifted her handbag from the floor and took out the key-ring with the clover-leaf medallion, handed it to him, smiling. 'I'm keeping it for my car when I get it.'

'You'd like a car?'

'Oh, yes, indeed. One has to dress oneself up warmly in winter on a Moped. That's one of the reasons why I wanted an apartment in Maurac. The journey to St Henri became tiresome in the dark.'

'I quite understood that was one reason.' He didn't look arch. He looked around. 'You've made your flat charming. Your taste is impeccable, of course. Don't misunderstand me. You have natural style as well as being beautiful. Everybody adores you at the store.'

She was flattered and pleased. 'Oh, what nonsense!'

'It's true. You set a certain tone in our establishment. You do your work well, you are light-hearted, and the very sight of you is good for us. That's what beauty does.' She had to believe him. He was quite naïve. His brown eyes were on her. He put down his coffee cup as if he had made a decision. 'I have a suggestion to make. It's been in my mind for some time but I should never have wanted to hurt Aunt Clothilde in any way. She always said when I visited her that it gave her great peace of mind to know that the books were in good hands.'

'Did she? Did she really say that?' She wished now she had made the effort to go and see Mademoiselle Derain.

'Indeed. But now that she's gone . . . ' He looked at her, and she saw what fine eyes he had but how pallid the skin was around them, how his suit had lost its rich original blueness. 'As I told you, Madeleine feels badly when I'm away from home. I must, of course, continue to go to Paris for furniture and carpets, but my father always dealt with a Toulouse firm for the bric-à-brac. I'm afraid I haven't been adventurous enough in that department. Crystel, could you take it on for me? It would only mean an occasional trip for you . . . we'll work that out later. Perhaps your assistant could be encouraged to take on more on the book-keeping side.'

'Perhaps'. Her heart was fluttering. 'She wants to extend herself.' Janine, plump, bespectacled, was also inquisitive. She remembered how she had barged in that day Tricia's friend had visited her. What a strange, charming man, not at all like Guy . . . 'I've discovered her looking through the books to see how it is done. But, Guy,' more and more in the last year she had found herself calling him by his first name, 'are you sure I'd be good enough?' She was excited at the prospect. For a long time she'd thought there was a preponderance of flowers on everything he bought from lampshades to *chaise-longues*.

'Far better than I am. Would you please try it? You would have a car, of course, at the firm's expense, and an allowance to run it. There would be an increase in your salary, naturally and commission.'

'I'm greatly honoured.' She saw in her mind's eye a clean sweep of the posy-strewn *bibelots* and in their place, simplicity, thick, square-cut glass ashtrays, more wicker work, cleaner lines in the lampshades.

'Our store deserves the best and I am unable to give it that, but with your help I could.' He wasn't bestowing a favour, he was begging for one, and his sad brown eyes decided her. And the thought of the car, naturally. There was room in Monsieur Rambeau's garage . . .

'I'd love to take on the job, Guy.' She put her hand to her mouth. 'I beg your pardon.'

'Always call me Guy, please. Your new position as my unofficial partner in the firm permits such informality.' It was the first time she remembered him speaking jokingly, and she laughed with him. They went back to Derain et Cie in the late afternoon, bubbling over with their plans.

The assistants all seemed to be genuinely pleased. Guy invited them into his office and offered them wine. Janine's spectacles winked, and she offered to take over the books at any time. Crystel said she would see. It seems, she thought later, bundling herself into her warm trousers, jerkin and scarf to mount her Moped, that I have become a career woman.

CHAPTER SEVEN
1972

ONE spring evening, when Crystel got back to her flat, there was a letter behind her door with an English stamp. Tricia, she thought, lifting it and going into the kitchen to put down her purchases. What a pleasure it would be to hear her news. They had started to correspond fitfully after Jake Russell's visit.

'I think he regards me as a muddled Mum,' she'd written, 'and that annoys me because I know I'm not, i.e., I'm a Mum but not muddled, or if I am it's only temporary.' Crystel thought of him sometimes, how alert he'd been, charming but not at all restful.

She decided to leave the preparation of her casserole until later. Perhaps Tricia would mention him in her letter. Am I interested? she asked herself. She poured some Pernod into a tall glass, put some water and ice in it, picked up the letter and went towards her favourite seat in the window, telling herself how lucky she was, not quite believing it. Did muddled Mums feel lucky? Mark Jolyon would be two in June, Emma Jane just three . . . such grand English names. She already kept a birthday book and was meticulous about sending cards to her friends' children. Clayton George Cook had been sent one with toy soldiers marching round it on his third birthday last December. Perhaps a birthday book is the first sign of becoming an old maid, she thought.

Spring was a time of longing. A career didn't seem so important when soft winds blew through the narrow street of Maurac, and Mademoiselle Coco started once more on her *arrangements*. She looked across the street. Yes, today it had been '*Le Pique-nique*.' She was rolling up a small carpet of artificial grass, and she had still to carry in the indispensable china dog with the one glass eye which gave it such a louche expression. She heard the door-bell of her flat being rung, it seemed tentatively. She frowned, deprived of her plan to read Tricia's letter, then got up hurriedly. Sometimes Papa had business to transact in Maurac, but not usually as late as this. She went to the door, opened it, and found Guy there. *'Quelle surprise!'* she said. 'Do come in.'

He followed her into the room, apologising. 'I'm sorry. Perhaps you're dining. Just say and I'll go away.'

'Of course not,' she said, 'I'm delighted to see you. I'm having a drink. Would you like to join me?'

'Yes, please. Anything.' He looked around, distrait.

'Pernod? That's what I'm having.'

'Parfait.' He didn't look interested in what she was having.

She went into the kitchen, wondering why he was here at seven o'clock when he ought to be dining with his wife. Perhaps since he was going to Paris tomorrow he had something to discuss. She had suggested that on this trip he should look out for more subtle tones, (she had put it carefully), using herself as an excuse. 'All my life I've avoided patterns. I feel I need a quiet background for my looks.'

'Have you come to talk about colours, Guy?' She brought him his drink, sat down across from him at the window. 'You see how plain this beige silk is that I'm wearing. At least it doesn't shout at my hair.'

'It is true your beauty needs no adornment,' he said, taking a sip from his glass.

'You're teasing me.' She smiled at him. 'Have you brought some swatches?' She couldn't see any signs of them.

'Yes . . . no, I regret. I left them in the car.' He took another sip. 'You talked of dove-greys, sage greens and so on, but there's nothing like that. They have ghastly names like "San Francisco", "Orinoco Gold", "Carmen". It is hopeless.'

'It was only a suggestion, merely to tie up the accessories with the carpets.' She looked at him. He seemed worn out. 'Are you on your way home for dinner?'

'No.' He shook his head. 'I left the house half-an-hour ago. Madeleine thinks I'm having dinner on the train.' He put down his glass and she saw that his hand was trembling. A few spots spilled on Tricia's letter. She saw the ink run. 'I'm tired, Crystel, to tell you the truth, tired of it all. I only go four times a year from home now since you took over Toulouse, but she makes it impossible for me. I know she has a lot to put up with because of Michel. We both love him so much but can do so little for him. Although it would be hard, I know he'd be better off in a place where he could train within his capabilities. I've found a special school in Calliac. I could pick him up each evening, but she won't hear of it. She says it would kill him . . .'

'Couldn't you get someone else to talk to her?'

'I've tried. The doctor, the priest, she just says it's impossible.' He lifted his glass, looked at it, took a long sip and put it down again. 'Mustn't drink too much. That's fatal. And then this evening she started again about me going away from home. What if something happened to him when I was in Paris? How would she get to me, what would she do? Actually,' he looked boyish, 'I had no intention of going until tomorrow, simply on account of Michel, but then I thought, I'll go, since she has keyed herself up for it. And so I came to you.'

Their eyes met. She had known for more than a year that he was in love with her. She pitied him. She longed to be loved by a man, but she didn't love him. 'You'd like to stay here, is that it, Guy?'

'Would you have me?' He pushed back the lock of mousy hair which had fallen over his forehead. 'It isn't fair to ask a beautiful young girl like you. There must be someone . . .'

'Not in Maurac.' She thought bitterly for a moment of René's mother. She leant forward and touched his knee. 'I want to be honest. I don't love you. And if we go to bed together it wouldn't be because you've been good to me in so many ways. It would be because I like you, and I'm . . . lonely.'

He got up and came and knelt beside her, put his head in her lap. She stroked his hair, thinking absently what a good colour it was. It would never go grey. He looked up at her, his brown eyes wet. She had never seen a man cry. 'I'm lonely too,' he said.

She enjoyed being in bed with him. It was more than an assuaging of hunger. His skin wasn't as smooth as René's, indeed it was rough and pimply across his shoulders, but he was a good lover. He had a lot of love to give and he had had experience of women.

Afterwards she showered and, while he showered, she made dinner for them and he helped her to serve it. He was as deft in the kitchen as he had been in bed. She lit the single Scandinavian lamp and they talked a lot as they ate. There was no embarrassment between them. It was like an extension of their business life together, only pleasanter. They discovered each other in a more intimate way, questioning, explaining, just as she had wanted to do with René.

He told her he would never leave Madeleine because of the children, and especially Michel, and she promised she would never let him stand in the way of someone she might fall in love with. Meantime he could come to her flat occasionally on his way home, or perhaps stay overnight when Madeleine went with the children to visit her parents. They would be extremely careful in the store and avoid comment.

'In any case,' she said, 'my reputation has already been spoiled by Madame Baron of *L'Hôtel de la Poste*. That's the way of small towns . . .' She told him of Tricia and Jan. 'We were all different, and I expect our towns are different too. Jan said that outward appearances were very important in hers. She said it was a kind of inferiority complex because they were a new country. And Tricia said they were what she called "reserved" in hers, possibly because they were old and had become blasé.'

'That's reasonable. What would you say was the peculiarity of Maurac?' Guy asked. He always seemed to listen attentively to her.

'Curiosity, without a doubt.' They laughed together.

'Jan never went back to America,' she told him. 'She's still in Paris and has a baby.'

'It would be what she wanted,' he said, 'I know what I want at this moment.' She'd hardly ever seen him laughing like that, opening his mouth and throwing back his head. Even his wobbling Adam's apple she found touching. And he had good teeth.

81

'We'll go to bed again soon.' She was enjoying so much having a man to talk to that she didn't want it to end.

'Whenever you want to,' he said. 'Tell me what the English girl looks like. We had quite a few English in the store last summer, you remember. They all seem to have the same face, long, like sheep.'

'It may be a general characteristic but Tricia wasn't like that. Her face was thin, certainly, but her eyes took up more room than eyes usually do and they were beautiful, a rich brown. Do you remember those curtains we got for Madame Recamé . . . the ones she returned? How in the folds they were purple? they reminded me of Tricia's eyes. I expect her husband fell in love with them. She doesn't mention him much . . . Guy, oh, Guy . . .' he was stroking her hair lovingly. His other hand was busy too.

'So beautiful, you're so very beautiful.' He was adept at small sweetnesses. It had been a long time since René. She got up.

'Afterwards,' she said, 'I'll read you Tricia's letter . . .'

'Dear Crystel, I should have written to you a long time before this to thank you for those lovely cards you send to the children . . . so French and pink and white like the fondants we used to buy in the confiserie.

'I'm kept very busy with the children. Emma seemed to resent Mark at first and once I even caught her putting a pillow over his face. "Send him back," she said when I smacked her. But now that she's three she's become fiercely protective of him which in a way is just as bad. There are no half-measures with Emma. I love them, but I do envy you your delicious little flat perched above Rue Boniface and your marvellous career . . .

'I've told you about Kingsley Heath before, haven't I? The Garden City our firm is building? It was my father-in-law's project, but he tends to delegate a little now . . . in Jake Russell's direction, Roger says. He gets the boring parts and Jake the overall planning and layout. He's Howard's blue-eyed boy and can do no wrong. Roger finds him difficult to work with but then their temperaments couldn't be more different.

Remember we used to talk in Paris about how our nationalities shaped us? Oh, those good talks we had! Poor Roger . . . as he says, his father never gives him any credit, as if he was expecting him to fail. Or is it Roger who expects to fail?

'*I get quite excited about Kingsley Heath. I wouldn't mind having a go at it myself, if I weren't so tied up with the children. My father-in-law bought the Estate when he was only twenty-three, but then, as Roger says, he had a father who believed in him, the great Jolyon Roger.*

'*This is stolen time and there are a hundred things to be done. Mercifully the children are sleeping but they'll be up and shouting any minute. Then it's shopping and tea and bath-time then Roger comes in, then it's supper then a hundred more things to be done when the children are in bed. How clever of you to avoid la ronde domestique.*

'*But there are compensations, I tell myself. I often think about Jan and how she manages in Paris. In some ways it's easier for her. At least they can live their own lives. Do you think she'll go back to the United States? Surely her parents must want to see their grandchild?*

'*We have such a strong bond, the three of us, forged I think by that strange night we spent in the police station. Remember Jean Paul? I think of you when I start up my Mini and see the clover-leaf on the keyring . . . I expect you have a smashing Renault. Shall we meet again sometime? Life puts you on a treadmill. I shouldn't say that. I'm really very happy. Write and tell me about all the beautiful things you buy on your trips and the beautiful clothes you wear and the men you meet. Write soon . . .*

'*Love, Tricia.*'

Crystel folded the letter and looked at Guy lying beside her. His eyes were closed. He looked happy. 'You've been sleeping,' she said, bending over to kiss him. 'You haven't been listening to a word.'

'On the contrary,' his eyes remained closed, 'I've listened intently. To me it's a window into the way the English live, your friend lives. I would say she compares this Jake with her husband . . . a little?

'You met him, remember, last August, in the store. In the bedding salon. You came to speak to me about . . .'

'Yes, a forbidding presence, I thought. He made me feel inadequate.'

'You inadequate? After tonight?'

'Oh, yes. I know myself. That's a help, at least.'

'You're lovable.' She was happy. And she knew he needed bolstering. Who didn't? 'What do you think of Tricia?'

'A strong character too. She longs to express herself. Babies aren't enough. She's happy with them for the moment, not even that with her husband. Or maybe she's ambivalent. She wants to protect him, and at the same time she doesn't *want* to have to protect him. Perhaps she's the kind of woman who will always have to take the role of protectress, I don't know. What comes through to me is that she hasn't got what she wants.'

She lay down beside him. 'Have any of us?'

'No, that's true. But when one has it for a little while you make the most of it, don't you agree.'

'Yes, I agree.' She wondered if Guy hadn't been married if she could have fallen in love with him. At this moment she felt she could. But, no, on second thoughts, he was a father figure to her, a delightful father whom she wanted to make happy. She put her cheek against his. 'Let's go to sleep. You've to be in Paris in the morning.'

'Sometime you might go in my place and call to see your other friend, Jan?'

'Could it be arranged?'

'Certainly. On the firm, of course. *Par la bonté de Derain et Cie.*' He laughed with her, drawing her close.

CHAPTER EIGHT
1972

WHEN Jan's sister wrote and said she was coming to Paris she was wild with delight. 'Rony's coming, George!' she'd cried, waving the letter in front of him in bed and he'd pulled her down beside him to nuzzle at her neck. 'You sho' are jubilant this bright and lovely mornin', Halleluia, praise the Lord!' Sometimes he spoke in what he called Mississippi River Boat, intended, he said, to break Clay's habit of speaking in French.

She had succumbed for a few minutes to the delights of his warm dark-brown flesh. It *felt* brown, even in the dark under the clothes, but Clay had disturbed them, climbing into bed beside them in his short vest and shouting, 'Ronee, Ronee!' copying her. 'Not Rony,' she'd said, taking him in between them, '*Aunt* Rony, Miss Veronica Sirica, if you like. Oh, isn't it goddam wonderful!'

The morning of her arrival, Jan dressed early and went to the market off the Avenue Lenine within sound of its thunder. They had grabbed at the flat in St Denis because it was on the west side of The Avenue and it would be useful to be near it when George got his car. Jan had visions of him slipping into the stream of traffic in a neat little Fiat or even a Renault, but it hadn't happened that way. Clay had happened first, and he'd used up all the extra money being born and being reared. They wanted to do their best for him.

In the market she bought things they couldn't afford, pineapples and avocados and a hunk of pink Auvergne lamb, and courgettes and sweet *petits pois* to go with it, and a carton of *moules* for a starter, and lettuce and chives for a green salad, (Rony would want a side salad) and hurried back laden to the flat to let George off to work.

Later on, when she'd scrubbed and polished until everything

was as clean as a whistle, and prepared the vegetables, and put the lamb rubbed with rosemary in the oven, she'd gone downstairs again with Clay and asked Madame Lu-Yang in the Chinese laundry to keep an eye on him while she went to Bondi's for pistachio icecream. If she ran very hard all the way back from the shop she'd get it into the Frigo before it melted. Rony had always liked pistachio icecream. She said she was partial to it. Jan could just hear her saying it.

Still, even scrubbed and polished, you couldn't say the place bore any resemblance to Cedars. It was so small for a start, and Cedars with its cool large lovely rooms and its parkland was a dream of delight. Dream was the right word. How often she'd lain beside George with her swollen stomach, (*enceinte*, he'd told her meant a fortified hiding-place, fancy that), and afterwards with Clay between them and dreamed about Cedars. *Oh, Momma, if you knew how my heart aches, you wouldn't say I was hard . . .*'

But then again, Rony wasn't one to make comparisons. She'd never felt about Cedars the way Jan had. She got away from home 'pretty damn quick' to live in her own way in New York. She wasn't afraid of Momma, and she only pitied Poppa. 'Live and let live' was Rony's motto.

She had written to Jan when Clay was on the way. 'Don't let her bulldoze you. You've chosen your bed so stick to it. It sounds a pretty nifty one to me with good mahogany furniture, so take my advice, keep the Atlantic between you and Momma.' She'd thought that was a terrible thing to say at the time although she knew it was true.

'*La voici! La voici!*' Clay shouted, jumping up and down on the chair where she'd put him to watch out for his aunt. His little bottom waggled from side to side like a puppy's. She ran to the window and looked down. He was right. Rony, tall rangy Rony, was paying the taxi-man, bending forward to speak to him, her carroty hair falling over her face, hitching up her shoulder bag with that characteristic gesture of hers. Something he said made her laugh out loud. She wasn't sexy; Jan had got all the boys, although her looks weren't a patch on Rony's. Maybe it was because she treated men as if she was a man herself.

She must have heard Clay thumping on the window because she swung round and looked up, saw them and raised her arm, straight up like the Statue of Liberty itself, Jan thought, America, here I come. She waved back, seizing hold of Clay's hand to waggle it from the wrist then, wild with excitement, she scooped him up in her arms and went running down the stairs into the street where she collided with Rony. They didn't kiss. Rony had never liked the kissing lark, but somehow there was a muddle on the pavement of Jan, Clay, and Rony, and in the background the interested faces of Mena in the Chinese laundry and the taxi-driver who was smiling and waving as he drove off. Rony had that effect on people.

'Oh, Rony,' she said, weeping copiously, leading her upstairs, turning round on every step with Clay in her arms to reassure herself that her sister was real.

'Still the same old Jan,' Rony said smiling up at her, 'cries when she's happy,' and then, 'say, this a helluva fella you've produced. Bee-ootiful . . .'

*　　　*　　　*

They were having a meal at the little restaurant where Jan, Tricia and Crystel had eaten on the tenth of May 1968. It was Rony's last night and George was taking care of Clay. He had said he didn't mind and in any case it made the outing cheaper. He hadn't said that to Rony, of course. He and Rony had got on very well right from the start. They teased each other, talked and laughed a lot and, well, you could never be jealous of Rony. George had summed it all up. 'I like her a lot but I'd never want to lay her.'

They had taken the Métro from St Denis to Montparnasse and then to St Sulpice, and walked along the narrow street where Jan showed Rony the plaque which gave the street its name. 'We loved it, even after the riots, maybe because of them. It made it kind of special.'

She pulled Rony from one side to the other to show her places she remembered, the Disco, the shop which sold the beaded dresses and fancy specs, the shop with the Mexican gear, the old courtyards with the *ateliers*. They zig-zagged so much that Rony said they'd better go in and eat or some mad Frenchman would run them down.

The waiter who wore the Mexican wooden beads said he remembered Jan. Who could ever forget *Les Événements*, or mademoiselle, he added, but that may have been to please her. He was certainly struck by Rony but in a different way. He showed her a wary, admiring kind of camaraderie and he talked to her about the food and wine although Jan was paying for it, but of course he wasn't to know that.

Rony said, 'Look at it this way. Momma couldn't help leaving Paris in a hurry when *Grand'mère* Leroy was dying. Maybe she was glad of the excuse, but it was a cast-iron one. She had to get back and so she missed out on seeing George.'

'Maybe it was the sight of Clay. Are the kebabs all right Rony?' It had changed to being Greek now. She remembered the terrible *ragoût*, and the noise and the shouting in the streets. 'She burst into tears when she saw him in the hospital. Her face was a screwed-up little nut of disappointment. Poppa looked ashamed of her.'

'Well, embarrassed, I'll bet, but afraid to say anything. Anyhow she did fly over to see Clay. That's the main thing.'

'That's the window where the stone came through and pole-axed me . . . but she didn't even call George, although she said she would. He'd been so glad for me. When he visited me at the hospital the night before he'd said, "Honey, I'm glad yo' lil' ole Momma's a-comin' to see yo'." That was to hide his feelings. Actually he's got a beautiful voice, don't you think so, Rony?'

'Very pleasant. If a voice could turn me on, his surely would.'

'He didn't say how disappointed he was, but I know. He was sitting in the office all day waiting for the call . . .'

Rony was speaking. 'Look, Jan, there's no point in going over old scores, huh? The thing is she's sent me as her envoy with a cheque to bring you all back to Maryland. I'm not pressing you. I know what I'd do in your place, but are you and George going to take it?'

She didn't ask Rony what she'd do in their place because she knew. Underneath all her mixed-up feelings about Momma she could see what she allowed Momma to do to her, reduce her to a quivering, spineless jelly. The only solution was to stay well away, keep the Atlantic between them. Wasn't that what Rony had said? She'd solved her problem. She'd cleared out. It was terrible seeing so clearly and yet going on making the same mistake. 'I don't think so,' she said, 'George and I have talked about it, oh, don't think we haven't discussed it, ad infinitum.'

'I've heard you discussing it,' Rony said, 'you crying and then the bed shaking.'

Jan waved her hands in embarrassment. 'He's passionate, George, he thinks everything can be solved by that. He's a superannuated flower-child. But he's also as stubborn as hell. He says he'll take me back when he's good and ready and with his money. Momma seems to forget that he wants to be back in the States just as much as she wants us back. He's been saving up for ages. We all go short to keep his American Piggy Bank full.'

'When do you think that'll be?' Rony asked.

'When he's got enough money.' They both laughed.

'I can see George's point of view. He's a proud nigger,' she didn't get offended when Rony spoke that way, because basically she was kind, right through to the marrow of her bones, 'he wants to do it under his own steam. If I can tell Momma you're intending to come she'll be happy. But would you take the cheque all the same?'

'I would, but George would kill me.'

'Well, I tell you what.' She tore the cheque into small pieces, put them in the ash-tray with all her mess. 'Tainted money,' she said. She smiled her wide rangy smile at Jan as she rummaged in her purse, got out her cheque book and wrote in it. 'There,' Rony said, tearing out the cheque, 'that's for half the amount, which is all I . . . no, dammit, semantics are the end, which is what I can afford comfortably. And don't start waving those hands about and going red in the face, it isn't for you, nor for George. It's for Clayton to buy him sneakers and overalls and a sack of his own to carry when he goes on the plane, and maybe a snazzy little scarlet raincoat . . . for Pete's sake, Jan, are you going to start crying again?'

Fortunately the waiter with the wooden beads and the not-quite-shirt appeared with the bill and Jan was able to flourish her fifty franc note at him. 'I'm sure I remember you,' he said as he took it. 'Did you come with a dark girl and another one . . .' he undulated one hand in the air and half-closed his eyes in remembered ecstasy.

'You've got it,' Jan said, 'that was Crystel.'

* * *

She saw her sister off, again weeping copiously. Rony wasn't going straight back. She was meeting a girl friend and going to the South of France for a week before she flew back from Nice. 'My heart's being torn in two,' Jan said, 'I want to go back with you. I miss Cedars so much, the space and the light . . .'

'Don't mix me up with Cedars,' Rony said. 'I live in an apartment block in the middle of Manhattan. I'm short on space and light but it suits me. Anyhow, home is where the heart is.'

She took Clay in her arms and hugged him fiercely, for Rony, that is. 'You don't know how lucky you are. People never know because they see from the inside-out.'

CHAPTER NINE
1974

IT was a blustery Saturday in March, too cold to take the children for a walk, Tricia decided, and the afternoon stretched ahead to be filled. I'll get through it, she assured herself cheerfully.

She'd long since realised that Roger required her to be cheerful. She knew she set the tone for the family. She'd stuck to her decision to have only two children . . . after the first wild careless rapture. It was a joke she had with herself. She'd give them all she had, but after . . . she didn't know what she meant by that, except that she knew her brimming energy would have to be directed *somewhere*. To bring up children wasn't the sum total of human existence, at least her existence.

Emma would soon be off to school, but Mark seemed to cling over-long to his babyhood. His push-chair was still used. The winter had been severe, and sometimes after their daily walks her fingers had been so numbed on the handle that she'd had to soak them in hot water to get the blood to circulate. She'd told Roger laughingly that she was getting frostbite, and he'd said absently, 'My poor love.' His own worries were dumped on her lap every evening.

Jake Russell was the chief cause of them. He'd been with the firm four years now and, except when he was away on his 'fancy fact-finding missions', as Roger called them, he only got in the way. She saw little of him. She didn't know whether she liked him or not. He interested her. No wonder, since he was in bed with them quite a lot . . . would he laugh if she said that to him? He was an unknown quantity. Last night he'd been at The Crescent for dinner, composed as always, a little more voluble than on their first meeting . . .

*   *   *

91

'Anyhow you're pretty well ahead with the overall planning, Jake.' Tricia and Mary exchanged glances as Howard spoke. Kingsley Heath was always with them. Jake Russell waved away Mary's chocolate mints.

'We're still held up by the rehousing of the factories, I find,' he took a sip of coffee, 'which is holding up the spine road.' Was there a hidden criticism of Roger in his words, she wondered. He always seemed impartial, only interested in getting the job done.

'How many still to go?' Howard turned to Roger.

She'd watched his compressed lips, the drumming of his fingers. 'It's difficult to say. I've offered Caldwell's two other sites and I think they'll bite. They've got to be near water for their effluent. Grubbs are the worry. They need a pretty large area for their repository. The manager's so damned nit-picking!' His voice rose.

'They're being feather-bedded,' Howard said. 'Tell them they're holding up the whole project by their shilly-shallying. What's the point in Jake submitting his detailed plans to the County Council if we've to build round a furniture warehouse? A fine focal point that would be!'

'I'm doing my best, Father.' He stared at his plate.

'Drink your coffee,' Mary said vaguely, 'it'll only get cold.'

'I'll go and talk to them!' Tricia had watched her father-in-law's colour rising. 'They'll listen to me.'

'It wouldn't do any good.' Roger was truculent. 'It's my pigeon. Leave me to handle it.'

'Roger's right, Howard,' Mary had surprised Tricia. 'You can't give him the job and then take it away from him. Besides you were told by the doctor to delegate. Delegate!' She looked round the table for support.

'Yes, take it easy, Howard.' This was Jake Russell.

He shrugged the remark away. 'I'm as fit as a fiddle. It's this damned frustration that's bad for me. When I think how long ago it is since I bought the Estate, over thirty years . . . you get off your backside, Roger, and speak plainly to that lot! I've set my mind on having the decks cleared for building by nineteen seventy-five and that's less than a year away.'

Roger's face was white. He'd pushed his plate away from

him and taken up his brandy glass. The aftermath would be played out in their bedroom. She dreaded it . . .

*　　*　　*

Emma was at her side, clutching her Paddington Bear which now rarely left her side. 'Where are you taking us, Mummy?'

'Somewhere nice.' The idea came. 'We'll go in the car to a lovely big house to see something special.'

'What kind of special?'

'You'll see when you get there. Go and find Mark's wellies and his fluffy bunny scarf . . .' You swore you'd never resort to baby-talk . . .

She strapped the children into the back of the car, got in and turned the ignition key with the clover-leaf dangling from it. She had a pang of nostalgia for her student days in Paris. We were going to change the world, she thought, as she backed expertly down the narrow laurel-lined drive.

She no longer worried about there being insufficient turning space, but over the years she'd built up an indentikit in her mind of the house she'd like, large sunny rooms, large gleaming kitchen, broad sweep of drive. A spatial quality. She read every book she could find on house design.

She stopped at the main road, turned into it when it was clear, in good spirits. We could have tea at Kingsley House if the café's open . . . her thoughts returned to Roger. He'd been irritable and carping this morning, going off early to keep an appointment with Grubbs' manager. 'Father doesn't even try to understand the difficulties I've been up against all along the line, then there's that upstart Russell criticising all the time . . . ' Would they have been difficulties for either Howard or Jake? It's a question of presence. Roger hasn't got it. But whose fault is that?

She stopped at the lights beside the Bowling Club, 'le feu', she remembered Crystel calling them. The green was deserted. She knew the rotation of the bedding-plants in the flower-beds like the back of her hand, wallflowers just now with a border of forget-me-nots, in mid-summer they'd be hauled out, rangy and woody-stemmed to make way for the dahlias. The old green-keeper wasn't imaginative. Maybe she'd be the same at his age . . .

'Green!' Emma shouted.

She turned right, drove slowly downhill through busy Stone-leigh Road with its bustling afternoon shoppers and underneath the railway bridge to the next set of lights. How that bridge had scared her as a child in case a train should run overhead! The children didn't seem to mind. Car children. Would this be her life, a child-minder, a husband-consoler? Sometimes she had great spurts of energy when she felt the house couldn't contain her. Perhaps routine was meant to be a corset or a crutch . . . 'Amber gambler,' she said to the two in the back. 'Always wait. Now off we go.'

She gathered speed a little. There were no more lights now, it was just a question of keeping a look-out for old people crossing waywardly, or dogs, the usual afternoon traffic. One of her bursts of joy exploded inside her.

I'm only a girl still, not twenty-five. There's lots of time yet. On the way back I'll buy something nice for supper, rainbow trout, and Roger and I will have a special dinner. This is my 'special' day. I'll light candles on the tables, make up my eyes. Perhaps I don't give him enough time, don't listen enough. It doesn't matter about Parky not coming much now. I couldn't bear anyone else in her place. She makes me laugh. And I like to hear about Royston and their love-life. Once Emma's at school maybe I could drop off Mark to play with Minnie and do something on my own. I wonder if I could do more for Parky's children . . .

They'd passed the Latham Town Hall now with what she thought of as its Hapsburg look, squared tower and fancy tesselations. She'd never been to Austria but maybe one of the town worthies had . . . that's another thing I'd like to do, travel . . . now she was turning by St Peter's. I could go sometime, pray for my soul. No, I'm better lighting candles for Roger. Besides, he never understood, being Protestant . . . she was careering at a fine speed along the leafy outskirts of Latham.

'Look,' Emma said, 'checked cows.'

'Friesians. They give a lot of milk. And, here we are, folks!' She drove with a flourish between the massive pillars crowned by stone pineapples, up the long drive and stopped in front of Kingsley House.

'It's only a house!' Emma wailed.

'No it isn't.' What if it's shut, she thought, then saw two other children with a girl in an anorak going up the steps.

She unstrapped the children, they clambered out and immediately started whooping and running about as if they'd been in solitary confinement for a year. She grabbed them in each hand.

'Stop that! You've got to behave . . . it's special. Take Mark's hand, Emma. I'll take his other one. We'll go up the steps nice and quietly.'

Their feet clattered on the black and white tiled floor. The lofty ceilings and the unexpected rows of showcases seemed to subdue them.

'Is it a supermarket?' Emma whispered.

'No, no. It's birds and beasts . . . but they're stuffed.'

'I don't like them stuffed. I'm frightened.'

'You won't be when I show you both this special thing. I used to bring my little brother here and he loved it.'

'Where's he now?' Emma looked accusing.

'He died.' She couldn't bring herself to say, 'He's gone to Heaven.'

'So where *is* he? Under the ground?'

'He's . . .'

'Is he stuffed?'

'Oh Emma! Here's the place. Now, you stand there. You'll get a good view and I'll lift Mark up.' His wiry little body was a ton weight. Emma was peering in through the glass.

'It's a piece of country! Real country. Look, there's stones, and ferns, and a beetle, Mummy, a beetle!'

'Yes, I see it. Don't bang on the glass like that. Now it's a hide-and-seek game. Do you see this poem stuck up there?'

'I can't read poems.' She pronounced it 'pomes.'

'I'll read it to you. What you've got to do is to find the little animals or insects. Ready?' She cleared her throat, feeling stupid, nothing had impinged yet.

' "Who killed Cock Robin . . ." '

'I can see him,' Emma shouted. 'He's lying there all over blood. Look, Mark, see, he's all over blood.'

'Don't frighten him. It's only red paint. Now, listen here's the next bit.

' "I said the sparrow,
  With my bow and arrow,
  I killed Cock Robin." '

She pointed. 'Do you see the arrow sticking in his little red chest?'

'It's a stick.'

'It's an arrow. Now see if you can find the sparrow with his bow . . .'

It came, the sense of *déjà vu*, as she spoke. In the background was the gleam of glass, the children's voices, but she herself was a child again. She could feel the tug of her plaits against her scalp, David's soft cheek pressing against hers. The feeling was sad and somehow sweet. How quickly my life has gone already, yesterday, it seems, a girl of twelve . . . she heard that girl's voice, 'I said the dove, I'll mourn for my love . . .'

Who is my love? I've never loved Roger passionately, completely, as a woman. I've wanted him, needed him, but any young man would have done. I should have gone to bed with someone in Paris as Jan and Crystel did, and then I wouldn't have rushed into marriage. I've still to experience love . . . the voices of the children filled her ears and she said, 'Shh, Shh! They'll put us out. Have you found the sparrow, Emma?'

'We've found the fly and the fish and . . . a great big dirty owl.'

'He isn't dirty. I'll read you his bit.' She looked up at the framed poem.

' "Who'll dig his grave,
  I said the owl,
  With my pick and shovel,
  I'll dig his grave . . .' "

All life and death are here, she thought. It's a Greek tragedy. I'm the chorus. Her arms ached from holding Mark and she put him down. The attendant came across the room to her. He was an old man, grey-faced, thin and bent in his navy-blue uniform, with peaked cap bearing a band on which was woven, 'Latham Town Council'. The outfit gave him authority. She imagined him stripped of it, thin, wispy grey hair, suit too big for him . . .

'It's a great attraction for the kids, that show-case. Can't tell you how many come to see it time and time again.'

'I came years ago with my brother, when I was a girl.'

His too-white, too-even teeth smiled at her. 'I wouldn't have said you was much more than a girl now. Them's two lovely kids you got there. Nice to get them when you're young. With all this Women's Lib going on means you can get back to work again all the sooner.'

'Do you believe in it?'

'T'aint nothing new, you know. Me missus always worked in other people's houses. Fancy talk most of it to let the women have a good time. 'Course, if there ain't much comin' in, stands to reason she has to earn a bit.'

'Yes, that's true.' It was no use saying there might be other reasons. 'I don't suppose the tea-room's open today?'

'Yes, it is. Experimental like. Starts in March now instead of April. There's a nice bit of subsidy from the LPT, you know. By Jove, they're goin' to make some changes here! Next time you come with the kiddies there won't be many trees and squirrels running about like now. There's goin' to be a grand housing estate for the best folk, leastways those who can afford their prices. That's the trouble with them schemes. Take me. Always wanted a garden. Strange enough, working here has made me keener than ever. That there show-case you was lookin' at, a little paradise, ain't it?'

'Yes, it is. Well . . .' she daren't tell him who she was. 'I'd better take those two off to the tearoom . . .'

'You didn't say about the bull,' Emma said.

'Never mind. We'll come back again.'

'That's right,' the man said 'you come back.' He nodded at the show-case. 'Don't know what it is about that there mock-up, but it gets me. "All the birds of the hair . . ." he peered at the framed poem, "fell a-sighin' and a-sobbin' . . ." '

'Did you write it?' Emma asked.

He turned an amazed look on her. 'A fine poem like that. I wouldn't be workin' here, Missy, if I did.'

'Yes, well . . .' Tricia said.

'Loo!' Mark's whimper rescued her.

When she went into the tea-room with the children she saw Jake

97

Russell sitting alone at a table. He'd seen her too and was on his feet, smiling. She was embarrassed, felt her cheeks redden, as she walked towards him, Mark holding her hand, Emma pulling at her skirt. Triumphal progress, she thought.

'Fancy seeing you,' he said when she got up to him. 'Are you having tea?'

'Yes, funnily enough.' She made a face, smiled.

'Great. Have a seat.' He pulled out chairs, helped the children into theirs. He treated them like adults, not making any fuss.

'Did you come to see Cock Robin?' Emma asked him. Tricia watched him. His eyes were amused.

'That and other things.' He beckoned to the woman behind the counter. 'I expect you'd like loads of chocolate biscuits, Emma?'

'Would I Mummy?' Her shyness gave Tricia confidence.

'They never refuse chocolate biscuits. Is that why *you*'re here?'

'Me?' He laughed. 'I've other fish to fry.' The woman was standing beside them, smiling. 'A plate of chocolate biscuits, please . . .' he looked enquiringly at Tricia, 'a pot of tea and orange juice for the children?'

'Yes, that would be fine.'

'We saw a fish in the glass case,' Emma said. 'It had a shell in its mouth full of blood.'

Tricia laughed. 'She heard you talking about fish. They like the gory bits best.'

'What was it?'

'A complete "mock-up", as the caretaker calls it, of poor Cock Robin, his life and death. I'm sentimental about it.' The woman was putting down a plate of chocolate biscuits and two glasses of orange juice, then the tea-things. 'Look at this! Say "Thank you" to Mr Russell, children.' Too fulsome, she thought.

'Thank you,' Emma said. Mark was engrossed in unwrapping his chocolate biscuit.

'Breathing space,' she said. 'Shall I pour out? I'm dying for a cup of tea. You begin to feel . . . fragmented. Conversations started and never finished. Sometimes I feel I don't even listen to Roger. Did you see him today?'

'Yes . . .' He seemed to hesitate. 'Was he all right when he left this morning?'

'So-so. Do you take sugar?'

'I'll help myself, thanks.'

'Why are you asking?' She stirred her tea, feeling apprehensive.

'You know about the bypass business, don't you?' How deep his eyes were. Impossible to see their colour.

'Howard's Government bogey?' She smiled at him 'Don't tell me Kingsley Heath is going to be cut in two?'

'It will be if we don't get the spine road fixed up and the firms off it.'

The apprehension was there again. 'That's Roger's bogey. Especially Grubbs.'

He nodded. 'It's the cash-flow situation that's worrying Howard. He's to meet all road diversions out of his own resources before the houses get off the ground, or on it.' Why was he stating the obvious?

'Roger knows that. He's worked terribly hard on it.'

'Surely . . .' His eyes were half-closed as he looked at her. 'I ran into Grubbs' managing director last night in the Lion, Jack Broadstone, and he fell in with a suggestion of mine . . . for another site.'

She felt cold. 'Roger's seeing him this morning.'

'I know. I've seen Roger.'

'So he knows about . . . your suggestion?'

'Yes. He wasn't as enthusiastic as Broadstone.' His mouth twisted.

'Can you blame him?'

'There's nothing personal about it, Tricia. The Trust comes first with me.'

'That's very evident.' She lifted her cup, saw her hand tremble, took a sip of tea. She was under Roger's skin for the moment, felt his mortification.

'I've upset you.'

She tried to speak calmly. 'Why should I be upset? The Trust comes first, as you say. But . . .' she spoiled it. 'Roger wanted to fix up Grubbs *himself*. It was important to him. His father . . .'

'I've been clumsy. I see it in your face.'

'Can you?' She raised her chin. 'You're imagining things. Was he still in the office when you left?' *She* could imagine things, Roger sitting at his desk, brooding.

'Look, Tricia . . .' He was sincere enough, but the hint of a smile showed round his mouth, as if it was all too piffling, Roger having the carpet swept from under him.

'You haven't told me why you're here?' she said, smiling too brightly.

'Mummy . . .' Mark became a baby, whimpering softly, and she took him on her knee. He settled his head on her breast, put his thumb in his mouth.

'Where's Emma?' She looked around and saw her talking to the woman at the counter. 'You need eyes in the back of your head . . .' Jake Russell was looking at her, making her embarrassed. 'This one,' she touched Mark's head, 'is softer. Like Roger.'

'Is he?' His smile was charming, boyish. 'You look . . . fulfilled.'

She laughed, still embarrassed. It was the depth of his look. 'Do I? Sometimes I feel I'm acting on the stage, that this is just a role, that I'll wake up and find myself Tricia Baker again. It wasn't the way I thought things would happen.'

'Better to go along with the tide.'

'I'm not complaining. I must have asked you a million times why you're here and each time I stop you from answering.'

His face was smoothed-out, relaxed, and she thought there was a certain fineness, even nobility in his forehead and the setting of his eyes. He's relieved I'm not going to make a fuss, she thought.

'I'm spying out the land.'

' "I said the fly, with my little eye . . . I saw him die." ' She felt a sudden heaviness of spirit, a foreboding. Roger, she thought, I must get back and ring Roger . . .

'Howard is dead-set on the first house being started this summer and having a slap-up do here. I've got the overall plans of the Estate ready, but not the individual one of each house. I'm here to have a look at where we'd site the first one.'

'So it's business after all?'

'Have I gone down in your estimation? Yes, but I didn't expect the pleasure of your company.'

'Thanks. I must be going.'

'You haven't finished your tea.' His voice had a satisfying

timbre. She didn't want to notice his good points. 'Howard wants to have the first brick laid with some ceremony.'

'How typical.' She laughed.

'And important. I'll leave the park more or less as it is with a play-ground for children added, and possibly tennis courts. But my idea is to build, say, five or six houses in a semi-circle round the lake . . . I'm not an artistic bloke, but I like to set the standard, as it were, with the first few I put up. It's a way of . . . making a statement.'

'*Very* painterly.' She liked teasing him. 'I was admiring the lake as I drove up. There's something about water . . .'

'It ties a house in, gives it an immediate look of permanency. Landscaping takes longer.'

She looked around. 'You'd use this place for the ceremony?'

'Yes, that's the general idea. Buffet tables in the hall. Plenty of champagne, of course. Howard has always seen Kingsley House as the focal point. He can't bear to see old houses pulled down and I agree with him. We'd leave the gardens largely untouched so that people can enjoy them. He's talked about a garden for the blind, sweet-smelling flowers . . .'

'Oh, I wish I could be in on it. I've all kinds of ideas!'

He smiled at her, surprised. 'Do you mean on the day of the ceremony or working in the firm?'

'Sour grapes, really. I don't know.'

'I think you'd be a decided asset.'

'It's a pipe dream. Roger wouldn't like it at all.' Her anxiety returned at the mention of his name. 'He likes women to be at home, bring up children, look after him . . .' She called across the room. 'Come along, Emma! We're leaving . . .' And then, 'I wonder who'll be chosen for the opening ceremony? Someone posh, I imagine?'

'No, that isn't Howard's idea at all. He wants someone who may be a future house-owner. He might even ask you.'

'That's nonsense!' She felt her cheeks redden.

'It isn't nonsense. Typical young mother with children, daughter-in-law of the man at the top. He thinks highly of you.'

'You're raising my morale and my hopes by leaps and bounds.' Emma was at her side, truculent. She silenced her with a look. 'I'll float home on air.' She shook Mark gently and made him get down.

'You really must go?' Jake Russell got up. 'I was hoping you'd walk down to the lake with me.'

'No, I've got to get back.' She hardly saw him. 'Take Mark's hand, Emma, and stop sulking.' She was suddenly fiercely anxious about Roger. Why had she wasted so much time? She had to be there when he got in, to comfort him. There was no possibility he'd have taken lightly the matter of Grubbs.

'It's been nice seeing you. Remember what I said about the ceremony.' He was smiling down at her. His eyes disturbed her.

CHAPTER TEN

SHE had given the children their tea, bathed them and tucked them up, read stories to them. And then she'd gone downstairs and sat at the window.

But still he didn't come.

She had prepared the trout in the kitchen, putting chives, butter and peppercorns inside them, wrapped them in silver foil, put them on a tray ready to go into the oven.

But still he didn't come.

It was eight o'clock now. He always telephoned if he was going to be late. Sometimes it was necessary to take some business associate to The Lion for a drink, so he said.

She thought of telephoning his father, but was afraid she would sound too anxious and needlessly alarm him, and certainly his mother. She walked about the house, impatient with herself and yet telling herself she was right to worry. He'd been gathering courage to make a definitive stand with Grubbs, and then to find out he'd been forestalled would be a bitter blow.

It's his father's fault, she thought, feeling angrily protective. He ought to remember how easily Roger's self-confidence is undermined. By choosing someone ruthless like Jake Russell, Howard has said in so many words, 'Look, this is how you should be.'

Was Jake ruthless? She was ambivalent about him. She'd seen him smile today, seen a softer curve to his mouth when he relaxed. But he was single-minded, disregarded personalities and, as far as Roger was concerned, constituted danger.

The secret of success is single-mindedness, she told herself, going quickly to the window because she imagined she heard a car. Roger hasn't got it. He isn't interested in the Trust. The job has been chosen for him. *I* would have been interested, she thought, given his opportunity. There's scope for my energy, my imagination.

She went racing upstairs, thinking she heard Mark calling her, but on the landing all was quiet. She stood and looked out of the leaded window and saw the trees tossing in the wind, dark masses of navy-blue against the paler sky. In my new house, she thought, I'll have slim poplars or light, feathery willows, no overbearing trees sucking the goodness out of the soil . . . she saw the headlamps sweep over the laurels giving them an oily glisten. She made herself walk calmly downstairs, breathing deeply, open the door without too much haste. She arranged her face in a welcoming smile as she heard the door bang. He came towards her, lurching. He was drunk.

'Roger . . .' He reeled past her and made for the staircase, stopped and held on to the newel post. 'Sorry I'm late,' he said, his voice slurring, 'stopped to have a little drink.'

'Where?' If he'd been at The Lion it would be all round the town.

'Don't know. Little pub down by the railway. Drove around for a bit. Found myself there. Sorry, Tricia.' He turned towards her; his face was white, wretched. His nose was running. He looked like Mark when he'd been crying.

'Wipe your nose.' He fumbled for a handkerchief, and she felt sorry for speaking sharply. 'Here's a tissue. You look ill. Why didn't you come straight home instead of drinking?'

'Why?' He rubbed his nose backwards and forwards with the ball of tissue, like a child. 'That bastard, Russell . . . doesn't give me a chance. I've tried, God knows how I've tried with Grubbs to get them somewhere suitable, and then that bastard . . .' he was swaying . . . 'comes along and says cooly, "I've fixed it." Can you beat it?'

'Never mind. You did all the spade work, softened them up. Come to bed. I'll help you. Lean on me.' His arm went round her neck obediently. How like Mark he is, she thought, as she put her arm round his waist. Together they went slowly upstairs.

'It isn't as if I haven't tried, Tricia. You know how I've worked on this bloody project, night and day, never hard enough for father, though, and then this bastard comes along . . . comes along and usurps me . . .'

They were in the bedroom. She made him lie down and bit by bit managed to undress him. His body was hot, as if fevered. She wondered if she should ask Dr Chapman to come and then felt ashamed to let him see her husband in this state.

'Roger,' she bent over him, 'have you a pain anywhere?'

'No, no pain.' His face was the same colour as the sheet.

'Did you drink a lot?'

'Drink's good when you're unhappy. No, didn't drink a lot. You know me. Too much makes me sick.' This was true enough. He had what his mother called a nervous stomach.

'I'm going to sponge your face and it'll make you feel cooler. Then I think I should phone Dr Chapman.'

'That bloody old woman? No, thanks.' His mouth went up at the corner and she smiled with him.

'Oh, Roger . . .' She put her hand out and stroked his cheek.

'There's nothing wrong with me physically. Sweating a bit, that's all.' He took her hand and held it over his heart. 'It's here. A constant ache.' He looked infinitely pathetic.

'You're tired and hungry, that's what's making you feel depressed. I'm going to get you something to eat and, when you've had a good sleep you'll feel better.'

'That bloody bastard . . . "By the way, Roger, your worries about Grubbs are over . . ." Other people there too . . . ' But the fire had gone out of him; his voice sank, faltered, stopped.

She flew downstairs and took the bread out of the bin, put two slices in the toaster, filled the kettle. Was tea the best thing, or black coffee? When she had a stomach upset, which was seldom, she couldn't bear coffee, but tea had tannin in it. Would warm milk be better? The truth of the matter is I've had no experience of husbands coming home drunk. I've led too sheltered a life.

The toast popped up and she buttered it, cut the slices into fingers and put them on a plate. She compromised by making a small potful of tea and putting some milk on the stove to heat. When it was warm she poured it into a jug, placed it on the tray with the rest and went upstairs. Her whole mind was concentrating on Roger. She was Roger, feeling his disappointment in himself as acutely as he did. It's fatal to expect too much from your children, she thought, as she nudged the bedroom door open with her knee and went in.

He was asleep. His pale hair had fallen over his brow and he was breathing regularly. She felt his face. It was no longer hot. One arm was thrown across the bed, the fingers clenched. She lifted it gently and put it beneath the sheet, then she went out quietly and shut the door. She went downstairs, put the jacketed trout in the refrigerator and sat down at the kitchen table.

Most girls would lift the phone now, she thought, unburden themselves to a favoured confidante but, although they were friendly enough with the young marrieds of Latham, she'd never seen much of the women apart from their husbands. They talked about 'something or nothing'. She'd been closer to Jan and Crystel in that year in Paris. They'd had the world before them, had trembled on the brink of their future, full of longings and dreams. Marriage was the last thing she'd thought of, but who would have imagined that Roger in only four years could have become so different from the engaging young man she'd wanted so much.

He's been crushed by his father's lack of trust in him . . . the slow anger which grew at the thought spread to include Jake Russell. That insensitive rock of a man, she thought, with his buttoned-up face that rarely smiles and eyes so deep-set that you can't ever imagine what he's thinking. He and Howard were two of a kind, able to ride roughshod over other people if it suited them. Roger hadn't a chance against them. I need to talk to someone, she thought, getting up . . .

She went into the hall and dialled her mother's number, stoking her self-righteous indignation and trying at the same time to dampen down the belief that *she* wouldn't have been so easily influenced. All very well to say that, but hadn't she felt Jake Russell's charm today when he came out of his absorption with the Trust and looked at her, really looked at her? What did he see anyhow? A practical young mother, or just a provincial lump?

'Hello.' She heard her mother's voice. Thank goodness. She couldn't have borne her father's chumminess.

'Hello, Mother. How are you? Have you your counselling

hat on?' Supposing she said that. No, her mother had never had a great sense of humour.

'Quite well. How are you and the children? I've meant to pop in and see you this week but there's been this and that . . .' And the other.

'I've got a problem. Roger came home drunk tonight.'

Not a moment's hesitation. 'Well, I daresay that happens to most wives sometime or other.'

'It's because he's unhappy in his job. You know how his father pushes him all the time, and then today Jake Russell did something which upset him badly . . .'

'Well, why didn't he come home and tell you about it instead of getting drunk?'

'I don't know. I suppose he wanted to think and he drove about and then he landed up in a pub. He hasn't been well all winter.'

'Get him to see a doctor, then. Take my advice, Tricia.' When her mother said 'Take my advice' it always made her feel truculent.

'I suggested him seeing Dr Chapman but we both dislike him.'

'I'm not surprised. He's quite out-of-date. The Newtons chose him for you, didn't they? That new young man, Peter Jobley . . . helps us a lot in the FPA. And he's more of Roger's age for a start. He's modern in his thinking, accepts the view that a lot of illness nowadays is psychosomatic.'

'Does he? Don't you think some doctors are too ready to say that?'

'It happens to be true. If you saw my case sheets in the Marriage Guidance Council . . .'

'I can imagine. Maybe I'll persuade Roger. He's ambivalent to doctors. Mother, what I phoned to ask you, was . . . do you think I should speak to his father about . . . everything? Maybe he doesn't realise how hard he leans on Roger.' She thought, that makes it psychosomatic. But on whose side? There was silence at the other end. 'What do you think?'

She heard her mother's considered, counselling voice. 'That situation existed long before you met Roger. People don't change. If I were you I shouldn't speak to Howard Newton.

107

Keep out of it, that's my advice.'

'But how can I?' She felt her anger rising. 'It's my husband we're speaking about. It affects me.'

'Bolster him up, then. I've had to do it with your father all his life . . .' so she had, come to think of it. Her father was a public figure. He was strangely diminished at home . . . 'but don't interfere in their work. They hate it.'

'Well . . .'

'I'd give the same advice to anyone, Tricia.'

'I suppose you're right.' She would have liked motherly advice, not advice she would give to anyone. But would you have taken it, she asked herself.

'I don't try to be right. I just try to see a problem objectively. Roger will have to fight his own battles.' Her voice softened. 'Don't worry too much. It'll sort itself out. Things always do.'

'I suppose so. How's Daddy?'

'He's at a meeting tonight. He's well.'

'I'd better hang up. I just had the idea I'd ring you . . .'

'You were quite right. It's good to externalise sometimes. Pop in and see me soon, not tomorrow, nor Thursday; but any other day. We'll have another talk.'

'Thanks. 'bye.'

* * *

The next morning she got up early, made an attractive breakfast tray for Roger with the best china and a single rose . . . she'd seen the idea somewhere . . . and took it up to him. He was sitting up in bed.

'Feeling better? You were still sleeping when I got up.' When she leaned over to kiss him she caught the stale smell of whisky.

'I won't go in today.' His eyes were dull.

'That's sensible. Have a good rest. I'll try to keep the children quiet.'

'You shouldn't wait on me.'

She sat down on the bed and ruffled his hair. 'Why on earth

shouldn't I? I like to. Shall I phone the doctor?'

'There isn't anything wrong with me. But I'm not hungry.'
He wasn't looking at her. I'd rather have him drunk and
obstreperous than this, she thought.

'We could change doctors. I agree with you about old
Chapman.'

'No doctors.'

She sighed. 'Well, drink some coffee at least.' There was a
loud wail from Mark. 'That's Emma teasing him. They're
having breakfast. I must go down. Would you like me to bring
up that book about Apollo Seven?'

'I don't want to read.'

'Right,' she said briskly, then wished she hadn't been so
brisk. There was a ring at the door bell. 'That's Parky. I must
let her in. I'll come up later and we'll have our coffee together
and a chat.'

'Take the tray back with you. The sight of food sickens me.'

'You wouldn't even like to eat my rose?' She looked at his
face. 'No, well . . .' She lifted the tray, went downstairs, laid
it on the settle in the hall and opened the inner door, heavily
leaded with languid ladies in stained glass like the window
upstairs. 'Hello, Parky! How are things this morning?' She
didn't know where this cheerfulness came from.

'Minnie's quite lively but Royston's off work with a boil on
his bum, excuse me, lovey. He gets them a lot. I tell him it
must be the bad in him coming out.'

'Oh, come on, you like him.' She was even breezy. I'm like
a nurse, a chameleon.

They were together in the kitchen now. Mark and Emma
were tucking into cornflakes, Mark in Roger's chair. 'Hello,
Sparky!' he said.

Emma sniggered. 'It isn't Sparky, stupid, it's *Parky*.' She
had a white moustache.

'He's a clever little lad, that's what he is, ain't you, lovey?'
She was tying on an apron. 'Just look at him sitting there like
Mr Newton himself.'

'We went to see Cock Robin yesterday,' Emma said. 'He
was all over blood.'

'Well I never!' She looked at Tricia.

'It's in Kingsley House, you know, in the Park. A kind of . . . exhibition. You should get Royston to take the children.'

'No,' she shook her head decidedly, 'that would be above his head. Nothing fancy. He just likes to sit around all day in a fug smoking and making cups of tea. He feels the cold, you see. But he's good with Minnie, fits and everything. That's a blessing.' She heaved a heavy sigh.

'Well, what's first?'

'My husband's in bed.'

'Oh, the poor soul. What's he got?' She folded her hands on her fat stomach. She liked discussing husbands.

'Nothing much, just a chill. Could you clear up here and keep an eye on the children? I don't want them going careering up and down to the bedroom. I've to zoom to the shops and it's too wet to take them with me. Then you could get away about eleven. I'll get anything in the supermarket you want.' I'm always guilty about having her work for me. I try to please her . . .

'No, there's nothing. I'm taking fish and chips back. Royston likes them. Says it's the best thing about England. I'll stay till twelve since he's there. The money's useful.'

'That suits me beautifully. Now, where's my purse, I had it to pay the milkman yesterday.'

'You put it in the bread-bin, Mummy,' Emma said.

'So I did . . . it's my new hiding-place. I'd better *zoom* away.' It was a word she used to amuse the children. Sometimes she clowned, put her arms out like an aeroplane. 'Be good, you two.' I'm like a clockwork toy which is wound up each morning, she thought, backing the car out of the garage and down the drive. I don't get time to think . . .

When she got back the kitchen was empty, but there was a note from Parky on the table. 'Did the dishes and the floor. Took the children back there. Royston'll play with them. Pick them up about twelve.' Sara P.

There's something intuitive about Parky, she thought, as if we're sisters under the skin. Did I look pale or worried, or did Roger call down to her to keep the children quiet?

Never mind. She had a breathing space. She'd make the

coffee now and they'd have it together. Perhaps they could talk sensibly about last night, and what they were going to do about 'things' . . . she meant his father's attitude and why Roger minded Jake Russell so much . . . the door opened and she turned round, kettle in hand. It was Roger. He was fully dressed.

'You're up!' she said brightly. He was white-faced, unshaven. His eyes looked bewildered, as if the kitchen was strange to him. The cold sense of foreboding she'd felt in Kingsley House came back to her. What are you going on about, she chided herself. He's alive, isn't he? His eyes wandered up to the high dim ceiling, down to the Klee posters she'd stuck on the walls. Anything to brighten the gloom. He sat down on the basket-chair and looked at the boiler. 'Feeling better?' She hated her bright false voice which seemed to have become part of her. 'I'm just making coffee. Parky has taken the children home.'

'My head's aching.' He drew his hand over his brow, ruffling the fine hair which he still grew too long. 'I made a fool of myself last night.'

'Rubbish. Every married man's entitled to stumble up the stairs once or twice in his life.' She smiled, feeling her lip tremble.

'Incentive and drive, father calls it.' He wasn't listening to her. 'You'll never get anywhere without incentive and drive . . . well, I haven't got it.' His fingers drummed on the table. He didn't look at her. The sight of him sitting there, figure slack, the pitifulness of him, suddenly couldn't be borne. She crossed the room quickly and knelt down beside him.

'Don't be such a defeatist! You're off-colour, that's why you're feeling like this. You weren't well all winter I know how you feel. Remember what I was like after Emma?' But that was purely chemical, she thought. She'd read it up later. With him it's a slow-growing thing, from childhood. 'I've been worried about you.' She stroked back his hair and his head sunk beneath her hand as if the small weight was too much for him. 'And then there have been those endless arguments you had with people to get them to move their factories . . . ' She could have bitten out her tongue.

'So Jake Russell steps in and ties it all up. Great! And no

doubt father could have done the same with his left hand tied behind his back.'

'Why must you always denigrate yourself? You've let this whole project get you down.'

'I've let my father down.'

'You shouldn't pay too much attention to him. He's obsessed by this Kingsley Heath. It's his baby. Don't you remember you said that once?' He wasn't listening.

'Everything has to move at a hell of a lick for him. He seems to forget it was easy twenty years ago. There weren't endless bureaucratic hassles. But it's a big company now. The bigger a company becomes the more unwieldy it is to handle.'

'That makes such good sense that I'm surprised you don't say it to him.'

'I have, often. He doesn't listen to me. He thinks I'm making excuses. God, I'm tired of it all.' He put his head in his hands.

She looked at him, feeling helpless. However bad things were, surely you didn't give up? They'd had this same conversation, or variations of it, for the past two or three years. My vision's clearer now, she thought. Perhaps that's what having children does for you. She remembered the Matron at the Nursing Home saying it did a woman good, washed out all the poisons. At eighteen Roger seemed to me attractive, even masterful. I got married in a cloud of veiling, orange blossom and illusions. I don't know him now. 'Listen to me, darling,' she said, 'you're run down, tired. You've still got the remnants of that 'flu virus you picked up last winter. That's what makes you . . .'

' . . . come home drunk?' He lifted his head to look at her. There were dark smudges on his cheekbones, his eyes had a full moist look as if he'd been secretly weeping. She was afraid, adopted the false brightness as the only weapon she knew.

'So you want to sign up for Alcoholics Anonymous? One little binge in five years! You know you've always come home as sober as a judge.'

'Because Mummy was waiting.' He'd lowered his head into his hands. They were trembling.

'My God!' She spoke sharply because of the fear. 'Oh,

112

come on, Roger, that isn't fair. You'd think I classed you with the children.' And yet as she spoke there were echoes of her own voice in her mind, 'Mark, Emma, Roger . . . come in from the garden . . . "Children, come down for supper. Bring Daddy . . .' " Like an older child.

'I'm joking,' he said. He lifted his face to smile at her. It was a trembling grimace. 'You're a wonderful wife, strong . . .' She didn't like that word. It had undertones. She didn't look strong. The mirror this morning had shown her a slight dark-haired girl who'd lost her girlish roundness, who had eyes like a lemur in her thin face. *That wasn't what he meant* . . . Tears roughened her throat.

'I'll phone your father, say you won't be in today, that you have a . . .'

He was looking at her, frightening her, the same look as he'd had when he came into the room. Her heart began to tap lightly on her chest wall, like fingers, cautioning her. She'd seen it before, put it down to abstraction, pre-occupation with the Trust. Even the children had noticed. 'Daddy,' she'd heard Emma say in her imperious treble, 'you aren't listening to us.'

She looked up uneasily at the Delft clock on the kitchen wall. It was a quarter to twelve. 'I've got to go. Parky will be getting fed up with the children.' She said, desperately, 'Would you like to come, Roger? Get some fresh air? It would do you good.'

'No, no,' he turned away his head, 'you get them.'

'Aye, aye, sir.' Her false foolish cheerfulness made her cringe. She remembered the big-chinned Matron. 'Come on, now, Mrs Newton, push harder, that's the stuff to give the troops. Heave ho, my hearties!' She'd hopped from parade ground to foc'sle deck with the greatest of ease. 'I haven't given you any coffee. I'm losing my wits. Make yourself some while I'm away.'

'No, thanks.'

'And you haven't eaten a thing. No breakfast.'

'Leave me.'

Give it up, leave him. He hates to be harried. He's had enough of it. You've had long enough with him to know he's

113

not a talker. His mother once told you he'd been a small secretive boy . . . her heart suddenly banged against her ribs, no light tapping this. Was she barking up the wrong tree? Had something happened on his way home last night? Like an accident, which he was keeping from her? That's wishful thinking, she told herself. An accident would be simple. This state of mind isn't new. It's of slow growth. At least her mother had been right there.

'Why are you looking at me like that?' he said.

'Am I? Sorry.' She felt too young for all this. 'You frighten the living daylights out of me at times. I feel there's something I should be doing to help, but I don't know what it is.'

'I'm feeling low, darling.' He was with her again, conscience-stricken. 'That's all. I'll snap out of it. I'm sorry to be such a misery. You must get fed up with me.'

'If you don't get fed up with me first. I'm always tearing about and we never have time to talk. I suppose every young married couple goes through this phase . . . horrid word.' She pulled a face at him. 'We ought to give ourselves a treat, Roger, get Parky in to look after the children, dine and wine in style.' She knew as she spoke that the last time he'd suggested that, it was she who'd been too tired. 'Shall I ask her?'

'Not today. But yes, we'll do that. Sure.'

'Okay. Back soon.' She kissed him, dashed out of the house and into her Mini which she'd left at the door. She turned the ignition switch, a shaft of sunlight made the silver leaf gleam. God, the sweetness of being just eighteen and not a care in the world, she thought, backing down the drive, (is my life spent backing down this drive), three girls on the threshold of their lives . . . she had an intense burst of nostalgia for Paris, the *croissants* and *essence* smell of morning in the Boulevard Raspail. 'Oh hell!' Swearing helped. This drive ought to be cleared of those horrible laurels. They had a graveyard smell, and look at the moss all over, like a graveyard too. It's always damp even on dry days, and there's fungus growing in the basement. I hate going down there . . .

She was in the road now. In my new house there will be no basement, there will be wide windows and a wide view, there will be so much sky to be seen through my picture windows that it will look like a Dutch landscape. I'll buy the children kites to fly from the front lawn which will be short dry turf, and where it meets the patio there will be no moss. I'll have an outside chimney to give it character . . .

CHAPTER ELEVEN

THE weather on the day of the ceremony was similar to the day in March when Tricia had visited Kingsley House with the children. It was blustery and only fractionally less cold.

She reflected as she dressed that it wouldn't keep people away. The town had been divided into sheep and goats, those who had received invitations to the reception at Kingsley House and those who had not. The hoi polloi would at least be able to keep out of the rain.

Since the night Roger had come home drunk he'd gone into a shell of his own making. He consistently declared that he was quite well, and she had to accept this. He was quiet but pleasant, drank sparingly, and was non-communicative about what went on in the office. He stopped complaining about Jake Russell, and she never mentioned him. He said he did want guests to dinner, and she took this to mean anyone from the office as well as their own friends. If she thought of Jake Russell at all it was with confused feelings. She wouldn't admit to herself the pleasure she'd got from his company.

They developed a pattern of living which would have suited a couple twice their age. Roger worked on papers he brought home, she cleared up after the meal and then did some tasks in the kitchen while she listened to the radio. She went to bed before him and was usually half asleep when he joined her. She couldn't argue or complain because he gave her no cause for complaint. Their love-making was spasmodic, brief, carried out in darkness, a silent coming-together which seemed only to push them further apart.

Everything in her told her the situation was impossible, but his strange flatness of temperament created in her the same kind of calm. Only once had there been any kind of a scene. She'd wakened suddenly one night and realised he wasn't beside her.

She'd snatched at her dressing-gown, looking at the illuminated dial of the bedside clock. It was three-thirty. The bed was warm.

She ran downstairs, fear stirring in her. She should have *done* something, broken the spell . . . he was sitting in the lounge, a book open on his knee. Their eyes met, and she recognised the familiar flatness. Her heart rapped on her ribs. 'Roger . . .' The bright light made her blink and she rubbed her eyes. 'What's wrong, oh, what's wrong?' She ran to him, removed the book and sat on his knee, putting her arms round his neck. 'I thought I'd lost you. What are you doing down here?'

'I couldn't sleep.' He spoke with his mouth against her neck.

'Roger . . .' her voice broke. 'It's not like what I expected. We're not close any more. I've a terrible sense of failure, of not having fulfilled my part of the bargain.'

'No, no . . .' His voice was muffled.

'You don't let me help you. You've built a wall round yourself. I mean to talk to you when you come up but you don't give me any encouragement . . . and then I go to sleep.'

'You're imagining things.'

She sat up. 'Look at me.' There was no vitality in his face. 'I wish I could believe that. Have you seen yourself recently? Why don't you tell me what's worrying you? It's got to be me or your work . . . unless there's another woman?'

'Only Emma,' he said, and the small joke cheered her.

'If you can't tell me, what am I to do? You're shutting me out.' She wept weakly because she was tired.

'I don't mean to.' His finger traced a tear making its way down her face. 'Look what I'm doing to you, making you cry. You're too good for me . . .'

'Oh, shut up! I hate you to crawl.' She was miserable at the hurt in his face. 'Can't you confide in me, tell me what it is you feel?'

'Feel?' He sighed slowly and heavily, turned his head away. 'The utter . . . fruitlessness of it all.'

'But that's . . . nihilistic!' The word came to her from somewhere. 'Is it your job? But even a job you don't like shouldn't make you feel like that. Nobody must feel like that. Nothing would get done! Think if I were the same. I wouldn't do a thing for the children, I wouldn't attempt to clean the house, I'd lie in my own filth . . .'

'Hey!' he said, 'stop it. And anyhow, what are we doing sitting here at four o'clock in the morning?'

'It was your idea.'

'We'd better get to bed.'

'Carry me upstairs,' she said, pouting, being feminine, feeling whorish. She shook back her hair, lifted her throat.

He stood up, keeping her in his arms, and walked towards the hall. 'Thank God you aren't Parky.' She trailed one hand, thinking, all the same, there's no real rapport, we don't laugh enough . . .

Upstairs he laid her on the bed and undid the cord of his pyjamas. She slid down the shoulders of her nightdress and they came together in a desperate kind of short-lived passion which left her unsatisfied and tearful. He lay heavily on top of her, seemingly asleep, and she had to roll him off her. The fear was back again as she tucked the clothes around him and lay down quietly at his side.

*　　*　　*

She stood back from the mirror to look at herself in the black and white patterned dress she'd chosen. The sheer black tights and black high-heeled sandals were right with it. Howard particularly wanted her to be smart; Roger liked her in anything she wore. She had decided not to wear the broad-brimmed yellow hat she'd bought. It would only blow off at the wrong moment, and she had enough to think about with the whole of Latham watching her.

Yes, that's it, she decided to put on more eyeshadow since there would be no hat. Marriage took a lot of practice, and not many got it right at first. She remembered Lyn Telfer telling her that her husband sometimes got up and went walking in the middle of the night. But it was a detail when you thought of Candy Roper's husband who liked her to wear only satin cami-knickers. Tricia had said it would have been worse if *he*'d wanted to wear them. And what about Myrna Gillespie, with her soignée elegance and fastidiousness, who was lumbered with a husband

118

who wouldn't take a bath? Beside those outré figures on the Latham landscape, Roger's behaviour was a mere nothing. He was a small secretive boy, she thought, fastening a thin gold chain round her neck, a small secretive boy grown up. He'd made an effort to charm her at the beginning and then he'd slipped back to being what he'd always been.

And what are you? she asked herself as she ran downstairs. You haven't even taken the trouble to find out . . .

* * *

'Isn't it quiet?' she said to Roger as they drove away from the house. The suburban road had a deserted air, and the only movement was in the branches of the heavy plane trees which dipped in the wind. He nodded. She turned to smile at the children, to enjoy them while they were good. They were more subdued than usual, probably awed by the sense of occasion. Emma was wearing a green dress with a yoke of broderie anglaise. Its attraction for her was the dorothy bag made of the same material. Mark was solemn in a pale shirt with a navy bow tie to match his trousers, his hair slicked back from his broad infantile brow. 'Good boy,' she said, loving him.

'Why didn't you wear your hat?' Roger said, stopping at the lights beside the Bowling Club. The dahlias were in now. Here and there she saw the tight fat buds amongst the broad leaves.

'I decided at the last minute not to. I had a dreadful vision of my saying, "I declare this stone well and truly laid," and watching my hat sailing over the crowds.'

'We'll see your pansy eyes.' She was touched, felt her heart swell with love for him and the children. Perhaps she could forget about the last three months, treat them as the tail end of the mysterious bug which had never been traced because he'd refused to see the doctor.

'Jake Russell will be there,' she said. 'The last time I saw him was at Kingsley House. We had tea together.' She was amazed how the secret held for three months came tripping off her tongue.

'Tea?' His voice was sharp. 'You never told me.'

119

'You make it sound like heroin.' She laughed uneasily. 'There was nothing to tell, and it was swallowed up in the general cafuffle that night . . .'

'You didn't tell me about meeting him. And he never mentioned . . .'

Emma interrupted. 'Who's Jake, Mummy?'

She rushed to tell her. 'Remember when we went to see Cock Robin and we met that man?'

'A big dark man, dark as night?'

'Dark as night . . .' She laughed, said to Roger, 'Isn't she the limit?'

'Dark as night, dark as night . . .' Tricia looked out of the window, the child's chanting in her ears. But when he smiled she remembered how his face had broadened, had lost its darkness and the lines at the corner of his eyes were laughter lines. And the timbre of his voice. 'You look fulfilled.' You couldn't analyse tone, it was a question of the senses. Nor expression, come to that, only by the effect it had on you.

And there was the depth of his look, as if he could see into her heart . . . don't go over it. It's of no importance. You're of no importance to him. Look instead at the pleasant prospect, the fields on either side waist-high in summer grasses. There would be branched buttercups and poppies in their depths. The sight aroused some childish memory of running through fields such as those and seeing a fine golden dust rising up around her. And of lying deeply down in the long grasses and hearing the insect noises in her ear . . .

The car was slowing down. Roger was muttering under his breath. Ahead of them was a procession of cars. She came back to the present with a stab of apprehension. 'Gosh, I hope the rain keeps off, gosh, I'm nervous, gosh, I'm glad I didn't wear that stupid hat . . .' She spoke like a schoolgirl to make fun of her nervousness.

'You'll rise to the occasion,' Roger said. 'My mother used to say that.'

'So did mine.'

He turned slowly in between the gateposts with their carved stone pineapples on the pillars. 'The whole of Latham,' he said, 'trust father to lay it on with a trowel.'

'That's my job,' she said, and laughed.

If it was Jake behind the planning, he'd done it well. The wide flight of steps up to the open doorway was banked on either side with masses of hydrangeas. Inside, the dark oak panelling gleamed between high fan-shapes of all the flowers of summer, and in between the more exotic stripe of orchids and the satin whiteness of magnolias.

Howard, Mary, the Mayoress and her husband were standing in a row in front of the Gothic stone fireplace. Roger and Tricia joined in the queue leading to them, each grasping a child firmly by the hand. 'Talk about Royalty,' Roger whispered.

'Your mother looks like the Queen Mother.' She could see Mary in fluttery chiffon, white gloves, a pink hat turned up at the front. The soft, faded face, the bow-shaped mouth which smiled so sweetly gave her a certain resemblance to the Royal Personage except that she lacked the aplomb. Her hands were as fluttery as the chiffon. The pink hat was slightly askew.

Howard was beaming and full of vitality when they reached him, handsome in morning dress, a carnation in his button-hole, his hair brushed sleekly to his head. 'Hello there! Stunning dress, Tricia. What d'you think of our nuclear family, Mrs Keswick?' He spoke to the stout woman at his side. The gold chain of office lay on her large chest as if on display in a shop window.

'Oh, is this the young Mr and Mrs Newton and their family? I've never had the pleasure.' She shook hands vigorously. 'No one will say *you* haven't the best of taste.' She gave Roger a prodigious wink. Now that Tricia remembered, wasn't she the owner of Keswick's Handbag Emporium in the Market Hall?

'This is my new dress,' Emma said, 'and a bag to match.' She swung it on her wrist. 'Mark hasn't got one.'

'Boys don't carry bags. Or perhaps they do now?' Tricia smiled at the woman.

'My dear, they're all the rage! Quite discreet, though, with a wrist strap.' She seemed to be looking at Roger to see if he qualified. Mary Newton interrupted.

'So elegant, Tricia. I feel like a Christmas cracker but Howard wanted me in something garden-partyish.'

'You look just right. Very regal.' Was she afraid of Howard as well?

'Yes, you do, Mother,' Roger said.

'Thank you, son.' Her eyes lovingly searched his face.

'Come on, children . . .' she gave Roger a discreet nudge. 'We're holding up the queue.'

They moved on and were given a glass of sherry by the waiter, who offered to fetch some orange juice for the children. She was looking around when she saw Jake Russell pushing his way through the crowded room towards them. She drew in her breath, thinking, 'the dark man . . .' His face looked grim, then he caught her eye and the darkness left it.

'The most important family here. Are you ready for the fray?' His look took her in from top to toe. '*Very* smart.' Was his voice admiring or mocking?

'I had a bet with myself,' he said to Roger, 'whether Tricia would be smartly dressed or prettily dressed.'

Roger looked down his nose at him. He didn't speak.

'Did you win?' she said.

'Yes, I won.' His face broadened with his smile, the lines showed at the corner of his eyes and she had to smile with him.

'Clothes are only part of it. I was fine when I got up this morning, but now, seeing all those people . . .' She looked around. 'Who's that man in the loud tweeds?' She was flippant because of her nervousness.

Jake glanced over her head. 'It's Rab Wilkes, a recent acquisition.'

'Of the Trust?'

'Yes.'

'You didn't tell me about him, Roger.'

'Didn't I?' She saw a muscle twitch at the corner of his mouth. There's nothing sinister in this, she wanted to say to him. Your father's surrounding himself with young men of ability. The only sinister fact is that you didn't tell me . . .

'Is he on the Kingsley Heath project?' For some reason she asked Jake instead of Roger.

'No. He buys up agricultural land, estates and so on, for the Trust. He was an auctioneer so he has a good background. You know how Howard likes money to keep on the move and he needs a lot of what it takes for the Heath.' He smiled at Roger. 'Right?'

'So *you* suggested Wilkes to him?' She saw the muscle twitching again. There was no colour in his face.

'Does it matter?' She could feel the tension between them as she checked up on the children. They'd been quiet too long . . . she looked down. Only Mark was there, placidly sucking juice through his straw, in some private orange dream.

'Roger, Emma's disappeared while we've been talking, the little imp.'

'Has she? I'll find her.' As he was swallowed up in the crowd her eyes met Jake's.

'I go round dropping bricks, it seems,' he said.

She shrugged, looked around. She wasn't going to discuss Roger with him. 'You must have a friend who's a flower arranger.'

He laughed. 'I hope I have a friend in the Almighty as regards the weather.'

'I'm drip-dry.'

'There's a marquee where the ceremony will take place, and I've parked a golf umbrella at the door.' He looked at his watch. 'One o'clock. We'll have to make a move shortly. Most of the guests have arrived now.'

She glanced at the reception line. 'Howard's in his element. Look at him. He's a public person.' And before she could stop herself, 'unlike Roger.'

'What else could you expect?' A vivid shaft of sunlight slanted through the glass-domed ceiling and lit up his face. His eyes became a deep, dark blue, surprising her. They gave a brilliance to his face, and then the ray of sunlight turned off like a searchlight and he was swarthy again, Celtic-looking. She knew she was staring, said quickly, 'I still don't know what the first stone or brick starts off. Roger doesn't seem to know either.'

'Doesn't he?' He was bland. 'It's a small court or mews for pensioners. Got to stay on the right side of the Town Council. I'm siting it near Kingsley House so that it can be used as a kind of Community Centre . . . for cups of tea.' His smile was mischievous. 'The sociologists are sold on the quality of life.'

'I'm too busy to think of that.'

'You should be aware of it at least.'

'Sometimes I think all my awareness took place when I was in Paris, at eighteen.'

'You should do something about that.' His eyes were suddenly the deep dark blue again in the fitful sunlight. It made the look he turned on her seem more intense.

'Have you got your plans finished yet?' She changed the subject, 'I mean, for the whole Estate?'

'A long time ago. This mews is to be called Kingsley Court, by the way. I'm looking for other names for the rest.'

'Russell Avenue, Russell Crescent, Russell Square?'

'Naughty.'

She pinned down her smile. 'I'm surprised you aren't building bungalows for your pensioners.' She didn't want their eyes to meet like that.

'I'm a firm believer in keeping them agile. Box them in a bungalow and you'll soon be boxing them for good.'

'You sound like Jolyon Roger.'

'Sound chap, that, a communicator. Of course there will be bungalows for those who want them, and terraces, and detached houses . . .' his face became lively . . . 'You really ought to come to the office and see the plans. You could give me some ideas.'

'I'd love to. I'm interested. And I didn't want to appear a complete clot today.'

'You'll never do that.'

'You think not?'

'I think not . . .' She felt her glance shift under his. She was still not sure when he was mocking. 'And besides you won't get a word in edgeways when Howard gets going. Your function is to look pretty, lay your brick with a silver trowel and murmur a few words.'

'Even a few words are too much, feeling as I do just now.'

'Oh, don't be so modest.' Did he think one denigratory person in the family was enough? She was relieved to find Howard at her side, not at all ruffled after having shaken hands with half of Latham.

'I think it's time we got going. Feeling nervous, Tricia?'

'A bit. Jake's been telling me all about his plans. Remember we're first on the list when it comes to family houses.'

'I thought you liked the one you're in?'

'You know I hate it.' She smiled at him.

'Well, you can't say it hasn't sharpened your critical faculties.

124

You get busy with your plans and then let Jake see them. He's open to ideas, aren't you?'

'I've already told her that.'

She was elated. 'I'll start tomorrow!' That's the first intellectual challenge I've had since I got married . . . She felt guilty, said to Howard, 'Where's Roger by the way?'

'With his mother, and Emma's with them. But what are we going to do with this little chap?' He looked down at Mark.

'Why not leave him with his mother?' Jake said. 'Nice family touch.' He grinned at Howard. 'That's what you want, isn't it, you old fixer?' They were easy together.

She stood under the marquee with her father-in-law, Mark at her side and said firmly and loudly, 'I declare this brick well and truly laid, the first step in the Kingsley Heath Garden City.' She remembered to smile.

Everybody applauded, Mark began to cry and she lifted him in her arms. Howard gave him the silver trowel, wiped clean by the foreman, and his tears dried like magic. He smiled and pointed with it at the Lady Mayoress whose golden chain was heaving gently in the front row. Howard stepped forward.

'I'm not going to bore you with speeches today. The champagne's waiting. Besides I'm not as pretty as my daughter-in-law.' Laughter and applause. 'I'd just like to say Kingsley Heath was my baby, but it's now on its feet, guided expertly by my planning manager, Jake Russell. Kingsley Court will be the foundation of what we hope to achieve here; an integrated community of different people, different in age, sex and occupation. The elderly come first, as is their right, but soon we'll be following on with family homes, homes for the newly-married, cottages, terraces, so that there will be something for everybody. I venture to predict that Kingsley Heath Garden City will become a model for similar enterprises in the future. Thank you for coming.'

The clapping was enthusiastic, probably at the thought of the buffet to follow. The crowd dispersed, began to trail in groups towards the house. The dresses of the women stood out brightly against the grey sky; the lawn was a bright wet green.

'You were just right,' Jake said at her side.

'I wasn't nervous at all. Isn't that strange?'

'Perhaps you like being in the limelight?'

'I was myself, not a . . .' she stopped herself, 'I must go and find Roger.'

'Thanks anyhow.' His gaze rested on her for a second, then he turned on his heel. She watched him pushing politely through the crowds, and then someone stop him, a woman. She was laughing up at him. She was joined by others. Someone shook him by the hand. Tricia looked away and met Roger's eyes. She went towards him.

'Was I all right?'

'Yes. You seemed quite at ease.' She would have liked him to be more enthusiastic. They were joined by a little group of people. She recognised the Pritchards, Ella in grey to match the day perhaps? She held out her hands to Tricia.

'You looked so confident! I should have died if I had to stand up in front of such a crowd.'

Mary Newton joined in the praise. 'You were so self-composed. I just said to Roger, didn't I, Roger, how self-composed you looked.'

'We'll have to put you on the payroll,' Richard Forsyth said. 'A decided asset to the firm.'

'You're all flattering me.' She was pleased. 'You saw, Roger, didn't you? I was as nervous as a kitten.'

'Were you?' He looked distracted.

'Come on!' Richard Forsyth said, 'show more enthusiasm. Little wifie's dying to be praised.'

'One enthusiast in the family's enough.' He didn't smile. There was a little silence.

'Well . . .' Mary broke it. 'Well . . .' she looked around. 'O, those grandchildren of mine are getting restless, poor things.' Actually they were well-behaved for once. 'And they must be starving. Come on, everybody.'

Tricia walked ahead with Roger and the children. He was looking straight ahead. 'Did you think I was too full of myself?' she said.

'It's all the *fuss* . . .' She could hardly hear him, felt her cheeks burn with anger. He couldn't bear her triumph, little as it was, and then again, what a childish thing to think.

'I'm going to take the children to the loo before we start.'

'Right.'

The man in the checked jacket was at their side. 'Hello, Roger. I'm Rab Wilkes, Mrs Newton. Just wanted to congratulate you. Never saw a foundation brick laid more prettily.' He had all the breezy confidence of a man used to dealing with the public. His eyes roved about as if he was afraid of losing a likely customer.

'Thanks.' She smiled at him. 'Good thing I didn't bring my hat today. I should never have got it on with all this praise. But Roger keeps my feet firmly on the ground.'

'Everybody likes a little pat on the back, eh, Roger?' Roger didn't answer.

'Are you married, Mr Wilkes?' she asked.

'Well and truly.' He emphasised each word. 'We've three kids. I'm going to bag one of the family homes; have Jake plan it. Why don't you?'

'We've talked about it. It's a good idea, isn't it, Roger?' She was getting tired of his silences.

'Perhaps.'

'Where do you live?' Wilkes asked. His eyes weren't missing a thing.

'In a cul-de-sac beyond the Bowling Green. Clifford Avenue.'

'Old-fashioned but good. A house will always sell there.'

'I imagine my father took that into account when he bought it,' Roger said. He didn't smile.

'Yea.' The man laughed. 'I never thought anyone could beat Rab Wilkes at his own game, then I met your father.'

They'd reached Kingsley House, gone up the stone steps and were in the big hall. It was milling with people. Through the door Tricia could see some of them already seated at small tables near the buffet.

'Excuse me,' she said, 'I'll be back before the champagne pops.' She hurried the children towards the cloakrooms, impeded at every step by people congratulating her, 'Lovely, Mrs Newton,' 'As to the manor born, I might say,' 'so natural', 'Your husband would be proud of you . . .' No he wasn't, she said to herself as she shepherded the children towards the door marked 'Ladies'.

'Mark's a gentleman,' Emma said.

'I can't take him into the Gentlemen's.'

'Why, Mummy?' The childish mouth had a smirk.

'You know perfectly well why.' She pushed them through the

127

door. 'And don't start giggling. Go into the cubicle yourself. You're a big girl now.'

When she washed her hands at the basin, the children busy turning taps beside her, the face she saw in the mirror was strange. Her eyes were brilliant and too big and her hair had a new vitality to it.

CHAPTER TWELVE

SHE sat with Roger, the children and her mother and father at one of the smaller tables. James was his usual self, talking a lot, laughing a lot. 'Have you been taking lessons in public speaking? You seem cut out for chairing a board meeting.'

'I know it,' Tricia said, 'don't tell me. I've made a terrible fool of myself and that's why everybody's saying I did so well. It's to cheer me up. Besides I hardly said a word.'

'Perhaps it was the right word.' Her mother said. 'I find this important when I'm dealing with my Deprived, otherwise you find your words coming back at you like a boomerang.'

'I know that feeling,' Roger said.

'This is a nice place,' Emma announced to anyone who liked to listen. 'Did you know Cock Robin is in the other room, all over blood?'

'Oh, Emma, really!'

Enid Baker turned to her grand-daughter, 'I don't understand, Emma.'

'Mummy took us to see him. He's lying on his back with his legs stuck up in the air and he's all *bloody*.'

Mark put down his spoon and began to cry.

'It's all right,' Tricia said, wiping his eyes. 'Honestly, Mother, she's the most ghoulish child.'

'Most children are at her age. Don't cry, Mark. Your tears will fall into your icecream and then you'll have a sorbet. Do you know what a sorbet is?' Mark shook his head and gave a loud sniff. 'A sorbet is a water ice. I used to make them quite often. Did I ever give you the recipe for the lemon one, Tricia? You could try it for one of your dinner parties.'

'We don't have any now. Roger's not up to it.'

He looked at her without smiling. 'I'm keeping her back from leading a madly social life in Latham.'

'I'm not complaining. I simply said you weren't up to it.'

He turned to Enid and James. 'I'm dead tired at nights. General dogsbody, that's me. I do all the running around while the others sit at their executive desks looking important. Take all this business today . . .'

'I thought Jake Russell was running the show.' James Baker liked to get his facts right.

'He gives that impression, yes.' Roger was eager to explain. 'In every set-up there are those who like to take the limelight. They aren't always the ones who do the work.'

'I daresay you all help.' Enid was impartial. Her eyes rested on Tricia for a second. She wasn't missing a thing. 'Your father's quite right to delegate his responsibilities, Roger, at his age.'

'You've got it wrong.' He leaned forward, his cheeks flushed. 'That's just it. He doesn't delegate. He's in the office every day checking up on things. Oh, he gives *favourites* their heads, but the sloggers never get a kind word. And yet it's the high fliers, the fly-by-nights, the wheelers and dealers . . .'

To Tricia's relief a waiter had appeared and was topping up their glasses. 'This'll drown our sorrows.' She smiled round the table.

'Your father must have a private line to Messrs Moet and Chandon, Roger,' James said. 'This is my third. I certainly shan't be able to go back to the Bank today.'

Enid turned to Roger. 'Why don't you take Tricia out for the evening? James and I could babysit for you. I cancelled everything for today and I'm quite free.'

He sipped his glass of champagne, twirled the stem in his fingers. 'What do you think, Tricia?'

'I'd love to.' She was grateful to her mother. But besides that she wanted to celebrate something which had happened to her today, a tiny step forward, something to do with the ceremony, the quality of life . . . Jake's words came back to her.

'Would you read us a story, Grandma?' Emma asked. 'Mummy always reads us a story.'

'Yes, I think I could manage that.'

'Could you bath my brother?'

'Possibly, but there isn't much wrong with a top and tail.'

'What's that?' Emma looked suspicious.

'Like gooseberries. Top and tail. It's what I used to give your Mummy when I was in a hurry to get out. Face and hands and bottom. For quickness.'

'Oh, we wouldn't like *that*.' Emma looked at Tricia, horrified. She laughed at her mother.

'You're being judged and found wanting. Many a top and tail I had, now that you mention it.' She remembered the expertise in getting her to bed, the firm, 'Be good.' It hadn't been a bad thing in retrospect. If parents were firm, children became decisive. She believed she was decisive, felt she was beginning to know herself as a person.

'Everything can be arranged satisfactorily,' Enid said to Emma, looking at her as if she were a difficult client. The child went quiet.

'Yes, high time you two young things painted the town red.' The champagne had made James jovial. 'When Enid and I were young we hit the high spots and no mistake.'

'Did you?' Tricia asked, laughing.

'Of course that was before . . .' he hesitated, 'before . . .'

' . . . David died.' His wife's tone was level.

Roger got up suddenly. He looked pale and strained. 'Excuse me. I'll be back shortly.'

When he was out of earshot Tricia looked at her mother. 'I don't think your idea went down very well.'

'What's wrong with the boy?' James spoke irritably.

'He's in some kind of stress,' Enid said. 'Did you persuade him to go to a doctor, Tricia?'

'No, he won't hear of it. He says there's nothing wrong with him. I get worried. I told you, that time on the phone.'

'Is he drinking?'

'Nothing to speak of. Maybe today more than usual. He's just . . . miserable, and he thinks he does the work and gets none of the credit . . .'

'What's credit?' Emma said.

Enid looked thoughtfully at the children. 'You take them next door and let them see that model again. Your father and I will have a talk with him when he comes back . . .'

131

'I don't want you to interfere.'

'I'm not interfering. I'm simply going to advise him to seek professional advice. It may be necessary for him to change his job.'

'What are you talking about, Enid?' James was irritable again.

His wife explained to him. 'It may be he's temperamentally incapable of getting on with his father. It's not unusual, especially when you've got a father as successful and seemingly well-integrated as Howard.'

'What do you mean, "seemingly"?'

'Don't sidetrack me, James. Anyhow for his own good something's got to be done. And for your good too, Tricia. You've lost weight and you look older than twenty-four. I thought that, watching you in the marquee today . . .' How they *watched* you, parents . . . 'In my experience in a situation like this the family suffers just as much as the patient.'

'You're frightening me.' She tried to speak lightly. 'You're treating him like one of your clients.'

'I'm speaking objectively, that's all. Here we have a rich young man not yet thirty with a wife and children who are a credit to him.' She caught the expression on Tricia's face. 'And don't smirk. I may not praise you a lot, but that's what you are, a credit. Don't you think there must be something wrong if he's *still* unhappy? I don't wish to pry, but it's probably something counselling could put right, if, and I emphasise that "if", the counselling comes from outside and not from members of the family, least of all from his father. On you go, Tricia. Take them next door. He'll be back soon.'

She got up, feeling relieved. 'Come on, children, we'll go and see Cock Robin again. You'd like that, wouldn't you?'

She seemed to have been in the adjoining room for a long time. They were the only visitors, and it was quiet except for the children's chatter and the distant sound of voices. Like a running brook, she thought, like a country noise, a suitable background for the enclosed little world they were examining through the glass. The unease was back again. '*Who'll carry the coffin, I said the kite . . .*'

Had she been wise in letting her mother speak to Roger?

Wasn't everyone supposed to deal with their own marital problems, because it *was* a marital problem, a failure of communication. Was the failure her fault, in that she despised Roger's attitude? Not despised, surely. That was too strong a word. But you couldn't turn away, as he was doing, become a victim. You feel superior, she told herself, because you recognise you would behave differently. But does that make you any better? *'Who'll bear the pall, I said the wren . . .'*

Her memories went back to Corfu, and sensations warmed her, the heat of the sun, the feel of the buoyant water on her skin, the naked loving, the smell of their sweat. I'm young, she thought, I need to live . . .

'What's the spotty one, Mummy, what's the spotty one?'

' *"Who'll sing the psalm,*
   I said the thrush . . ." '

There was a new kind of noise coming from the other room, at least the tenor of the previous noise had changed. Perhaps Howard was going to make another speech. She ought to go back now. She thought of her mother's earnest face, her father's embarrassment, and thought, they'll get nowhere with him. He doesn't want to listen.

'Can't hear you,' Emma said, 'can't hear you!'

'It's the noise outside.' It wasn't a happy noise. It was as if a cold wind had spread amongst the guests and they were reacting to it by shouting it down, not angrily, but fearfully. She took the children hurriedly by the hand, turned to go, and saw her father at the entrance. He came half-running towards her, his footfalls echoing and clattering on the chequered tiles.

'Something terrible has happened, Tricia.'

'Emma, Mark!' She saw her mother at the archway, beckoning, white-faced.

'Go to Granny.' They ran obediently, Emma's dorothy bag bobbing up and down on her bare arm, Mark's shirt a little tail of blue where it had worked loose.

'What is it?' She turned to her father. He put his hands on her upper arms, his mouth open. No words came. She wanted to scream at him, 'Get on with it!' 'What is it?' Her neck muscles were rigid, her tongue clumsy.

'Howard's been found dead . . . in the Gentlemen's.' His

133

voice was hushed on the last three words, shameful. She had an intense wish to hoot with laughter, found decorum somewhere.

'Dead . . . who found him?'

'One of the young clerks . . . Mathers, was it? He creased his forehead. 'No, Mathieson, I think. I'm not sure . . .'

'It doesn't *matter*.' Why had she this terrible impatience with him when he was doing his best? 'Was it his heart?'

'We don't know. He'd fallen. I went in. He was lying on the floor. Terrible . . . Dr Chapman's there. He'd been invited, fortunately . . .' She interrupted him, frantic with anxiety.

'Are you *sure* he's dead?'

'Oh, he's dead. There's no doubt about that. You should see . . .' He swallowed, she saw the greyness round his mouth. 'It's going to be a terrible shock for you, Tricia.'

It was already. It was so terrible that she couldn't take it in. Her mind was zig-zagging about . . . had Howard told anyone he was feeling ill . . . but he'd looked so well . . . had he gone to the toilet *because* he was feeling ill . . . and if so had anyone seen him . . . her heart seemed to stop there. *Roger*.

No sound came. She tried again. 'Roger . . . he excused himself. He might have seen him before . . . maybe they were talking . . . didn't you ask *Roger* when he came back?'

Her father looked at her. His eyes had fear in them. 'He didn't come back.'

'What?' She thought she screamed.

'He didn't come back. We've looked everywhere but we can't find him. He's disappeared.'

'Disappeared?' She daren't think any more. 'What do you mean, *disappeared?*' Why was she standing here shouting at her father? 'We'd better go.' She touched his arm, apologising. 'Perhaps he's there now. We'd better go, Father. We'd better see . . .' She walked beside him, restraining herself from running.

*   *   *

Her father hadn't succeeded in preparing her for the sight which met her eyes. People had stood aside as she went in,

134

Richard Forsyth, Jake Russell, she didn't recognise any others. Dr Chapman was kneeling beside her father-in-law's body on the floor. He turned a moon face to her as she came in, shook his head.

'What's happened?' She heard her voice choking. The place was a shambles. Pieces of broken porcelain lay on the floor, some spattered with blood, one ugly jagged piece close to Howard's face. She saw a large gash on his left temple. It was the first dead person she'd ever seen. The set *deadness* overwhelmed her at first, but as she made herself look she saw there was an expression in the features, a pulling of the muscle at the left side of the mouth, the eyebrows lifted, giving him a surprised look as if death had bludgeoned him at the last. The fists too were clenched, one had several small cuts across the knuckles, blood was smeared on the back of it. She moved her feet, feeling sick, and there was a crunch of glass under them. 'What . . .?'

Dr Chapman, still kneeling, half-turned and indicated the remains of the basin above where Howard lay. The back section with taps and a piece of soap still hung crazily from the wall. The plug dangled on its chain. She heard Jake Russell's voice behind her, low, level.

'He must have grabbed it when he fell.'

Dr Chapman got up stiffly, dusting his knees. She saw splinters of glass fall on to the tile floor. He turned his face to Tricia and she saw the sad downward lines in it. Howard had been an old friend as well as a patient. 'It's better not to say anything at this stage, Tricia. I've sent for the Police. If I were you I'd take the children home and get away from all this . . .' Was there a slight distaste there?

'Can't I do . . . anything?'

'No. See to the children. I'll keep in touch.'

'Come on, Tricia.' She heard her father's voice. 'I'll drive you home. Your mother's in the car with them.'

'All right.' She turned, saw a gobbet of blood still wet on the splash-back above the broken basin. There hadn't been any on Howard's face. Was that because it had been wiped clean by Dr Chapman, or did blood stop flowing when someone died? 'Where's Roger's mother?'

'The Pritchards have taken her home. She's in a bad way.'

She was reluctant to go, felt there was something being held back from her. She met Jake Russell's eyes and he nodded at her as if he understood. 'I'll stand in, let you know everything. You go with your father.'

Dr Chapman walked with them through the hall. Everybody had been banished. She saw the white coat of a waiter behind a pillar. 'Poor Mary,' Dr Chapman said. 'A terrible blow. I'll phone MacKenzie to call and give her a sedative.' That was his partner, a thin, dour Scot. She looked at him, saw the worry in his face. Why hadn't he mentioned Roger? Asked where he was? She walked meekly between the two men, hardly able to bear the fear inside her. Later she would grieve for Howard, but not now. *Nobody had mentioned Roger . . .*

CHAPTER THIRTEEN

SHE came downstairs, having put the children to bed. Dealing with them had kept her calm. But the fear was there while she answered their excited questions. Grandad had had an accident, she told them. A little at a time was enough. She couldn't risk them having nightmares on top of everything else.

She had heard the door bell earlier and voices in the hall. When she went into the room she found Jake Russell there with her father and mother. He got up when he saw her.

'Your mother's made some coffee, Tricia. Have this chair.'

'Thanks.' She looked up at him. 'What happened? Did Roger come back?'

'No.' His mouth was grim. 'I shouldn't worry too much. There will be some explanation.'

'Yes . . .' She breathed deeply. 'And . . . Howard?'

'The police sent for an ambulance. He's been taken to the mortuary.'

'Is it usual to send for the police? I thought Dr Chapman . . .'

'In cases of sudden death, yes.'

'I see . . .' Fear was leaping about inside her. She daren't ask any more questions.

'Mr Russell's been to The Crescent, Tricia,' her mother said. 'Mary's sleeping.'

'Oh, good.' Where did this composure come from? 'Who's with her?'

'Ella Pritchard. That's right, isn't it, Mr Russell?'

'Yes, she'll stay the night. Although I don't think Mrs Newton will wake. The doctor's seen to that.'

Her mother gave her a cup of coffee. 'Drink that. And I've made some sandwiches with a piece of ham I found in the fridge.' She held out a plate.

'No, thanks.' How typical of her mother calmly to make sandwiches at a time like this. She looked at Jake Russell who was sipping his coffee; couldn't bring herself to ask the question. All the time upstairs, while she'd been attending to the children, thoughts had been going through her mind, too terrible to admit. Roger and his father were together when he died . . . *Roger had disappeared.*

She watched her father nibbling at a sandwich, saw the misery in his face, his guard down. Her mother was looking straight ahead, sitting with her back straight, her chin pulled in. That was how she'd met every crisis since David had died. Implacable.

'What . . . what did he die of?' She'd asked it. At last. She felt the blood draining from her face as Jake Russell looked at her. His eyes were dark, no colour but darkness.

'Dr Chapman didn't say. The police asked the staff to leave the place exactly as it was.'

'You mean . . . where my father-in-law . . . was found?'

'Yes. It's routine procedure. I shouldn't worry.'

Her fingers slipped on the handle of her cup. It clattered into the saucer, slopping the coffee, and her mother got up and took them from her. 'You nearly spilled it on your pretty dress. I'll pour out another one.' She went out of the room briskly.

'Why . . . why would they want the place left exactly as it was? Is there some doubt?' She found her mouth was trembling so badly that she could hardly speak.

'Mr Russell's told you,' her father said, 'standard procedure. My guess is he had some kind of attack, grabbed the basin.' He was repeating what Jake had said.

'But why should it *break* like that?' She remembered the jagged piece lying near Howard's face. 'And he was so fit. You saw him.' She looked at Jake, was aware that her father got up and left the room. 'Where's *Roger?*' She heard her voice rise despite her efforts.

He shook his head. 'I don't know. I looked all over for him. His car wasn't at Kingsley House.'

'Did anyone see him go? Any of the staff?' I sound like a Private Eye, she thought.

'I don't honestly know.' His eyes held hers. 'Maybe he got

enough of the show today and took off, just cleared out before it happened.'

'Yes . . .'

'Look, Tricia, leave it, eh?' There was no doubt now about the sympathy in his eyes. 'You've had a shock, and naturally you're anxious, but everything's being taken care of. The first thing is to find Roger. I've looked in the obvious places, the Lion, and so on, before I came here.'

She responded to the warmth in his voice. 'You're right. The thing is, when we were eating, he excused himself and went, I presume, to the lavatory. He was . . . pale. Howard would have been there.' She bit her lip.

'Don't jump to conclusions. He may have gone out for a breath of air instead.'

'Yes, that's true.' She smiled apologetically at him. 'I've been thinking all kinds of things.'

'Don't. He'll soon be back. And then you'll have to comfort him about his father.'

That was another thing. She felt the sharp pain of loss for the first time. Howard was dead. She'd never see him again. There had always been a rapport between them, and she'd admired so much his vitality and charm. Tears gathered behind her eyes, began to choke her, and then the shambles in the toilet came into her mind again, the broken porcelain, the blood and glass, the ugly gash on the dead face. Roger *couldn't* have left him like that . . . the door opened. She looked up, her heart leaping. It was her parents.

'We'll stay the night if you'd like us to,' James said. 'Or at least until Roger comes back. Is there any place where you think he might be? Any friends he might be with?' He sounded as if he was repeating words he'd rehearsed.

She shook her head. 'There's no one he'd go to. He didn't drop in on people. He needed to come home. It was his refuge.'

He looked at her as if surprised at her choice of word. 'Well, we'll wait with you in any case. You don't think you should notify the police, Mr Russell?'

'No, I shouldn't. Not yet.' Tricia thought he looked uncomfortable. 'I'm sure there's a rational explanation.' He glanced at his watch. 'It's seven already. I feel I'm in the way. I'll go now.'

She didn't want him to go. 'Please stay for a bit.' The thought occurred to her that it was rational for Roger to behave irrationally, but she couldn't say that. There was that other time he'd come home drunk . . . an idea flickered. 'I've just remembered. There's a pub by the railway. I don't know its name. Roger went there once before.'

Jake looked interested. 'Anything's worth a try. We'd soon find it.'

She felt hopeful. 'He went there before when he was under some stress. It's just possible . . .'

' . . . he might go back?'

'Yes. And then The Crescent's nearer the railway than here. He could go on to his mother. They've always been close.'

'It sounds logical,' Enid said. She looked hopeful too. 'I should start with this pub first, Tricia, if Mr Russell's willing to go with you, and then look in at The Crescent. I've a feeling you'll find him.'

'So have I,' Jake said. They were trying to cheer her up, she knew, and she appreciated it. But they didn't know Roger as she knew him. The ceremony today had upset him, because it had been organised by Jake Russell. He was sensitive to imagined insults. It's not the complete answer, she thought. He's always sensitive to imagined insults especially where the Trust is concerned. Something had happened today, with his father, something he couldn't bear . . . her mind refused to be pushed any further. She got up.

'I'll go upstairs and change,' she said. Action was the best answer. She went up two at a time, stripped off the black and white dress, got into jeans and a sweater, peeped in at the children to make sure they were asleep and was downstairs in ten minutes.

'Quick work,' Jake said. She tried to smile at him.

'The spare bed's made up if you get tired, Mother. I'll phone you in any case, when I get to The Crescent. Since you're here I might stay overnight, to help Mary. It depends . . .' She steadied her voice.

'Good luck anyhow,' James said.

Her mother saw them to the door. She kissed Tricia, which

was in itself unusual. 'It'll turn out all right. My guess is you'll find Roger at The Crescent. He'll want to be with his mother.' Are you presuming he knows about his father's death, she wanted to say. 'I hope so.' She started to shiver.

'Remember to phone me.'

'Okay.' She went down the steps with Jake to his car. 'Are you good at backing out?' she said.

'The best.' He reversed down the curving drive faster than she'd ever managed it.

The Railway Inn wasn't seedy, as she'd thought. It was a working men's pub, shining with old brass and had the original mahogany counter, but it was spoiled by plastic-covered tables in a loud red and white check. There were a few men in railway uniform drinking, and a sprinkling of others in plain suits.

'You go and sit at one of the tables,' he said. 'What would you like?'

She said, surprising herself, 'Brandy, please,' and then added, 'but make it small.'

She watched Jake talk to the bartender, the man listen intently as he polished glasses, then shake his head decisively.

Jake came across the room to her with a glass in either hand. 'I'm having the same. No, he doesn't remember Roger being in, certainly not this evening. He says it's mostly railway men as they knock off shifts, and reps.' He sat down.

'He doesn't remember Roger at all?'

'No.' He shook his head. 'Take it easy.' He looked at her over his glass. 'I know it's a double blow, your father-in-law, then Roger missing.'

'Oh, don't start pitying me!' Now she was being rude. 'Sorry. Is it a double blow, though? It's terrible, Howard dying like that. But Roger . . . maybe I, we, are making too much of it. I know him. He was miserable. Maybe he just decided to clear out early as you said.' She drank some brandy, 'I'm frightened of my own thoughts.'

He didn't reply for a second, then put down his glass. 'You think they might have been together when Howard died?'

'I told you. He . . .'

'Yes, you told me. And you're thinking they may have had

141

an argument?' If that were all . . . if he could know how her imagination ranged ahead . . .

'I don't know . . .'

'Don't, Tricia,' he said. She wouldn't meet his eyes, 'Dr Chapman knows Howard's medical history, remember.'

'Yes, but calling the police . . .' She tried to smile at him. 'I'm being stupid. Roger . . . he isn't aggressive at all. I think that's what angered his father most. He wanted a pushing man for a son, a driving force, like you or Rab Wilkes.'

'Do you think so?' He was non-committal.

'Is *your* father still alive?' she asked.

'Yes. He's neither aggressive nor unaggressive, just normal. I've no complaints.'

'That's lucky for you. Would he like you to be married? He and your mother?'

'They don't say. Yes, I'm sure they would, but they don't go on about it. They're so reasonable that nowadays I feel I have to apologise for them.' He smiled at her.

'My parents wanted me to be married.' She stopped. 'I say that so often that I believe it. It's convenient for me to believe it . . . to find a scapegoat.' She stopped again, looked at him. 'Isn't it strange I should sit here talking in this fashion when my father-in-law's just died violently and my husband's missing.'

'Trivialities are the lifeline to sanity.'

'Is that your own?'

He smiled his brief smile. 'Surprisingly, yes. I'm not a great talker. I get on with the job, I get on with most people. If I don't, I don't blame myself, I blame them.'

'And you don't get on with Roger?'

'He won't let me. I like Roger.'

'I like Roger,' she said. 'I like him very much.' Tears rolled down her face. He handed her his handkerchief. 'It's a shame,' he said. 'It would do you good to get into a corner and have a howl instead of having things to attend to.'

She mopped her eyes. 'I like you better when you don't get soft. We'd better go. I've made up my mind. I'll stay with Mary. I'm sure Roger will come back there.' She handed him back his handkerchief.

'Always back your hunch.' He got up and drew out her

142

chair. They walked out to the front of the pub, his hand on her elbow.

It was still light, and the children were playing in the cul-de-sac flanked by wooden sleepers. One of them had chalked squares on it, and three girls were waiting in a queue while a fourth jumped over the lines in an intricate hop-scotch.

'Strange how children organise themselves, isn't it?' she said.

'Playing's serious.'

A boy came careering towards them on a skateboard, swooping and curving from one side of the road to the other, and they both dashed out of his way in opposite directions.

'You couldn't see us for smoke,' she said. She watched his face broadening as he smiled and thought, there are two persons in him. I'm beginning to know them.

He drove back over the railway bridge, past the Latham High now Comprehensive, and turned into The Crescent. It was a strange place for Howard Newton to have chosen to live. The houses were large but terraced. They had handsome balconied fronts but there was only a narrow strip of garden at the back.

'Howard should have had an estate in the country,' Jake said, drawing up at the gate.

'He never wanted it. He was Latham born and bred, a small town man.'

'You think it's a type?'

She nodded. 'I discussed it once with Jan and Crystel, the friends I had in Paris.' He moved his head impatiently. 'Sorry, but of course you visited Crystel. You liked her, didn't you?'

'Yes, very much.' He looked away from her, repeated in a softer voice, 'very much'.

'You haven't talked about her, but then we don't meet very often.'

'No.' She could scarcely hear him. She thought for a moment, has he been smitten? But then everyone was smitten by Crystel.

'It was a pity you couldn't spend more time with her.'

'It was my own fault.'

'There's always the next time.' He didn't answer. He isn't a man to discuss his feelings, she thought, nor for that matter, reveal them. She didn't want to go in, to wait . . . she searched her mind for another topic. 'Small towns,' she said, 'Jan came from Johnstown, a small town in Maryland, and you know what Maurac's like.'

'A small town.'

'I remember saying Latham was "reserved", Crystel said Maurac was "nosy", and Jan that Johnstown cared too much for appearances.'

'Small towns are all those things.' His voice was level.

'D'you like them?'

'I come from one. And when I go to France I never stay on the coast. The small market towns show you the true character of the country.'

'And Maurac was like that?'

'Typical, the main street bustle, the Frenchness . . .'

Without meaning to she said, 'Didn't you think Crystel was lovely?' The angle of his head altered. The voice was clipped.

'She was like the part of the country she lived in.'

'*Sauvage*?' She smiled, remembering Crystel's word for it.

'No, more a kind of lushness, richness. And yet a French practicality, business-like, mistress of the situation . . . I felt in the way a little. A man appeared and called her . . .'

'That's Crystel. She was the organiser. Before we left she took us to a *Parfumiers* in Rue de Vaugirard. We wanted some kind of souvenir, a symbol of our friendship and of . . . something more we learned in Paris . . .' Someday she would tell him.

He didn't reply. He never listened unless it suited him. He was autocratic . . . his voice surprised her when he spoke, there was a new tone to it. 'I remember her perfume.' She waited. He didn't speak. The conversation was over. Typical. It was very quiet in the car. She could see the sun setting through the tall chestnuts which framed The Crescent. She recognised the beauty of the terrace for the first time. Perhaps Howard had seen it all along . . .

'I'll go in now,' she said. 'If Roger's there I'll come back and tell you. If not I'll stay on. Oh, Mrs Pritchard's there. Would you take her home?'

He raised his head, immediately practical. 'You wouldn't

like her company? Supposing your mother-in-law wakes and is distressed?'

She shook her head. 'That doesn't worry me. I can comfort her.' It was Roger who worried her. What he would say and what he would look like. What worried her was sitting in dread throughout the night if he didn't turn up. She got out and spoke to Jake through the open window of the car. 'Thanks for everything.'

'For nothing. I'll sit for a bit. Send Mrs Pritchard out when she's ready. And remember to phone your parents . . . look, Tricia,' he put his hand on the door, 'I'll come in with you.'

'No, don't. I have to manage.' She turned and went up the steps.

CHAPTER FOURTEEN

THE telephone was ringing as Ella Pritchard opened the door to her, and she said, 'It's all right, Mrs Pritchard. I'll answer it.'

'Oh, my dear, you look worn out! Your mother-in-law's fast asleep . . .'

She went to the hall table and lifted the receiver.

'Tricia? You didn't find Roger?' It was her mother.

'No, I'm just in.'

Dr Chapman's been on the phone. He says he's reported the death to the Coroner and he's ordered a postmortem. There will be an inquest.' How like her mother not to mince words.

'Does that mean . . .' Fear was alive again, constricting her throat, 'does that mean they think he *didn't* die of a heart attack?'

'It doesn't mean anything of the kind. He had a history of heart trouble, don't forget. The pathologist will soon find that out.'

'That means Dr Chapman's withholding a death certificate? Do you think . . . ?'

'Look, Tricia,' her mother's voice was level, 'I don't know anything more than he told me. He sent his commiserations.'

'Did you tell him Roger couldn't be found?' There was silence and then the calm voice.

'He knows that. They'll be sending round a policeman from the Coroner's office.'

'Mother, I'm terrified. You know Roger went . . .'

Enid interrupted her. 'Don't say any more. Try and calm yourself. I'm sure Roger will turn up soon.'

'All right.' Her heart was beating so heavily that it was making her sick. From the kitchen she could hear the clatter of dishes. Ella Pritchard would be making a cup of tea. Was she listening?

'Are you there, Tricia?'

'Yes.'

'I'm going to make a suggestion. Do you remember I mentioned Peter Jobley to you? I told you I thought highly of him. Did Roger ever consult him?'

'No, but I registered the family in his practice. I took Mark that time he had a sore throat. I liked him.'

'I'm glad. Now, wait where you are. If Roger comes back and he's in any kind of state, phone Peter and ask him to call. He'll help you. He's reliable, discreet. Will you do that?'

'Yes, I could do with some advice.'

'Professional advice. You know what I think of well-meaning amateurs.'

'But maybe I should be at home because of the policeman coming?'

'He'll have to be instructed by the Coroner first. It won't be right away. If it is I can give him any information he wants.'

'All right.' Her mother could deal with that side of things much better than she could. She'd be in her element giving clear, concise answers. 'All right,' she said again. 'I want to give Roger a chance to see me alone. Too many people will frighten him.'

'You're quite right. I might ask James to drive over to the house later, give him something to do.'

'There's no need. Poor father . . .'

She ignored this. 'You'll do what I say, about Peter Jobley?'

'Yes.' It was a gleam of hope. His opinion would be ethical, informed, what she needed.

* * *

Mrs Pritchard had long since gone with many protestations of sympathy. 'Died in his prime,' she said tearfully, and it was a suitable epitaph for Howard.

Tricia slipped up to her mother-in-law's bedroom and found her deeply asleep, the cupid-bow mouth half-open. Dr MacKenzie had made a thorough job of the sedation. She had looked up Peter Jobley's house number in the directory. She wouldn't use it unless she had to.

Now the house was very quiet. She sat in the Victorian

grandfather chair beside the Rococo fireplace and listened to silence. December, she thought, it was six years ago in December since I was in this room, pregnant, listening to Howard pontificating in front of that fireplace, his champagne glass in his hand.

'I said I had good news. We have received formal approval of our project, the Kingsley Heath Garden City.'

The chestnuts rustled outside like ghostly hand-clapping. She felt his presence in the heavily-ornate room. There was no sign of Mary here, except for the high polish on every surface, and perhaps the little Chesterfield near the window where she liked to sit.

That time when he'd had his first warning . . . the glass he'd been holding had fallen and rolled on the carpet. She looked down at the close red pile under her feet. It would cushion any fall. But in a men's lavatory, with tiles or marbled floors . . . a fall would be a different matter. And there were no hard sharp edges such as broken pieces of wash-basin, only fluid curves.

You're frightening yourself, she thought, letting your imagination run riot. It's only routine procedure as far as the police are concerned. *They* aren't looking for Roger. Sudden death always has to be investigated. Dr Chapman would have told them that Howard had a heart condition.

There were so many questions she would like to ask. Someone like Peter Jobley would answer them. She remembered the square-chinned young man, a Rugby player's face except for the tired eyes, and in contrast the thin clever fingers as he felt Mark's throat. And his straight-eyed look, none of the old-fashioned pomposity of Dr Chapman.

Stress, for instance. Wasn't it supposed to trigger off a heart attack? Had there been stress in that cold tiled room which she was constantly seeing in her mind's eye, Howard washing his hands at the row of basins, looking up to see his son's white face in the mirror, turning round . . . 'Roger! You look as sick as a sick calf. Has the champers been too much for you?' Where was she getting those words from? Or could it be quite different, a congenitally unsound heart which had to fail sooner or later regardless of stress? But why the shambles, the blood, the broken basin, the violence? Why had Roger run away?

At first she thought it was the wind rustling in the high trees, and then the noise altered, became a steady scraping. It came from behind the heavy red velvet curtains draping the french windows. Ella must have drawn them earlier. She listened intently. There was no doubt about it. It was a scraping, like finger-nails being drawn down the glass. It couldn't be her father obeying instructions to see if she were all right . . . he would come to the door.

She stood up, and this time there was a further noise, a squeaking, like a handle turning, and a thudding. That could be her heart. She strained her ears and heard the voice, 'Mother . . . Mother . . .' Her heart froze. She stood stock-still for a second, her nerves seeming to make a jangling sound inside her head, and then she ran to the window. Her hands were so clumsy that she fumbled amongst the folds of the curtains before she found the draw cord. And then they were sliding back, and Roger was there, on the other side of the glass. His face and hands were white in the darkness. He was shaking at the handle, like a child.

'Roger!' she called. He looked up and saw her, stopped obediently. And then he did something which stabbed through her heart like a knife. He put his arm up to his face as if to shield it. Like Mark. 'Wait, Roger! I'm opening it.' She turned the heavy key, dragged at the glass door, and he staggered through, blinking in the light.

'Where's Mother?' He looked around as if he were blind. 'I didn't think . . .'

'Sit down first. You're shaking.' She helped him to the small Chesterfield. 'I've been so worried about you . . .'

'Mother . . .'

'She's sleeping. The doctor's given her a sedative.'

'She knows about . . . father?' His eyes were wide, staring. He's in shock, she thought.

'Yes. She was there in Kingsley House, remember? They had to tell her. Shall I get you a drink, or something to eat? You look terrible.'

'No, I'm not thirsty, or anything. I've been driving for miles, I don't know where I've been. It seems like a million years, and then I thought of mother. I wanted to comfort her . . .'

149

She took a rug from the back of the sofa and put it over his knees. 'You're cold. I'm going to make you some . . .'

'No, don't, don't leave me Tricia.' He clutched at her hands. 'I can't bear to be left. It wasn't so bad in the car. There was the noise of the engine, and the lights of other cars. I'd like to have driven for ever but I knew . . .'

'You knew you had to come back?' He didn't answer. His eyes were fixed on her face. He had a naturally fair skin. Now it looked transparent. She could see the blue veins standing out on his temples. 'Roger . . .' she sat down beside him, put an arm round his shoulders. 'You've had a terrible shock. You have to tell someone. Try and tell me. I love you. Did you see your father die?' His eyes didn't leave her face. 'Roger,' she said, as if she were speaking to Mark, 'tell me, please.' He shook her arm off roughly, bent over his knees.

'Yes, I saw him. Oh, yes, I saw him die.' '*I said the fly, with my little eye, I saw him die . . .*' Was she shocked too?

'You went into the toilet and found him there, didn't you?'

'Yes, he was there. You *know* I went, Tricia. You were sitting at the table with me, you and your parents. And the children. I had to go. I suddenly felt sick . . . sick of it all . . . all the praising, all the glory . . . but none of it for me.' His voice broke. He tunnelled his fists into his eyes.

'Did you quarrel?'

'He started it!' He looked round at her. 'He said, "Well, son, this is our day of glory . . ." '

'Were you standing near him? Looking over his shoulder?'

'Not all that near. What makes you say that? I'd come out of the cubicle where I'd been sick. I was at another basin. Nobody else there. I don't know how many basins there were . . . it's a row, you see . . .' his voice dwindled. 'You've never been in a men's. I've never been in a ladies', funny, isn't it?'

'Yes, funny. What did you say when he spoke to you?'

'Nothing at first. I thought, my God, here I've been puking my guts out and he hasn't even enough fatherly interest to ask me, must have heard me . . . just says, "Well son, this is our day of glory . . . ' "

'What did you say?'

150

'I told you I said nothing. I ran the water, and I splashed some on my forehead . . .'

'But *after* you said nothing?'

'After? After?' He raised his head, his fists tightly clenched, 'Oh, yes, *after*, I felt anger rising up in me like the bile had risen up in me. And I shouted at him. "Whose glory? Whose glory, you bastard! It's not been mine. Maybe your bumboys, your Russell's and your Wilkes', but not mine, by God. I've been humiliated . . ."' He stopped, not looking at her. His body was tense, as if it was in the grip of a rigor.

'Go on, Roger.' She had to know.

'His face . . . he turned his face to me . . .'

'Don't say any more, Roger.' Tricia swivelled round. His mother was standing at the door in a wide-sleeved kimono, vaguely twentyish, beneath it there was the bedraggled pink hem of her nightdress. Her hair was hanging loose round her white face.

'Mary, what are you doing here?' Tricia jumped to her feet, went towards her. 'You should be in bed.'

'I heard my boy.' She turned to Roger who was staring at her, held out her hands to him.

'Oh, Mother . . .' He covered the distance between them, and then he was in her arms. His weeping was hopeless, helpless. 'I'm so sorry . . .'

Mary raised her head and looked at Tricia. 'You aren't to question him. I know you mean well but he's had enough, all his life. Leave it.'

'I wasn't meaning to upset him, but . . .' she saw Mary stagger, and Roger disengage himself, keeping an arm round her.

'Poor Mother,' she heard him say. He turned a tear-stained face to Tricia, 'Poor, poor mother . . .'

'Yes, Roger.' She was infinitely gentle with him. 'Would you help her upstairs? I'll make a hot drink for both of you. Sit with her till I come.'

When she heard them at the top of the stairs, their slow passage to the large bedroom at the front of the house, she went to the telephone. Her fingers shook so badly that she could hardly dial Peter Jobley's number.

CHAPTER FIFTEEN

THE Coroner's Court was hardly bigger than the board room of the Latham Development Trust, and surprisingly, considering the Bavarian aspect of the town hall, it was new, built across from the shopping complex. Two walls were of stripped pine, two of glass covered by that favourite accessory in modern town planning, louvred blinds. The carpet was of shaved hair, like a pig's back, only green. There were too, the inevitable pot plants, ivy, geranium, and a sharp-leaved purple one which Tricia didn't recognise.

There was no judicial atmosphere, in fact hardly any atmosphere because of the functional rows of long tables of light wood, the steel-framed chairs, the square lights set into the ceiling tiles, but no doubt it would grow its own with age. It was people and events which added something, like the patina on old wood.

The Coroner hadn't a special desk or podium. He sat in a non-judicial light suit at the table at the top of the room. On his left was a man of about the same age, the pathologist, a friend of Peter Jobley's.

What would she have done without Peter during the last few months, the anxiety of Roger's removal to a psychiatric hospital, and the impending inquest? He was sitting beside her now, and when she turned to whisper something to him, she saw again the bags under his eyes. Leila, his wife, must have been 'creating' again last night. He'd told her recently that she would have to be admitted to an alcoholic unit. 'Sometimes it's difficult to remember it's a disease.'

Tricia had seen her in the shopping complex one day recently, her hair untidy, a farouche air about her. The two assistants at the check-out desks were exchanging amused looks. When Tricia had gone to help her she'd given her a look full of suffering . . . but it had gone in a second and she had been extravagantly grateful, talking too loudly, stuffing notes into her purse, letting some of them fall.

Mary was on Tricia's other side. She had insisted on coming. Some inner steely strength had kept her going through Roger's illness. Her life had become busy with the daily visits to the 'Nursing Home' as she called it. So far he wasn't showing many signs of improvement. He still preferred to be with his mother, but he was generally gentle when Tricia visited him, if remote. He showed little interest in the children. Sometimes they sat without speaking because there was nothing to say.

The Coroner had stopped his consultation with the pathologist. He beckoned to the officer, and the first witness was escorted in. It was Roy Mathieson, the young clerk who'd found Howard. 'I swear by Almighty God to tell the truth, the whole truth . . .' He looked spruced, excited, pleased to be the centre of interest.

'Now, Mr Mathieson,' the Coroner said, 'I want you to tell me exactly what you discovered when you went into the gentlemen's toilet in Kingsley House on the 26th July 1974.'

'Yes, sir. I had excused myself from my friend, Janice Reid . . . she works in the Trust as well . . . and I hurried . . . I mean I went to the toilet and when I pushed open the door I found Mr Howard Newton lying on the floor.'

'Would you describe the scene to me, please?'

'Yes, sir. There was blood on his face, what looked like a nasty gash on his forehead, and he wasn't moving. The hand-basin was pulled out of the wall. There were bits on the floor, a big piece near his face, blood-stained. And glass everywhere. It gave me quite a turn.'

'Quite so. What did you do then, Mr Mathieson?'

'I thought the sooner I got help the better, sir, so I ran out and found Mr Russell.'

'Have you any idea at what time you entered the toilet, Mr Mathieson?'

'Yes, sir. My friend, Janice, told me to look at my watch when I got back and told her. Best to know the time, she said. It was two-thirty-five, so I reckon I found poor Mr Howard around half past two.'

'Thank you. That will be all.'

The young man gave Tricia a gratified look as he walked towards the door.

The Coroner turned to the pathologist. 'Could I hear your report, Dr Best?' Their voices were low.

'Yes.' He read from his notes. Phrases reached Tricia from time to time . . . intensive infarction . . . history of heart trouble corroborated by family physician . . . gash on his left temple . . .'

'How would this gash be sustained?'

'It could be that he struck his head on the wash-basin as he fell, wrenching it at the same time from the wall.'

'*Could* be?'

'It is possible. Pieces of porcelain were found in the gash.'

'This would cause a lot of blood?'

'Yes, sir. And of course there would be flying splinters of porcelain. There were several small cuts on his hands . . .'

The horror of the scene came back to Tricia as the pathologist went on speaking. Her heart started to beat rapidly as she watched the two men. What verdict would the Coroner give? Peter said Dr Best was reliable, kind, the Coroner fair. Dr Chapman had confirmed Dr Best's findings, said that Howard had ignored his warnings to go slow . . .

'Thank you,' the Coroner said at last. 'There's another witness, officer,' he raised his voice, 'Ask him to come in.'

'Yes, sir.' The young officer strode to the door. Tricia heard him call, 'Mr Taplow.' She watched as an elderly man appeared and made his way slowly to the top table. There was a pause while he fumbled for his spectacles in a steel case which he then shut with a loud snap in the quiet room. The officer held the Bible beneath his nose.

'I swear by Almighty God . . .'

'Sit down, Mr Taplow,' the Coroner said. 'You are employed as a porter in Kingsley House near Latham?' He smiled reassuringly.

'Yes, sir.' Now Tricia recognised him. He'd spoken to her the first time she'd taken the children there. Memories flooded her mind. The children's eager faces, Emma's piping voice, 'He's all over blood . . .' And Jake Russell, across the table. 'You look fulfilled.' His eyes had softened.

'. . . Will you tell me, please, Mr Taplow, what you were

doing on the afternoon of the 26th July 1974, at Kingsley House?'

He drew himself up. 'Attending to me duties, sir. Standing at the door. Mr Russell had told me I had to direct the people coming from the . . . that there big tent . . . to the buffet in the 'all. They was all in eating and the champagne was flowing, like, and everything was going fine. I stayed at my post in case of, er, late-comers.' He looked pleased with the word.

'Go on, Mr Taplow.'

'Then when they was all inside eating and drinking Mr Roger came running down the side corridor. I asked him if there was something, but he didn't answer so I opened the door for him. He ran down the steps and got into his car and drove away.'

'When you say "Mr Roger", you mean Mr Roger Newton, the son of the deceased?'

'Yes, sir, that's it, the young un.'

'You know him?'

'Not to say "know him", but I knows him when I sees him. He comes about the Estate quite a lot. He's well-known in Latham, Mr Roger is.'

'Did he look . . . different on the day under discussion?'

'Well, he's always different, Mr Roger. Pale and quiet like his mother. Not as you might say jokey, like the others. And he was in a hurry. Didn't speak.'

'Quite. Could you tell me what time approximately Mr Roger passed you at the door?'

'Not to a minute, sir, but I reckon around half-past two, give or take a minute on either side. I keeps my eye on the clock and Mr Russell told me he wanted them all to be in and attended to by two o'clock at the latest.'

'Thank you, Mr Taplow. That will be all.' The old man took off his spectacles with a small flourish, put them back in their case with the same loud snap. He saluted before he walked away. His words came back to Tricia. 'There's something right sad about that there mock-up . . .' But it wasn't a mock-up now . . .

'Is Dr Jobley here?' The Coroner smiled at Peter as he stood up. They were more than acquaintances, he'd said.

'I understand you have a letter from Mr Roger Newton's psychiatrist at Norwood Hall?'

'Yes, sir.'

'Will you come forward and take the oath, please?' He was friendly, although decorous. Justice would be done, but in the nicest possible way.

'I swear by Almighty God . . .' Peter's level voice was heard clearly in the court room. Fear stabbed her. Soon they would know . . . she looked out of the window and saw the Hapsburg shape of the Town Hall, and towering above it the steel and glass shopping complex. Why did they do it, she thought, her mind swerving away from the fear. Couldn't they have built something Teutonic to match, oak-beamed, perhaps white-washed? What they'd built was soulless. She looked up and counted the square lights set into the roof tiles. Twelve, and blazing away in spite of the fact that the sun was shining outside. Peter's voice came to her in snatches, in waves . . .

'My patient for some time . . . debilitated all winter . . . too conscientious to stay off work . . .'

'This letter says,' the Coroner tapped it, 'that Dr Weatherby cannot as yet estimate a date for Mr Newton's discharge.'

'That is so. His improvement is gradual.'

'Quite so.' The Coroner looked down at the letter again. 'It says that Mr Roger Newton is a sensitive man who has allowed his health and spirits to become severely affected, resulting in a depressive state. But that his cure is certain, given time. Do you agree with that view, Dr Jobley?'

'Yes, sir.'

'And with his statement that it would put a severe strain on his patient to appear in this Court?'

'Yes, sir.'

'Thank you. I have no wish to distress Mr Newton further if it can be avoided. That will be all, Dr Jobley.'

Peter returned to his seat and sat down, looking straight ahead. The room was very quiet.

'Dr Best,' the Coroner turned to the pathologist, 'you have already stated that Mr Howard Newton suffered extensive cardiac infarction?'

'Yes, sir.'

'In your opinion was that the cause of death?'

'Yes.'

'And the injury sustained on the left temple . . . would this

156

have any bearing on his death?'

'I should say not, sir.'

'However it was sustained?' Did he emphasise that 'however'?

'That is correct, sir.'

'At what time would you estimate death occurred?'

'At approximately 2.30 p.m.'

The Coroner nodded, looked straight ahead. Tricia put her hand on her mother-in-law's arm. 'Don't say any more . . .' Mary had said to Roger on that awful night. Had she been living in terror ever since? Tricia had tried to find words to comfort her but she'd always said that she didn't want to talk about it. Her composure had been frightening.

Silence, except for the faint buzzing of the electric clock above the Coroner. Was he wondering about the blow on the left temple? She stole a look at her mother-in-law's face. It was ashen, and she could feel the rigidity of her body through her arm. There was the sound of papers being rustled. Mary didn't move. The Coroner was gathering them up, putting them together in a neat pile. He folded his hands on top of them, said almost conversationally, 'The verdict is death by natural causes.'

Tricia pressed Mary's arm. Her head swam for a second with relief.

'Thank you, Dr Best.' The Coroner bowed his head to the pathologist then turned to look across the tables at Mary. 'Mrs Newton. Would you take this certificate of registration to the appropriate office and obtain the death certificate?' He passed a folded paper to his officer who came forward and gave it to Mary. She kept her head lowered.

'Thank you for coming.' The Coroner stood up. Dr Best followed suit. They bowed and went out of the Court together.

'Are you all right, Mary?' Tricia said, afraid for her.

She turned a haggard face. 'All right?' she repeated the words vaguely, then seemed to pull herself together. 'Oh, Tricia, the relief . . . I can't tell you . . . yes, I'm all right.' Tricia helped her to her feet. The three of them walked out of the courtroom and down the wide staircase.

'Let me drive you home,' Peter said, his hand on Mary's elbow. 'Have a nice hot cup of tea and put your feet up.'

She shook her head. 'I've no need for cups of tea, Dr Jobley.'

Her voice shook. 'I must go right away to the Nursing Home and tell Roger . . .'

'Don't say too much. Just that it's all over.'

'Would you drive me there, Tricia?' She looked pathetically at her. 'You understand, don't you? I want to be with my boy.'

'Yes, I understand.' They were now in the car park behind the building. The wind which blew had an autumn tang in it. She saw the trees had lost their summer fullness. Through the branches the sky was a serene blue. 'We're very grateful, Peter . . .' sudden tears choked her . . . 'for all you've done behind the scenes.'

'I've only told the truth.'

Tricia helped Mary into the car. As she went round to her seat Peter put his hand on her arm. 'The time factor helped.'

'Yes. I could see that.' How long did it take to strike someone down? She was horrified at her thoughts. 'He was just, the Coroner, but not implacable.'

'Humane.'

'Shall we ever forget . . . all this?'

'It's over and done with. Put it out of your mind.' He bent forward and kissed her cheek. She was touched. 'See you.' He strode off and she watched the broad-shouldered figure, a Rugby player, one would have thought, from his back.

Mary sat with her eyes closed on the way to Norwood Hall. Tricia didn't disturb her. I must try and do what Peter says, put it out of my mind. But it's not so easy. It's crowding in on me. Perhaps it should be taken out and looked at, for the last time. She drove automatically in her swift, careful fashion. The fields and autumn woods blurred past, the road was clear in the centre of her vision, but on either side the pictures crowded, the words, from that night . . .

*   *   *

She was in the drawing-room of The Crescent. Peter was there, and she'd persuaded Roger to come downstairs to meet him. He'd come like an obedient child, accepted a drink from her, sat down, silently looked at Peter.

158

'You remember Dr Jobley, Roger,' she said. 'He's our doctor now.'

'We've never met.' He was sitting on his mother's Chesterfield, the glass cupped between his hands. He didn't raise his head.

'He's going to help you, Roger.' He still didn't raise his head. The glass trembled. She saw the liquid moving in it.

'Is your mother asleep?' Peter Jobley asked him.

'She dozed off. I was going to tell her . . .' he sighed, 'about father . . . but she dozed off.' He turned his head away.

'Tell Tricia.'

She wanted him to look at her. 'Remember, just when your mother came in, you were saying, "His face . . . he turned his face to me . . ." '

'Was I?' His smile was one-sided, sly. 'Was I saying that? Not like Dad to be struck dumb, not like the great Howard.' He looked serious, confiding. 'But I had provocation. Talking like that to him. You know I had provocation, Tricia . . . especially that day . . . with his precious Jake Russell.'

'Yes.'

'You're agreeing now, eh? Russell. He's so bloody presentable. Sometimes I thought if he's so successful one way he could well be the other . . .' He laughed, looking at Peter Jobley, a man's look.

'Your father was staring at you, Roger, not speaking . . .'

He nodded at Tricia, again serious. 'Yes, that worried me. I said, "Dad . . ." Wonder why I started calling him *that*, then . . .?' He let out a bark like an animal, tried to take a drink from his glass, slopping the liquid over his jacket. Peter Jobley took it away from him.

'What happened, Roger?' Her voice was trembling.

'Have you ever seen a tree struck by lightning? That's what happened. Except for those eyes on me those terrible eyes, bursting out of their sockets. I . . . I . . . No . . . !' His voice rose in a scream. He put his hands up to his face, wept great, childish spluttering sobs.

'Tell me, Roger, please tell me.'

'Nothing to tell. Noise, clatter, ringing in my head.' He spoke through the sobbing. 'Basin broken. Blood. All over blood . . . watched an arm twitch . . . then stop.' He raised his

159

head and said pitifully to Tricia, 'Why didn't you come to help?'

'I didn't hear.' She could hardly speak. 'No one heard. It's at the end of a long corridor. What . . . what happened then?'

'I knelt down. That awful stare . . . eyeballs glazed, full of blood . . . that terrible cut on his forehead . . . I wiped it and wiped it but the blood wouldn't stop. I said, "Father, I was going to say I was sorry, I didn't mean . . ." but the cut had stopped bleeding. I knew, oh, my God, I knew he'd never hear me!' His voice suddenly wailed, he put his hands to his face again and rocked his body backwards and forwards. She saw the tears spurting through his fingers. 'He'll never know . . .'

'Shh, shh,' she said, bending over him, putting her arm round his shoulders, 'Oh, darling, don't weep, try not to weep so much . . . he'd know you were sorry. He'd know. You panicked. You meant to tell someone when you went out but when you saw all the people you ran to your car. You meant to drive to the hospital to tell them, you hardly knew what you were doing, poor Roger . . .'

'An old man, the porter, I think, opened the door for me. I could have told him . . .'

He sobbed in her arms for a long time while Peter stood there. Sometimes when she met his eyes he only nodded. After a time Roger seemed to be half-asleep, waking himself suddenly with deep indrawn breaths, then sighing with an infinite weariness. She lifted his feet on to the sofa, having to double up his legs because it was too short for him. She saw Peter Jobley leave the room, and then heard the ping of the receiver being lifted. 'Is that Norwood Hall?' she heard him say.

* * *

Mary spoke, as if she had been following Tricia's thoughts. 'They've been good to Roger at the Nursing Home. But nobody could help liking him. He's gentle. Never lost his temper . . . well hardly ever.' She stopped. Then, 'Not like Howard. Often . . . frightening. We were two of a kind, he said, Roger and me . . .' her voice trailed away.

160

Tricia stole a look at her. The woman's eyes were closed. Her lids were swollen with sleepless nights. 'You never . . . ever thought . . .' she kept her eyes on the road,' . . . that he had anything to do with his father's . . . death?' She waited. Waited.

'I wouldn't have blamed him if he had.' The quiet venom in the voice shook her. Now she understood. It had been a loveless marriage. The outward show, Howard's bonhomie, had been a shell. No wonder he'd put so much into the Trust.

She drove extra carefully for the next few miles before her heart steadied. Roger had spent a long time with his mother. Would there be, for ever, a secret shared only by them? I am caught, she thought in this situation. There is no freedom. Is that how it always is? She thought of Jean Paul's brave words.

CHAPTER SIXTEEN
September, 1976

JAN woke knowing something good was going to happen today. She lay beside George stretching her limbs, smelling his smell which was clean yet musky, enjoying his nearness as always but with an added edge of pleasure. So often each day stretched forward with nothing to pinpoint it, early marketing while George was still at home to mind Clay, making breakfast, seeing George off and taking Clay to School. He was going all day now and she started to look for a job.

Madame Lu-Yang in the Chinese laundry downstairs had said she might take her on part-time from ten to three, as Mena, her assistant, was pregnant. She'd tried to catch a glimpse of Mena's stomach through the window to discover if there was any sign of swelling, but she kept it hidden under the counter and a flowered smock. Jan prayed she wouldn't abort.

The money would make a difference. George, since he'd obtained his degree at the Sorbonne, had been with a large conveyancing firm on the Left Bank, but they didn't pay well. She believed it was because he was black and rode a bicycle that he hadn't been promoted, but George said this was silly. It all took time. He dreamed of having his own practice some day in America when they'd saved enough money.

It had been difficult to live, but not as difficult as the first two years. If Momma could have seen them then . . . she got up on one elbow and gently bit George's ear, saw his flat-bridged nose twitch, then his hand with the pink palm come up to brush it as if to scare a fly. She loved his hands, the black strength of them on one side, the baby-pinkness on the other.

She bit his ear again and this time a slow smile spread over his face. She liked his smile even better than his hands. His face had such gaiety, such pure joy. Your 'All-American smile', she called it. He opened his eyes and turned his body towards her, his pelvis pushing forward as if waking and having to touch her were one action. 'What's the game, baby, huh, what's the game?' She'd never forget the Big Apple when he was around.

'Oh, George.' She put her arms round his neck, curved her body back from his so that there would be the pleasure of slowly coming together again. 'This is the day Crystel's coming!'

'Crystel?' He emphasised the last syllable. 'Now I want you to tell me, who the hell's Crystel?'

'You know perfectly well.' Closer, closer . . . now they were together. He was inside her. It had been just as easy and natural that first time at the party so long ago . . . she swallowed, closed her eyes. 'Don't move or I'll kill you. I want to talk. Crystel's coming today! Isn't it fantastic? I did all the marketing yesterday and Madame Bombel gave me two melons for a franc. They were over-ripe, but I've cut the bad bits out. You and Clay can have one each if I'm not home in time. I'm meeting her at the Boulevard to see if it's all still the same, the shabbiness, the iron gates, the kiosk in the courtyard, the cars parked in front of the bill-boarding. It's all fixed up, I told you. I can hardly wait . . .'

He was cradling her in his arms, rocking her gently. 'Now, I'm sure as hell sorry, honey, but it's all washed up. I can't mind Clay. I've got to be off early on an assignment. Some rich chick out at St Cloud who wants my advice on her saleable property. I believe it's a beautiful apartment . . .'

'I said don't *move*. Wait . . . wait. Oh!' She sighed slowly, carefully. 'That's better . . . For a minute you had me worried, George Cook, but you wouldn't do that to me. Gosh, I've been looking forward to meeting Crystel all week. I could have died of shock when I got her letter after all that time. I guess she must have quite an important career if she's coming to Paris to buy for her firm. I never thought she'd be a career woman. I remember her saying in that Midi accent of hers, "I want to find a man to love me, a lovair." It was Tricia who had all the liberated ideas.

163

'She was good-looking, Tricia, plenty of style, but I guess she was inhibited. It's living in England that does it. On the face of it they're full of bigotry, racial, political, religious. You can't blame them, living on an island and with their history. They have to learn to integrate, not dominate, see people in the round, black people, teenagers, old people . . .'

'Hey, you're not at a Convention! She was sweet, though. Her legs were really elegant.'

'It's her eyes, I remember. They could eat you up, those eyes. There's hope for her with those eyes . . .' He stopped speaking, began to run his hands slowly up and down her spine, keeping his body cupped against hers. She felt the strong tweak of his body inside her, groaned.

'Don't start anything, for godssakes. Clay will come in.' She had to talk quickly to dampen down the lurch of desire in her own body. 'But Crystel hadn't any problems like that, had she?'

'No, I guess she was integrated, even in her looks. She knew what her body was for. The French are born mature. The English have to acquire it. And every black man is a philosopher. God knows why I didn't fall for her instead of you . . .'

'But you didn't.'

'No. I took one look at you, and you were for me. It was as simple as hay-making on a summer's day. Everything fell into place. I gave up nothing and got everything. It's you who had to do the giving up.'

'No . . .' It was difficult to speak now. The lurch had steadied, but desire was mounting in her, swamping her. Supposing Clay came in . . . if Momma could really understand that George and I have something that will last, but I think she's coming round to it. The last letter she wrote she was suggesting that father could fix up something for George. It isn't that I'm not happy, I like Paris and even St Denis with its crowded streets and squashy vegetables at the end of the day . . . we'd never sell them like that back home . . . but to go back, to be in Cedars, and the cleanness, no corners, no twisted pipes under the basin, to feel at home again, not in a foreign land. 'Oh God, oh God, George . . .'

'*Maman*,' Clay said from the doorway, his curls in a fuzzy

164

red-brown aureole against the light, 'C'est l'heure pour partir à l'école. Maman . . .'

Jan turned slowly to look at her son. She was drowsy, filled, fulfilled. No one could help liking him, could they? 'Oui . . .'

George kissed her ear and sprang out of bed, lifted Clay in his arms and raised him on his shoulders. 'You've got to talk English at home. Remember Momma said it? Let's see you salute the flag?'

Jan watched his hand go shakily up to his brow. He was smiling like his father, richly, blackly.

'Now, sing!' George threw back his head, opened wide his wide mouth, bawled, ' "Oh, say, does that star-spangled banner . . ." '

' ". . . yet wave . . ." ' The treble voice joined in.

'That's not singing. That's a baby squeak from a clittermouse.' He bawled again in his Paul Robeson bass. ' "O'er the land of the free . . ." Give it all you've got. "And the home of the brave . . ." '

Jan set up in bed, pulling the covers under her arms. At the end of the song she said, 'You might have put some clothes on, George.'

* * *

Crystel was more beautiful than Jan remembered, in a dress of pleated chiffon with crocodile shoes and bag which didn't dim the red-brown of her hair. Was it a shade richer? She had a smooth look. Jan had seen that look on her own face this morning, a shiny, slightly spotty face. Her shoulder blades stuck out like little wings and her bosoms didn't swell. Nor was she cocooned in a gorgeous perfume, a red-brown velvet feel to it, earthy but sweet.

George didn't know she went short on her own to give Clay the best of food, fruit from the market bought at its freshest, and on rare occasions, pieces of expensive steak which he and George shared. 'I don't feel like meat,' she said. 'I'm into vegetables and grains.' She felt nowadays she would throw up if she attacked a real juicy steak, other times, watching George eating, she would have liked to tear it away from him and sink her teeth in it. When she thought of the big shining kitchen at Cedars, and her mother watching Dorothy trim off the fat from a piece of sirloin with the rich blood oozing from it, it made her salivate.

'Just a salad, Crystel. *Gardez la ligne*. When I got your letter I was so happy! I've thought of you often. Where we live isn't much of a place. It's on the main route out of Paris, above a Chinese laundry. I wouldn't like to ask you there.'

'You are stupid, Jan,' Crystel said, with that ravishing smile. She'd put her white gloves on the table and her nails were varnished petunia like her dress. 'I am a peasant. My home is a cottage in St Henri and luxuries mean nothing to me. I can take them or leave them.' This was her time for taking, evidently.

'It's difficult to believe. That peach of a dress you're wearing! Look at mine. It's been washed so often it's shrunk up to my *derrière*.'

'I thought it was a girl of eighteen coming to meet me. You've got younger instead of older. Now, tell me everything about you.'

'George and I are still together. We haven't got married. At first he said contracts were for the fearful, but now I think it's stubbornness because he knows my parents wouldn't like it.'

'Or perhaps to leave you a loophole?'

Jan looked at Crystel. George was right. She was no age, any age, her lovely curved mouth had a maturity about it. 'Maybe. I hadn't thought of that, nor of ever leaving George. There's Clay . . . I don't think much at all. Each day's so full of work and shopping and taking care of Clay. And I'm slow.'

'Your French is fabulous anyhow. Boulevard Raspail could do nothing for me.'

'I'm glad it couldn't. I like yours. It's throaty and sexy and suits you . . . and your perfume. Jungly.' She laughed. 'My fluency comes from haggling in shops. Until you've been angry in French you don't know the language. The test is when you and another woman grab the same cabbage. I guess you don't have that kind of problem in Maurac. Are the people still as curious as ever?'

'It's I who have become curious. I watch from the window of my apartment to see who goes along the street, when *le Syndicat* is busy, when Mademoiselle Coco puts out her *antiquités*, when the *Charcuterie* pull down their sunblinds . . .'

'I do that too.' The salad had left her ravenously hungry. 'Shall we have an icecream?'

'Yes, please. A knickerbocker glory?' She must remember to tell George how she said that. Delicious. 'Oh, it's another world, those days . . .' She sighed, raising her hand to the waitress, a young girl with teetering heels and a pompadour. 'Two American knickerbocker glories, please.' She had it now, a little pause in the middle. The two French girls were laughing together. She's just as easy with women as men.

'My, it's lovely to see you, Crystel . . . we don't go out much because of Clay and then we're saving up to go home soon. I guess that's why I like seeing life from the window. Clay's seven now. He's really beautiful.'

'Like his father?'

'Yes, oh, I didn't mean . . . yes, I guess I did. I think George is beautiful.' She thought of him this morning, naked, holding Clay. 'It seems funny to my mother, that . . .'

'Because he's black? I thought they'd got over that in America?'

'Not in Johnstown.'

'Hasn't she met him?'

'No. She was shocked when I told her about the baby. She wrote bitter letters . . . anyhow my father must have talked her round and they came to see me in hospital. But she never met George.'

'Why was that?'

'Grand'mère Leroy was dying and she had to rush home. She was the only one who could dominate Momma. She lived in New Orleans and came to stay at Cedars every summer. She had a black ebony stick with a silver leopard's head and when she was sitting she leant her two tiny claws on it, that's how I thought of her hands, with narrow nails painted blood-red. She always wore dangling drop earrings, and when she had her first small stroke it never showed except in those earrings when her head trembled. It fascinated Rony and I. She was a real *grande dame*. I haven't met anyone so grand in Paris, certainly not in St Denis.'

'She sounds fascinating, but cruel.'

'Cruel, yes. She was dead when they got home. Sometimes I think Momma blames me for that as well.'

'Only if it's in her character. How is your sister?'

'Rony's just fine. She comes to see us, *en passant*. Once she gave us money, well, to Clay to fit him out for going to US of A . . . that's what George says . . . but he had bronchitis that year, and every year. I guess Paris is pretty damp. Rony I love!' She waved her hands and had to push back the heavy silver ring George had given her which had fallen over her knuckle.

'Is she like you, skinny with long hair?' They laughed.

'No, she's big, much bigger than me, bone-wise, rangy, with carroty hair like Poppa used to have and she's down-to-earth and acts as a kind of buffer between Momma and me. I try to keep the peace with Momma by calling her long distance when I can. When I hear her American voice I cry . . . sometimes I speak with father too. He says he's looking out for something for George. There will be no problem. That's Poppa, always no problem. George is paid badly where he is. I can't understand it when he's so clever.'

'Paris is parochial.'

'What a thing to say about Paris!'

'It's composed of *les coteries*. It's only tourists and the aristocrats who think it's cosmopolitan. No longer even the artists. He'd be better in the south, like Toulouse, where I go to buy sometimes. There they are broadminded . . .' her smile was rich, sensual, 'or in the States. He could become a famous black lawyer hired by the Mafia.' They laughed together. Their sundaes came and they laughed again at their hugeness and colour.

'It's like being eighteen again! Do you remember those parties? Nothing parochial about them . . . but George would never be a lawyer to the Mafia. He's full of principles. Oh, Crystel, do you remember those lovely walks we had, all over the place . . .'

'Père Lachaise, and we couldn't find any of the famous tombs.'

'And we asked a man who was tidying up and he pointed out Oscar Wilde's away up at the top. Someone had scratched on it, "I love you, dear."'

'Sad.'

'Do you remember Tricia's face in churches?' She made hers go long and solemn. 'Churches don't turn me on unless the glass is good. Light pouring through stained glass. That's truly religious.'

'Tricia and I started to write after a friend of hers called to see me . . . Jake Russell.'

'I expect he's been back again. One look at you . . .'

'No. It's five years ago. I think we got off on the wrong foot. Is that it?'

'Yes. I can't believe it. You must have been wearing a ring. *Are* you married?'

'No, I'm not.' She poked delicately at the sundae with her spoon and Jan saw a square-cut amethyst winking on her finger. It was too big to be real, surely. 'There was a man when I got back from Paris. His mother owned *L'Hôtel de la Poste* and I didn't want it to own me.' She smiled up at Jan. 'And so I decided to become a career girl.'

'Who needs men?' Jan said, smiling back. Her beauty was so enjoyable. The people she saw around their *quartier* were ugly. They had raucous voices and they fought over cabbages.

'*I* do,' Crystel said. 'And don't tell me *you* don't. It's written all over you.'

'Is it?' She was pleased to have it written all over her. 'I love George very much. He . . . excites me. But Clay, well, that's different. I flow over with protective love for him. He's a gift I don't deserve, my hostage to fortune. I want to cherish, keep him from all harm . . .' She stopped herself from waving her hands again. It was too French.

'You have a mothering instinct. I never had it.'

'But you like your job?'

'I like it for what it gives me, independence, a flat of my own, clothes, a car . . . I travel quite a lot buying for Guy, that's my boss.' Her smile flashed. 'As a matter of fact I'm here *par la bonté de Derain et Cie.*' Her amethyst flashed too and Jan wondered. 'That's a joke we have between us, *you* know?' She did. 'He has a wife who doesn't understand him.'

'So you sleep with him?'

'Didn't I tell you I needed a man? Yes, he's sweet and he needs some happiness. So do we all. I'm a hedonist. I've learned that word.' I don't know what I am, Jan thought, a mother first and foremost, then a lover . . . 'How are your parents? Who never stood in your way.' They both laughed.

'They still live in St Henri. I go home each week and take off my makeup and my smart dress and bake and cook in the big kitchen and feel like the peasant I am under the skin. And sometimes I take them in my car to see my mother's two unmarried sisters, Angelique and Justine, and I feel I'll end up just like them, doting on my father because he wears a moustache. Then I go back to Maurac with my bunch of country flowers and cream and butter . . . so different from Paris.'

'Oh, Crystel, remember Jean Paul that night . . . you said he opened our eyes . . . and all our talks and dreams . . .'

'Our dreams . . .' The beautiful eyes shadowed for a second. She beckoned to the waitress. 'Two coffees, chérie.' She pointed to her half-finished sundae. 'Parfait.'

'Listening to you talking about your life at St Henri makes me feel awfully homesick. Not so much for Johnstown. It's Cedars, the high ceilings, the candelabra, the bathrooms with no cockroaches . . . George calls them the Parisian indigent . . . my horse, the car they gave me on my eighteenth birthday . . . I've still got my clover-leaf key-ring, have you?'

'Yes, and a car.' She laughed.

'I can see it that sunny morning, standing waiting for me, the tonneau cover down . . . Oh, God, I can wallow in self-pity.'

'As long as you don't tell George what you gave up for him.'

'I'd never do that.' She shook her head. 'He gave me Clay. I want to take him back so much and let Momma see him. I really think we'll be going back soon, maybe not to Cedars, George says. This month particularly, in the sticky heat, with the shops shut and the factories closed down, I think of Johnstown and the kids round the swimming-pool and the trees and the high blue sky and I know I *have* to get back. And now there's this letter from Momma. I really think it's influenced George . . .'

'Talking about letters . . .' Crystel opened her crocodile bag with the gold fastenings and took out an envelope. 'I had this from Tricia the other day. It was in my flat when I got back from Grimaud.'

'How fabulous! Grimaud . . . I wrote to Tricia when I had Clay. I had a letter back saying she was married and had a little girl. I was so surprised at her getting married so quickly after all she said.'

'I think it was a surprise to her. We've written to each other for a long time now. She's had a bad time.'

'What happened?'

'Marriage happened, I guess.' She waved her hands, smiling, mimicking Jan. 'You've been luckier than you think with your George. Here,' she handed her the letter, 'read it while I go and do my face. I've an appointment at four o'clock with a wholesaler.' She got up and as her silk skirt swished against the table, Jan got a whiff of her perfume. Crystel in essence, she thought, sophisticated but earthy, orchids, and the smell of the park at home when you went riding before supper . . .

'12th September 1976. Such a long time since I last wrote to you that I'm ashamed, but so many things have been happening. But, first, your letter.

'I'm glad you're happy with Guy and enjoying your job. It's so strange. I always thought you'd marry a French Comte and have two beautiful children called Marie Laure and Christian. You'd give stunning parties and you'd have to fight off other French comtes trying to persuade you to have an affaire on the side.

'It's now two years since my father-in-law died, and things haven't been easy for Roger. That's an understatement. It started by his father having no confidence in him and ended in tragedy.

'When Howard died, Roger went to pieces. It was terrible for everyone, terrible for his mother who worships him. He was in a psychiatric hospital for six months. He felt life wasn't worth living. He wept a great deal. He was never violent, just unutterably sad. Even the children made no impression on him.

'This is becoming a very gloomy letter, Crystel, I'm sorry.

Someday when we get together I'll tell you the whole story. It's too painful.

'And here's where I cheer up. "Begone dull care . . ." I work in the family business now, the Latham Development Trust to give it its proper name. It was Jake Russell's idea. Did you ever hear from him? He's like an oyster about that visit.

'It may have been Jake's idea, my working, but it's very much to Roger's chagrin. Isn't it nice to find a word I don't have to struggle over? I work with Jake and Rab Wilkes, who was appointed by my father-in-law not long before he died. He's what we'd call here a "cheery chappie".

'Jake has got it into his head that I've some ideas to give to the Project . . . our name for Kingsley Heath. He says it's what Howard would have liked, and oddly enough, he left me equal parts in his Will with Roger, his mother and Mr Deakin, an old friend of Roger's grandfather.

'At first, when Roger was in the Hospital, I only went to the office occasionally, but now that he's recovered he still doesn't want to work. Peter Jobley, his doctor . . . he's been marvellous . . . says not to push him, that, although he's cured of his depression, the shock of his father's death has left a psychological scar.

'So now I work every day and love it. Emma and Mark are both at school and, if I'm not back when they come out, Roger picks them up. He seems to fill in his time in an amazing way, reading, gardening, visiting his mother . . . they're very close. At first the situation frightened me . . . he wasn't the Roger I'd married, and then as each day passed I discovered I was becoming more and more immersed in my work and I didn't worry so much. I suppose you have role reversal situations in France too. Maybe not in Maurac! But sometimes it's like a bad dream, my marriage . . . no, that's not true. I have to remind myself he's been ill, that it will all come right, given time.

'Oh, dear, what an egotistical letter this is becoming, and it could be even more so if I went into details about how much I enjoy working on the Project. It's like our baby, Jake's and mine . . . what a stupid thing to say, far too extreme.

'If you do have the chance to visit Jan when you're in

Paris, please give her my love. How different our lives are from what we planned! Have any of us gained that freedom of the individual we discussed so often perched high in our room in the Boulevard Raspail? Do you think you have to lose your freedom first to gain it? Jean Paul could have told us, or is he like the rest of us, caught up in day-to-day living?

'*I must stop. I'm writing this after the children have gone to bed. Roger is at his mother's, and he may be in any time. He finds a kind of comfort and solace from her I don't think I can give him, and that saddens me.*

'*I love your letters, Crystel, like reading "Clochemerle", only nicer. Has Monsieur Rambeau still got his Fiat nestling beside your big Citroen, and does he still talk politics but refuse to come into your parlour? And is the nasty René Baron still regretting he did what his mother told him and took anyone else but you for a wife? And aren't you glad?*

'*Give my love to Mamselle Coco and all the people of Maurac whom you watch from your patio. I long to visit you sometime, but perhaps Jake will get there before me. Once he told me he remembered your perfume . . .*

'*There's Roger. Must go. Much love.*'

'What did you think of it?' Crystel said, coming back looking smoother and more beautiful than ever.

'She says Jake Russell remembers your perfume.'

'Yes. One wouldn't have thought so.' She looked away for a second, then turned back, her face lively. 'Are you surprised at Tricia becoming a career woman?'

'No, she's doing what she wants.'

'Guy said to me once, it was the first time he slept with me, that we all know what we really want.'

'I think that's true. I want to go back home with George and Clay. I want Clay to grow up to be an American boy, to play baseball and have a peaked baseball cap. There are no French boys, only little adults.' She looked at Crystel. 'I don't think that's too much to ask. How about you?' She watched the beautiful face downbent as she pulled on her gloves, the thick, springing hair with its depth of colouring. Someone like you could have anything, she thought . . .

173

'It's difficult.' She looked up at Jan, her lips parted, her eyes soft. 'I'm not unhappy, that's true. All I know is that I haven't got what I want.' She smiled brilliantly, flicked her eyelashes. 'Don't think I'm wiping away tears . . .'

CHAPTER SEVENTEEN
December, 1976

THEY arrived at Cedars just before Clay's eighth birthday, tired, bewildered, not believing that Paris was behind them and that they were now in the US of A as George put it. The long journey by train from Kennedy Airport to Baltimore and from there by coach to Johnstown had made Clay speechless and George's copper face grey with fatigue. Jan was light-headed, a curious mixture of tiredness and elation.

She had gone home after meeting Crystel and burst into the living-room. 'I had a wonderful time. I was telling Crystel how much I want to go back home.' George had got up, kissed her and said, 'Okay, when we get things together, we'll go. I've got the money.' And that was it. He said afterwards it was her radiant face that had done it.

The only person in the family who hated leaving Paris was Clay. *'Qu'est-ce-que je vais faire sans mes copains?'* he had said from time to time. Jan who thought very little of the scrawny urban children he played with had tried to cheer him up with stories of swift-footed boys with bats, of swimming pools as blue as the sea, of fishing, of barbecues under the stars, of the garden and park at Cedars and the possibility of a pony, but he remained faithful to Paris. *'Chez grand-père, je ne connais personne,'* he said.

'Talk English!' George had roared, and to Jan, 'Don't blow him up with that fancy talk about Cedars or he'll think that's our home. It's where we'll *stay* until we get a place ourselves.'

So here they were now, getting down from the coach, travel-stained and hungry, and father was waiting there to greet them. It took her a minute to recognise him. He had a paunch, and yet his face had shrunk, he was grey at the temples, and he carried a walking stick. She remembered something about a troublesome cartilage of the knee and was ashamed that she had never given it a

175

moment's thought. But when he raised the stick and called out, 'Hi, Jan!' and set off towards them, hardly limping at all, he was handsome Carl Sirica again. She ran into his arms. 'Oh, Poppa, Poppa . . .'

'Jan, little Jan.' His voice was rough in her ear. Then he sniffed, said, 'This won't do,' and held her away to look at her. She saw the good silk of his shirt, the Yale tie. 'You're just the same girl who went away and left us. Even your hair's the same.' He lifted one long strand.

'It's awful, Poppa, stringy. We've been travelling for so long! This is George.' George was busy gathering their cases together and all that was to be seen of him was a denim rump. He straightened and turned round, stuck out his hand. George would always make the first move. He said that being black he over-compensated.

'Glad to meet you, Mr Sirica.'

'So you're the man who stole our little girl? I shouldn't speak to you at all.' She watched her father taking in George. He was used to dealing with people, all colours, all nationalities, in his job as timber exporter.

'Well, it's a long time ago, Mr Sirica. Let bygones be bygones, huh? This is Clayton, our son. Clay, say hello to your grandfather.'

'*Comment allez-vous?*' Clay said, looking suspicious. 'George, this is not my grandfather. He should have *une barbe blanche*.'

'What's that?' Carl said to Jan.

'A white beard, Poppa. I think he's been shown pictures at school of grandfathers . . . Clay, speak English if you don't mind. It's impolite when in America not to speak the same language.'

'The boy's dead tired,' Carl said, 'let's get him into the car.'

'Is Momma there?' Jan lifted one case, took Clay by the hand and George followed with the other two. Carl fell into step beside her, walking easily. She wondered if the stick had been adopted as a mannerism. He'd always been what she and Rony called a snappy dresser, enamel and gold cuff-links, a signet ring with a single diamond. 'Momma . . . ?' She looked at him.

'No, she stayed behind to see that Dorothy had a good meal ready for you.' His voice sounded unconvincing.

176

'Have you still got Dorothy? She must be a hundred and ten. I thought she would have retired to her wonderful Vermont long ago.'

'She's close on seventy, but to tell you the truth I don't think it's going to be that easy to get rid of Dorothy. Your mother and I have come round to thinking we might sell Cedars instead, move into something smaller.'

'I didn't think you'd ever do that.' She didn't know if he were serious or not.

'People change.'

The car was a new Cadillac, there had probably been two or three new Cadillacs since she'd left, large and luxurious and Clay's tiredness was temporarily banished when he was allowed to ride in the front. Jan and George sat in the back, hands clasped, listening to the rapid fire of his questions.

'Do you have *les freins* in US of A? Tell me, please, is this the stick? That's right, George, isn't it, stick?'

'*Oui, certainement.*'

'George, not you too.' Jan nudged him with her elbow.

'I'm suffering from culture shock,' he whispered.

'Does the kid call you "George"?' Carl asked, steering with the tip of one finger and half-turning.

'Yes, I guess if we'd had more children he wouldn't, but we've grown together. And he hears Jan saying it.'

'Your mother won't like that,' Carl said, meeting Jan's eyes in the mirror.

'If that's all she doesn't like . . . Rony and I used to call her Ettie behind her back.' As a mother she could say what she liked, surely. George had warned her about being browbeaten or patronised. 'Where is Rony? I thought she might be home.'

'She's working in New York in Public Relations. She got herself a really good job after College. She's coming home as soon as she can to see you.'

'Great. I've missed Rony.'

'We've all missed you. It's been far too long. Now, after supper you and I are going to have a chat, George. I'm sorry you didn't make out in Paris.'

'I could have changed jobs, but Jan had set her heart on coming home.'

'Yes, yes . . .' he wasn't used to being interrupted. 'I hope to get you fixed up in a good firm in Baltimore. I have plenty of connections there. Of course you could have walked into my attorney's office in Johnstown, but Mrs Sirica didn't think that would be advisable.'

Jan looked at George. His face was grim. She liked him best when he was smiling. He smiled easily and often. Clay had fallen asleep against his grandfather's shoulder. She could only see the top of his fuzzy head. She had a sudden acute sense of loss, of having made a terrible mistake. Paris had been their home. She'd been chasing a chimera to imagine she and George could live anywhere near Johnstown. Momma wouldn't like it. She might not even like George . . .

She looked out of the car window, saw the long, straight Johnstown road which ran past Cedars, the occasional large white house with its pillared porch and parkland. They looked so settled, so secure. That was the Emersons. Rony had once said if the Emersons had grown squashes in their front lawn the Jeffersons would have done the same. There was the Ogdens' place, bigger than either of them and set up on a knoll so that their windows looked down on everyone else. Those terrible Ogden children . . . 'Our drive is two miles long. How long is yours?' How far away those days seemed, the children's parties, the coming-out balls, the sledging in the Ogdens' park. How sunlit.

Soon they'd be turning in at their drive, not two miles long, but wide and bordered by spruce and . . . she shut her eyes because they were stinging with tears. All those dreams of Cedars, the pool, the tennis courts, the riding, were childhood memories, nothing to do with a girl of twenty-six with a black man who wasn't her husband and a black child. None of these things belonged to her any more.

The sense of loss turned into a deep-seated pain in her ribs. She had made a mistake. Her day-dreaming and nostalgic longing had made her lose sight of reality. There was no place for them here in this ordered landscape, in those white Colonial houses. In America, perhaps, but not here. You couldn't go back in time, and you couldn't take the present, which was George and Clay, back into the past. She put her head on George's shoulder until the pain went.

178

She raised her head when they turned into the drive. She remembered how beautiful it was in the fall when the shumacs, now stripped of leaves, were on fire. The spruces were straight, unbending, the sky above was a cold blue. It needed snow to soften it, make it a familiar picture. 'Look hard and you might see a red squirrel,' she said to Clay. He'd sat up when his grandfather had swung the car round. He drove too showily and too fast for his age. Was that why he had married Momma? Seeing her as another accoutrement? Or that she could be the provider of them? And had she fallen for his showy good looks? What on earth was she thinking mean thoughts like that for?

'What is that, Maman, what you have just said. Speak in French, please. I cannot understand.'

'You wouldn't understand any better in French because you've never seen one. *Un écureuil.*'

'Yes, I have!' He turned round, triumphant. 'They are in our school-books. They hold a nut in their paws, *comme ça.*'

'They've all gone,' Carl said. 'We're becoming quite suburban out here, worse luck. They're building a new housing estate between us and Johnstown. Of course the Emersons and the Jeffersons and the Deeres, Leo Wigner, all the old people, have lodged protests, and I carry a bit of weight in the town as you know, but it's gone ahead. Nowadays there are all kinds in the office, blacks . . .' he stopped suddenly, laughed and hit the wheel, lightly. 'No offence, Mr Cook.'

'George.'

'George. I'm an old-stick-in-the-mud. Things change too fast for me.' He turned with conspicuous dash round the last curve and drew up in front of the broad flight of steps leading to the columned porch. He leaned back like a conjuror who has played his ace and was now waiting for the applause.

Jan looked and her heart filled with love. The four pillars supporting the balcony of the master bedroom. The mansards which had been hers and Rony's rooms looking over the park. Like looking down a telescope she had an image of the view in her head, the wide grassland, the clump of spruces at the pool, the winding drive . . . how gracious, how ineluctably right the house was. This was what she remembered, its spatial quality, the cool white exterior, and the cool interior with its black and

179

white tiled floor when you came in from the baking heat.

She waited for George to say something complimentary, or even polite. He didn't. His eyes rested, took in, that was all. His head was held slightly back so that he looked down the broad plane of his nose. Her father had been waiting too because he gave a light tap on the driving wheel with his gloved hand and said, 'Well, that's Cedars. She's got her welcome smile on.'

'Is it a *Musée?*' Clay asked.

'No darling.' She laughed uncomfortably. 'It's grandfather's and grandmother's house. Mine . . . it's where we're going to stay . . . for a bit.'

She saw his head nod once. He had become a real little French adult. It was a good thing she'd taken him away in time. Then he'd slipped off his seat, opened the door remarkably skilfully considering he'd never been in a Cadillac before, and was helping George with the cases. She got out too and walked to the back of the car. George had the trunk open and was giving Clay the handgrip he'd taken care of throughout the journey. He put the strap on his skinny shoulder and looked shyly at her for the next move.

'On you go with grandfather,' she said, 'George and I will bring in the rest.'

'Come on, Clay.' Carl held out his hand as if he needed support. 'We'll go on in together.'

Her mother was in the hall, small, quite French-looking, Jan thought for the first time in her life, elegant but never beautiful. 'Momma, oh, Momma!' She ran to her, feeling awkward and too tall. She put her arms round her and felt the stiff, corseted body, smelled the same heavy hyacinth perfume which she'd never liked. 'I'm so happy to be home.' The tears had run down her cheeks when she'd embraced her father. She'd wiped them surreptitiously with a long strand of hair. Now her eyes were dry. She straightened herself and looked at her mother's face. She was smiling stiffly, nervously, and *her* eyes were wet.

'I can't believe it, Jan. I simply can't believe it . . .' There were runnels of tears in her thickly madeup face.

She said foolishly, because she wanted so much to weep and

180

couldn't. 'You're wearing *Grand'mère's* earrings.'

'They were left to me.' She was dabbing carefully under the mascaraed eyelids with a lace-trimmed handkerchief. 'There's a bracelet for you but I didn't risk sending it, the little seed-pearl one. Oh, dear . . . ' she smiled bravely, putting away the handkerchief. 'And I kept on thinking you'd be home any day. How could you have stayed away so *long* . . . ?'

'Momma, I can't explain. Clay was ill . . . ' and the money got used up again and again, and why didn't *you* come? But she couldn't say that.

'*Je suis* Clayton.' She heard the composed little voice. Perhaps he'd been drilled secretly by George.

Her mother smiled, no longer stiffly. Her two prominent front teeth showed, her nose wrinkled charmingly. 'Oh, come and give Granny a kiss, you little dear.' She held out her arms and Clay came forward and kissed one cheek, then the other.

'How very French.' She took the boy by the hand and faced George who was standing beside the suitcases. Faced was the word, Jan thought, inwardly shaking, and yet thinking, she can't *do* anything to me. I'm not hers any more.

'This is George, Momma.' She put her arm through his and led him forward.

'George,' her mother said, the smile stiff again, her eyes sliding away from him, back to him, away again. George kissed her as Clay had done then pumped her hand.

'It's fine to meet you. We deeply regret it's been such a long time.' He must have composed this too, Jan thought. It had an unreal sound.

'Even a long time passes,' her mother said. Her eyes now stayed on George, and as if with relief she smiled and gave her head a reproving little shake. The diamond earrings trembled. 'What am I thinking of keeping you standing here, you poor souls? You look tired to death. Come along upstairs and I'll show you your rooms. Carl, help George with the bags. Clay, come with me. I've got a lovely room for you. It was your mother's, and all her old picture books are there.' She took his hand and led him to the staircase. 'That's it, now, watch the steps. They're broad for your little legs.' She turned to Jan who had followed them. 'He seems small for his age. Why, here's Dorothy to say hello.'

Jan turned also. The green baize door to the kitchen was swinging. Dorothy was coming towards them. She would have scarcely known the woman. She'd changed far more than her mother, who'd hardly changed at all. She was bent and her face had sunk into grooves making her squaw-like. Her hair was still jet-black, smooth, parted in the middle and drawn back tightly behind her ears.

'My own lamb,' she said, reaching Jan and putting her arms round her. 'Why did you stay away for so long, you wicked girl? You nearly broke your mother's heart . . .'

'Dorothy,' Ettie said, 'don't gabble. You're making it sound like "Gone with the Wind".' Jan remembered her mother's often cruel sense of humour. 'Say how do you do to Jan's husband.'

Dorothy's face stiffened. She put out a limp hand which George pumped briskly, then gave her a kiss on either cheek. She drew away as if she'd been bitten.

'I'll scurry right back to the kitchen now, Mrs Sirica. I can smell the roast.'

'We all can. Off you go.' When she'd disappeared behind the baize door she said to George. 'We make allowances for her because she's old now. I hope you will too.'

George, looking mystified, said, 'Sure, sure.'

Her eyes have lost George again, Jan thought, or rather, as if that one glance had been as much as she could take. She seemed to speak to a point in his throat, and then she withdrew her eyes altogether and began to climb the stairs with Clay. She'll get used to him. *I* never think of him as black . . .

'Isn't it lovely?' she said to him as they went up the wide curved staircase together. 'Just stop a minute to look at the view from the landing window. I've dreamt of this. Look, there's where Rony and I used to ride . . . that path through the park . . . and you can just catch a glimpse of the swimming pool behind the spruces. Is it still heated, Momma?'

'Oh yes. Your father likes his swim every morning before he goes to the office. He can't start his day without that. Then his shower, then his fresh shirt and everything just so. Isn't that the way of it, Carl?' She turned.

182

Carl was behind them like a dutiful dog. 'Your Momma says I could keep a laundry going on my own.' Her mother had never allowed them to keep dogs, she thought, which was strange. Horses were different. Every well-brought-up girl in Johnstown rode. What else would there have been to talk about?

'You'll be able to join your grandfather in the morning for a swim, Clay,' Ettie said.

'I'll try it with George first, thank you.' He was trudging manfully upwards, lugging his hand-grip.

They had missed Rony who had been home for Christmas, but she came to see them early in January, and then Jan did weep at the sight of her sister in a woollen hat pulled half-way down her face, her red hair spread on the shoulders of her leather coat, her scarves, her shoulder-bag bulging, her huge fur gloves, her high boots and her wide rangy smile. As soon as possible they took themselves up to the top of the house where their rooms had been and settled themselves into two old chairs with faded cushions.

'Momma's a pack rat,' Rony said, arranging her long legs over the wooden arm of the rocker. 'She ought to have got rid of this stuff long ago. Well, tell me how she's been?'

'Just fine. We've had one or two dinner parties so that George could meet the local people.'

'The Emersons and the Jeffersons?'

'No, they're in Europe. That's still to come. And she got the family silver out and Poppa laid on champagne and Dorothy scuttled around like a crab and with a face like a crab-apple. She doesn't like George.'

'Dorothy doesn't like George!' Rony's tone was mocking.

'She thinks he should be in the kitchen with her, cleaning shoes or something.'

'She's demented, poor soul. *Folie de grandeur*. You should know what that means, Frenchie. She always was a pale copy of Momma. What does *Momma* think of George?'

'She's getting used to his blackness. At first she took sneaky looks as if she could only stomach a bit at a time.'

'Yes, I've seen the sidelong glance, as perfected by *Grand'mère* Leroy. And what does George think of her. That's the question.'

'He doesn't say. He's coiled up into a tight ball of frustration waiting for the job Poppa's going to fix up for him in Baltimore. Poppa took him to the city and introduced him to Mr Wendell, a friend of his own attorney. Mr Wendell said he hadn't any openings right at this minute but he would pass the word along and he was sure something would turn up. It's a month now, but nothing has.'

'Father always exaggerated his influence in Baltimore.'

'Or Momma did. You can't see through façades when you're small. George goes long walks on his own and doesn't speak much. He hasn't even got Clay now because he's at school. He drives him to Johnstown every morning in Momma's roadster.'

'I bet she tells him to hurry back in that oh-so-delicate way which gets you just where it hurts.'

'She likes it for ten o'clock. He doesn't discuss Momma or Poppa, he just clams up. All he talks about is work, when is he going to get something to do . . . ' Jan waved her hands. 'I'm going on about us all the time. It's great to see you. I've missed you more than Momma and Poppa, now it can be told.' She laughed. 'Even more than Cedars.'

'You always were a homebird, Jo-Jo.' The childish name made Jan's eyes sting. 'I don't come back here very often. I've made my own life in New York.'

'Don't you miss here?'

'What is there to miss? Oh, I know you mean the place, but that's not important. I've grown away from it. Let me tell you what happens if I do come back. The first day or two Momma calls all her cronies and gives them tea and shows me off. Acts out a scene about this wonderful girl of hers who's making out so well for herself in New York, then she gets tired of it and retreats. You know what she's always been like. She disappears into the little sitting-room, her boudoir, as she calls it now. She's even got Dorothy trained to say, "Mrs Sirica's in her *bood*war," for godssakes! I get the feeling that the curtain's been rung down and I'd better push on, so I do.'

Jan winced. It described what she was beginning to feel herself. 'Of course we don't intend to stay long. It's just that George is committed to waiting to see what Mr Wendell can do for him, and you know Poppa. "Any day now, George."'

He likes everybody to think he's so important. Momma started it, now it's a second skin. George is no fool. He's beginning to suspect that. Then there's Clay . . . '

'How does *he* like being here?'

'He doesn't.' She laughed, feeling miserable. 'Don't pay too much attention to me, Rony. I'm letting my hair down. I think this room does it . . . ' she looked around, 'old memories. Remember we used to quarrel about that doll's house? You put cars in the kitchen . . . '

'And you were always fussing around in the bedrooms, putting dolls to bed.'

'Yes, you're right . . . Clay's a city child. I didn't realise it before. He misses sidewalks and street markets, isn't that ridiculous, and being allowed to help Madame Lu-Yang sometimes with her laundry. And he even misses Mouchou, a dirty old cat that pee-ed on our stairs and I had to wipe it up, and most of all his *copains*. George says he bossed them around because he's bright, that his identity has been taken away from him. He does a frightening thing, Rony. When he comes back from school he right away climbs the stairs and goes into his room across the landing, and shuts the door. The first time he did it I went up and he was lying on the bed staring at the ceiling. He wasn't crying, or anything. When I asked him what was wrong he said, *'Je suis fatigué.'* Can you beat it? A boy of eight saying he's tired. He doesn't run about, he's taken to and from school. The only one who can get him to romp is George.'

'His spirit's tired. You get worn out trying to adapt. When I first went to New York I was always tired. Now I love it.'

'Yes, you're right. I was homesick in Paris. That's what it is, homesickness. My goodness, I seem to be complaining about everything but I feel so guilty. George didn't like his job in Paris but he could have got another one. He has to be working. He's lively. He gets so frustrated he wants to kick things. He chops wood for Momma and he offered to repair a fence in the paddock but there's Jason who comes every morning and he doesn't want no nigger burstin' in . . . '

'Don't talk like that. You're tired too.' Rony got up and stretched herself, walked over to the window and looked out. 'Such a beautiful place, Cedars. Poppa's choice with Momma's

185

money. He likes it for show and she likes it because it's her proper background. Do you remember *Grand'mère* and all her mannerisms and that ebony cane of hers?' She turned round and her hair was on fire from the light behind her. 'I hated her.'

'*Hated* her? Why?'

'Because she was reactionary, snobbish and mean-minded. She believed in the wrong things, the old, worn-out things. She brought Momma up believing in them. It isn't honest here. Everything's covered by a thin silk veneer except when Momma pierces it with one of her cruel barbs. If you stay here, Jan, she'll destroy you. She didn't want you back for *you*, it was only to show the Deeres and the Jeffersons and that lot that you *came* back. She'll come between George and you, she'll criticise endlessly with those little shafts of hers which hurt two seconds after they've been fired, and go on hurting. Some I remember to this day. Take my advice and get out of it.'

She didn't like what Rony was saying. Was it because it was near the bone? 'You're . . . hard.'

'I'm a clearer thinker than you. But look, you instinctively shook yourself free. You didn't know why you were doing it, but you did it. And being you, you had to go all the way, get pregnant by a black man. Oh, Miss Sirica of Cedars, Johnstown, Maryland, how could could you?' She was laughing, and Jan felt her face redden.

'Stop it, stop it, Rony! It's not fair, I was young. You've always tried to tease me. I'm not going to fight with you the minute you arrive.' When they were children they'd often fought, seriously at first, Jan often weeping, but ending in gales of laughter.

Clay came in. 'George has gone for a walk, *Maman*.' He looked shyly at Rony.

'Well, look who's here!' She came towards him. 'My favourite young man, Mr Clayton Cook from Paris, Europe, the World, What an honour! I'm mightily impressed.' She took him by the arms and swung him round. He kicked his feet, squealing with pleasure.

'Rony, Rony . . . you'll break something! Rony . . . '

'*Aunt* Rony,' Jan said.

'Just listen to your mother.' Rony stopped, breathless, put

him down. 'She wants everything to be conventional, at least she thinks she does.' She staggered back theatrically to the rocker, fell into it. 'And how do you like Cedars, Monsieur Cook, or may I call you Clay? Here, sit down on the floor and have a rest. You don't have to stand to attention like Napoleon.' She stuck one arm across her chest and Clay sat down beside her, giggling.

'She's very *drôle*, isn't she, Maman? I don't like it here. Neither does George. It's too big. I lose the way and I haven't any *copains*. They tease me at school.'

'Well, tease them back. Boast that you are Parisian, a real swank. Lord it over them. They don't know a thing, the *copains* in this part of Maryland, just the back end of a horse from the front.'

Clay nodded, looking up at her, fully approving. He was sitting with his thin legs crossed like a Yogi. 'I don't like riding either. I prefer the Métro.'

Jan and Rony laughed together. 'See what I mean,' Jan said, 'I haven't got a chance.'

'Well, get the hell out of it. If you'll pardon my French, monsieur.' She bowed deeply to Clay.

CHAPTER EIGHTEEN
January, 1977

ETTIE had one of her parties while Rony was home. There were originally twelve guests invited, but an unexpected heavy fall of snow caught the snow-cats on the hop and a few people called off.

Clay had stood mesmerised at the window almost all day. 'So much. Look, George. Here at least the snow is decidedly better.'

The girls helped Dorothy to set the table, and George was despatched upstairs at five o'clock to shower and dress in his best suit. He had been busy clearing snow around the stables.

'See if you can get some of the black off,' Rony shouted at him. He gave her his melon grin, turning round as he bounded up the wide staircase.

'That's not very nice,' Ettie said. She was seated at the table folding napkins into water-lily shapes.

'He likes it,' Rony said. 'He's black. He knows he's black. You can't shut your eyes to it.'

'And who is shutting their eyes to it?' Ettie pulled out a white peak with stubby fingers loaded with rings. 'Sometimes I don't like the way you talk, Rony, since you went off to New York. It's kind of brash.'

'New York *is* brash, you call a spade a spade there . . .' She stopped, put her hand to her mouth and laughed. 'Did you hear that Jan?'

'Change the subject, can't you?' she muttered, as she went round the table placing the heavy Georgian silver cutlery. The handles were intricately chased, the design wound round the letter 'L', *Grand'mère's*, of course. She'd never minded or thought of George's blackness until she came here. Now it

188

hardly ever seemed to be out of the conversation. Even this morning her father had said he hoped Wendell wasn't going to make any difference on account of . . . then stopped short, wiping his lips with his napkin and staring out of the window. 'Is Mr Wendell bringing his family, Momma?' she said.

'Yes. Harvey's at Yale now, he's nineteen, and Miranda's in her last year at High School. Lisa has trained them to be so beautifully mannered. It's a pleasure to have them at Cedars.'

'Who else is coming?' She'd seen Rony turn up her eyes.

'The Deeres, of course. Such a pity they haven't a family, but Joan was saying to me the other day that sometimes she feels it's just as well, so many things can go wrong . . .' The concealed barb. 'She does the most beautiful needlepoint. She's just finished one of the Battle of Antietam which they've hung above their fireplace.'

'So welcoming to southerners,' Rony muttered.

'Then, Leo Widgery, one of the gayest bachelors I know . . . there's no need to smirk, Rony. I'm aware of what the term can mean nowadays. Leo's perfectly normal, thank goodness.'

'Some of my best friends are gays,' Rony said.

'I daresay.' She stopped pleating. 'Both you girls have led lives away from Cedars which totally amaze me. Oh, I'm fully adjusted to it, but believe me, it isn't without a great deal of heartache. Look at Jan, disappearing in Paris. A lifetime. Unable to come back to her old home.'

'We hadn't the money.'

'I offered it to you, I sent Rony with it, but you wouldn't have it. You preferred to turn it down rather than come back to where you belonged.

'It was George who turned it down.'

'Ah, well, *George* . . .' there was a wealth of meaning in her voice. She carefully lifted the completed linen water-lily and placed it on one of the fine Rockingham plates, then looked around. 'I wonder where Carl's got to. I want him to set out the drinks. He *knows* he takes a long time over it.'

Jan got up. 'I'll go upstairs and see if Clay has settled down.' He had been deeply affronted at being banished before supper. 'It wouldn't be like this in Paris,' he'd said, making great reproachful eyes at her. 'George and I have our best talks at supper-time . . .'

*   *   *

George was sitting on Clay's bed. They were talking happily in French, and the sound of it made her fly into anger.

'I asked you to speak English with him, George, you're just encouraging him, and you haven't even dressed yet!' He was in a short bath-robe, and his slightly bowed black legs looked muscular, almost anthropoid. He wasn't abashed at her rage.

'Oh, come on, *Maman!*' he pulled her down beside them and started to tickle her. She squealed, Clay squealed, and the three of them rolled about the bed, kicking and panting like puppies at play. He never kept an argument going, she thought. She could feel his hand occasionally touch her breast. If he couldn't resolve a row he walked away from it or made love to her.

'Look at *Maman's* hair!' Clay shouted. 'It's all over her face.'

'And I'd done it so carefully for the party.' She pulled her self free from their clutching hands and sat up. Her flurry of bad temper had gone. 'Good thing I hadn't on my dress. It's all frills and things.'

'You look lovely like that, doesn't she look lovely, Clay?' George said.

'*Ravissante.*' Like a gigolo. 'You should stay up here with us. You'd have much better fun.'

'I'm not staying, neither is George. The guests will be here in ten minutes. Do you realise one of them might give George a job? You would't like him to miss that.'

'In Paris?'

'No, silly, we've left Paris. In a big city called Baltimore. You like cities, don't you?'

'No, not any city. But we aren't staying here, George says. It's just till he finds work. He's going to try New York. I think New York's a good city. It's got a fine Métro and Rony lives there.'

Jan turned to George. 'Have you been talking about this to Clay before discussing it with me?'

He smiled at her. 'He's my legal adviser. I never make a move without consulting Mr Clayton Cook, the well-known attorney-at-law.'

'The well-known attorney-at-law,' Clay said, jumping up and down on the bed, 'that's me, the well-known . . .'

'Stop it, Clay!' she shouted, and then seeing the sudden fear in his eyes she hugged him tightly. 'Be a good boy. You've had fun. Now it's our turn.'

'There didn't used to be "turns".' He lay down and pulled up the clothes. Only his fuzzy head was visible.

'Well, it's different now.' She bent over and kissed him, but he didn't move. His thin body hardly made a mark under the bedclothes. They screwed you up, children, she thought, following a silent George into their room.

When they went downstairs three of the guests had arrived, Joan and Randy Deere . . . Rony said his name was a joke since they were childless . . . and Leo Widgery. Her mother was talking to them and her father was making cocktails with an imposing battery of silver equipment.

'Bring on the fatted calf,' Leo Widgery said, which was a cue for everyone to laugh, except her mother who had her stiff nervous smile on.

'You may well say that,' she said, rising. 'Now I want you to welcome Jan's husband, George Cook.' George smiled hugely, turning his pink palms outwards as if on exhibit. There was a slight pause. Ettie went on 'He's been busy in Paris for the last few years, climbing the ladder of fame.' George laughed.

'Glad to know you.' He went round the group, pumping hands as if it were a good joke, extravert as always. Jan followed, kissing Leo and Joan but not Randy. Rony said he always had a free feel if Joan wasn't looking.

'What's your line of country, George?' Randy asked.

'I'm a lawyer.'

'Oh, I do envy you Paris,' Joan said. 'No wonder you didn't want to come back to stuffy old Johnstown. Tell me, George, what do they call attorneys in Paris?'

'*Notaires*, I guess.' He gave her his brilliant, impartial smile.

191

'I wouldn't like to tell you what they called me at times. I was only a dogsbody.'

'Still . . .' Randy said, 'I mean with the economic situation as it is. And in your case . . .' He was like an old woman, Jan thought, the way he pursed his lips and tilted his chin.

'Now, don't be so fuddy-duddy,' Leo said. 'If he didn't like his job he was quite right to quit it and come to the Land of Promise. Right, George?' He looked across the room. 'Carl's not listening to us. He's inventing a new cocktail called, "Long Time a'Comin".'

Joan screeched. 'Leo! You say the cutest things. Besides Carl's cocktails are so good when they arrive. Worth waiting for.'

'Yes, he's got one called that too.' Leo Widgery was a rounded balding man with a sweet mouth and a high domed forehead. Jan had always liked him. He had shown endless patience listening to her when as a child she would confide in him sad tales about her dolls, or later, her pony, and he always complimented her on her dressing, although she knew she had no style. 'That's a really becoming dress,' he said to her. 'Is it Parisian?'

'No.' She was embarrassed. 'As a matter of fact, Momma bought it for me.'

'She has absolutely no flair, Leo,' Ettie said, 'and living in the midst of *haute-couture* you'd imagine . . . but then Jan was always so woolly, living in a romantic dream.' Her eyes rested briefly on George, slid away.

'With a figure like Jan's who's worrying?' George said. Jan saw the slight look of distaste pass over her mother's face.

'And so say all of us.' Leo smiled back at George, a half-smile in comparison to his. 'Ah, here's the man of the house with the drinks. Lovely, Carl. And there's the door-bell ringing, Ettie. It's all happening.' He raised his glass to his lips. 'It's going to be one of your lovely, lovely parties . . .'

The Emersons and the Jeffersons had one thing in common, their private opinion of Carl and Ettie, and their envy of Cedars. The women gushed over the table, the food, (served by Dorothy in a white overall and wearing a lugubrious expression), the men on the view from the long windows of the dining-room.

George, whom they seized upon with glee, had been heaven-sent to redress the balance. They welcomed him effusively, plying him with questions about Paris, flattering him. Jan saw impatience in her mother's strained smile, heard embarrassment in Carl's laughter. He, in turn, kow-towed to Mr Wendell, his wife, Lisa, and the two grown-up children who were like stone effigies with a built-in Baltimore indifference to this hovel in Johnstown in which they were obliged to spend the evening.

'We could do with George to help us over this housing estate problem,' Clyde Emerson said, sipping wine from the fragile Venetian glass . . . 'still a full set after thirty years,' Ettie had said to Jan earlier, making her butter-fingered . . . 'a good lawyer's what's needed to frighten them off. Now, George, you must have had plenty of experience back there in Paris.'

'Not with housing estates,' George said. 'We only dealt with the best of property, l'Île St Louis . . .'

'L'Île St Louis!' Baby Emerson's soulful blue eyes had faded somewhat in the last few years. 'Oh, it's *darling* there! I remember thinking on the *bateaux*,' she giggled, 'pardon my French, that if we could get to live there I'd be truly happy.'

'It's plagued with rats,' George said.

'All the same,' Bruce Jefferson came into the conversation, 'I'm surprised you left Paris. Someone like you . . . well, I imagine you'd integrate better there than some places . . .'

'Jan wanted to come back home,' Ettie said. 'Try some of this sauce, Bruce. Dorothy puts clams in it and pounds them with cream and makes it absolutely delicious.' She gave a mock sigh, 'What am I going to do when I lose Dorothy?'

'You could move to the housing estate,' Linda Jefferson said. She was a big woman with a big nose and a flying chiffon scarf. Jan remembered the puckered scar of a thyroid operation when she'd come to bathe in the pool.

'Scarcely my milieu,' Ettie said. '*Grand'mère* would turn in her grave.'

'I had an English friend in Paris,' Jan said. She knew her mother was watching her. 'Her husband's firm are building what Tricia calls a Garden City.'

'Jan made some nice friends when she was studying in Paris,'

Ettie said, 'girl friends. What was the name of the French girl you told me about?'

'Crystel. I could never imagine why George didn't fall for her instead of me. She lives in the South-west of France.'

'I went there with a man from Yale,' young Harvey Wendell said, sitting straight and elegant in his elegant chair. 'Bannister Williams from Kentucky. Banny, we called him.'

'Oh, the Williams!' Ettie said, ecstatic, 'I think I met them at one of *Grand'mère's* balls. The Ellisville Williams?'

'Right. Banny's taking a law degree so that he can manage the estates.'

'Banny's so . . . so . . .!' His sister looked as if she was going to swoon over her clam pie.

'Miranda's stayed at their place,' Lisa Wendell said. 'Of course she's young yet . . .'

'He's so . . . so . . .!' Miranda looked round the table for help.

'Cute?' Rony said.

Her lips pressed together, her little nose went ceiling-wards in disgust. She sighed, shook her head and went into a trance again.

Her father, looking impatient, addressed himself to George. 'Had any luck yet?'

'What kind of luck?'

'With a job, with a job.'

'Well, Mr Wendell, I understood you were . . . er . . . passing the word along.'

Mr Wendell digested this with a piece of pie. 'Yes, yes. I mentioned it at the Club, of course, but you can't just come home from the other end of the world and jump into a job first time round. Besides, you'll have to sit State exams.'

George looked at Carl, who immediately began waving his hands, laughing in deprecation. 'Oh, he knows all the difficulties. Got a head on his shoulders, young George. But he was dead set on Baltimore and I said I'd put in a word for him with you . . . for goodness sakes, he never expected he'd just *jump* into a job, no sir!'

Bruce Jefferson waved his fork at George. 'Lawyers are a shifty lot as you should know, being one of them. Wriggle out of things like eels. If I were you I'd go right off to Baltimore and have a look-see for myself.'

'Now, now,' Ettie said, laughing her special social laugh, 'you're one of the best for handing out advice, Bruce, but it's scarcely in your line of country, is it? Grain stores and law practices are quite different, aren't they? The matter is in Carl's hands, and Craig's.'

Randy Deere pursed his little mouth, his eyes gleaming. 'I'm inclined to agree with Brucie here. There's too much nowadays of young fellows being helped into jobs. Oh, I know I'm on shaky ground not having a family of my own, but I use my eyes and ears.'

Jan looked at the boredom on Harvey Wendell's face. Miranda was still in a Kentucky dream. She caught Leo's eye. 'You've no children either, Leo. What do you think?'

'I don't think at parties, honey. Fatal, absolutely fatal, ruins the digestion. Rony tell me about New York. What's on at the Met?'

'I wouldn't know. It's far too highbrow for me. I get my kicks in the single bars in my own neighbourhood. You ought to visit with me, Leo. You'd love it.'

'I guess I'm too old . . .' Jan looked across at George. He had stopped eating. His black face had a purple tingle. She knew the signs. He had a quick, fierce temper which had to be given an outlet. She tried to catch his eye but he was studiously looking at nothing in particular. She watched his shoulders square and felt a sick sensation in her stomach.

'Mr Wendell,' he said cutting across the conversation he was having with Ettie, 'You don't think there's too good a chance for me in Baltimore, then?'

Craig Wendell looked at him. He frowned. 'I wouldn't put it as bluntly as that, Mr Cook. I just hope Carl hasn't been too optimistic. Those things take time, as you know. You have to sniff out the territory, find out who's leaving, it all takes time.'

'Like how long?'

'Who can say? Three months, six months, it depends on circumstances. Jobs don't grow on trees.'

'Fine. That's all I wanted to know.' He took up his knife and fork. 'In a way I'm relieved.'

'You don't mean *relieved*, George,' Ettie said, laughing the laugh again. 'He's been speaking French for such a long time . . .' she took in the people round the table with a sweeping glance, 'that he's lost his touch. You mean "disappointed", surely?'

'I mean relieved.' He speared a piece of pie and stuck it in his mouth, chewed vigorously, vulgarly, with a fair amount of teeth and gum showing. 'I never liked the idea of Baltimore anyhow.'

'Don't be hasty,' Carl said, hastily, 'come *on*, George . . .'

George ignored him. 'That's why I've put off studying for the State exams. It depends which State I find myself in, doesn't it? I've wasted too much time already, hanging around here . . .'

'George . . .' Carl's hand flew up.

'No, no,' Craig Wendell said. 'Don't put a brake on him. I quite agree with Mr Cook. He doesn't want to let the grass grow under his feet. Let me put it this way, Carl, if I wanted to get Harvey into the office in Baltimore I couldn't do it sooner . . . well, not *that* much sooner.'

'Now, Craig,' Baby rounded her eyes at him. 'That's a qualified statement. "Not *that* much sooner." There are wheels within wheels but not for Jan's husband. Isn't that what you're saying?'

'It is not what I'm saying, Baby. You're putting words into my mouth.'

'They were *your* words.'

'Leave it, Baby,' her husband muttered.

'I just said . . .'

'That's husbands all over.' Joan Deere joined her, looking suddenly outraged. 'Always correcting you at table, when you're having a drink with friends, always right, think they know best, making you look a fool . . . it makes you sick!'

'And telling you what to wear all the time.' Linda Jefferson threw her chiffon scarf over her shoulder, defiantly.

'Has anyone read any good books lately?' Leo Widgery said. His bald dome was shining.

CHAPTER NINETEEN

JAN wept when they got up to their bedroom that night, and
George took her in his arms, took her in his own body,
wrapped his legs round her.

'Don't upset yourself, honey. It's better to get it straight. I
never thought your father could do much for me. He's a loud
mouth . . .'

'You shouldn't speak of my father like that.'

'I'm not insulting him. Your mother is the one that does that,
so he has to shout all the louder.'

'Now it's Momma you're criticising.'

'Look, honey, I'm telling the truth. I went along with your
idea. You wanted to come here. I haven't got a home now
since my mother died, so we came to yours. I know what
homesickness is. I felt it in Paris too. I never intended to work
there if I hadn't met you. So we're home. We're in Cedars.
Tell the truth, is it how you pictured it in your dreams?'

'They were summer dreams,' she said sniffing.

'Well, what do you want me to do? Wait till summer till you
can ride and swim? But you're no longer the girl who lived
here; you've got a black lover and a black child. There's no
room for them in Cedars. If your mother could blot out Clay
and me, then you could start all over again.'

'You're cruel about my mother.'

'She's a cruel woman.'

'She's taken us in here.'

'Only on her conditions. Your sister realises this. She's got
enough sense to make her own life far away from here.'

'How come you're so wise about everything, mister?' she
joked, feeling better now.

'I don't see them through a romantic mist. Do you want to
bet on something?'

'What?

'In six months you'll be dreaming about Paris. You'll say to people, "When I was in Paris . . . " It won't be the scratchy existence you had in St Denis. It will be a wonderful writer's and painter's Paris, made up of what you've got from pictures and books and that time you had when you were with the two girls. You'll skip the bad bits. Everybody does it.'

'I'll never skip you or Clay. He's my life.'

'Don't get too hooked on him. You'll lose him too.'

She shivered and buried her face in his neck. 'Don't say that.'

'You always lose children sooner or later. Look at my mother. She lost me when I went to Paris, and she died when I was there.'

'You hardly ever spoke about her.'

'Because you were all the time speaking about Cedars.'

'That's cruel.'

'It's true. Anything that's true, Jan, you call cruel. Wait till you see what Ettie's going to be like tomorrow. Then you'll know what's cruel.'

'She was all right after the people went. Remember?'

'That's because she has to plan first. She has to think and then tell Carl how he has to handle it. Just wait . . . '

He was stronger than her. She half-believed him. Besides she was sleepy, and she wanted to be loved in a sleepy, semiconscious way, one of the best ways, when she slowly came out of her first sleep to find she was being loved.

*   *   *

When they went downstairs for breakfast the next morning, only Carl was in the dining-room. Dorothy had a sour face and was banging dishes about on the sideboard. 'The ham's ruined and the eggs is like rubber. Some folks have no sense of time.' She gave them both a baleful glance.

'I've told you we never eat breakfast, Dorothy,' Jan said. 'In Paris you only have coffee and a roll . . . '

'Oh Paris!' She sniffed loudly, gathered up some dishes and stalked out of the room.

'Sleep well?' Carl said. He was wearing a mauve silk shirt with a cravat of a paler mauve tucked in at the neck. The silver hair at his temples seemed to have a faint violet tinge as well. He looked very handsome.

'Yes, thanks, Poppa. Did you?' She poured out coffee for herself and George, sat down beside him. 'I guess Mr Wendell was quite right to say what he thought.'

Carl waved his hands. 'Craig! The super-pessimist! He thinks the Bomb's going to fall any minute. You don't want to pay too much attention to Craig. With my influence and his know-how of what gives in Baltimore George won't have long to wait. Eh, George?'

George nodded, hunched over his cup.

'Besides George is useful about the place. He can shovel snow all day now if he likes.' He laughed heartily but seemed to have some difficulty in looking directly at George.

'Carl,' George had no difficulty in looking directly at him. 'If I were working at my job I'd still shovel snow in the mornings and evenings and weekends, but I don't want to make it my life's work.'

'Only a joke, George.'

'Okay. You're very kind putting us up here, and I wouldn't have minded for a few weeks. But it's practically two months now and Mr Wendell says it could be six.'

'I told you he's the original Doom Watch.'

'Maybe so.' George leant back in his chair. 'Let's put it like this. I'm not too keen on Baltimore. I said so last night. I've never been keen on Baltimore but I have affinities with New York. I'm going to take myself up there and have a look around, register at the University and get myself a job. I'd greatly appreciate it if you could give Jan and Clay a roof over their heads while I'm doing that. It shouldn't take longer than a week.' He spread his hands. 'You understand, Carl?'

'Oh, sure, sure, George. I . . . we . . . like having you all around. It's quiet here, just Ettie and me. And the little chap's a real oddball. But you see . . . ' he looked uncomfortable, stopped speaking, took another piece of toast on to his plate but didn't touch it.

'What is it, Poppa?' Jan said.

He looked up at her, his jowls loose. His handsomeness had gone and she thought, this is what he'll look like all the time in another ten years, when he's sixty. 'You know Ettie, Jan. She likes everything clear-cut. We talked about it last night after we'd gone to bed. I don't think she would like you using Cedars as a base, so to speak. She said as much. Either you all stay here with a view to George getting a job in Baltimore, or you . . .'

' . . . clear out?' George said.

He nodded. 'You know your mother, Jan. No loose ends.'

'But why? Oh, I don't mean she can't do as she likes, she always has, but I don't see why . . . I don't see her reasoning.'

'It's easy,' George said. 'She's got to hold the whip.'

'You're coming on a bit strong.' Carl bridled. 'And you came on a bit strong last night, George, don't forget that. I haven't mentioned it but it upset Ettie. She loves the little lad, and it's just great for her to have you back home, Jan, seeing you in your old haunts, and everything . . .' Jan heard Rony's words in her ear. *'She'll destroy you. Don't let her.'* 'Sometimes I think you girls get your mother wrong. She's always thinking of your welfare. Even this morning she was thinking of you. She wants you and George to go and have a little chat with her in her boudoir, to discuss, er, things.'

'Sure,' George said. 'Well, honey, if you've finished breakfast, shall we go and see your mother?' The face he turned to her was like a mask. I'm tied to this man, she thought, this black man. It's *he* who holds the whip . . . for a second it was Ettie speaking inside her and then she was horrified at herself.

'Into the den of lions, eh, Poppa?' She smiled at her father, seeing him with new eyes too, a man who'd been destroyed.

*   *   *

Her mother was seated at the rosewood desk in the bay window. The boudoir was a prettier room in summer because then its cool green-based chintzes made it like a flowery arbour. But in the clear cold light of December it looked drab as if the brilliance of the snow outside had sucked its colour away.

'Good-morning. Come and sit down.' She put down the letter she had been reading. 'Where's my little Clay?'

'Playing upstairs,' Jan said, going and looking out of the window. There were tracks across the park, too small for a horse's hooves, and they hadn't any dogs. A fox? She sat down on the window seat. 'I think he's in Rony's room. She romps about with him. Come and sit here, George.'

'No, George, take that one opposite me. It's more comfortable. Yes, I expect she does. There's always been something undignified about Rony. Between you and me, Jan, she gets worse as she grows older. She'll never get married if she goes on the way she does, so . . . inelegant.'

'I don't think she wants to get married, Momma. Everybody isn't the same.' I'm not married. She couldn't possibly say that.

'Well, let's leave Rony out of it. She's a dear girl. I wanted to have a little chat about last night. Are you comfortable in that chair, George? It's really a woman's room this, and, no, please, I never allow smoking here.' George put the pack of cigarettes back in his pocket. She smiled at him. 'I'm beginning to understand you, George. You don't have much time for finesse, do you?'

'It depends what you mean.'

'You as a lawyer should know very well what I mean.'

'I keep my work and my temperament separate. One is a skill, the other is how I am.'

'You never cheat?'

'Oh, Momma,' Jan said, 'what *is* this? You're making it sound like a seminar. You think George offended Mr Wendell, that's what you're getting at, isn't it?' George would be amazed if she told him what had crossed her mind right at this minute . . . Mouchou, that sneaky cat who pee-ed on the stairs never when you were looking . . . its round blameless face with the button nose was like Momma's! She giggled, put her hand up to her mouth, said, 'Sorry.'

'I can see you're following in your husband's footsteps, Jan. No respect. Anyhow, I'm glad we know where we stand.

201

Now, George,' she smiled with great charm, 'you're going to settle down here, aren't you, and wait, like a good boy. The job in Baltimore when it comes will be a good one, and it might be much less time than you think. Craig always plays safe.'

George shook his head sadly. 'I'm afraid I'm not going to settle down and wait, Mrs Sirica. It isn't in a black man's nature. He's impulsive, his blood heats up, and he's gotta do what he's gotta do. I'll set off for New York first thing tomorrow morning.'

There was a pause. Her mother sat upright in her chair, her eyes lowered. She seemed to Jan to take a deep breath, then the smile was in place again. 'All right, George. Everyone must be true to their own background. However, no recriminations. I'm not in favour of you using Cedars as a base, but I'll stretch a point. Leave Jan and Clay here till the spring. Winter's the wrong time to be trailing a wife and child about. Then you can send for them . . . always provided you've got a job. Don't you think for their sakes that's sensible?'

George didn't reply. He put his head in his hands, not in an attitude of despair, but as if he was thinking hard. When he raised it his hair was standing up like wires. He'd combed his fingers through it, as he used to in Paris sometimes, to make her laugh. 'The nigger's coming to get you!' He looked at her. Was he going to say they weren't married? It was the wrong time for that.

'There's a sensible proposition, Jan.' He was straightfaced. 'You'd be in your family home, lapped in luxury until spring comes round. New York can be mean in winter.'

She couldn't tell whether he was joking or serious. She wasn't clever enough. Was he saying that *that* was what had brought her back from Paris, the luxury as compared with their life in St Denis? Everybody liked luxury, my goodness. Think of a cold-water apartment in New York in weather like this. And the snow was always grey there . . . there was a knock at the door.

'Come in,' Ettie said in her 'chatelaine' voice. That was Rony's word. 'I asked Dorothy to bring coffee in here . . . ' Clay put his head round the door and then tip-toed in.

'*Excusez-moi*,' he said.

'I beg your pardon!' George roared. 'I made you repeat that about twenty times only the other day. What have you up there instead of a head, a block of wood?'

Clay giggled. '*Excusez-moi* is much simpler, George. It is less words.'

'It doesn't matter about that. You're in the US of A, not frog country.'

Clay giggled again, then caught sight of his grandmother's face and stopped suddenly. 'I search for *Maman*. My blue trousers are missing and they are the warm ones.'

'Did you look under your bed?' Jan said. 'I've told you before. Always look under your bed if anything goes missing,' and hardly pausing, she turned to her mother. 'I can't stay here that long, Momma. It would be impossible.' She started to weep.

George got up and came and sat down beside her, took her in his arms. 'You go off and find your trousers, Clay,' he looked up, 'and remember, don't barge into your grandmother's boudoir again. See how you've upset your mother.'

'Right, George.' He teetered, looking at Jan, then slipped like an eel round the door.

'Come on, honey,' George helped her up. 'Thanks, Mrs Sirica.'

'Yes, thanks, Momma.' She tried to swallow the tears. 'For everything. We surely appreciate it.'

The face her mother raised was ugly, dark red, the rabbit teeth showed. 'Appreciate it? You've never appreciated anything I did for you in your whole life! Jason's got more appreciation in his little finger than you've ever had.' There was spittle in the corners of her mouth. 'All you can appreciate is rolling in bed with a black man, having a black child by him, rolling in your own filth . . . you disgust me! Get out of my sight!'

'Momma, Momma!' She wrung her hands in fright. 'Please don't say things like that. Please . . . '

'Come on, Jan.' George put his arm round her. 'She'll feel better now she's got that off her little ole system.' He stood looking at Ettie for a second, then led Jan, weeping, from the room.

They went that same day. Ettie didn't speak to them again, remaining closeted in her boudoir, and Carl, who had come home to find them packing, had little to say, as if the stuffing had run out of him, George said. Dorothy gave them a baleful look when they met her in the hall as they were leaving. 'Some folks have no consideration,' she said. She was carrying a tray set with tea-things. Jan was to think of that tray afterwards as epitomising Cedars, and chased silver showing through the lace cloth, the Rosenthal china cup and saucer with the graceful pot, the silver sugar and cream.

CHAPTER TWENTY

RONY put them up in her own apartment near Memorial in First Avenue, and never once said, 'I told you so.' They decided it was useless to send Clay to school until George got a job fixed up, and for the first week the three of them went out every afternoon until George had classes. He had enrolled right away. In the mornings, when he was free, he went to the Public Library nearby to scan the papers, then came back to write his applications. There were so many vacancies that he was optimistic.

They were all buoyed up by the fact that they'd made a definitive move and that Clay seemed so much happier. Jan kept quiet about her bad dreams. Sometimes in them she saw her mother like Mouchou, the cat, the small round face spitting at her, other times in her boudoir, the words tumbling from her mouth, shattering against the walls, 'Rolling in bed with a black man, rolling in your own filth . . .' George would hold her tightly when she awoke, tears streaming down her face.

'Never mind,' he'd say, 'Clay is happier, that's one thing. He's a city child, just like me. Detroit, Paris, New York. I like the smell of gasoline, hot bread, I like litter, I like the feeling of everybody pushing to get on.'

Clay loved the free exhibitions, the heady elevators which took him up, as he said, 'to the top of the world.' The Eiffel Tower had been his yardstick and now the Trade Centre left it well behind, '1350 feet, George! It's the greatest!' He was ecstatic when George took them to Coney Island to the Aquarium, and talked about the dolphins for days. Rony encouraged him. 'You're too bright for the country, fella. You're a city slicker. The country's only for red-necks.'

Their evening meals, so different from the stiff formality of

Cedars, were the highlight of the day. She and George shopped for them, prepared them in Rony's tiny kitchen, Clay set the table. They welcomed Rony when she came home like a messenger from Mars.

But as the weeks passed, and George hadn't found a job, the routine became broken. Rony had friends whom she liked to see. Sometimes she dined out, other times she had them to the apartment, men and women who seemed strange to Jan, used to the formal patterns of France. Sometimes her head ached with trying to follow the drift of the conversation as it darted from one person to the other. They were like birds skimming over the ocean, she thought, sometimes dipping down for tempting scraps, then soaring away again. She felt they were speaking a new, secret language.

George became quieter, and thinner, and started going to the Library in the afternoons to work. He said it was too cold for excursions now, and she suspected he didn't want to spend the money. But she was glad to stay indoors. It was the last gasp of winter, and it ate into their bones like icy maggots.

Their funds were running dangerously low, but they hid this from Rony, sometimes buying exotic food they could ill afford. Jan insisted George must keep himself well-dressed for the interviews which rarely came, and the week when they had to buy him a new shirt was calamitous.

Clay, missing the excitement of excursions, pleaded to be allowed to go to school, and she snapped at him because she knew he was right. 'Don't be silly when George is on the point of getting a job. You know how big New York is. What's the use of going to school in this neighbourhood, then losing your friends?'

'It's better than having no friends at all,' he said with French logic. She was touched.

'Let's ask George tonight, shall we?' Rony had said she wouldn't be in, and Jan was having what she called a 'picnic supper', which meant using up odd scraps from the refrigerator.

'Clay's wondering if he ought to start school,' she said later when they were eating their bagels and cheese.

'School?' He looked at Clay. 'You were ahead of your friends in Paris, and at Johnstown you said the kids didn't have

206

a look in. Surely you can wait?'

'It seems I have waited a long time, George, Momma's busy (he had dropped calling her *Maman* now), cleaning the apartment, and I'm hanging around waiting . . .'

George's quick temper flashed out. 'So what the hell's wrong with that? You're like your mother. Never satisfied. Next thing you'll be saying you'd rather be back at Cedars!'

'Don't speak to him like that,' Jan said, 'you forget he's only a child.'

'I don't forget anything. But don't make him like you, thinking the grass is always greener anywhere but where you are. He's living on sufferance in his aunt's apartment, his father has no job and his mother's getting fed up with the whole thing.'

'I never said that!' She was furious with him. 'You're right we're here on sufferance. It's quite natural for me to want a place of my own and for Rony to want it to herself.'

'We don't fit in anywhere at the moment. We're occupying other people's space.'

'Couldn't we go back to Paris?' Clay said. 'I'd have my *copains* . . .'

'Look, Clay,' George's voice was dangerously quiet. 'If you say that word once more I'll flay you alive, so help me. And if you start whining when I'm trying to make out as best as I can . . . get off to bed out of my sight!' The boy slid off his chair, weeping loudly, and went running out of the room. They heard the bedroom door bang.

'Now look what you've done with your black temper!' Jan said.

'So it's all coming out?' His smile was wide but not pleasant. 'You really agree with Miss Ettie all the time. My temper's black as well, is it? And probably my soul. I'm all black, knee-bone, thigh-bone . . .' he got up and stomped out, singing in rhythm, 'What a pity you didn't stay in White Man's country w'en you got the chance.' He spat the words out. 'Cedars! That monument to white supremacy, the porch with its four columns, yea, I've counted them, *four*, its park, its pool . . . well, if you want to go back, go back, crawl on your knees to her. You aren't married to me. My God, if she knew that she'd wet

207

herself. But at least you can leave me if you want to . . .'

She got up, weeping as loudly as Clay, and ran out of the room.

They all finished up in the same bed, weeping and snivelling, and from that they went on to laughing, and when Clay was asleep they made silent love.

*　　*　　*

It was May before George got a job in a seedy Private Crime Investigation office in Harlem. It was near where he worked for nothing in a Legal Aid Bureau as part of his course. Before he came home he rented an apartment round the corner from West 142nd street and they moved out of Rony's with their last few dollars.

'I'll kill you two if you don't tell me if you run short of money,' she said. She put an envelope into Jan's hand. 'That's a loan so don't throw it in my face. I'm going to charge a fancy interest then George can sue me.'

'You've been so good to us, Rony. We'll never forget it.' She was sick at herself for continually weeping.

*　　*　　*

Clay liked his new school. Almost all the boys and girls were black, but that wasn't the reason. He had craved mental stimulation, and he had a young teacher who saw his potential and whom he quickly came to adore. Mr Newton became an invisible guest at their table.

Jan didn't like the apartment. It was on the seventh floor, and looked out on other apartment blocks which seemed to menace her from every window. The owners used their balconies for drying clothes, growing pot plants, keeping caged birds, squabbling in, laughing in, sitting in, listening to transistors in.

Her mother's words began to dim in her memory, she began

to make excuses for her. She had been upset at losing them. And when you thought of it, George was no one to talk. He'd always been good at shooting off his mouth. She felt starved of fresh air. She was different from George and Clay, she thought. She needed space and lightness to survive, like a plant. At least in St Denis the buildings had been lower. There had been a little park close by. 'In six months you'll be saying, "When I was in Paris . . ." ' She remembered the bet George had wanted her to make.

She'd had a letter from her mother in reply to the one she'd sent (she hadn't told George), saying she was glad they were fixed up at last. Perhaps Rony would bring them to visit if they hadn't a car. Carl hadn't been well all winter, some kidney trouble, and he'd lost a lot of weight. It was tantamount to an apology. She decided she'd go and see him as soon as she could.

George didn't like his job. That's two he hasn't liked, she thought, the one in Paris and now this. He worked long hours, and as he had to ride the subway a lot to see his clients, he came home silent and grey. He listened to Clay's stories about school without his usual lively interest. His vitality seemed to have been sucked dry.

As the weather grew hotter, they took to sitting out on their small balcony at nights. The thought of walking in the baking streets was too much for them. Clay would bring out his school books and lie on a rug beside them as if he felt a need to complete the family picture. She saw him look anxiously at George from time to time.

On a June evening, when the first fierce heat had got its grip on the city, she said to him. 'I'm thinking of going to see Poppa. He's ill.'

He looked at her in amazement. 'Would you go back there?'

'I told you Poppa's ill. And I've had a letter from Momma. An apology. Everybody loses their temper sometimes. You do.'

'I never insult you, humiliate you . . . Hey,' he pretended to be simple, 'maybe you think she was telling the truth?'

'I've forgotten what she said now.' She lied. 'Would you come with me to see Poppa?'

He looked at her as if there was something strange about

209

her. She shifted uneasily. 'I can't get time off, honey. And there's studying . . . God knows how I'm going to fit it all in.' He rose from the kitchen chair, walked to the edge of the balcony and put his hands on the rails, his back to her. She saw the thin shape of him. He had become angular in the last six months, his backside was flat, he had no hips.

'I know. Maybe I'll take Clay off school.'

'No!' Clay looked up. 'Mr Newton doesn't like boys to stay away unless they're sick. We're colouring in the Amazonian Forest.'

'Well, I guess I'll have to go myself,' she said. 'I can't compete with the Amazonian Forest.'

George turned round, leaning his back against the rails. 'Can't you call him instead? We've got the rent this month. And there's going to be a wedding shower for one of the typists. Ruth says I'm expected to give five dollars.'

'Ruth says you're expected to give five dollars? My, my!' She knew there was a sneering note in her voice. 'I can't get to see my Poppa who's ill, but Ruth says you're expected to give five dollars!'

'Next month, honey, huh?' He wasn't going to be drawn. 'This is a tough one.'

'He might be dead next month.' She wasn't all that worried about her father. Her mother had always used illness as a lever. She was worried because she was prisoner on a small balcony in Harlem. If he'd been more patient, a job was bound to have cropped up in Baltimore. Part of her said, 'You're twisting the facts,' but she didn't want to listen. 'All right,' she said, 'I'll wait till next month, but remember, if he dies before that it'll be your fault . . .' She heard a slight noise and turned round. Clay had gone. His books were lying sprawled on the rug.

CHAPTER TWENTY-ONE
July 26th, 1977

'Do you believe in coincidences?' Tricia said to Jake. They had come out to Kinglsey Heath to talk about the layout of a Play Centre. She'd been glad to go with him. Even in the office she'd been aware of the summer day outside, its warmth, the feeling that they had now passed the crown of the year, that there wouldn't be many more like this.

'Who doesn't?' The sun was shining into his eyes as he turned to her, searching out their blueness. The depth of the colour always came as a surprise to her. 'I met you by coincidence at Kingsley House long ago, remember?' His eyes were friendly, she thought, nothing more.

'I remember.' 'You look fulfilled,' he'd said. Mark had been on her knee. Was that the first time she'd noticed his eyes, or the variability of his face, sometimes broadly smiling, sometimes grimly dark.

'You were with Emma and Mark showing them one of the exhibits.'

'Who killed Cock Robin . . .' She felt a shiver go through her. 'I think you fired my interest in Kingsley Heath that day when we had tea together.'

'Did I? Was that the coincidence you were thinking of?'

She nodded. 'And another one. It's three years today since Howard died. I was reading a rhyme to the children when my father came looking for me. Sometimes it haunts me.' She laughed at herself.

'You had a worrying time.'

'Don't let's talk about it.' She meant to change the subject, found herself saying, 'I took the children to Kingsley House because I remembered taking my brother who died.'

'You're looking for some kind of pattern?'

'Is there one?'

'Always.' He smiled. 'You working for the Trust, for instance. With me.' Their eyes met and she looked away from him, embarrassed. Roger was part of the pattern.

'I like it.' She looked around. 'All this, being in on it . . .' They were standing in Crow Drive on the brow of the hill. It had been her idea to name the drives and avenues after birds. 'That there mock-up,' the old man had said . . .

The land ran away from them in a gentle slope and half-way down she could see the sham-Gothic towers and pediments of Kingsley House against the skyline. From there it flattened out and there was the glimmer of the lake through the trees before it began climbing towards the heights again.

'Away up there,' she said, pointing, 'beyond the Estate, that's magic country. The old Latham road runs along that ridge. You can imagine packmen and travellers walking it, long ago. Roger loved it.'

'How is he?'

'I think he's well. Except that he doesn't want to work.' She'd had a long talk recently with Peter Jobley about it. He'd said to accept it. 'Sometimes I feel he's been born out of his time.' She tried to speak lightly. 'He even finds tape recorders difficult.'

'Everybody's different. I'm no psychologist but I think you'll have to be patient.'

'I've been told that.'

'Some men aren't suited to the cut and thrust of business.'

'Maybe there's too much cut and thrust.' She didn't think so. She loved the excitement of it, longed to go abroad like Jake. 'Roger should have been a country gentleman. He's always found the Trust too much for him. Now it's worse than that. He finds it meaningless. Maybe he's right.'

'Could be.'

'At first he coped, but Howard was hard on him, as you know. Now it's grown too big for him. He's afraid of it. In a way, he's quite happy with the way we live, that I go out to work, that he dabbles in this and that. He's happy with his mother. He's always got a rested look when he's been to see her.' I sometimes feel they're glad Howard's gone . . . 'I try to tell him that it doesn't matter if he doesn't fit into his father's pattern, or Latham's, for that matter, but I haven't convinced him . . .' And you haven't convinced yourself, she thought. You want it both ways, a dominant man and freedom to be independent . . .

'Is he interested in the new house?'

'I think so. He puts up a pretence anyhow.'

'He never discusses it with me although I've often asked him round to the site.'

'You know why, don't you? You're like chalk and cheese. You can't communicate.'

'I got off on the wrong foot with him from the start. I have a habit of doing that.' She wondered why his eyes darkened. Then the swift shake of the head which she had come to know. 'The house will be ready to move into before Christmas. Are you excited?'

She smiled, ready to leave the subject of Roger. 'Yes, I'm excited. It's absolutely the first thing I've seen through from start to finish.'

'How about Mark and Emma?' He grinned at her.

'I could do that without study. But the house . . . I had to work at it, pore over plans, learn to draw, learn about elevations and drainage and siting and materials, read, read, read . . . can you imagine I hadn't even heard of Corbusier, and then I find he thinks like me!'

'Such conceit!'

'Yes, isn't it? Oh, I've enjoyed it like nothing else. The only thing that's left now is to find a name.'

'Mon Rêve?'

'Don't tease. But it is in a way. Clifford Avenue showed me everything a house shouldn't be. Howard was right about that. I made up my mind the next one would be light and airy with lots of sun and wide views . . .'

'Wide View?'

'No.' She shook her head.

'You said, no clumps of trees.'

'Because I've had experience of them cutting out my light.'

'I've ordered a willow from Carrington's for you. It's quite well-grown and from a good stable or wherever well-grown willows come from. They're planting it tomorrow.'

She was touched. 'That's kind of you, Jake. I must arrange to be there. I don't want them to place it dead centre. I know the exact spot where it won't obstruct the view of the lake. I may have to go out in a boat when they're planting it.'

'Or swim out.' He laughed. 'You're a perfectionist. Shall we get moving now? I haven't too much time. I want you to give me your impression first-hand of this site.'

'Lead the way. It'll have to have a name too.' They left Crow Drive and walked on to a wider road. On their left a row of houses curved away from them. Tricia looked at the name on the low wall to confirm her memory. 'Yes, Lark Crescent. I like the curve there.'

'Rests the eye, doesn't it? It's one half of a semi-circle. Kingsley Road bisects it. I should have brought the plan with me.'

'No need. I can remember it. Thrush Crescent is the other half, and Kingsley Road leads straight through to Kingsley House.'

'Yes, that's the bus route. They're running a half-hour service. At first they offered an hourly one but I turned that down. I want to cut out cars as much as possible. I'm encouraging tenders from mini-bus firms as well, once the Estate's fully built-up.'

'Another five years?'

'Around that.'

'What will you do then?' She laughed. 'What will *I* do then?'

'We're too valuable to be lost. Rab Wilkes is busy buying property all over the country. There will be new projects, new ideas. I've even sown seeds abroad.'

'You wouldn't have me leave my lovely house?'

'Don't get hooked on houses. I've never done it.'

'But then you aren't married.'

'No . . . look, that's nice, isn't it?' He pointed to a terrace built in echelon so that no window was overlooked by another. 'You'd be surprised how many people are afraid of being "detached", as they say. You can tell people by the houses

214

they inhabit. Lots of people like to have neighbours. They're afraid of their own company.'

'Are you trying to tell me you're a loner?'

'I used to think I was. I'm not so sure now.' His smile was warm, almost intimate, and she thought, ours is a kind of business marriage, devoid of sex. And yet there's a communication because we think alike and there's the intellectual respect . . .

Was he really a loner? He was heterosexual, she would bet on that. The only woman he'd ever mentioned was Crystel . . . goodness, that was ages ago! She'd shown him a picture of herself Crystel had sent, lying in a deckchair on the patio of her flat, the sun shining on her gorgeous hair, deepening her eyes. 'Guy must have taken it,' she'd said. 'Her lover.' And he'd handed it back, face expressionless. 'Yes, I met him.'

Now they were walking across an unused piece of land. The path was narrow, and they had to go in single file. The long grass swished against Tricia's trousers, and she wished her legs were bare. I'm happy, she thought. With this man I'm happy. No sex, she thought again. But I'm married to Roger. He makes love to me, not as often as before his illness, but we're man and wife. Catholics don't often divorce.

The ground was dry, and the fine dust which their footsteps raised was gold-moted, stirring that childhood memory again, poignant, all the summer meadows she'd ever known . . . there isn't a marriage now, she thought, we cohabit. Its back is broken, it's propped up by convention, by the children's needs, by my pity, by occasional sex. I'd like to tell Jake just once about the agony we went through that night Howard died. I'd like to have his reaction . . .

'This is it,' Jake said.

'Thank goodness we aren't building here.' She looked around, blinking, 'this view . . .' she drew in her breath, felt the tears recede, 'views should be preserved. You could have seats in that corner there . . .'

He'd taken off his jacket, put it over his arm. He looked muscular, there would be hair on his body. 'You've talked me into it. I thought one open space round Kingsley House was enough.'

'Too far for mothers to walk with toddlers, or old people, or

215

disabled people. They need a park on their doorstep.'

'My Octavia Hill.' Again the warm smile. 'But they've gardens!'

'Gardens are not always lovesome. They can be lonely.' She looked around, 'Where would we put the Play Centre?'

'No rusty old cars. I draw the line at that.'

'You've no pop art in your soul. All right, something sculptured with lots of holes in it.'

'To see the view through?'

'To climb up. And benches arranged in groups with wooden tables . . .'

'What about dogs?'

'We'll have a Dog Section.'

He held his forehead in mock despair. 'Where's all the money coming from?'

'You know the Trust is rolling in it. Look,' she took his hand and led him, half-protesting, laughing, across the grass.

'You're abducting me!'

'What a hope! There's your ideal spot for the Play Centre.' She stopped beside a clump of trees. 'Sheltered from the wind. There could be the usual stuff, climbing frames, wheels . . .' she realised she was still holding his hand, released it quickly. 'Sorry.'

'Don't be sorry.' She looked at him. His eyes were dark. His face had the thinness of repose. And was there sadness? 'I liked that, Tricia . . .' she smiled uncertainly at him. 'I thought for a minute I was one of your toddlers.'

'Oh, you!' She looked away. 'There must be broad paths for the older ones for cycling or skating, but don't make them without lazy policemen . . . and a fair amount of this long grass should be left wild, just have it scythed occasionally. It has a country feel. I was happy for a minute walking through it, far from everything . . .' she met his eyes again. 'This heat's addling my brain. But you understand, don't you? I'd like people to get that feeling too.'

'Take on the designing of the whole area, then. There's approximately twenty acres. Let me have a plan, have it costed.'

'Is that why you brought me here? Yes, I'd like that. We'll

call it . . .' the name dropped into place. 'Robin View.' 'Who killed Cock Robin . . .?' Dark thoughts of Howard's death were with her, her elation disappeared.

They went back to where he'd parked his car and drove slowly through the drives and avenues. It was like looking at your own child. The gardens of Kingsley House were bright with dahlias, people and children were sitting outside at white-painted tables. An Ideal Place, like a dream. You might organise the exterior, but never what went on underneath.

'Scene of my entry into public life,' she said.

'You looked elegant.'

She remembered the black and white dress, the success and elation, and then her father's face as he drew nearer, white with shock. 'Something terrible has happened, Tricia . . .' Something terrible had happened. Her marriage had died. Nothing would ever mend it again. 'Try to understand, be gentle,' Peter Jobley had said. But love would be better. Tempestuous, demanding love . . .

'We put the gardens in order for them first,' Jake said. In front of them the lake gleamed, and on the far side there were one or two houses already built, their new gardens running greenly down to the water. One had a red-painted rowing-boat tied up at a wooden jetty.

'I like to keep the foreshore looking attractive. It would never do to spoil the view.' She felt him looking at her.

'It's lovely,' she said, her eyes on the water. A duck rose, and dropping its wings, projectiled to the far bank. She couldn't see properly. An Ideal Place. A house, not a home . . . She took out her handkerchief. 'Fly in my eye . . . that's better. That's Rab Wilkes', isn't it?' She pointed to a long, low, white-washed cottage which looked as if it had grown there.

'Clever, isn't it? Good repro. And they've done wonders with the garden. They've had the benefit of a good summer.'

'Madge is a cottage type.'

'That's what I said, wasn't it? You can tell people by their houses. They're quite well on with yours.'

She looked, saw the outside stone chimney which she had always wanted, and how the smooth lawn curved down to the lake. 'I can see exactly where I want the willow to go,' she said. She turned to him in the car. 'Why not come along tomorrow and see it go in?'

His face was expressionless. 'I think that's Roger's job.'

She turned back and stared straight ahead. The lake had a cold metallic gleam. The stark outlines, the angles, the modernity of the house looked ugly. Like her? Anyhow, it would never be a home.

CHAPTER TWENTY-TWO

IN September Roger's drugs were stopped again, and this time the experiment, except for a shaky start when he had one or two bad nightmares, was successful. The psychiatrist said he should go back to work. Peter Jobley, over-worked as he was, took time off to drop in and have a chat with Tricia, having first made sure Roger wouldn't be there. He'd gone to the new house to supervise the landscaping of the garden.

'I think we're home and dry, Tricia,' he said, accepting a sherry. 'It's been a long haul for you as well as for him.'

'I've had my work, and the children. I'll be forever grateful to you for helping us . . . that terrible night . . . I think of it as Roger's Gethsemane. And the inquest. I don't know how to thank you for everything.'

'There's no need. I did what any doctor would have done. Try and look forward, not back.'

'Do you think Roger will manage to do that?'

'The psychiatrist thinks so. He told me it was time to draw back the curtains, to let in life.'

'Did he say that? It's true. I feel I've been in darkness . . . nothing to the darkness Roger's been in.'

'Watching someone suffer can be just as bad. I know. But you're a positive person, Tricia. You'll be behind him.'

'I'm a bit worried that the psychiatrist thinks Roger should go back to the Trust. It all started there, in a way.'

'It started in Roger's head. Unless there are any more Howards there?' He looked at her.

'No. Everybody's well-disposed towards him. It will be only in his imagination if he feels threatened.' She thought of Jake when his face wasn't broadly smiling, when he had a dark, grim intentness on the job in hand, an offhand way of dealing with people because of his concentration. She'd have to ask him to be careful . . . 'I wonder how he'll take to us both going out to work. Will he be diminished in any way? He's been brought up in the old school. He's had the excuse he was ill.'

'If he's sensible, and fully cured, he shouldn't feel anything wrong. It's not an unusual situation for a married couple to work in their own business, virtually. And he's a director too, isn't he?'

'Yes.' She had insisted on that.

'It's coming on, that place. You tycoons . . .' He knew more about it than he pretended. 'I'm thinking of setting up a surgery there, say two or three mornings a week.'

'We'd like that. Howard always viewed it as being more than a Garden City. Would you like me to put it up at the next meeting? There are some nice houses . . .'

'No, no!' He laughed. 'I'm not in the smart set. Besides, I like old Latham. But I'm thinking of taking on a new assistant. He might be in the market.' He shook his head, smiling, 'you never miss a chance to do business, you people.'

'It's not my department. It's Jake Russell's. You know him, don't you?'

'Yes.' He could be reticent when you wished him to talk, or was it that she wanted to talk about Jake, since he was in the forefront of her mind?

She gave up waiting. 'I'm in planning and design. They tell me a woman's point of view is invaluable.'

'Yours should certainly be.'

'Thanks. I'm happy in my work. Peter . . . I'm going to ask you a straight question. Do you think Roger will ever be completely back to what he was?'

'What he was?' His eyes were baggier than ever this morning. He must have had a bad night with Leila. 'That's a different matter. I think you've probably got an erroneous impression of him. Remember, you met him when he was twenty-three and five years older than you, isn't that right?' She nodded. 'He held all the cards then. He was the son of the local tycoon, he hadn't been tried out in the fire, and he was pressing his suit. From personal experience that's when a man's most aggressive.

He's got to be if he wants to get the girl. But he isn't like his father.'

'I know that.'

'He'll never be. He's his mother's son. Anyhow, you wouldn't like another Howard Newton, would you?'

'No . . .'

'You've got the drive, Tricia. He knows that. But you can complement each other, make a good marriage.'

'Is he likely to get another depression?'

'We're all allowed one,' he smiled, 'except hard-working doctors. Besides, there were peculiar circumstances . . .' his eyes dropped away from hers for a second. 'But you know Roger better than anyone else. He can't take a lot of pressure. You can protect him there without him knowing. That's your role. We're all stuck with our roles. Look at mine.'

'Yes.' It was hard on him that it was he who had the bags under his eyes and she went around looking like a smooth-skinned angel . . . when she appeared. 'It must be hard, constantly listening to other people's gripes.'

'It takes my mind off my own. Besides, we've all got to grow up sometime.'

She smiled at him. 'I can remember myself at eighteen . . .' she felt the aura of Paris, dimmer now, the regret. Had any of them achieved that freedom of soul Jean Paul had talked about? Did it exist? She met Peter Jobley's eyes. Could you give me a prescription, Peter? It wouldn't be found in the Latham Development Trust. She was clear-sighted for a second. 'I'm a different girl,' she said, 'from the one Roger married.'

'That's a long time ago. There would have been something to worry about if you'd stayed the same.' He got up, was at the door before she knew it. It was a special trick of his. He could be away while you were blinking. He put his head round the door before he shut it. 'It's over to you, now.'

* * *

During Roger's first week back, in the middle of September, he attended a board meeting. Richard Forsyth gave a little speech

221

of welcome, saying Roger had timed it well since business was booming. Bob Pritchard seconded that and said Roger was welcome to have a look at the books any time.

They all sobered when Jake, who was chairing the meeting, announced the death of Malcolm Deakin at the ripe old age of ninety. The last link with Jolyon Roger, Tricia thought. She remembered the first sight of old Malcolm wheezing in his chair at The Crescent, four months after her marriage. 'Small profits and quick returns, eh, Malcolm?' She could hear Howard's lively voice. At least he'd paid homage to the man who'd financed the Trust at the beginning.

'We all owe a great debt to Malcolm Deakin,' Jake was saying. 'He gave financial wings to Jolyon Roger's ideas. Without his help there would be no Latham Property Trust as we know it.'

Roger knew Francis Crane, the firm's architect for Kingsley Heath, but he hadn't met the two men who'd been appointed recently, Jack Crowther and Martin Brigsteer. Jake introduced them.

'Glad to know you,' Roger said, shaking hands. Tricia was relieved she'd told him of the appointments. He was touchy. But Jake had it in hand.

'I know you'll be thinking, Roger, that the staff has grown, but the fact is we'll get a greater variety of styles if we have a greater variety of architects. You can see we're quite a nice mixture now, Francis is grey at the temples . . . very distinguished, Jack's black-haired, and Martin . . . is that a toupé you're wearing, Martin?' He had the right light touch. 'There have been one or two developments you should know about. The Trust has now taken away the running of Kingsley Heath from the surveyor who liaised between us and the Town Council. They've agreed that we're capable of managing our own affairs now . . . anyhow I'm sure Tricia has kept you in touch with our progress. The overall plan's in the main hall, so have a look at it. We've been careful to leave open spaces . . . at your wife's insistence, I may say . . . and we're going to donate a piece of land to the first church which asks for it.'

'That'll get you into deep water, Jake,' Bob Pritchard said.

'How about an Ecumenical Centre, built like my new kitchen?'

Tricia smiled round the table, 'Spin it around for the religion you want.'

'I must say that's the first time I've heard a Roman speak like that.' Richard was Catholic too. He looked faintly shocked.

'You've got to be broad-minded nowadays.' And quickly, in case she'd made a gaffe, 'while I have the floor, I had a chat with Dr Jobley the other day. He might be opening a surgery in Kingsley Heath.'

'That's fine,' Jake said. 'It'll go with the other applications. We have one in from the Bank . . . our own, of course.' That got another laugh. 'Now to the more serious business. You've had the balance sheets, Roger, so you know that the industrial estate we've developed alongside Kingsley Heath is our most profitable commercial property holding. We've to thank you, Rab, for getting the firms settled in, although Roger did the spade work. What you may not have noticed is that the rental income from the industrial side now produces more than what the Estate originally cost Howard back in 1942. I'm sure if he's listening that would gladden his heart.'

'Anything to do with profits gladdened his heart,' Roger said. 'It was when I became a liability that he had no time for me.'

No one spoke. Tricia looked at Jake. His face was impassive, the others round the table were restless, tapping their pencils, riffling the papers in front of them. Richard Forsyth, perhaps the oldest there, spoke for them.

'We don't look back, Roger. We're going to put you to work because we need you.' He looked at Jake, nodded. Jake went on.

'The selling side of the Kingsley Heath houses and the general buying and selling for the Trust can no longer be done by one person. Rab has been on sorties often, but he prefers to localise his activities now, getting long in the tooth, I think . . .' he smiled across at Rab. 'Since I'm the only unmarried member of the board . . . don't all look so envious . . . and therefore more peripatetic, I'm proposing to concentrate on the general side of the business. As you know there are our overseas interests which I built up with the full connivance of Howard. We have to keep our folio lively. Our branch offices need advice and support from time to time. You've already agreed that I should take on this roving commission, and we'd be glad, Roger, if you'd take charge of the selling programme of Kingsley Heath. You're suited for it. It's a post for a family man. You're going to be resident in the Estate soon. Rab would be at hand to give you advice if you wanted it. What do you say?'

Tricia sat very straight. I'll miss him. The seed of what she knew would be a constant ache seemed to implant itself in her breast. She tried to ignore it, to concentrate on Roger. Would he prevaricate? When you've lived with a man who can't make up his mind, she thought, you suffer more than he does.

He got up to his feet, looked around the table. 'I'm meeting with kindness on all sides . . .' His voice broke. There were sympathetic murmurs. 'I'd be happy to take on the job if you all think I'd be good enough.' He sat down.

'You'll be good enough,' Jake said. 'Those houses are selling like hot cakes. All you need is a croupier's rake.'

While the motion was being carried, Roger looked at Tricia. She saw the eyes, so like his mother's, searching for her approval, and she nodded. The ache in her heart was still there, it had grown, had settled as if it belonged. It had nothing to do with Roger. He'd do the job all right. All he needed was a croupier's rake, she thought, remembering Jake's remark. How often she'd been stung too.

She recognised now, not with a flash of intuition, but as a result of a natural growth, that during the three years she'd been working for the Trust, something more than mutual esteem had grown between her and Jake, a compatability, an empathy. It wasn't simply that they thought the same. That would have been too easy.

She'd grown to like the look of him, had been more than ordinarily rewarded when she could win one of his smiles, see his eyes deepen into their intense blue when the light, or was it some inner light, illuminated them. She'd applauded at the same time as she'd been mortified by his harsh criticisms, because they were fair. She knew his hands intimately, so often they had pored over drawings and plans together, the strong-boned, big-knuckled hands that were so sure, that never fumbled, that matched his mind. I've been given Roger back and he's been

224

taken away. The ache was in her throat now, making it difficult to swallow. She heard his deep voice as he wound up the meeting.

'The policy which our founder, Jolyon Roger Newton, set up is carried on, small profits and quick returns. We don't have to put advertisements in the papers to catch business. People come chasing us. And they wonder how long we can retain our other policy, that of renting property. We didn't give this up during the property boom after the War when many long-established companies were being taken over. We've kept our image, to use the popular word. Stock market analysts have wondered how long we can go on picking up the remnants of the private rented sector. Well, we've done our sums too.' He looked up. 'We believe it's possible to keep the Latham Property Trust buying and selling and renting property for the next two and a half centuries at least. Anyone think they're going to live longer than that?' There were guffaws round the table. 'Our success is built on a solid foundation, an unbroken record of good tenant-company relations. We're following this policy in Kingsley Heath. It will be, I hope, a matrix for the virtues which LPT stands for.' He sat down to enthusiastic clapping.

CHAPTER TWENTY-THREE
1977/1978

'I had a letter from Jan Sirica this morning,' Tricia said. It was a gloomy November day and they were driving to the Trust offices at Latham Cross in Roger's car. She was careful about small things like that. She knew they mattered to him. It was a new Saab, and he was inordinately proud of it. 'It's got power,' he'd said when he chose it. He meant it gave him power.

'Had you?' He emulated now what had been his father's style of driving, casual, leaning-back. She wasn't as happy about his driving capabilities. 'Has she got married yet?'

'She doesn't say. She went back to Maryland, you know, but it didn't work. Her mother's unbearably bossy, and then she never approved of George.'

'She wouldn't like the black child any more than the black lover.'

'That's a silly remark. America's used to it. We get more and more immigrants here too. Mother was telling me about a new Racial Integration Society she's set up in Latham.'

'Trust your mother.'

'Well, she gets things done, and she isn't paid for her work which is more than I can say.' They were going down the long hill towards the main street and she looked at the speedometer, closed her eyes.

'I don't think it would make any difference to you. It's the work you like, the feeling of power.'

'Like you with that Saab.' The Hapsburg tower of the Town Hall was pushing up behind the houses and shops lining the main street.

'You win,' he said, slowing down. He looked well this

226

morning, she thought, taking a brief glance. The job was suiting him. He'd put on a little weight and he was sleeping well.

'Jan's in New York now but she's had a terrible summer. She says it's been so hot and the job George has found is pretty poor. He works for some kind of Crime Investigation Bureau.'

'A Private Eye?'

'I suppose so. We're lucky in comparison. Both in good jobs with no money worries. Yes, we're lucky.' She thought of Jan in her seventh floor apartment in the humid heat of a New York summer.

'I get awfully tired, and I always seem to be nagging at Clay. The kids he plays with are so rough and I try to keep him in. Once, I guess he was bored, I found him playing with my keyring, our keyring. He'd taken it out of my purse. I snatched it from him and threw it over the balcony, can you imagine? But it was our symbol. He wept and wept, holding on to my legs. I felt terrible. "That was to teach you not to be a magpie," I said.

'When George came home he took him down to the street and would you believe it, they found it lying in the gutter. "Is it all right now, Momma?" he kept on saying. What good is it to me anyhow. I thought. I used to have such high hopes, oh, nothing to do with a car, just, everything. "You shouldn't have done that to him," George said. "You've given him your problem."

'He gets so fagged out with travelling in buses and on the subway. We sit on the balcony at night to get some air and I remember the wide-open countryside round Cedars, and forget how I couldn't stand my mother when I was there. And then George and I go to bed and make it up . . . thank God that bit is as good as ever.'

It wasn't with her. Roger, as if he had to discipline himself in his sex life as well as his work, had become a twice-a-week man, Wednesday night and Sunday morning. There was a lack of spontaneity about the performance from the first touch of his hand on her left nipple (like starting the Saab, she thought), until the last flurry of his orgasm.

Often she lay and thought of Jake. He had become an obsession with her. She told herself she was like a child who'd missed its opportunity to buy sweets when the shop was open. Now that she saw him rarely she realised she'd been in love with him all the time Roger was ill. She couldn't understand herself. How had she *not* known it when she couldn't get him out of her mind?

There had been countless times when they'd been alone together, and neither of them had put a foot wrong. She faced the fact that he might be indifferent to her as a woman, rationalised by telling herself he'd had a sense of loyalty towards Roger. And tried to convince herself that her present feeling might be no more than regret at the loss of a valued friendship.

'Do you think Jake's missed in the office?' she asked Roger, so that she could use his name.

She could see him trying to be fair, the furrowed brow, the casual steering. At last. 'He's like father. The same presence and charm . . . but no, I don't think so. Generally speaking he's doing good work for the Trust, but, actually, in the office . . . well, no-one's indispensable, as I found.'

'Oh, you're doing a good job, Roger.' As usual she was over-anxious in her reassurance. 'No one could do it better.'

'I remember your precious Jake saying all anyone needed was a croupier's rake.' He hadn't missed it after all.

'I must write to Jan. Maybe now that it's winter, things won't be so bad for her. And Crystel. I must write to Crystel. It's my dream I'll have them both over to visit me sometime . . .' she laughed. 'Otherwise they *will* become dreams. I expect Crystel's still living with her married man.'

'I wouldn't say your two chums have done very well for themselves.' He was driving now behind the Trust buildings, very slowly, so that he could find a big enough place to accommodate the Saab.

'It depends what you mean.' She watched his cautious movements, his too-nervous turn of the steering wheel which botched it up. She, or Jake, would have swung the damned car in without all this manoeuvring. 'They're doing what they want to do, that's the main thing.'

228

'Didn't you once tell me Jake had met her?' It was as if he knew Jake was in the forefront of her mind.

'Yes, briefly, a long time ago.'

'If she's as beautiful as you say she must have made an impression on him.'

'I'm sure she did.' He seemed to be needling her for some reason.

'Anyhow, you've certainly kept in touch, the three of you.' He had now parked his car successfully which perhaps made him generous. She lifted her brief case from the back and got out.

* * *

She said to Gillian Farquharson, her secretary, when they were sorting out mail. 'Is Mr Russell missed in the office, Gillian?'

Gillian was a more composed person than the girl who'd blushed and stammered years ago in Howard's house. Perhaps that was because she'd become one of the senior secretaries when Miss Baines had died suddenly of a cerebral haemorrhage a few months after Howard's death. At the time Tricia had wondered if her death was circumstantial. 'Jake?' Gillian said surprisingly. 'Oh, yes, very much. We all adored him in the typing room. He was such great fun.'

'Was he? I always thought he was a man of, well, few words.'

Gillian didn't hide her surprise. 'You must have known a different Jake! There was nothing randy about him, but he was a great favourite. He had . . . charisma.' She nodded, satisfied. 'Those eyes . . . maybe you frightened him, Mrs Newton?'

'Frightened him?' She was piqued. 'How could I frighten him?'

'Well, you're . . . top brass, and terribly efficient, and I think when Mr Roger was ill you were anxious . . .'

'How do you mean, anxious?'

'Well, anxious about him, of course, and that made you sort of over-anxious about your job.' Her voice was kindly.

Out of the mouths of the Miss Farquharsons. 'Maybe I was.' She made herself smile. 'Well, I hope I've learned to relax now. But before I go limp, will you take some letters while you're here? Some of those firms are very slow about tendering. I want Robin's View completed and open for spring.'

'Yes, Mrs Newton.'

Robin's View, the recreation park at Kingsley Heath, had become her solace while Jake was away, an expression of her creativity and organisation. She'd asked Emma and Mark endless questions, had used them as guinea pigs in Latham Park, a sorry place full of dark laurel bushes where the swings and a squeaking wheel were the only attempts at amusement for children. She'd visited play-grounds and spoken to youth leaders, visited other Garden Cities, read innumerable pamphlets. She had perused even more erudite works and become a fan of Ebenezer Howard. She had found that as well as being intellectually satisfying, research was a good antidote for the ache in her heart.

Was planning a Utopia, she asked herself, for this was how she sometimes saw Kingsley Heath, or even Robin's View, a search after power, or was she trying to create a Utopia for other people since her personal life was unsatisfactory? She remembered reading that everyone creates out of what they lack, not out of what they have.

*   *   *

At the beginning of December, Jake appeared unexpectedly one evening in the office, just before five. Gillian had brought in Tricia's letters to sign and gone away, and when she heard the knock at the door she called, 'Come in,' thinking the girl had forgotten something. She looked up and Jake was standing there, taller than she had remembered, swarthier. His smile was broad, she saw the laughter lines round his eyes, she thought, what a satisfying kind of face it is to me, the feeling of strength, of integration.

'Jake!' She knew the blood had swept over her cheeks as she

half-rose, holding out her hand. 'What a surprise! I thought you were Gillian.'

'Do I look like her?' His grip was warm. 'I thought I might find you here. I've been with the architects.'

She sat down, glad of the support of the chair. Her head felt giddy with emotion. 'It's lovely to see you. I've got so much to tell you.' She stopped looking at him with difficulty. 'Wait till I sign those letters . . .'

'I'll wait if you promise to have a drink with me.'

'Oh, dear! I've to go to my mother-in-law's. We always have dinner with her on Friday.'

'Phone and say you'll be late.'

She looked at him, considering, tapping her front teeth with her pen. The utter delight of seeing him . . . She smiled, lifted the telephone and dialled Roger's office. As she thought, he'd left. It was his job to pick up Parky and Minnie to sit in with the children. She often thought Emma and Mark had more fun than they had at The Crescent . . . especially if Minnie had a fit. 'Minnie had a fit!' Mark had told them with shining eyes last Saturday morning at breakfast. 'There was soapsuds in her mouth.'

'Is this the Play Park?' Jake was looking at the plan on the wall.

'Robin's View, if you don't mind . . . oh, hello, Mary. Tricia. Um . . . how are you? Oh, good. Look, Mary, I'll be a little late in arriving. I've got held up . . . no, the children are all right. It's business . . . yes, eight or eight-fifteen at the latest. Yes, I might be earlier. It's an unexpected complication. Yes, goodbye, see you.'

'What will you tell Roger?' he said when she hung up.

'That a conference with the architects blew up.' Tacitly they were agreeing that Roger must be guarded from the truth. 'It quite often happens. I'll mention you were there too, of course. The new boys love discussing things over a gin and tonic.'

'I can see what the attraction is. Mind if I sit down?'

'No. What do you mean, you can see . . . ?'

'I've never seen you look prettier. Those great eyes of yours. There's hardly any of your face left.'

231

'It's an optical illusion.' She bent her head to put her signature to a letter. 'Roger used to tell me about my eyes . . .'

'Not any more?'

'He can't see them in the dark.'

'I see what you mean.' His tone made her redden again, and yet she'd asked for it. She felt sweat on her back, making her blouse cling.

'Let me sign those letters, please. Don't utter.' She read them rapidly or hoped she appeared to be reading them rapidly. Gillian's neat typing was a blur before her eyes. 'There,' she said, sitting back, At least she'd had time to collect herself. 'I'll hand them to Gillian on the way out.' And then joy overtaking her again, 'Are you really going to take me for a drink? I've got so much to tell you. I miss you for discussing things. Robin's View is finished now.' A labour of love. 'Do you like the lay-out?'

'It looks adequate, more than adequate.'

'I had fun doing it. My mind's a hotchpot of Froebel and Piaget, but I've tried to remember . . .' she laughed, 'that play is part of a child's response to his environment. I think I've got it right.'

'And that the child is father of the man?'

'You've read the right books too. D'you think we should have a plaque somewhere for Jolyon Roger?'

'Or a Jolly Roger Paddling Pool?'

She laughed, excited and happy. 'You always tease me. Why not Deakin's Dell for the shrubby part while we're at it. Oh, thanks.' He'd taken her coat from its hanger and was holding it out for her. When she slipped into it the touch of his hands was exciting. She was behaving like a sixteen year old . . . 'I've talked about myself all the time. I know you're doing important things for the Trust. I hear from the others. Something very hush-hush.'

'No more important than Kingsley Heath, only bigger . . . another Garden City. And we're thinking of going public. I've bought up two large tracts of land, one in Scotland, the other in Nottinghamshire, 15,600 acres including villages, church, colliery rights . . . it's that one I'm working on.'

'Sounds exciting.'

'It is. This Nottinghamshire project is going to be the Garden City to end all Garden Cities,' he smiled at her, 'a concept of civic design and architectural harmony, as they say.'

'Well, you've got it all there according to the book, an industrial outlet for the residents, even a church.'

'I hope so. Richard and Bob think it's a good chance to float shares. I'm going to America again. They're well ahead there with greenbelt towns.'

'You lucky thing. Will you be away long?' He was quite right. Her eyes were large, and full, and tender . . .

'No, only a few weeks. Come on, give up tittivating yourself. I'm dying for that drink.'

She walked through the outer office with him, caught a quizzical look from Gillian, said, 'Good-night' gaily, went down the wide staircase to the main hall as if she was stepping on air. She waved to the clerks behind their grilles, and smiled at Simpkins, the porter, an OAP of her mother's who'd been bored stiff collecting his pension. She felt light of foot, light-headed, as if she'd been born again. In the car she had to restrain herself from gushing, her happiness seemed to spill over . . .

They had two gin and tonics apiece and she hardly stopped talking. Once she interrupted herself and said, 'Do I have a blanketing effect on you? Gillian told me you were the life and soul of the party otherwise. What is it I do?'

He smiled at her. She longed to see his eyes deepen to blue, but they were in shadow. 'Do to me?' His eyebrows went up. 'I find you stimulating and I like listening to you. I admire your mind. You cut corners, take leaps. You think in flashes of intuition but there's a hard practicality too.'

'Is that all?' She was disappointed.

'You really have grasped the basic concept of the Garden City. You're a reincarnated Fabian. I saw that from the beginning.' His eyes were mischievous.

'It amuses you. I can see that. But everybody wants a paradise on earth. I know environment isn't everything, that it can't cure, only alleviate. I see this in the work my mother does. Maybe when I'm her age I'll take to social work . . .'

'Are you unhappy, Tricia?' He'd never asked her a personal question before.

'No.' She shook her head. 'I tell myself I'm lucky.'

'That's no answer. Come on, we've known each other a long time. Are you unhappy with Roger?'

Tears filled her eyes. She kept her head down, was grateful for the dim light of the lounge bar. 'Yes, I am, fundamentally, but not so as I can't cope with it. It's a matter of having got married too soon, and then changing . . .'

'Couldn't you make a break?' She raised her head and looked at him. His hands came out and went over hers lying on the table. 'No one as beautiful as you should be unhappy . . .'

'Old worn-out clichés.' She was suddenly angry with him. 'You're so smooth. You don't care tuppence whether I'm unhappy or not, beautiful or ugly.'

'Don't I?' His eyes were still in shadow. 'You're a lovable girl, sometimes too lovable. I've watched you for a long time, watched you turn on the charm . . . no, that's not true, you're not aware of your own charm, that's why you're so lovable. And you're not a whiner, thank God. You've coped with Roger's illness . . .'

'Roger had to cope with that.' She felt tremulous, unused to praise. Lovable? She'd never thought of herself as that, didn't like herself too much at times . . . 'The thing is, Jake, I couldn't ever leave him. He needs me. His father saw it before I did. And then, there's the religious side of it. You're never going to believe this, but I've got an old-fashioned belief that marriage is sacred. I tell myself that a clear thinker like me should have overcome that taboo long ago . . .'

'Taboos have nothing to do with clear thinking.'

'I should know that. Coming backing to the Trust, I love working in it. To hear you say that I do all right is high praise. I never feel I do well enough. But I do know I'm *used* up to my capacity, and sometimes I wish it was the same in my personal life. Even Jan and Crystel,' she apologised with a downward grimace, 'here I go again . . . are luckier than me in that way.' She suddenly remembered Roger's remark this morning. 'Do you ever think of her, Jake, remember her?'

'In what way?' His voice was level.

'Well, any way. She would be difficult to forget, Crystel.'

234

'I . . . wrote to her.' Now she heard a slight hesitation, 'Some time ago . . .' She was surprised at the fierce flame of jealousy which shot through her. She said lightly, but not able to look at him.

'Did she reply?'

'No . . . perhaps it wasn't the kind of letter that needed a reply. I'd hoped . . .'

She didn't want to know what he'd hoped. 'I suppose in comparison with Jan and Crystel my intimate life has been a failure.' She didn't like herself, saying that.

'You mean your sex life?'

'Yes.' She looked at him, loved him. Any thought of Crystel disappeared. Crystel was the past. This was now. She looked at him, and seemed to enter into him through his deep, dark eyes. The windows of the soul, she thought, bemused . . . the voices of the other drinkers seemed far away, a constant running sound like water. All she was aware of was Jake's hands on her own, the warmth which was flooding her, an exciting warmth which spread through her body. Her cheeks burned. 'I'm crazy,' she said, 'it's the gin.' She took away her hands, looked at her watch. It wasn't even seven o'clock. 'Are you dashing away somewhere?' She tried to speak lightly.

'Not till about the same time as you are. Martin Brigsteer's asked me to dinner. They're putting me up.'

'Our house is finished, Jake. We move in next week.'

'Is it? Great news. Are you pleased with it?'

'I am. It's me. I don't know if you'll like it.'

'Why not let me see it? We've still time.' And as she hesitated, 'It's business after all.'

'By a long stretch of the imagaination.' She laughed, was grateful that he wouldn't be leaving her yet. 'All right. But I think we'd better take separate cars. The Wilkes' are next door, remember.'

'Whatever you say.'

'And don't park outside. Better to leave it round the corner. Madge has eyes like a lighthouse beam.' And, weakly, 'Perhaps I'm doing her an injustice.'

'You're making it sound very cloak and daggerish.' It was the mocking tone again.

235

'You don't know Latham. It's a town with eyes in the back of its head.'

'Well, you're the local girl.'

She giggled like a child as she stood up. The warmth was still in her veins, a potent mixture of happiness and gin. 'I can't get over you praising me,' she said.

'Can't you?' Now that he was on his feet a light caught his eyes and they were deeply, intensely blue.

A fine rain was blowing as she put the key in the door and opened it. Behind her Jake reached forward and switched on the hall light. They stepped inside. 'Shh!' she said, over-acting because she was so happy.

'I feel like a burglar,' he said. 'Lead the way.' He was tip-toeing behind her when she looked round at him, and he grinned. 'I like games.' Then casting his eyes about, nodded. 'Mmmh. The right size.'

'D'you think so? I wondered if it was on the small side for a hall, but I wanted all the space for my lake room.' She led him up into it.

The room was filled with a pearly grey luminescence. As her eyes adjusted to it, she saw it had the same tone as the pale sheet of water they could see through the long windows. The room was right. She had counted on the reflected light, hadn't seen its effect so late in the evening.

'A lovely space.' He was standing close beside her. 'Water's a tremendous asset. And you've got the proportions right. I can feel it. What happens at the other end?'

'There's a step up to the dining area and off that a paved square the same size, the outside dining-room. Come and see.' She thought, I ought to put the lights on, was reluctant to do so. She knew every inch of the house by heart, and he seemed to follow her with the same sure-footed confidence.

'The sliding windows slide,' he said, 'good. Let's stand outside for a minute. I want to get your view.'

'There's a light outside.'

'Leave it.'

They went out together and the soft greyish light seemed to swim round them. The rain had stopped. There were far-away bird noises, maybe water-hens, a solitary bird-call, a clap of

236

wings. They stood silently. He put his arm round her shoulders and she shivered.

'Cold?'

'No.' She shook her head. In the sky above the horizon there was a faint glow which made the trees densely black, and when her eyes lowered again to the lake, its pearl-like evanescent quality had increased. 'It's so perfect . . . why can't we have everything? Why do we always want more?' She turned towards him and his arms went round her closely.

'You're shivering, poor thing.'

'Well, who wouldn't be?' She spoke against his shoulder. 'Standing outside in the middle of December. It's asking for pneumonia.'

'Come inside, then.' He laughed and released her, too quickly. 'I haven't seen the house properly.' They went in and he carefully shut the sliding windows and locked them, sure-fingered.

'You must see my kitchen, my *tour-de-force*.' She spoke gaily to convince herself that nothing had happened. She led the way and switched on the lights. 'Enough of being in the dark . . .' The strip lighting was harsh, and when she looked at him his face was strongly etched in black and white, the lines deep. She shook her head. 'Oh, cruel light.' And then, 'What do you think of it, Jake?' She was blinking. The light seemed to pierce and hurt her eyeballs.

'It seems to have everything.' He swivelled on his heels. 'It's the centre of the house, isn't it?'

'Yes, that's the idea; the heart of the house, home is where the heart is . . . I thought of continuing it through the roof and making a circular viewing tower . . .' she couldn't bear the brilliance any more, she couldn't bear the gleaming kitchen with its shelves and cupboards, its soulless efficiency. 'I'm getting a headache with those lights.' She was nervous, irritable. 'Come and see the bedroom wings. I'm quite pleased with them. The carpets are laid there.'

The main bedroom faced the lake, and the deep carpet under their feet was soft. 'It's white,' she said, 'everything's white. I don't want to distract from the outside in any way. The lake draws me like a magnet.' She laughed. 'I lift my eyes beyond the lake and see the view.'

'Howard's View?'

She was surprised, pleased. 'The name of the house?' He nodded. 'Ebenezer?'

'Why not? Isn't he number one on your reading list?'

'Yes, he is. Then, Roger's father . . . I like it. Yes, I'll have it. Thanks.' She turned to him, laughing, and again she was in his arms. She didn't know who made the first move, but this time there was no warm, comfortable embrace, but on her part a desperate clinging, on his a strength which overwhelmed her, didn't surprise her. Her hands were clasped behind his neck, she was shaking, stammering, 'Jake, I've wanted you for so long. It's grown . . . each night I've thought of you . . .'

'No . . .' his head went back. She tightened her grip.

'Yes . . .'

'Are you sure?'

'So sure, so very . . .' his mouth stopped the words, she felt her head reeling, knew that she swayed, that her knees buckled, that they were on the floor together.

'Is this rape?' she said, trying to make some kind of joke out of it. The softness of the carpet was under her.

'It isn't rape if you're willing.' His voice was terse as if there was no time to talk. 'Aren't you . . . afraid?'

'Of committing adultery?' She didn't know what he meant. She was only afraid he wouldn't make love to her.

He didn't speak. Roger spoke all the time, sighed, murmured endearments, demanded reassurance. This man only demanded love. His fingers were sure on her clothes. She felt like a willing doll being undressed, except that a doll wouldn't have had the feelings she had. They were new, strong, as if her skin was going to burst, a good match for his loving which was full-blown, mature, sophisticated, what she'd wanted from Roger and had accepted she'd never get. What surprised her was not Jake's strength but her own, a will to prolong as well as to give. She was laughing weakly at herself when it was over, saying, 'Oh, oh, oh . . .' again and again.

'It's a nice carpet,' Jake said, stretching out beside her, making her laugh even more weakly.

'Shag pile,' she said. The laughter overwhelmed her, she was hysterical now. It was incredible that little more than an hour

238

ago she'd been an ordinary human being and now she was different, she'd added a new dimension to living whether it was good or bad, moral or immoral. 'That bit's as good as ever,' Jan had written. Now she knew what she meant.

She had to wait for quite a time until the laughter stopped. It was as if her whole body which had been contained neatly for so long had disintegrated, broken into facets of pain, delight, sensation, laughter, and it had to be collected with her clothes and made into a neat parcel again.

She said good-bye quickly to him in the hall and let him out. In a second or two she followed him, locking up and walking swiftly towards her car. She heard his starting up and then the noise of the engine slowly dying away.

Madness, she thought, getting into the driving-seat, putting the key in the ignition. The silver clover-leaf swung before her eyes. Now I know what it's been like, Jan with your black lover, Crystel with your married man. To think that I'm the last to know . . .

She drove circumspectly towards Latham, feeling her body settle into its normal rhythms again, the blood recede from her nerve centres, become cool. She watched out for traffic, drove carefully but quickly because it was eight o'clock. The guilt would come later. And the other thing that was nagging at the back of her consciousness, not to be recognised at this moment . . . that would come later . . . had she started it?

*   *   *

She made an excuse and went to London to meet Jake, using the pretext of Christmas shopping. Mary was more than willing to look after the children, and even urged her to go. 'Take a few days off, Tricia. You deserve it.' But she said, 'Three days at the most,' firmly, with a mixture of guilt and elation.

London was transformed in her eyes. She joined in the Christmas crowds strolling down Regent Street, allowed herself to be swept down an escalator to a department store where the dresses were trendy and slightly shoddy to her eyes, used to the staid *haute couture* of Latham where the shop which she patronised kept 'County' clothes at County prices.

She bought dresses in deep jewel colours with revealing décolletage, sheer tights and costume jewellery, bright scarves and brighter makeup, all for Jake. She had saunas and her hair and nails done, she bought shoes with high heels whose price was in direct contrast to the amount of fine kid used in their manufacture. Everything was bought for Jake.

She met him each evening of her three days. They had dinner together and then went to his flat where they made love. He offered to take her to the theatre, to take her dancing, but she made the excuse that they'd have to rush dinner. To sit with him in his favourite French restaurant lingering over the meal, offering him samples of her choice on her fork, drinking more than she usually did, being cosseted by the waiter, was like being a courtesan on a small island. People came and went, there was the sound of voices, cutlery, the sharp French command of their chef sometimes, all like some distant sea surrounding their white-covered table.

When they came out of Tottenham Court Road, walked to his car and drove through the Christmas lights, she sat in silence beside him, her body on fire. Her one piece of decorum was not to stay the night with him, but to return to her hotel. Roger might phone her, or the children might be ill and they wouldn't be able to get in touch with her. Occasionally, when she was being driven by taxi to her hotel, guilt would overwelm her, but only for an instant. It didn't alter her love for Jake. She was possessed by him, not only physically.

She was, she told him, on the pinpoint of desire. 'Even my language is changing,' she said. 'I search for words to describe this feeling I have for you, this intensity of living, of loving. I'm not too intense for you, Jake?' She would search his face. Sometimes she imagined he looked not sceptical, but anxious, but she would reassure herself. He liked her to go overboard. He told her he'd never known anyone like her. 'You throw yourself into lovemaking the way you do into your work.' She was afraid of frightening him with her love. One evening, when she got back to her hotel, she sat down and wrote a letter to Jan.

240

'This is to wish you a merry Christmas from London, England. I'm here shopping for the family, and spend my days in Hamleys and Harrods and my nights with my lover. Does that surprise you? Remember how prudish I was in Paris when you and Crystel were having a good time with all those students? Even after I married Roger I still felt I didn't know what it was all about. Then I realised from your letters that there was something between you and George that I'd never known, except for one brief time in Corfu.

'But now I do. It's heaven. I don't use that as a catchphrase. It simply is heaven to me. I see now the whole point of my life. If I died now I'd be happy. I never thought I'd experience heaven on earth but when I watch his eyes on me, feel his hands on me, listen to his voice . . . I smile at everyone all day long, the shop assistants, the taxi-drivers, the bus conductors, people at bus-stops, the maid who brings me my morning tea, I feel my skin taking on a moist bloom, and when I catch sight of my face in a mirror my eyes smile back at me full of love.

'Why have I had to wait so long before I knew this heaven, knew it existed? I realise now that there has been this lovely secret behind quiet faces, people whom at times I've pitied because they haven't been, as I thought, so fortunately placed as I was. I want to join hands with all the women in love all over the world, I want to be with my lover all day and every day, but instead I have to go back home tomorrow to my dream children and dream husband, for that is how they seem to me, writing in this quiet room.

'My happiness tonight, Jan, was so great that I had to share it with someone and I thought of you. Now I know why you gave up your home to be with George. You know that saying about happiness being akin to sadness? As I write a cloud descends on me and I think . . . something will happen. No, that's nonsense. I love my lover, I love the whole world. Nothing can touch us.

'Forgive those outpourings. I'm tempted to tear up this letter and throw it in the wastepaper-basket, but no, I'll be honest, and self-indulgent, and send it. My love to you, Clay and

241

George. I have so much love . . .'

She told Jake about the letter when she was in London again early in March the following year. 'I had to get it out of my system. Goodness knows what she thought of it.' But she hadn't changed. She was deeply, irrevocably in love with him.

'Are you trying to tell me it's all over?' he said. He was in a light-hearted mood, handsome, debonair, full of his plans for the Nottingham project. Half the time their talk had been of business, not of love. She had registered this at the time.

'I'll never fall out of love with you, Jake.' She wanted to be honest with him. 'Maybe I've steadied a little. Heights are dangerous.' She smiled at him. 'I missed you terribly when I went back to Latham at Christmas, but my life swallowed me up. The children were ill, and some of the staff were off with 'flu . . . Roger had it . . . and I hadn't time to think of you during the day.'

'Work will always be your salvation.' His face was dark for a moment. 'I've no worries on that score . . .' She wondered what he meant.

'Are you trying to tell *me* that it's all over?' Her heart was thudding painfully.

'You're very intense, Tricia . . .' And then as if he sensed her slight stiffening in his arms . . .' but very lovable. All the same, I sometimes feel a bit of a heel . . . Roger.'

'He gets most of me. Loving you doesn't make him suffer. I'm fair about that.' Fair yet trying not to be sexually provocative, making the excuse of sleeping near the children during their sessions of childish ailments. Almost glad of them although it meant sleepless nights for her.

'The next few months are going to be hectic,' he said over dinner the following evening, She was surfeited, in a happy haze of alcohol and love, 'We'll have to plan very carefully. I shall be more than busy.'

'Where there's a will there's a way.' She opened her handbag and took out her diary. 'Shall I put you in as "hairdresser"?' She laughed at him.

'You're very beautiful.' Was his admiration reluctant? She brushed the thought aside.

'Oh, Jake. How am I going to get through the spring? It's a loving time. I'll want you so much on those soft spring evenings, I'll want to be with you . . .'

They compared dates. Yes, they could coincide their London trips, and yes, there was a possibility of meeting halfway, and yes, it would be a good idea if they both took their holidays in August.

'Where will you go?' he asked her.

'I don't know. Sea and sand for Emma and Mark, some nice shops for Mary. She'll come too. Bournemouth, perhaps. I don't care. Where will you go? On some madly expensive cruise to meet a rich widow?'

'No,' he said, 'I rather think I'll get into the car and drive to France.' He was withdrawn. She wouldn't worry, she told herself. He was complex, there were times when she knew she shouldn't ask questions.

In the train the next morning she thought of him constantly. The people in the compartment were like ghosts. *I'm a ghost,* she thought, this wife, going back to Latham, is only part of me. My love if anything is stronger, only more contained. I can run my life at home and in the office, I don't any more have to sit down and pour out my heart to Jan. She knew it wasn't yet the same for Jake because he'd never said it was, and he was honest, some people thought, ruthless. But men had a loyalty towards each other. He was perturbed about Roger. Sometimes he cut himself off from her, like yesterday.

Don't worry. They would grow closer, and when he needed her as she needed him he would suggest a divorce. *Don't worry . . .* She closed her eyes the better to think of him, felt the small aches in her body where he had been.

CHAPTER TWENTY-FOUR
August, 1978

CRYSTEL was in her kitchen cooking. She'd taken a shower when she came in, put on a short towelling robe and tied an apron on top of it. Her feet were bare. She liked to curl her toes on the cool tiled floor which she kept as clean as a whistle, liked her sleeves rolled up to the elbow, she adored the rich smell which was filling the kitchen . . .

The cassoulet was in its final stages. Three days ago she had bought the garlic sausage, the smoked bacon, the salt pork, the pig's feet, the goose pieces she needed were in her store cupboard preserved and bottled at Christmas when she had been at St Henri. Two days ago she had soaked the haricot beans, last night she had cooked them with herbs and a piece of gammon, and tonight was what she called the *grand assemblage.*

And all because of Guy. Madeleine, he'd said, was becoming so neurotic that she never took time off to cook. The care of Michel monopolised her time. 'She's turning him into a baby,' he had said a few nights ago. 'The rest of us are neglected. I don't mind about myself, but the other children need her care. Already they're showing signs of rebellion. And the food is scrappy and always bought from the supermarket. Do you know, Crystel, the last cassoulet I tasted was before I was married.'

Hence the cassoulet. It was far too big for two people, but tomorrow as it was Saturday she would wrap it up carefully in tinfoil and take it to St Henri. She, her father and mother could enjoy it over the weekend. Perhaps, even better, she thought, I'll take them and the cassoulet to see Angelique and Justine at La Mothe Fenelon. It must be a long time also since they've tasted one.

She finished chopping up the meats and started layering them with the beans in the deep earthenware pot, the smell of garlic strong in her nostrils. Too much? No, not for a Toulousaine dish. She reverently lifted it with gloved hands and put it into the oven. *Mon Dieu*, it's heavy, you could feed Napoleon's army with this.

She straightened up and looked at her watch. Five forty-five. Guy was coming about eight, and he would then be able to enjoy the final rites, the opening of the oven, the stirring of the crust formed by the beans into the mass, the rich aromas, the gentle shutting of the door again, the delicious waiting for the final crust to form.

'We shan't be able to eat until about ten o'clock,' she had told him, 'and if you take too much you won't be able to make love to me.' Madeleine was spending the weekend with her parents. He had taken time off from the shop to drive them to Limoges. He would be able to stay with Crystel overnight.

'As long as I don't belch too much,' he'd said. 'Otherwise it will give me strength to perform.' he liked to speak frankly at times coarsely. He said that in the shop, when they were being formal, it gave him a *frisson* to remember his remarks. In any case it seemed to release tensions in him, and for her part, brought up in the country, it was natural.

She went out on to the patio with a Ricard in her hand to cool down after her labours. She lay back in her *chaise longue*, sighing with content. Over eight years, she thought, I've been in this flat, and I'm happy, not totally happy but I have most things I want. She sipped her drink, feeling reflective.

Perhaps I should be more demanding of life, like Tricia who drives herself, and yet against that I think of Jan who has been driven by circumstances . . . she watched Mademoiselle Coco carrying in her *Arrangement des Funèbres*. One of these days it will be her own. Look at that hunched back, and her arms and legs are like matchsticks. She can't manage to lift the broken-nosed grand'mère any more.

She watched intently while Mademoiselle Coco rolled the plaster model on its plinth as if it were a milk-can. Monsieur Raoul, René Baron's hairdresser (he was a farmer's son from Soucirac), came out of his shop wearing his white jacket with its mandarin collar and began to help her, rather reluctantly. He'd never liked farm work. His father had told Crystel's father that Pierre couldn't even lift a bale of hay.

Perhaps she would have her hair done by him one day. She was happy with Yvonne, but it was good to have a change occasionally . . . no, on second thoughts she wouldn't. Men, even poor specimens like Pierre Carinac, always wanted to cut too much hair off, snip, snip. They went crazy when they had scissors in their hand.

I have no future all the same, she thought, not feeling too unhappy about it. Guy can never leave Madeleine because of poor Michel, and in any case I shouldn't like him as a husband. He's too unsure of himself. It's only in bed he has confidence, and you can't be in bed all the time, much as I like it. There must be a man somewhere whom I could respect, dressed and undressed. Perhaps I should take the bull by the horns and go to Paris to work, leave *Derain et Cie*, leave Guy, but she knew she wouldn't. The discomfort would be intolerable, a poky flat in some dark apartment block, travelling by Métro every day, the *circulation* being too awful to contemplate driving, the lack of fresh air, the tattling girls in some back-street office.

And worst of all, no St Henri to escape to at the weekends, to be able to work in her mother's big kitchen, to walk over the fields, to visit neighbours and hear the village gossip, to take her parents for a drive in the new Citroen. Guy had insisted this year that she should replace the old one. Her father, particularly, was captivated by it. He twisted the knobs on the facia board like a child with a new toy.

She heard a car stop in the Rue du Château and wondered if Guy was coming earlier than he had said. It took him three hours to get to Limoges and back, allowing for the necessary stop at Madeleine's parents' house. It couldn't possibly be him. Then she saw the dark head bobbing between the hedges . . . it will be a new boy-friend for Monsieur Rambeau, she thought. He'll have quarrelled with the fair one. But it wasn't a boy. The head had a squarer, more mature look. And then she knew who it was, wearing a corduroy jacket and jeans, foreign-looking, taking the steps cut into the rock two at a time, as if his legs were too long for them. She got up as he came towards

246

her, thinking he looked at ease, as if he knew where he was going. Everything about him was decisive, the clipped voice, the dark face, English but not sheep-like, squared-chinned, the straight glance. He bowed.

'Is this a terrible intrusion, Mademoiselle Romaine? I was passing . . .'

'Non, pas du tout.' Her English forsook her. 'Quelle surprise! It's Monsieur Russell, isn't it? I can hardly remember . . .' She knew him right away. She held out her hand and he took it in a warm grip.

'Jake. I felt my last visit was too abrupt . . .'

'But you wrote.' She still had the letter. There had been something about it which intrigued her, as if some of his personality had been caught in the short phrases . . . 'I was a boor,' (whatever that was), 'regret any impoliteness . . . hope to rectify it in the near future . . .' It had been an unnecessary letter and yet touching, as if there was more behind it than the words conveyed.

'Yes, I did, and you didn't reply, so here I am.' He smiled charmingly at her. Although she herself was quite boulversée underneath, she admired his ease of manner. Fumbling in any shape or form she couldn't abide.

'I was thinking of Tricia only the other day. How strange . . .' Something in his look made her feel shy, a rare experience for her. 'Excusez-moi,' she said in a rush of French, 'en effet c'est difficile de parler Anglais. Your coming here . . . it is so sudden.'

'I should have warned you. Have I been rude again? Would you like me to go away?'

'Non, non!'

'Would you like me to speak French? I can stagger along . . .'

She laughed. 'No, I have now my breath back, thank you.' She looked down and saw that her robe was parted too much at the front, remembered its shortness, her bare legs and feet. 'Excuse me again. I've been relaxing. I've been busy.'

He nodded. 'Yes, Tricia told me you have a very important job.'

'No, no!' I'm laughing like a hyena, she thought. 'I've been preparing a cassoulet. Much more important.'

'Ah, that's the delicious smell . . .'

'Perhaps too much? Some people say the smell of the cassoulet is sufficient . . . will you excuse me for a moment, Mr Russell?'

'Jake.'

'Mr Jake. Ah, pardon. The English rush into *prénoms*. I learn. I was on the point of dressing but had to cool down after having been in the kitchen. You will sit in my chair and I will get you a drink. What would you like?'

'What are you having?'

'A Ricard.'

'That'll suit me, thanks.' He looked around, smiling. 'It's like an eyrie here, isn't it?'

'*Comment?*'

'You have a bird's eye view of the whole town. Tricia told me about your flat. She'd love this. She's mad keen on views. Her house . . .'

'Telling me all about Tricia will take a long time because there is much I want to know, so first I get your drink?'

'Thanks, yes.' How deep-set his eyes were. But what colour?

In her bedroom she found her heart beating rapidly as she pulled on a fine cashmere sweater in her favourite pale mauve, then eased on linen trousers of the same shade. She brushed out her hair and looked at herself in the mirror. Her eyes asked a question of her, and she nodded. Yes, I'm excited. Excited at the sight of him, surprised and yet not surprised . . . She put on the shoes she liked most, pale mauve high-heeled sandals. She liked very much to have shoes in the same colour as her clothes. Guy teased her about this and often asked her how long it took her to find them. 'Anything worth having is worth spending time on,' she had told him. Guy's image in her mind seemed tired and worn in comparison with this Jake.

In the kitchen, pouring from the Ricard bottle, she found her hand shaking . . . She breathed deeply, and now the aniseed superimposed on the smell of the cassoulet. She carried the drink carefully through her lounge and on to the terrace.

She found Jake Russell sitting on the stone wall which surrounded the terrace. He smiled round at her and she now saw his eyes were deeply blue, like jewels. Tricia had never said how handsome he was, but then she had seemed to stop speaking about him altogether in the last year. Her letters were full of her work and her plans for her 'Kingsley Heath', of the children, sometimes she mentioned her husband, Roger.

'I hope I'm not holding you up in any way,' he said as he took the glass from her. 'Thanks. Just what I needed. I'm passing through Maurac on my way to Carcassonne . . .' he met her look, 'well, I deviated somewhat. You were on my mind . . . I mean, I felt . . . I always felt my last visit didn't strike the right note.' She had no idea Englishmen were so punctilious. 'I'm staying at *L'Hôtel de la Poste* tonight.'

'Ah, yes,' Crystel smiled, tried not to look down her nose, 'it's a very fine hotel. I know the proprietor well.'

'The woman at the reception desk was a bit surly. Could it be Madame, the *patronne?*'

'It could be.' That was all she would permit herself to say. That was dignified. 'And please don't talk about right notes. This is wonderful for me. Tricia sometimes speaks of you . . . not lately. Tell me about her.'

'Tricia's all right, blooming, in fact. We've become . . .' he looked down at his glass . . . 'close friends.' What does he mean, Crystel thought. His eyes were now looking in the direction of Mademoiselle Coco's boutique. His face was grim.

'You help her in her work?'

'No.' He didn't look at her. 'Actually I'm not based in Latham now. I'm in the London office quite a lot. We opened one there this year, and also I'm supervising a new project in Nottingham, profiting from the experience we gained at Kingsley Heath . . .' he stopped, turned towards her, smiling slightly. 'How boring for you. I'm sure you aren't interested in this meaningless gabble of mine. What I meant to say is that I don't see Tricia very much at Latham. Sometimes we have to meet in London . . . on business.'

'I see. Is she able to get away from home with her husband and children there? In my case,' she shrugged, 'I just pick myself up and go, but she's very conscientious, isn't that the word?'

'Yes, that's the word.' He was still looking at her. Her heart for some reason started to beat rapidly again. She had no bra on. The sweater was tight. Would her bosom show her agitation?

She waved her hands in front of her chest. 'Jan and I were the frivolous ones, but Tricia was stern, upright, like a schoolmistress, only far too pretty for that. Those wonderful eyes of hers . . . she had a good sense of humour but it struggled against her religious and moral principles.'

He took his eyes away from her and she breathed more easily. 'We all have to drop some of them along the way, don't you find?'

'In my case, yes.' She laughed a little. 'I had a different outlook. I believe to be happy is a principle of life since you make other people happy.' She was surprising herself, if not him.

'Try telling that to people with strong moral principles.'

'But I don't.' She waved a hand. 'Why should I? I lead my own life and let others do the same.' The agitation had died down now. 'Here in Maurac we're backward. Even for a girl to live in her own flat, unmarried, is considered not quite *de rigueur*. But, look, I can entertain whom I like, it's all mine, I am proud of my little eyrie, isn't that the word you used? Come inside and see it, Jake.' She smiled at him. 'I find that strange. Is it *Jacques*?'

'I was christened John, but it's always been Jake since school. Perhaps you grow to suit your name.' He got up from the wall. His smile was so charming, and she liked how the wrinkles appeared at the corner of his eyes. He was just as she remembered him, only thinner. She realised now that he had been at the back of her mind, remembered perfectly, with all the attributes of René's charm combined with Guy's sweetness, but a virility which was all his own. 'Tricia always goes by the feel of a house,' he said. Tricia again. But then she was the link. '"if the location's right, it's right," she says. She's more like Roger's grandfather than Roger is himself.'

'Really?' She led him into her salon. 'I expect she'd see plenty of faults here, but I like it. I make rooms suit me, with comfort first and then, if possible, a certain amount of elegance. Perhaps I'm lucky because I work in a furniture store. My boss lets me have things more cheaply.'

'Yes, Tricia told me.' What had Tricia told him? That Guy

was her lover? Why should he mind, or indeed why should she mind him knowing? She met his eyes. The lively face he had turned to her on the terrace was again replaced by a grimness and a darkness, as if he had shut himself off from her. She'd seen this in English people before, a sudden withdrawal as if they had given too much of themselves and regretted it.

'I've known Guy for a long time. He's been kind to me, a good boss . . .' And then she disliked herself, apologising for Guy in this way. 'He's coming this evening, as a matter of fact. Perhaps you would care to stay and meet him?'

'No, thanks.' His voice was abrupt, even rude.

'Oh, please do. It would give me pleasure.' And before he could answer, 'Come and see my bedroom.' She felt her cheeks redden, she who rarely blushed. What a ridiculous thing to say, as if that was going to change his mind for him. He was standing in the doorway, glowering, that was the word which occurred to her. 'Please enter. Simple again, as you see, but of course the best of materials, and I like the antique. I pick up pieces from Mademoiselle Coco who has a shop in Rue Boniface, just across from here. This charming little *escritoire* is my latest purchase.' She ran her hand over it. Old wood had a different feel, a satiny smoothness.

'Very charming,' he said. He was communicating his uneasiness to her, and he seemed to have no taste for antiques. She had obviously made a mistake in inviting him here, something Tricia would never have done. A quick shaft of envy ran through her. Tricia had the key to this strange man's personality. He couldn't be her lover, surely? She stole a look at him. He was standing beside her little Boule bedside table with its squirrel design, completely ignoring it, his gaze resting on her bed with its sprigged cotton cover as if he'd never seen a bed before. And yet there was no lasciviousness in his look, merely a dark kind of sadness. Was there something he wanted to say? Had he something to tell her? About Tricia?

'Tricia is quite well?' she asked timidly.

'Quite well.' He spoke as if the question wasn't worth answering.

In the salon once more she asked him to sit down and excused herself. She went into the kitchen and set the fan in motion, and from there went to the bathroom where she brushed out her hair again and sprayed it with her most expensive perfume. How could she explain to him that there was no *double entendre* in showing him her bedroom? What with that and the strong smell of onion, pork and garlic probably clinging to her, he must think she was a peasant. When she came back he was sitting in one of her Louis Quinze chairs so carelessly that it might well have been a rush stool. He turned and looked at her, unsmiling. 'What a delicious perfume.'

'Hadn't you noticed it before? Let me refill your glass, Jake.'

'Thanks.'

She refilled her own also, sat down opposite him and crossed her legs. They'd struck the wrong note again. The debonair man who'd come bounding up her steps had changed into someone who was wrapped up in his own thoughts. It affected her deeply, and she reflected that he was the only man who'd ever done so. Now that she thought of it the bedroom incident was trifling. A man of this calibre wouldn't normally give it a moment's thought. He would know his way about bedrooms. She looked at him. Their eyes met. He sipped his Ricard, holding her glance, seemed about to speak, then looked away.

'Tell me about Roger,' she said. She was inspired. 'I read between the lines in Tricia's letters. She's had a bad time. Is he well now?'

He seemed relieved at her remark, turned and spoke to her as if she'd thrown him a lifebelt. 'As well as he'll ever be. She copes with the situation in her own admirable way. Things haven't been easy for Tricia . . .' his voice faded away. 'But tell me about *you*. And the American girl.'

'Jan.'

'Jan. The three of you seem to have a close bond. I've often thought that.'

'Yes, it's true. We shared an experience together which we thought would change our lives.' She smiled at him. 'It didn't. Perhaps that is the bond. None of us has what we said we wanted.'

'I thought *you* would have. You seem so . . . complete in every way. Beautiful,' he didn't smile, 'happy . . .'

'I'm not unhappy,' she said. 'But I'm waiting.' She decided to be absolutely frank with him. She would tell him about Guy, about the understanding there was between them, but how she knew in her heart Guy wouldn't last, how he had always said she must feel free to go when she wanted . . . from outside the salon she heard his voice.

'*Chérie, c'est moi!* I can smell the cassoulet in Rue Boniface!' He came through the door from the terrace and she saw him clearly not for the first time, but how she had seen him at the beginning and had forgotten, a thin, worried man with a slight pot belly, a sweet smile, a greying beard, a crumpled suit. A stepping-stone in her life.

'Guy,' she said, 'this is a friend of Tricia's from England. Monsieur Jake Russell. You remember you met him a long time ago?'

He nodded, bowed. 'Yes. You called once at my store.'

'That's right. I was passing through Maurac again and I decided to . . .'

'Monsieur Russell works in the same company as Tricia, Guy. Isn't that interesting?'

'Very,' Guy said. 'What a road that was to Limoges, *chérie!*' And then to Jake. 'What do you think of the French roads, *monsieur?* I was taking my wife and children to Limoges, and the hold-ups! It's a hilly road, you know, from Brive, a switchback. And just as bad both ways. Someone will have to do something about those roads . . .'

'We have the same problem,' Jake said.

'I'm sure you have. But you're well-disciplined.' He sniffed, an air of satisfaction on his face, 'That smell, Crystel! It wafted me here, I assure you!' He laughed, pleased with his joke, and repeated it to Jake. 'All the way, *monsieur.*'

'Jake's going to join us,' Crystel said. 'Help yourself to a drink and fill up his glass . . .' She saw Jake get to his feet, wave away Guy's hand.

'I'm sorry.' He looked sternly at Crystel. 'I can't stay after all. I'm sorry . . .'

'Don't apologise,' she said. She was mortified. 'Naturally I'm sorry too. I should have liked to hear more about Tricia.'

'Are you staying in Maurac?' Guy asked.

'Tonight only. But I have a lot to do . . .' he waved his hand vaguely, ' . . . work.'

She walked with him to the door. The mortification had gone but in its place there was a sense of desolation. She didn't want him to go. There were so many explanations, they would have to talk and talk, get to know each other, he would have to be as frank with her as she had intended to be with him. They shook hands. She tried to clear her eyes as she met his. 'Give my love to Tricia,' she said. 'It's been a . . . pleasure . . . to see you again.' I had *wanted* him to come back. The realisation struck her. There was a tight feeling at the top of her nose, the beginning of tears. She blinked, smiled.

'Crystel . . .' He kept her hand. 'You must think me rude . . . a boor . . .' There it was again. Her heart ached, and yet buried deep in the ache there was a glimmer, some kind of realisation.

'No, it's quite all right. I understand you're busy.'

'No, it isn't that. I'm just . . .' he shrugged, ' . . . astonished at myself. Any *savoir faire* I had is gone. I'm like an awkward schoolboy. I had so much to tell you. I couldn't get started. I've always been bad at words. They don't come easily to me. Do you like me? Even a little?'

'I like you very much.' She had never been coy.

'Something . . . conclusive has happened to me today. I'll go back to the hotel and write it all down. I'll bring it to you and say, "Read that. That's what I couldn't say." But then again you might not want to hear it. There's Guy . . .'

'I'll want to hear it,' she said. Their eyes met, held. There was so much to know about this man. He wasn't easy. It would take a lifetime. He turned awkwardly away from her. She watched him running down the steps cut out of the rockery, saw his head bobbing between the hedges, listened for the slam of his car door.

She went back into the room. Guy held out his arms to her. 'You and cassoulet, *chérie*,' he said, 'what bliss.' She went to him because it was her nature to please, and sat on his knee thinking, while he told her of Michel being sick and how upset Madeleine was and how she had talked of turning back . . . 'Thank goodness the Englishman didn't stay,' he said, 'he would

254

'Because of Guy?'

'In a way. One doesn't make the effort to meet new people, the mental effort, when one is with a man. Like me being with Papa. We're married, of course, which makes a difference. I never tried to sway you because there's always a base of humanity in what you do . . .'

Crystel put a hand on her mother's. 'You've been good about that, *Maman*. You understood. I should have said so before. You've been good all the time, you and father, at understanding . . . and yet you've made this house a refuge for me.'

'It's just there, *cocotte*. We've never made it anything. Do I know this man?'

'No, he's English.' She laughed. 'Your eyebrows are lost in your hair. Don't you remember me telling you how he came to the shop one day, years ago . . . Tricia sent him.'

'The English girl?'

'Yes.'

'I remember now. But didn't you say at the time he was rather abrupt, impatient?'

'Yes, he was, and I dismissed him from my mind. Then slowly he began to creep back into it, year by year. He acquired in my mind all the virtues I think a man should possess.'

'Oh, if you're looking for virtues!' Dominique said with a sniff.

'The virtue of occupying my mind, perhaps,' Crystel said. 'Then some time ago I had a strange letter from him, as if that first visit had stayed in his mind . . . a kind of apology. And that made me think of him even more.'

'Did you write back?'

'No. I didn't know what to say to him. I thought I'd like to wait and see . . . if he wanted to come back, if he had to come. And he did. Yesterday. I found I'd remembered him perfectly, everything about him, an air, a combination of sureness and handsomeness and rightness and abruptness. No, something far more . . . did you feel like that about Papa?'

'Not immediately, but it grew. But then it comes in all ways.'

'Certainly. We talked, we laughed and enjoyed each other when he came yesterday. We were instantly at ease with one another. I was happy, only worried because Guy was coming.'

'Did that chase him away?'

'I don't know. Even before that I'd sensed a sudden unease in him, a withdrawal . . . as if he was regretting coming.'

'So, why?'

'He'd see evidence of Guy about the place. He would have permitted himself to hope that Guy no longer existed . . . for you.'

'There was a change of mood certainly. Do you think there might be an English custom that if you show a man your bedroom it's an invitaiton to . . . use it?'

'What an idea! Did you learn that rubbish in Paris?'

'You're right, Maman. I dismissed the idea around three o'clock this morning.' She laughed, then grew serious. 'I heard a fox barking in the far copse. How lonely it sounded. Lying awake last night I began to doubt *myself*. I wondered if I had imagined the rapport. It was the strange fashion in which he became wrapped up in himself, didn't even want to admire my *bibelots* . . .'

'Perhaps because he was thinking that someone supplied them. You have expensive tastes, *chérie*.'

Crystel looked at her mother, and then smiled. She felt the broadening of her face, the sheer pleasure of the smile, like a release. '*Maman*, for a country-woman you're very *mondaine*. But I've never taken anything from Guy as you know.'

'Except reduced prices on everything you have.'

She tossed her head. 'That's a business arrangement, a perquisite which is even given to my typist, but,' she couldn't stop smiling, 'how wise you are! Why didn't I think of it? I couldn't understand the change in him, I thought he had suddenly grown tired of his visit, that the situation bored him. The English can be arrogant in a peculiarly English way. I've seen it in the shop. "No, thank you," ' she put her nose in the air, mimicking, ' "It's not what I'm looking for." '

'The shopkeepers in Maurac don't like them.'

'But they like their money. Guy always says that.'

'Poor Guy.' Dominique sighed.

'Guy to me is like . . . a comfortable chair, one is at ease with him. But this strange man, Jake . . .'

'Is that his name? It's strange too.'

258

'It's like *Jacques*. I find it distinguished. When we were at the door the rapport was there again. I swear it, *Maman*.'

'I believe you.'

'He stumbled over what he was saying, apologised, said he would write when he got back to his hotel. *L'Hôtel de la Poste*, if you please. What puzzles me is that I don't think he's ill at ease with women. I think there was something else . . .'

'Perhaps it was the smell of the cassoulet?' They laughed together.

'It's no laughing matter, *chère Maman*. This is different for me, quite different . . . by the way, I should stir the cassoulet again. Papa will soon be back from church. Praying gives him a good appetite.'

'Fortunately, there's plenty to satisfy him.' Dominique got on her knees and opened the oven door. The smell came out in heady waves. 'Ah, it's a good one, Crystel.' She put the spoon to her lips, blew on it and then sipped carefully. *'Parfait.'*

Crystel smiled and her eyes strayed to the window again. She saw a man pass it, the eyes straight ahead as polite people do when passing someone's window. Her heart leaped. '*Maman* . . .' she thought she was going to faint. The blood pulsed in her cheeks. 'Maman, it's . . . it's . . .' she heard the determined knock at the front door. He would knock like that.

'Who can this be?' Her mother straightened, stood up, her face red from the heat. 'What's wrong with you?'

'It's . . .' Words wouldn't come. 'I'll answer it.' She opened the kitchen door, ran down the narrow corridor, stood for a second then opened the door on to the street. Jake stood there, darker and grimmer than ever it seemed.

'Hello,' he said, 'I've run you to earth.'

'Yes.' She swallowed, tried to compose herself. 'I saw you pass . . .' It would have been so much easier to have thrown herself into his arms.

'Did you? I've been walking over the fields trying to summon up more courage. I came to St Henri about ten . . .'

'How did you know I was here?' She was as tongue-tied as he'd been yesterday.

'Look,' he said, grimmer than ever, 'I don't want to have to speak to any of your family yet. Would you come for a walk with

259

me? I've a lot to say. I've been up all night thinking about it.' His face became rueful. 'I couldn't write that bloody letter!'

'So have I. I heard the fox barking . . . for its mate.' She was confused, happy, but first there had to be a lot of talking, a lot of explanations. 'A moment, please.' She went running back along the passage and into the kitchen. '*Maman*, I'm going to make a little promenade. You'll never believe it but it's Jake, the man I was telling you about.'

'I have only to look at your face.'

'I must have laid a trail with the cassoulet.' She laughed. She was delirious, happiness came in waves swamping her, making her head reel. 'May I invite him to luncheon if he would like to?'

'Why ask me? It's your cassoulet.'

'It's your house. And you're teasing me . . . oh, *Maman*!' She kissed her mother. 'I feel like Crystel at fourteen.'

'You look like her. But fortunately you have more sense.'

* * *

Sunday gave the fields a special look, she thought, calm, golden. The houses nestling in the hollows were pink-roofed, the trees swayed more circumspectly. A gentleness permeated the air.

'You asked Monsieur Rambeau about me?' she said, smiling at Jake, feeling vulnerable, child-like. He hadn't taken her hand nor touched her in any way. He seemed to want to talk, to begin right at the beginning.

'Yes. First thing after breakfast I decided to call to explain my rudeness, to explain everything. I'd decided that at dawn. But you weren't there. Then I heard the noise of an engine under my feet as I stood on your terrace. I looked over the wall and saw this *monsieur* backing out of his garage. I called down to him and he said you always went to your parents early on Sunday.'

'I'd just left. He gave you their address?'

'Yes. He said I'd have no difficulty in finding it. I hadn't. What I had difficulty in finding was the courage. I've been walking about for the past hour.'

'What is it you find difficult, Jake?' Her voice was soft in her ears, as if the Sunday gentleness was in her too.

'Why I've waited for so long. You've been in my mind since that first time, at the back of it to begin with, but still there . . .'

'You could have come again.'

'I could have, I should have, but I was abroad a lot, career-orientated, we call it. I thought a beautiful girl like you would be married, or tied up . . . I knew about Guy,' he looked at her, grim and dark. 'Then Tricia and I became lovers.'

She felt no surprise. 'So that's why you didn't want to talk about her yesterday?' She kept her voice soft.

'Yes, I suppose so. But there has to be honesty. I don't know how it started . . . that's the first lie. Of course I do. It was inevitable, the moment was propitious. Once it started it was difficult to stop. She would have been hurt . . . now I'm putting it all on to her which is wrong. I've always admired her, thought she'd had a raw deal with Roger. He's ineffectual, won't ever amount to much. That may sound arrogant. I don't mean it to be. Or maybe I *am* arrogant. Well, I was until last night.' She met his eyes. They were deep, dark, anxious. He would have to scourge himself first, poor darling.

'Go on,' she said. My voice, she thought, is as soft as the breast of doves.

'Roger . . . I was talking about Roger. His father overawed him from childhood. I don't think Tricia realised it at first. She was very young when they married. Very pretty, as you know. Her eyes . . .'

'Now you're speaking more sensibly.' She was trying to make him smile, but he was far too anxious, English-anxious. No Frenchman would take a whip to himself like this. Guy had had no compunction about Madeleine.

'She's not a girl you try to make,' he was saying. 'Do you know that word? She's always just a little straight-laced, maybe because she's a Catholic.'

'I'm a Catholic.'

'Are you?' She could feel his surprise. He wasn't using his wits. 'Maybe if you're a native of a Catholic country . . . One night, when I came back to Latham I dropped in at the office to see her. She . . . emanated pleasure. You think she's calm and disciplined, only interested in business, and then she looks at you with those eyes . . . Do you want to hear all this, Crystel?' My dear, dear Englishman, it is you who want to tell me.

'I want to hear.'

'I was flattered, of course. I make no excuses. She was beautiful, and intense. You know how she is, in her work . . . '

'She was intense in her loving?'

'She needed to be loved. Crystel . . . ' his troubled eyes were on her.

'And then?'

'We met in London sometimes, halfway stops, sometimes I came to Latham.'

'And then?' She spoke a little sharply, the way she spoke sometimes to Janine in the office. She waited. The air was full of summer sounds. The wind was like a cool hand on her cheek. She said, deliberately. 'Guy and I were always frank with one another.'

'Yes . . . what happened was this. I hadn't the courage to break off with Tricia and yet you were increasingly in my thoughts. I know it's hard for you to believe. You're so straightforward.' His voice was gentle. 'It was as if the affair with her stirred up my feelings for you. I tried cancelling appointments with her. I avoided any discussion about divorce. I hated to hurt her, knowing how proud she was . . . I thought maybe my preoccupation with you would go away. It didn't. I had to face it. Usually I've no difficulty in being decisive, but it was my regard for Tricia which held me back, for the sterling quality of her and the fact that she said again and again how happy she was with me. Can you understand a little?' He stopped and looked at her.

'I can understand you hated to hurt Tricia. Was the decisive thing coming to see me?'

'Yes, I had to be sure. If you were free. If you'd feel the same about me. When I saw you I knew the feeling I had for Tricia was only a reflection of her passion.' He put his hands on her shoulders. His face was dark red, his composure gone. 'Look at the state I'm in, my hands trembling and my stomach churning, but as well there's the feeling of having stopped

262

searching at last, of knowing that this is what I've been waiting for, Crystel, dearest, my God, you must feel the same otherwise it couldn't be as strong, as certain, as sure, this feeling . . .'

She put her hands on either side of her face to steady her own body. From here to my toes I'm trembling . . . 'Do you feel jealous of Guy?'

'Horribly, sickeningly. When I saw that bed you'd slept on with him I could have torn him limb from limb. D'you feel the same about me?'

She took her hands away from her face and held them out to him. 'I didn't sleep all night, either.' When his mouth closed over hers the sky tilted but she spoke sternly to herself. Don't be such a fool, Crystel. This is the most wonderful moment of your life. You can't afford to miss it . . . she put everything she knew into returning his kiss.

When he released her she wanted to tell him about the happiness. 'I feel . . . I feel . . . a strange *beginning* feeling. I am going to start counting my age from this second. Does that seem bizarre to you?'

He smiled at her, his face broader, his eyes smaller against the sun, but deeply, intensely blue. 'I know exactly what you mean. I'm thirty-four and I feel about ten. I feel like I did one summer day long ago when I ran along the beach with my kite and thought I'd discovered happiness.'

'What is this kite?'

'A . . . *jouet*. I don't know its name. Like this.' He ran away from her in a circle, his arm above his head, came back to her, laughing. So handsome. It was sad about Tricia, sad about Guy, but *c'est la vie*. He was hers.

'A *cerf-volant*. You were ten years old once with a "kite" . . .' she stumbled over the word. 'It is so wonderful to me. You enter my life only yesterday and now I know everything about you. I want to tell you everything about me, how sad I am perhaps to break Tricia's heart. I don't think so. She has strength. Shall I tell you . . . yes, let's walk, put your arm round me . . . that I knew you'd come to St Henri? No, I must be like you, honest, I *hoped* you'd come. I'm like . . .' she waved her free arm . . . 'those cows. I believe in the slow turn of events, like the seasons. I can accept the suffering of others more readily than you because I'm used to the necessary suffering of animals, especially in this part of the country where we put them in the pot.' She liked what she was saying. It prevented her from imagining Guy's face when she told him it was all over. 'That cassoulet I was cooking yesterday meant the killing of quite a few animals. I'd wrenched herbs roughly from the ground for it . . . here they scream, you know . . .' she smiled mischievously at him, 'men had worked hard to press grapes for wine for it, poor Spaniards who have to leave their wives and children and cross the Pyrenees, poor pigs had their feet cut off for it, a goose had its neck wrung for it . . .'

'Stop,' he said, 'you bloodthirsty girl.'

'It's part and parcel of life. I keep close to my roots. It makes it easier.'

'What I'll do,' he said, as if he wasn't too interested in her philosophy, 'is to tell Tricia we're in love as soon as I get back. That it was inevitable, a once-in-a-lifetime chance for us, that we have to be selfish about it.' He looked at her. 'How do you think she'll take it?'

'She won't commit suicide, she isn't the type, but it may shatter her for a time. You were her escape.' His brows were drawn together, his face was longer, leaner. 'And she'll hate me.'

'You think so?'

'I should hate me if I were Tricia.' She didn't want him to wallow in self-pity. 'Don't forget I shall have to do the same to Guy.'

'Yes . . .' He was *distrait*.

'Poor Guy, I have been his only happiness, no, that is not true, he loves his children and *Derain et Cie*, but I've been his only joy. I shall have to give up my flat, my weekends here where I love to be, my job . . .'

He looked at her. 'What are you talking about?' This is how he'd be at work, brusque, almost rude. She was impatient with him, like a wife. *Toujours la politesse*, she wanted to say but it was too soon for that.

'I must make it easy for Guy, keep his self-respect intact. He's grown used to our arrangement. He jokes and says he'll miss the flat and my cooking when it's all over, but it isn't so. I prop him up. The flat is his refuge, just as St Henri is mine. If I say I have accepted a more important job in Paris, that will make it easier for him.'

'But you don't want to go to Paris.'

She sighed. Men . . . 'I hate the thought of it. But there are compensations. You will come to see me there and court me, and you'll have time to think as I shall. In an important matter like this, when it is for life, I have to be courted.' He stopped her speaking by taking her strongly in his arms.

'There's a wood back there. Do you want me now?' His face was stern, dark with passion, there was no blue in his eyes. She doused her own of desire, shook her head. She'd had enough of that with René.

'I have a much better idea. We'll go back and you'll meet my parents.'

'My future parents-in-law, I hope?'

'That is a proposal of marriage?'

'It is.' He was smiling at her, sure.

'Don't tell them right away. They are country people and don't like to be rushed. If you eat my cassoulet with a good appetite that will impress them much more.'

'What am I marrying into?' His face broadened as he laughed. 'Have I to be the champion pie-eater of Maurac before I can win your hand?'

'We'll see.' She laughed with him, and then they kissed, and then they walked back to the cottage.

CHAPTER TWENTY-SIX
1977/1978

THE winter had been trying, with Clay off school a lot because of his bad chest. Since the key-ring episode he'd become quieter, but then as Jan reminded herself, he's growing up now, it would soon be his tenth birthday. It was all the more shocking, therefore, when he began to wet the bed. She'd lost her temper the first time, used words which made her eat her heart out with shame and guilt. 'Clay, honey, I'm sorry, sorry for what I said.' He wouldn't look at her, and she only knew he'd gone out of the apartment when she heard the door bang.

She'd waited in terror at the window most of the day, telling herself, he'll be with the other kids somewhere, it'll be all right. When she saw him coming along the street with George her heart lifted and then plummeted again. He'd gone to George. It was she who'd had to deal with the sodden sheets and pyjamas in the basement wash-place, who had to put up with other women's suspicious looks.

Around March, when it was still happening, George said it would have to be brought out into the open. 'You started something with that key-ring of yours,' he said. 'He knew how much you valued it.' She was astounded at being accused like this. 'He was worried sick that we wouldn't find it. You gave him your problem.'

He brought the subject up one supper-time, in a light way. When he smiled now his cheeks went into folds. Sometimes his face looked like a black man's skull, especially when he came in cold from the street and his blackness had turned grey. 'It's no big deal this. More boys do it than you think. We're constructed differently.' She saw the old gleam in his eyes, there so seldom.

266

'I know that.' She was being put in the wrong again. 'I'm sorry if I blew up that first time, Clay.' She'd called him 'a stinking brat.' 'As George says, it's no big deal.' He struggled to get out of his chair. George put a hand out and held him where he was.

'You sit there. You've been sick with bronchitis most of the winter, in bed more than usual. This has become a medical problem. Tomorrow Momma will take you to see the doctor.'

'Will he fix it?'

'Sure as hell he'll fix it. They've got pills for everything nowadays. A dose of those pills and you'll find it difficult to go to the men's room even in the day-time.' Clay didn't laugh. 'Now you're doing really good at school, and we want you fighting fit for Mr Newton, so you just go with Momma tomorrow and see Dr Fixit.'

'You won't tell Mr Newton why I'm going, George?'

'What do you take me for? You tell him it's the aftermath of your chest troubles that took you to the Doc.'

'Is that what it is? The aftermath?'

'Sure. You don't think you've sprung a leak, do you? It's the doctor's office you're going to, not the plumber's.'

Clay started to giggle hysterically, the tears running down his face. He kept on eating his corn and hash, shovelling it in through his tears. George spoke casually. 'I'm planning to take a trip to Bear Mountain when I get some time off. The boat goes under the bridge at Tapanzee. That's some bridge. Want to come?'

The boy looked up through his tears, his eyes shining. 'Bear Mountain? I've read about that.'

'We'll have a picnic,' George said.

Jan looked at her son's face, her eyes stinging. 'Well, who's for pie?' She tried to smile, to sound as light as lemon chiffon.

The doctor examined him and said there was nothing physically wrong, then told Clay to go into the waiting-room and look at some comics. He was young, black, and new to the district. Jan thought he was almost too sure of himself.

'This is not uncommon, Mrs Cook,' he said. 'The boy's all right where it matters. He must be worried about something. How about school?'

267

'He loves school. He's bright. And his teacher and he are really close. No, it can't be that.' She thought he hadn't started off very well.

'No trigger?' She thought of the key-ring.

'No, no trigger.'

'How do you and your husband get along, for instance? Any problems except the obvious one? You're white and he's black.' *You gave him your problem* . . .

'That's never worried me.' He made her feel defensive. 'My parents, naturally, at first . . .'

'They objected, did they?'

'I met George in Paris when we were both studying. Clay was born there.' And then, 'We aren't married.'

'Does Clay know that?'

'I don't know. It would mean nothing to him.'

'Do your parents?'

'Parent. My father died last fall. I wanted to go visit him but we . . . well, we couldn't afford it at the time.'

'So you took it out on the boy's father?' He laughed to show he was making a joke. She was beginning to dislike him. He's defending George because they're both black, she thought, although he knows nothing about it. Mother always said they stick together, blacks . . .

'I did nothing of the kind,' she said, speaking like Ettie. 'George has enough worries. He's got a job that doesn't pay well, and he works really hard, studying as well. Sometimes he has to stay late at the office, making his reports . . .' She saw the gleam in the doctor's brown eyes. Ruth, she types the reports. This man was making her thinking stupid . . . 'He's dog-tired when he gets in. Then we live in this crummy apartment. It's so different from my own home. There's a kind of . . . airiness . . . and space there.'

'Wealthy background, have you?' he said easily.

'I didn't mean that. Well, I guess so. But it's the country I miss. Somehow it didn't matter so much living in Paris, but New York last summer . . . that was really something.'

'They come every year, summers. You just have to get used to them. Unless you want to go back home?'

'No. My mother would like it, I guess, and she gets lonely

268

but, no, I wouldn't leave them. Clay likes it here. He really loves his school.'

'He really loves his school,' the doctor said. 'Well, then, if he loves his home just as much there's nothing to worry about, is there?' He got up as if he'd had enough of her. 'Come and see me again in a month with the boy.'

'Aren't you going to give him any pills? George told Clay he'd get pills.'

'Did he now?' He stroked his sparse goatee beard which seemed to have grown by accident on his young black face. 'Well, he's the psychiatrist.' He bent down, wrote rapidly on a prescription pad and gave it to her. 'These are only sugar, but tell Clay they'll work if he takes one every night before he goes to bed. Okay?'

'Thanks,' she said. She felt mystified, cheated, as if he'd been prescribing for her, not Clay.

'And what I'm going to tell you,' what a sing-song voice he had, 'is that a boy of ten isn't ready to shoulder grownup problems so you just try and be happy, okay?' He dismissed her by sitting down abruptly and beginning to write at his desk.

It took a long time to clear up, but once they were into spring and Clay could play in the streets with the neighbourhood kids it was almost gone. If it did happen occasionally, she gathered up the wet pyjamas and sheets and got them out of sight as quickly as possible.

She didn't keep happy as the doctor advised her. How could she? She'd taken Clay to visit his grandmother at the Easter vacation, and the sight of the broad park, the white façade of Cedars, but mostly the countryside around it, made her dread going back to the stuffy apartment.

'You're still living in Harlem?' Ettie said. She had grown thinner since Carl had died. She was like a bird, a small, pecking bird. 'No wonder your husband doesn't come with you to visit. I guess he's ashamed to have taken you away from all this.' Old Dorothy was in the room serving and she nodded sourly in agreement.

'He works hard, Momma. It isn't his fault. Scratching a living in New York is difficult. It's all he can do to keep his head above water.'

'Some manage it. Even Rony does well, although I wish that girl would get married. She's got a nice apartment and good clothes but . . .'

'She'll never marry, Momma.'

'You keep on saying that. Maybe when she looks at you it makes her more careful. No, I shouldn't say that, honey.' Her hands were like blood-tipped claws. 'Sometimes I get lonely here on my own thinking about you two girls so far away when I need you. Do you remember Miranda Wendell who came with her parents for dinner when you were here?'

'Yes.'

'Lisa, her mother, called last week, and she's just got back from the Williams' place in Kentucky visiting with her. She married the son, Bannister.'

'Banny . . .' She remembered the elegance of the dinner table that evening, the silver, the Venetian glass, the shining mahogany of the round table, the women's voices chattering, Baby Emerson, Joan Deere, Linda Jefferson, (Momma's gang), remembered Mr Wendell saying pompously, 'Jobs don't just grow on trees.'

'Harvey's running the business now since Craig had his stroke.'

'Oh.'

'We had a nice long girlie chat. She said she admired George very much and how he'd spoken up that night of the dinner party. She says she never had the nerve to cross Craig herself because he used to fly into such rages. Well, Harvey's much more amenable, and as I told her, George at least has a degree from the Sorbonne, Paris. Then he'll soon have his State Registration. It would add lustre to their practice, we both thought, a Parisian-trained lawyer. Lisa says there are some black clients who might prefer their lawyer to be the same colour. She could fix it up with Harvey, Jan. He's always been a mother's boy.'

'Fix what, Momma?'

'Get George a job in the Wendell practice. I know he said he didn't like Baltimore, but he was up against it that evening, you couldn't blame him. Over-awed . . .'

'He's never over-awed.'

270

'Look, honey, you talk it over with him. Women have to be diplomatic at times, you know what I mean. I had to work on Carl to get him to do what I wanted. Say you'd like to be out of that terrible apartment, that it's ruining your health and not doing Clay any good. He's like a skinned rabbit. And while you're looking around for a house you could come here. What do you say?'

What did she say? She looked out of the tall windows, saw the broad park, the blue gleam of the pool through the cypresses, the wide sky. 'I dread another summer in New York. It's so humid and we get bad-tempered with the heat and sometimes I feel I can't breathe. Oh, Momma . . .' she put her face in her hands.

'There, there, my darling.' Ettie got up and pressed Jan's head to her hyacinth-perfumed bosom. 'You come home and be looked after. Leave your sister to do what she likes in dirty old New York, but you come home. It will be like old times . . .'

It was like eating milk and honey. It was like being back in her childhood again, all the worries taken away, no more decisions to make. After all, she wasn't married to George. The Maryland countryside out there was like a mirage, beckoning. Clay would be able to ride, swim . . . She sat up straight, wiping her eyes. 'I'll ask him, Momma, I'll call you and tell you what he says.' Not being married to George cut both ways. She could leave him if she liked.

She told George when she got home that Harvey Wendell could fix him up with a job in Baltimore. That his father, Craig, had had a stroke and he was in charge, or that his mother was in charge. He'd come in very late looking grey as he often did, the way a white man looks pale, she thought. He listened until she had finished, and then his temper flashed like lightning.

'Are you out of your mind, just tell me that, are you out of your *mind*?'

'Keep your voice down. Clay's asleep. He waited and waited for you tonight. He says you promised to take him to Bear Mountain for a picnic. He says you were going to show him the Tapanzee Bridge . . .'

'Leave Clay out of it. I haven't forgotten. But have *you*

271

forgotten that dinner party with those stuffed shirts and those macaw-like women and all of them patronising me? And Craig saying jobs don't grow on trees! *Their* trees. Have you forgotten what *I* said?'

'No, I haven't, but . . .'

'What was it, what did I say?'

'Don't shout at me! Every word you say isn't molten gold. I don't treasure every sentence that falls from your lips. You told them you didn't like Baltimore or something like that.'

'Great, great! Well, it still goes. Nor do I like being put up and patronised by your mother. I suppose she offered you that again?'

'Just till we get ourselves sorted out. Why are you so selfish? You never give me a thought, nor Clay. You promise him things and then don't keep your word. You know the city doesn't suit him, look at the trouble we've had, you know I hate this apartment, that I dread the thought of another summer cooped up here with the smell of rotten garbage and stink rising from the street . . .'

'Who's shouting now? And you know you're talking lies. Clay likes it here. And he'll get to Bear Mountain when I get the money together. We could all be happy if you'd accept it. I'll get a better job. I'll work myself up in the one I've got. It isn't so bad . . .'

'Especially with Ruth there,' she said. She saw the greyness leave his face. It became a deep plum colour.

'What's that you said?'

She shouted because she was afraid. 'I said especially with Ruth there, typing your reports for you, making it pleasant to come back to in the evenings so that you don't bother to hurry home to me . . .' he came towards her and she backed away from him.

'I'll kill you if you don't stop that!' He grabbed her by the shoulders and shook her till her head was ringing. 'Don't you ever say that again, just don't ever open your mouth and say that again! When I think how I work . . . and just you get right to that telephone in the hall and call your mother. Say I *still* don't like Baltimore!' He shouted the words at the pitch of his voice. 'And if you like, say that since you aren't married

272

you'll come and live in stately old Cedars with your dear old Momma. But one thing I'm telling you . . .' he came towards her again but this time he didn't touch her. *'You aren't going to take Clay!'* She went running out of the room and fell over Clay who was sitting in the passage in his pyjamas.

'What's making George angry, Momma?' he said.

'Nothing, nothing . . . get back to bed.'

'We're all right here. The doctor fixed it . . .' his eyes slid away from hers for a second, 'and there's the kids, and Mr Newton, and George coming in for supper. Doesn't matter if he's late, and sure we'll get round to going to Bear Mountain. George said it. He's okay.' She stumbled over his legs and opened the outside door of the apartment, ran for the stairs.

*   *   *

When she got back George was sitting on Clay's bed telling him some outlandish story about a man on the subway. 'It was in his pen pocket, this white mouse. Every now and then this little pink nose would come up then it would burrow down again.'

'Why did it do that, George? Come up?'

'What a question to ask. It wanted to see which station they were at. Didn't you know mice can read?' He looked up and saw her standing at the door. 'Well, did you call Miss Ettie?'

'Yes, I said you didn't like Baltimore.'

'That's that then. So you're going to stay on with Clay and me in little ole New York?'

'Yes. In US of A.'

'Great. Tell you what. Tomorrow when I get back we'll have a picnic in Central Park. Get us into training for Bear Mountain. I'm working on that, kid, just as soon as I can take a whole day off.'

'I can wait, George,' Clay said.

'I know you can. So we'll go to Central Park meantime.' He looked at Jan, the old gleam in his eyes. 'There's a folk group, all white boys. You'd like that, huh?'

She ran to him and he put his arms round her. She heard him

273

say to Clay while she wept. 'This little ole Momma we have is sure a heap o' trouble, but we kinda like her all the same.'

'Yea.' He sounded tired out.

'And we're going to stay like a happy family right here till I can get more bread and then we'll buy a ritzy house on, maybe, Fire Island.'

'I like it round here, George. We don't have to move.'

'Now, you've got to have more ambition than that. Folks would think you'd been brought up in the sticks. You've got to be more like your Momma.'

But in bed later he didn't joke. He made love to her silently, and his face was wet with tears.

CHAPTER TWENTY-SEVEN

It was August now, and one of the hottest days of the summer. She'd left the apartment at the same time as George in the morning so that she could shop while it was still cool.

'I'll make something really good for tonight,' she told him. 'Iced fruit cup to start with, and a chicken salad, and maybe a dessert. They've got a meringue one in the supermart.'

'Right,' he said. 'That'll keep me cool, just thinking of it. See you honey.' He'd strode away from her, thin as a bean-pole, but still broad-shouldered, his brief-case banging against his skinny legs.

There was no sun. It was buried somewhere in the yellow blanket that was the sky. There was only the humid heat suffocating her, so that she went around the apartment like an animal looking for a cool place to be. Even Clay didn't want to play with the kids. A lot of them were on holiday including his best friend, Baseball, and he mooched about the apartment getting in her way.

'For goodness sakes, Clay, find something to do,' she said, exasperated. 'Couldn't you read a story, or write one? Didn't Mr Newton say your essays were good?'

'It's too hot to do any of those things.' He looked grey-pale, like George.

'Well, put some chairs out on the balcony. Or, look, stir this for me.' She had emptied cans of lemon and orange concentrate, two bottles of ginger ale and a tin of what was called 'Hawaian Punch' into a large bowl. 'It's a new kind of drink. I read the recipe in a magazine.'

'What's it called, Momma?'

'Punchbowl Delight. It should be really good.'

'Do I get to have any?'

'Well, maybe a small glassful. That Hawaian Punch was bought in that liquor store, remember.'

'I'd get drunk?'

'No, not drunk, it's too well diluted, just a bit tipsy.' You've got to be tipsy to live in this place, she thought. Her head ached, her period was due, and she felt the usual deepseated discomfort in her loins, and the tension. On an impulse she said, 'You go on stirring and I'll go call Rony. Maybe she could come over and help us drink it.'

'That's a good idea, Momma.' His voice sounded lively at the mention of his aunt.

At six o'clock Rony arrived in a sleeveless black top and tightly elegant trousers of white linen. Her makeup had an orange glow which teamed with her hair, a bit weird, Jan thought, but it suited her. As usual she was full of life.

'Hi, Clay. How's every little thing?'

'Just great, Aunty Rony. I'm glad you stopped by. Momma's made a special punch for George coming home.'

'She has?' She collapsed in a chair, her long legs straight out in front of her. Jan could see the beaded moustache of sweat on her upper lip.

'If you could stay for supper it would be just fine,' she said. 'It's a celebration.'

'What for?'

'That I stay alive, I guess. Could you, Rony? I've got a chicken salad ready in the icebox and a meringue dessert.'

'I'd love to, but it's impossible. I'm heading out to Long Island tonight. A friend's joining me. I have to pick her up at her apartment in an hour.'

'Well, never mind.' She sighed. 'Long Island . . . the ocean . . . come outside anyhow and we'll have some of this punch Clay's talking about.'

The heat on the balcony was overpowering, and yet perversely Jan wanted to be outside. The apartment had depressed her all day with its dingy drapes which cried out to be renewed, and the stale smells from all the previous tenants which seemed to be trapped in it. She couldn't stand the bathroom. There was a perpetual smell of urine there which all the bleaching and disinfectants she used failed to shift. Once, scrubbing away, she remembered a girl saying at school. 'Black people's urine is stronger. Did you know that? More yellow. Something to do with the colour of their skin.'

They sat on chairs and sipped the punch, Clay being allowed a little as well. He sipped and tipped back his chair against the railings of the balcony the way George did. 'I went to see mother at Easter,' Jan said. 'I guess I told you.'

'No.' Rony looked surprised. 'How did you find her?'

'The same. A little pathetic. I think she's lonely.'

'She said she would buy me a pony if I came to live there,' Clay said to Rony.

'That's some offer.'

'Yea, if you like riding. I'm like George, scared to death of horses. I guess I'm truly urban.'

'Yea?'

'He's heard George saying that,' Jan said. 'He repeats everything he says.'

'We're going to Bear Mountain for a picnic, just as soon as George can get a whole day off.'

'If pigs could fly,' Jan said.

'What does that mean, Momma?'

'Sometime never.' She met Rony's level gaze, felt ashamed. 'Yes, I thought she was missing us. Well, it stands to reason, without Poppa . . .'

'She's got heaps of friends, and Dorothy. Is old sourpuss still there?'

'She says she doesn't like boys. They're coarse and rough,' Clay said.

'Dorothy's getting on.' She looked at Rony, trying to win her favour again. 'She used to say she was going back to Vermont to retire, but she can't bring herself to it now. Cedars means more to her than Vermont.'

'Cedars,' Rony said, 'is like one of those flowers . . . I forget their name . . . but if anything settles on them, like an insect, they fold in on themselves and suck it right in. A kind of vampire flower.' She sipped from her glass. 'Ettie, it has just dawned on me, is a vampire flower.'

Clay giggled. 'Ettie is a vampire flower,' he repeated.

'Stop that!' Jan was annoyed at both of them. 'I'm surprised at you talking like that, Rony. You've got really hard since you came to live in New York. As a matter of fact, Momma thinks about us a lot. She would like you to get married.'

'What are you niggling for, Jan? You know perfectly well I'll never be married. Why don't you tell her?'

'Tell her what?' She met her sister's eyes and looked away. She didn't need an answer. 'Anyhow,' she cleared her eyes, 'she's been speaking to Lisa Wendell, and Craig had a stroke, you know, and Harvey Wendell is running the business now.'

'That whitened sepulchre? God!'

'Lisa thinks they could easily fix up a job for George in Baltimore.'

'I hope you told her it was no use fixing up anything for George in Baltimore or anywhere else. That woman's a tryer. Are you never going to learn, Jan? I credited you with a lot of sense when you met George in Paris and stayed there. You haven't got the guts to stand up to mother. Your only hope is to keep well away from her or you'll get sucked in too . . .' She stopped to look at Clay. 'Hey! Your eyes are shining . . . yea, you'll get sucked in by the vampire flower. What do you say, Clay?'

'George doesn't want to go to Baltimore. He likes it here. I like it here. Baseball, that's my best friend, is on vacation right now, but once he comes back it will be fine.'

'That's great.' She nodded at Jan as if to say, 'See how lucky you are,' sighed and jumped to her feet. 'I've got to go. We were supposed to hit the trail at seven o'clock and it's that time already.' She looked at her watch. 'Gee whiz, five past. Will George be in soon?'

'Any time now,' Jan said.

'I'm sorry I have to miss him, but give him my best. 'Here, Clay,' she fished in her pocket-book and brought out a five dollar bill, 'put that towards a glove ready for Baseball coming back.'

'Thanks, Aunt Rony. Say, that's too much. Isn't it, Momma?' His eyes were pleading, anxious.

'If your aunt cares to throw five dollar bills about like paper who am I to say? You go downstairs and see her to her car. You might run into George.' She smiled at Rony. 'Sorry I was

278

needly.' She pressed her hands on her stomach.

'Sure. But remember the vampire flower bit, Clay. Come on. There's a project for you during your vacation. Get yourself to the library and look up the name of the flower that eats insects. I'd surely like to know.'

* * *

When Clay came back alone they carried out the chicken salad to the table on the balcony, laid plates, knives and forks beside it. The meringue dessert was to remain in the icebox until George came in. 'Sometimes when you dish up food it makes them come. Grandmother used to say that when I lived at Cedars.'

She offered Clay some of the chicken salad but he refused, although his eyes dwelt hungrily on it. She flicked over a magazine feeling the tension swell and grow inside her with the ache in her pelvis. She heard a noise and saw Clay with his feet on the bottom rung of the chair-back, trying to peer over the rail. 'Clay!' She shouted at him because of the ache. 'Don't do that. It's dangerous.'

'The back makes a ladder. I was trying to see George.'

'Well don't. He'll be along any minute.' She filled up her glass.

'Can I have some, Momma?'

'Just a little.' Rony had said it was as weak as water, that she'd been done by the liquor store with the so-called Hawaian Punch. The stuff now had an unpleasant metallic taste, probably from the inside of the cans. He spoiled everything, George. All this expensive food and drink going to waste in the heat. At Cedars there was a cool porch at the back of the house with an electric fan, and the cedars cast a welcome shade. The painting of the house in the hall showed their tops above the roof . . .

At nine o'clock the light had turned to a dull copper. She and Clay were silent, listening to the noises around them, the street noises, someone's radio blaring out an old Beatles song, 'She loves me . . .' It made Jan think of Paris when she and George had first met, those parties in the high old buildings of

Montparnasse, the staccato French chatter. He was suddenly there, his smile gleaming in the semi-darkness.

'George!' Clay was just as suddenly wide-awake.

'Hi, fella. Hi, Jan. Say, you're never going to believe this. The subway broke down between Lennox Avenue and 135th. We had to sit for an hour while they mended it. Was I mad?'

'Was the man with the mouse in his pen-pocket there?'

'No, worse luck.' He flung himself down on his chair. He looked worn to death, as if in greeting them he had expended what energy he had left.

'You seem to attract bad luck,' Jan said. 'Let's have this chicken salad. I covered it with a napkin but goodness knows what it will taste like now.'

'It's a special treat. I helped Momma set it out here.' Clay's vitality made his father look sucked dry. 'Aunt Rony came, George. She didn't wait too long. I went down to the street with her hoping we'd see you.'

'Well, it was that subway, I told you, and then I had to get my reports typed up.'

'By Ruth,' Jan said. She poured a glass of punch and gave it to him. Their eyes met.

'There is only Ruth, or rather, only Ruth who's willing to stay on. All the kids want to get off by five.'

'Is she old, then?' The ache was like a hurting ball between her legs.

'The same age as you.'

'Black?'

'Yea, black. Isn't everybody? Say, what is this, an inquisition?' He took a long, deep drink, sighed. 'That's good, that's really good. Now I know why you're so full of pep, Clay. This has got enough punch in it to knock over a horse and cart.'

'Is that why it's called punch?' He giggled. He went on and on, snorting and snuffling.

'Clay, stop that!' Jan shouted. 'You're behaving like a fool. Now pull in your chair and eat your food. It's spoiled, but eat it!'

'Okay, Momma.' His eyes slid to her, slid away again.

'So what was your Aunt Rony saying?' George asked, his face grim.

'Can't remember.' Clay muttered into his food.

'Didn't she give you a project?' Jan said.

'Yea, that's right, she gave me a project, George. She says I've to go to the library and find out what the flower's called that eats insects that land on it.'

'Isn't that really something?' George was pretending to be interested. Or was he really interested? Everyone wasn't as mixed up and complex as she was. 'I used to know that flower. I remember reading about it. Maybe it will come to me. Why does she want to know that?'

'It was something to do with grandmother and her house, wasn't it, Momma? Momma, I'm not hungry. I don't like this chicken salad.' He got off the stool he'd been sitting on and went back to his chair.

'Who said you were to leave the table?'

'Leave him, Jan, leave him. It's past his bedtime. Let him sit there while we have ours. When I've finished mine I'm going to start on your chicken salad, Clay. Say, thanks a lot for deciding not to eat it.' He grinned his great empty melon grin.

She meant shining melon grin, surely. She would have said shining melon grin last year. The whole disappointment of the evening was crystallised in the mess of chicken and corn and peppers in the middle of the table.

'I'll tell you why you don't like it,' she said, raising her voice, looking across at Clay where he sat. 'It's hung around too long waiting for your precious George to decide to come home. Okay, okay, it'll all go into the garbage bin where it belongs. And don't you eat it either.' George had lifted his knife and fork. 'You've most likely had a snack with Ruth in any case when you were dictating your reports, like a hamburger, or a toasted sandwich . . .' She saw his eyes, saw that he mouthed, 'Bitch.'

'Cool it.' He turned to speak to Clay who was sitting behind him. 'About that vampire flower, it's coming back to me. I'm beginning to get vibes.'

Now he was ignoring her. She screamed at him. 'You're getting at my mother now, don't think I don't know it! That's why you're bringing it up, to get at Momma. You think Rony was very clever, don't you, to use that analogy, is that the word . . . pardon me, but I've been out of the world so long . . . that idea about Momma being a vampire flower? Well, she isn't the only one. There's the same situation right here! I've been sucked into it, taken in by a lot of fancy talk and pillow talk, dumped in this trash-heap which you know I can't bear in summer . . .'

George pushed back his chair, got up, came round the table towards her. She backed away from his smile. 'Cool it, honey, huh?' His voice was quiet. 'You're only raising your temperature. The way to stand up to the New York heat is to play it cool, not to get yourself in a hassle. Accept it. You accepted far worse in Paris.'

'Paris was different. I was young. Everything was good in Paris. Far from Momma. There was just you, then you and Clay. You should have seen that, you shouldn't have brought me back.'

'God Almighty,' his voice was still quiet, 'you wanted to come.'

'I can't stand it here. It's so ugly. The ugliness gets at my insides, the dirt and the squalor and nothing happening. You're away all the time . . . enjoying yourself . . .'

'I'm away working for us! You know that. I keep telling you it'll be all right!'

'The days are too long. I feel isolated. I can't wait. I could have waited in Baltimore, but not in this place. It stinks in summer, all the time it stinks . . .' he was suddenly shouting at her, the quietness gone.

'Bloody well put up with it.' His face was ugly, thick lips, flaring nostrils. 'You can't leave me because of Clay. You'd lose him. You know that. You're trapped. In a cage way up on the seventh floor in Harlem, New York, US of A. We all know you'd like to go back to Cedars. We're sick and tired hearing about it. You're never off the subject.' He was close to her, blocking her way. She could only see his broad black shoulders covered by the light suit he washed at the Automat himself every week.

'I called Momma and said you didn't want to go to Baltimore, didn't I?' She heard herself whining, thought, this isn't me, it's the tension . . .

282

'How long ago was that? Three whole months. And was that the matter closed, the book shut on the dear old Maryland saga? Not on your life! The first hot day we get you're whining on and on about the heat, making everybody hotter just listening to you, just looking at you with your hair all anyhow and your miserable face . . .'

'And Ruth's isn't miserable, is that it? Now we're getting right into it!' This tension was going to kill her. She couldn't stand it a second longer, she had to find something really bad to hurt him with, something that would make him stop getting at her. She was all right if he could only see it. She loved him under all this, this . . . but she had to be kind of cosseted, nursed through the bad times like when it was too hot . . . 'Oh, came the dawn!' She waved her hands, deliberately dramatic, 'Realisation at last! Oh, yes, I get it now. Ruth's face isn't miserable because she's black! Why didn't I see it before? Well, all I can say it's a great damn pity Clay wasn't yours and hers . . .' she had to take a breath, 'instead of mine!'

'You're out of your mind.' He was shaking his head at her, a look of stupid bewilderment on his face.

'All right. I'm out of my mind.' She clutched her hair. She would act like a mad woman, then, since she was out of her mind. 'What am I to do?' She heard herself moaning. 'I'm trapped, trapped, trapped . . . I can't live my life the way I want to. I'm torn here in New York because Maryland is near. It was better in Paris. Ah, yes, you're right. Rony was right. She said I should have stayed there. It's terrible not knowing what you really want to do . . .' she must stop this moaning somehow. It wasn't really her, it was some demon inside her, ' . . . terrible when you can't make people see it. Do you know, George,' thank God she was weeping now, not moaning, 'sometimes I wish I'd never *seen* you. Or Clay.' What was she *saying?* Clay was her love, her life . . .

In the silence there was a thin, high scream. She was frozen, watched George swing round. She made herself raise her head. Watch him lunge forward at Clay who was balancing on the top rung of the chair-back. Watch Clay topple out of their sight, quietly, before George could reach him. He just wasn't there any more. She looked, looked, *looked,* her hands on either side of her head where she had been clutching her hair. The chair was *empty*. Its back was tilted against the rails of the balcony. *Don't do that . . . it's dangerous . . .* she'd warned him, warned him. A great wave of shock brought her to her knees. Her stomach lifted. 'George!' she screamed at him. He was like a stone image, then suddenly his lips were moving.

'God tell me it hasn't happened God tell me it hasn't happened God tell me . . .' It was like a jungle chant. He clutched the rails, looked over. She heard him retch. Then he turned, not looking at her and went like a blind man towards the door, feeling for it with his hands. She flung herself down on the floor and gave way to the blackness, the despair and the desolation.

*   *   *

A long time later she was aware of someone lifting her up, two people, and carrying her into the bedroom, laying her on the bed. She saw black faces. One belonged to the old man who lived on the ground floor and shouted at the kids, the other one to the fat woman with the gold ring earrings who sometimes spoke to her in the basement. 'George . . .' she said. She could hardly speak for the sickness. She saw the woman's thick lips open. She had splayed white teeth.

'He's gone in the ambulance with your little boy. We got it real quick. Don't you worry now, honey.'

'Don't worry!' she screamed, then feeling so sick said, 'Forgive me . . . we were talking. We got wrapped up in . . . what we were talking about. He was behind George . . . the chair had a ladder-back he'd been warned, warned . . . he's always been sensible. Maybe we expected too much. He called my . . . he called George by his first name . . . George. I couldn't see . . . broad shoulders . . . forgot about Clay . . . talking . . . I forgot . . .' She looked up and saw the doctor whom she'd gone to see with Clay. Now it didn't matter, the key-ring, clover-leaf, wasn't it, the bed-wetting. He knelt down beside her and took her arm in his black fingers. 'I'm going to give you a good shot.'

'Clay . . . ?'

'Your boy's dead. He didn't stand a chance.'

'I saw him,' the old man said, 'flat as a . . .'

'Hold your mouth,' the doctor said. And to Jan. 'You're going to sleep now, Mrs Cook. When you waken up you'll have to deal with it, but have a sleep now . . . have a sleep now . . .'

She opened her mouth and started to scream. She saw the fat woman move in to hold her down. She screamed and screamed . . .

CHAPTER TWENTY-EIGHT

At the beginning of September 1978, the Latham Property Trust went public. It would have happened long before but Mr Deakin had always said he saw no commercial reason to go for public flotation, and Howard had eventually given up trying to persuade him. 'If anything happens to me, Howard,' he'd said often, 'you can do what you like.' In the event Howard had gone first.

They had missed the boat, the accountants in Latham, headed by Bob Pritchard, had decided. If old Deakin had given into Howard in the early sixties when a stream of privately-owned companies were queuing up to go into the stock market, they would have avoided Capital Gains Tax. Now they'd be as well to remain as they were.

But Bob Pritchard and his laissez-faire attitudes had been replaced by the new young accountants based in the London office. The issue accordingly opened for public subscription and was successfully completed, not without his knowledge, certainly, but perhaps without his blessing. He was tucked away in the provinces. He was past his prime.

Jake was elected Company Chairman, Bob Pritchard retired, and after a fairly rocky passage in the stocks straits, the Trust had settled down and continued to do as it had done before with such success, kept out of commercial property dealing and traded only in residential estates.

Jake's work in securing the new estate at Nottingham had been instrumental in gaining him his appointment. It was causing a furore amongst the more traditional type of planners. He had read, thought, planned, travelled widely, and with his own original ideas he was well thought of in the vanguard of Garden City development.

Tricia was immensely proud of him. In him she'd found a man who seemed to answer her every need. He was sexually mature, hardheaded, supremely confident. He gave her everything she had always dreamed of. If there was one flaw it was that she didn't see enough of him, for business with him always came before love. Sometimes she wondered if it was she who made the running. Once, desperate, she'd rung him at his flat to fix a meeting, after Roger was in bed.

'I'm not too much for you?' she'd asked him when they met, but he hadn't answered her directly. She had to accept that he was the kind of man who could take a love affair in his stride, whereas she was in a tremendous state for days after she had been with him. She felt it must be apparent to everybody.

The last time they'd been together was in the middle of August, over six weeks ago. It was the longest time they had ever been apart, and she craved for him in every way. She was incomplete without him, a cypher. She had taken Emma and Mark on their annual summer holiday to Bournemouth, Jake had been in Europe, and when he'd come back he'd been thrown into the activity of the Trust going public. It had been necessary for their affair to take second place.

Had she been simply a housewife it would have been unbearable, but the days were never long enough for her. Fearful always that the children would be neglected because of her work, she ferried them to swimming, riding, parties. At the office Kingsley Heath claimed more and more of her time. It was beginning to take shape. The sense of community was already strong. It was as far removed from the housing estate type of development as it was possible to be.

She believed wholeheartedly with social reformers like Howard and Unwin that there should be a master plan so that the project shouldn't develop in a haphazard manner. The idea of each 'hamlet' being completed before moving on to the next meant that at every stage there was a degree of unity. She helped to prepare a brochure, she went up in an aeroplane when they were taking photographs.

But she wasn't blind to some of the flaws. In long letters to Jake she said he was lucky at Nottingham. He was profiting from the mistakes which had been made at Kingsley Heath.

She told him that the joy of meeting him was not only the joy of coming together physically, but the stimulation of exchanging ideas, which like the tremulousness, lasted for days afterwards. This, she told herself, is the peak of my life. I shall never feel again this keenness, this love, this intense creativity.

She was sure Roger didn't know of their affair. He had settled into the job of selling houses, a sinecure, but Roger could always find difficulties in whatever he did, make mountains out of molehills. She tried to be patient when he got sidetracked by what she considered to be trivialities. All she had left for him was a kind of affectionate pity.

She felt guilty and to remove this guilt, she realised, she must be honest and ask him for a divorce, but her relationship with Jake hadn't got to that stage. She told herself he was hesitant about breaking up her marriage because she still harboured religious scruples. But she knew she could have been persuaded, although her spirit sometimes failed her when she thought of Mark and Emma and how they would be affected. Lying sleepless at nights beside Roger, she would tell herself to be patient. Wasn't it enough that she had this richness of living in her life?

*   *   *

On a mellow Sunday morning the telephone rang at Howard's View. She was in the garden with Roger and the children, and in a mellow way, she was happy. In the garden Roger was at his best. In nine or ten months he'd made it a thing of beauty, smooth lawns, beds of flowers, rock formations, a boldness of line and intention he didn't show in his own life. She was admiring a clump of petunia pink asters he'd grown at her request.

'Mummy, the phone!' It was Emma, standing up to wave. She and Mark were playing with the Wilkes' children at the lakeside.

'I heard it!'

'My hands are dirty. Will you get it?' Roger straightened,

holding them up. A colourless lock of hair hung over his brow. He looked like his mother.

She ran towards the house. Mary came for lunch every Sunday, but always rang to make sure she 'wasn't in the way'.

'Hello,' she said, lifting the receiver in the hall.

'Tricia?'

She knew the voice. 'Oh, Jake . . . where are you phoning from?'

'London. I'm sorry I haven't replied to your letters. I've been tied down by all the spadework over the shares, and before that I've been abroad . . .'

'Yes, I know.' She wouldn't say he might have sent a postcard at least. She looked round, lowered her voice. 'Jake, I've missed you . . .' She had to sit down. Her heart was thudding against her ribs. She waited. It was his turn. There was a pause. Then . . .

'I didn't want to write. I'm hopeless at it anyhow. I've something to say to you, something important.'

'Have you?' Now the thudding was in her ears. She could hardly hear him.

'Could you come to London? They'd all be glad to see you in any case. Everybody's excited about the way the shares have gone.'

'So am I. I'd like to meet the whizz-kid who brought it off.' She tried hard to be business-like, cool.

'Ronald Asyl. He's a good man.'

'I'm intrigued about why you should want to talk to me . . .' He'd made up his mind to persuade her to marry him, ask Roger for a divorce. He'd had time to think about it. There would be a lot to discuss, the children, how to tell Roger . . . obviously it couldn't be done by letter.

'Look, Tricia,' he was business-like, or eager? 'Let's fix the day and time now.'

'Okay. Monday I've all-day meetings with architects and town council people.' She was glad she could appear not too eager. 'Tuesday?'

'Right.'

'Shall I meet you in the office?'

'I shan't be there, unfortunately. I've an appointment. Tell

289

you what, meet me at our restaurant. Eight o'clock.'

'I could go to your flat.' She didn't like the idea of the restaurant, intimate as they'd found it, as a place to talk over such important matters.

'No, I mayn't be back there in time. Get a taxi to Tottenham Court Road. Okay?'

'You're a tyrant.' She spoke softly into the mouthpiece. 'I love you.'

'I . . .' his words were lost. He'd been cut off.

'Who was it?' Roger said when she went back into the garden.

'Some dreary woman about running a Play Group in the Health Centre. Fancy ringing here.'

'I thought you liked to be available at all times.' Was he giving her some of her own medicine? But he was bent over the rockery.

'Yes, I do, of course I do. But Sunday . . .' She was amazed at her own perfidy. 'Children!' she called, so that she would distract him. 'Who's coming in the car to fetch Granny Newton?' The guilt was back. As she walked across the lawn she knew there was only one thing which would banish it, and that was to be with Jake, to share the power, the pleasure and the abundance of her love.

*   *   *

She spent a lot of time deciding on what to wear for London. She wanted him to be overwhelmed, to be more in love with her than ever. But she had to be in the office first, she had her role of business-woman as well as lover to play. And didn't she now hold one-sixth of the new shares? At barely twenty-nine she was a wealthy woman.

She bought a belted coat in South Molten Street, brown with a black fox trimming, chose a black dress to wear under it with a bronze velvet cravat tucked in at the neckline. 'Exactly like your eyes,' the woman said. 'You know how to make the most of your best feature.'

She enjoyed herself in the London office. All the men there were about twenty years younger than those in the Latham office, and the combination of respect and admiration in their eyes was heady stuff. She stayed on until six with Ronald Asyl talking about shares. She wanted to be able to discuss the new development intelligently with Jake.

'Jake calculated almost to a penny what they'd be worth on the open market,' Asyl said. 'He's got a flair, that chap, a real Renaissance man, good at everything he touches. The Stock Exchange adviser corroborated his figure and they're holding more or less at Jake's price. That's all we ask for.'

'So his appointment was unanimous?' she asked.

'No, but the ayes have it. He doesn't suffer fools gladly. You probably know that. If he has anything unpleasant to tell you he wades right in. People who can't take this get the sharp edge of his tongue.'

'He's better off here than in Latham,' she said. 'It was too small a pond for him.'

'Well, if there's someone like you running things we don't have to worry, eh? Brains and beauty.'

'They never tell me that in Latham. I'm glad I came.'

'I could tell you more. How about a drink after a hard day's work?'

'And charge it up to LPT?' She enjoyed the admiration in his eyes. It stimulated her, prepared her, in a way, for meeting Jake. And it was very agreeable to be taken to the Caprice by such a smart young man, to have a Campari soda, to flirt mildly in between business talk and to be put in a taxi at half-past seven because she said she had a dinner engagement.

'I'm surprised your husband lets you out of his sight,' Ronald Asyl said when they were shaking hands. 'I wouldn't.' She thought his eyes were more knowing than they should be.

Jake was waiting for her in the cocktail bar. They kissed briefly, and then she excused herself, saying she had to tidy up. Her eyes were deep, luminous, when she looked in the mirror, her face pale. She thought without vanity that she'd never looked better. When she came back to the bar he helped her off with the successful coat and they sat down facing each other.

'Jake,' she said, overcome at the sight of him, stretching her hands across the table to him, 'Jake . . . why do we need to eat?' The bar waiter was at her elbow, holding out the menu.

'What would you like to drink, madame?' His smile was friendly. 'Nice to see you again.'

'A Campari soda, please.'

'The same for me,' Jake said, and when the man went away. 'He recognised you. No wonder. People don't forget those eyes in a hurry.'

'I'm being showered with compliments today, and Campari sodas. Ronald Asyl gave me a drink at the Caprice.'

'I'm not surpised. You look more beautiful every time I see you.'

'If I am it's being in love, my darling. When Ronald was singing your praises I had such a sense of loving pride. I wanted to break in and say to him, "He's mine. We love each other." Sometimes I want the whole world to know. Don't you?'

'Two Campari sodas.' The waiter was there again with a tray and the two drinks. 'Have you chosen, madame?'

'Yes, thank you.' She hadn't looked at the menu. 'Cantaloupe and trout, please.'

'Sir?'

'Salad and a filet steak. Medium rare.'

She laughed up at the man. 'All your wonderful chef's efforts are wasted on us.'

He shook his head. 'It takes a good chef to cook plain fare well with no sauces.'

'Oh, but I insist on my shrimps.' She was talkative with joy.

'You should try *sauce des amandes* for a change, madame.'

'No, thanks. I can't be coaxed.' She was almost flirting with him. He took the menus, bowed and went away. She smiled at Jake. 'All French waiters try to direct your eating.'

'I was in France.'

'Yes, and Sweden, and America.' She teased him. 'Really, it's too bad you should get all the perks while I have to stay in Latham and earn the money to pay for them.'

'I work for my perks, don't forget. I've got a lot to tell you about Garden Cities, *Cité-jardin*, *Gartenstadt*, *Tuinstad*, to name but a few variations on the theme.'

'Tell me later,' she said. 'I'd rather hear about this important thing we have to talk about. It's silly, Jake . . . when I heard your voice I thought I was going to have a heart attack. I had to sit down on the chair in the hall. And when I went back to the garden I told Roger it was a woman about a Play Centre. The lie swam into my consciousness and I let it out without feeling the merest smidgeon of guilt, or almost . . .'

'D'you still feel guilty about cheating Roger?' She didn't like the word. It was like a splash of cold water.

'I don't call it cheating.' She sipped her drink. 'I haven't given away anything belonging to Roger. And he isn't able to give me what you do. It doesn't harm him either way.'

'It would harm him if you told him.'

'Yes, but that would only occur if . . .' The waiter was there again.

'Dinner is ready.' He pulled out Tricia's chair for her.

And when they'd been led to their favourite corner table and there was an element of privacy she said, 'I have the same joyous feeling as I had in Paris with Jan and Crystel. When I felt all the world was before me . . .'

'I told you I went to France.' When she looked at him his face was bleak.

'Was it that bad?' She still teased him. 'Did they overcharge you in Paris? Did it rain cats and dogs? When I was there long ago it was beautiful all the time. Or so it seems now . . .'

'I was only in Paris for two days then I went to Carcassonne. I had an idea I might write a series of articles on the first Garden City.'

'Carcassonne? But it's fortified, isn't it?'

'Yes, it is, but supposing that became the plan for the garden city of the future? The nuclear garden city? Underground fortifications, shelters, *galeries souterraines*. I had the idea I might visit and study some of the *bastides* in south-west France, Villeneuve-sur-Lot, Montauban, Villefranche-de-Rouerge . . . after all they were called new towns in the Middle Ages and the garden city is a comparatively new development . . .' His face was bleak, without the usual lively enthusiasm.

'Ronald Asyl said you were a Renaissance man.' She still spoke lightly. 'You can plan, calculate stocks and shares, write.

293

Do you paint?'

'Sometimes.'

'Play an instrument?'

'Drums at school. It would be useful in a *bastide*.' He smiled. It was all right. 'What will you have to drink?'

'Vouvray?'

'Right.' He called the waiter, reminded him to see it was properly chilled. Another waiter came and placed her melon before her.

'I feel like a pig eating this when you have nothing.'

'I'm not hungry.' His eyes were on her and she felt faint with love. Her head swam. She took one spoonful of melon and pushed it away.

'I'll wait with you,' she said. She had to swallow, sit calmly. The wine came. It was poured out, Jake tasted it, nodded, their glasses were filled.

'I should start on that,' he said. When she looked at him his face was dark, his mouth grim.

'Why?'

'It'll brace you. Go on.'

She did, swallowing with difficulty, laughed. 'Why should I need bracing?'

'I met Crystel when I was going through Maurac.'

She put down the glass, feeling a wave of relief. 'You met Crystel! You mean you called on her?'

'Yes. Remember the last time I saw her in her store? This time I called at her flat.'

'Good for you. How was she looking?'

'Lovely.' His voice was so clipped that he seemed to bite off the words as he spoke. 'She was in a white bathrobe with bare feet. She'd been cooking. But she changed.'

'Did she? Into what?'

'Trousers and jersey. Pale mauve. And shoes, pale mauve shoes.'

She laughed. 'How like Crystel. Pale mauve. She had always exquisite taste. And yet she's so beautiful, and the least vain person I've ever known.'

'Yes.' His eyes were bleaker than ever. There was a painful tuck in her heart. She felt it when she breathed.

'What did you talk about?'

'You, part of the time.'.

'Oh, I loved Cystel!' She heard herself gushing. 'To tell you the truth I used to envy her. Such beauty. And that hair . . .'

'You've no need to envy her, Tricia.' Why was he so kind? And his eyes so . . . tortured?

'It's sweet of you, but I know I can never hold a candle to her. She has a completely natural, unconscious type of beauty. She's . . . womanly in the best sense. She was womanly at nineteen.'

'Yes.'

'You were lucky to get her in.'

'Yes.' There was a pause. 'I was stopping off for the night at Maurac . . . I had to go . . .' *Had* to go? 'That place of hers . . . it's quaint, built on the side of the hill, full of character. I met Guy.'

'Her lover?' She was relieved for some reason. 'Isn't it surprising a beautiful girl like that should be wasting her time with a married man?'

'I don't think she sees it like that.'

'And I expect no one else has turned up. A small town . . .' Why was he sitting so still, and straight? 'So you couldn't take her to dinner when Guy came.'

'No, I left.'

'What a pity.' Had she meant, what a relief?

'The next day I went to see her at her parents' house . . .' The waiter came and put their food in front of them. 'Your shrimp sauce, madame,' he said, placing the silver boat to one side of her plate.

'Thank you.'

'Salad, monsieur.'

'Thank you.' He went away. A coldness had settled round her heart. The jabbing pain had gone. She would have preferred it.

'You were saying you went to see her at her parents' house?' She lifted her glass and drank slowly from it. She should have chosen a claret. It would have been warmer. 'It's a pretty village, St Henri.' she said. 'She's told me about it often. She has a great affection for her parents, and the countryside. It's an unexpected side of Crystel. She used to say she was a peasant at heart.' She met his eyes. They were full of suffering. The cold was now like a cold hand pressing on her heart, making it difficult to breathe. 'Why did you want to see her again, Jake?'

He pushed back his plate. 'How can I tell you this without seeming heartless?' She made a noise, encouraging, deprecating, it wasn't a word. 'There's no other way . . .'

'Don't . . .'

'I'd fallen in love with her. This is terrible for you.' The same awful, clipped speech . . . 'Lovely,' he had said, 'she was looking lovely . . .' 'I'd known it for years, wouldn't admit it. Then there was you, loving . . . It became clearer to me. I couldn't believe it at first. One meeting. Ridiculous. I tried to ignore it but it wouldn't be brushed aside. Even when I was loving you. The thought of Crystel began to obsess me . . . say something for God's sake.'

'Go on.' Her voice was harsh in her ears. 'Finish it.'

'There was only one way to settle it and that was to see her again. I knew when I met her it was the real thing. No doubt. I couldn't sleep all night in Maurac. Thinking of her. I literally didn't sleep!' He sounded amazed. When would *she* ever sleep again? 'The next day, I told you, I saw her at St Henri, and we talked. She feels the same.' She kept her head down. It was easier that way. It was swimming, although she'd had only two sips of wine. Like a roundabout, faster and faster . . . if she toppled sideways people in the restaurant would lift their eyebrows and say, 'She'd drunk too much . . .' 'Tricia, please, could you look at me?'

She raised her head. It was a ton weight. Her eyelids were as heavy as lead, as heavy as her heart, a dull numbing heaviness which made her brain the same, unable to think, to realise . . .

'There's no easy way to do this,' he was saying. 'It's better here. I know. I've had . . . other difficult things to do. Keeps it . . . civilised.' She wasn't interested in his views on protocol.

'This is the important thing you wanted to tell me?' She felt as if she was speaking a strange language.

'Yes.'

'That you've discovered you're in love with Crystel. And she with you?'

'Yes. It's real. It will last. We know.' The expert on love. 'But it doesn't affect how I feel about you . . .'

'Why did you make love to me?'

'You were entrancing, Tricia . . . still are. And I told you how . . .'

'You still want to sleep with me, then?' It sounded like a logical remark.

'No.' Did he wince? 'I was foolish, and now I'm being heartless . . . unavoidably. But everything has to be tidied up before we're married. We won't rush it. She'll tell Guy. She'll move to Paris. She's heartbroken too at causing you this hurt.'

'Is she?'

'She's an essentially kind person.'

'You must know her well . . . two brief visits. Or was there a night as well?'

'No.'

'You've got to marry her first?'

'Cut it out.'

'You weren't so . . . *tidy* with me. God, I shouldn't say that. I've no right . . . oh, oh . . .' the moans escaped. She bit her bottom lip so fiercely that she tasted blood, had to wipe her mouth with her handkerchief. She even managed to smile. 'Would it be terrible if I disproved your theory that a public place was the best place . . .'

'Easier. There's no best place. Nothing's good about it.' She looked at him, saw him suffering.

'I always envied Crystel, a deep-seated envy. No, it wasn't just her looks. She was complete, somehow. But I never thought, in my wildest dreams . . .'

'How could you? How could any of us? And don't envy her. Look at it logically. You and I would never have made a go of it. We're too alike.'

'How convenient. But it doesn't wash. She's a career girl too.'

'No, she isn't. She's a Frenchwoman first and foremost. She could give up her career without a backward glance.'

'So could I, if it were necessary, if I'd been asked . . .'

297

He looked away. 'That's not what I meant . . .' and then turning to her again. 'I mean it isn't important to Crystel. It is to you. When you get over this you'll agree with me. It's the only consolation I have.'

'But you've got Crystel!' Tears seemed to burst from her eyes. She mopped and mopped again, heard herself make queer, sucking noises.

'Tricia, darling,' his voice was tender, 'is there nothing between you and Roger, nothing at all? If I could feel you could make some sort of life with him . . .'

'You want everything, don't you?' Her eyes were suddenly dry, hot and burning. 'Crystel, and consolation. No guilt. Well, I can't give it to you. Roger has nothing I want. He doesn't fulfil me.' 'You look fulfilled,' Jake had said long ago in the tea-room of Kingsley House. Mark had been on her knee, his head on her breast . . . 'I class him with Emma and Mark. But they'll grow up and no longer need me, and perhaps Roger could learn . . . I came today prepared to ask him for a divorce, if you'd wanted it. I'd even got rid of my religious scruples, wasn't that nice? Ready and willing. There, I've humiliated myself enough in front of you. I would have given up anything for you.' She met his eyes, turned away. 'I can't stand any more of this. Could we go?'

'Yes.'

He took her back to his flat. She stayed the night because she was in no fit condition to go anywhere else. She abased herself. She wept and pleaded, pleaded and wept, loathing herself but unable to bear the pain of losing him, and eventually was put to bed by him and made to swallow two sleeping pills.

She slept fitfully, waking and weeping, seeing him sitting there. Once she knew she sprang up because of a dreadful shaft of pain going through her, and she knew he put his arms round her and held her. Once, lying stiffly awake she felt his hand on her cheek and she turned and kissed it. In the morning when she struggled up, her first sensation was of her heart being broken inside her, a physical sensation so enormous that she had to lie down again. But she knew by his grim face that it was true.

He brought her breakfast, helped her to get up and dress,

then saw her on to her train. She hardly spoke. She was intent on guarding her broken heart. Besides, there was nothing to say. It was over.

CHAPTER TWENTY-NINE
1978

DURING the time when her affair with Jake had been going on, Roger, a creature of habit, had continued to make love to her. At first she'd felt a burning sense of guilt, but after a time she hardly felt ashamed. 'He'll touch me there but it'll be different . . . If Jake were doing that I'd be mad with delight . . .' She used him.

All that was behind her now. In this dark winter when she'd lost Jake, Roger's timid advances became more than she could bear. And as the year dragged slowly towards another December she came to dread the obvious signals; the shower running, Roger coming into the bedroom wearing only his bath-robe, his anxious smile like his mother's, as if he expected to be rebuffed.

The fourteenth of December came. She woke to the awareness that it was exactly a year since she and Jake had made love in the empty Howard's View. It was ringed red in her diary. The whole day in the office she was tortured by thoughts of him. 'You're looking awful, Mrs Newton,' Gillian said, 'maybe you're sickening for 'flu.' At four o'clock she gave in and told Gillian she was going to collect Mark and Emma from school. No one had told her that jealously could make your bowels run like water, give you a constant feeling of nausea.

The children's delight at seeing her only added to her misery. Had she been neglecting them in the last year? Parky had left because there was another baby coming. The woman they now had in the house, Mrs Cooper, a widow, was efficient but devoid of a sense of humour.

But they certainly didn't look neglected. Emma was beautiful in her zipped scarlet jacket and trousers, her large eyes dark beneath the white fur bonnet. Mark was obstreperous and untidy, his socks round his ankles, his tie knot under one ear. Neither of them was going to have their father's temperament, although at one time she'd thought Mark might. They had a directness totally lacking in him.

'Is it a treat, Mummy?' Emma asked. 'You never come to meet us at school.' She felt chastised.

'Yes, it's a treat.'

'Could we go Christmas shopping?' Mark was dancing with glee beside her. 'Could we?'

'He's greedy, Mummy. He wants a Chopper. I've told him we can't afford it.'

'I've thought of bicycles for both of you.' She was amazed that she could talk like this when her heart was aching so badly, feeling swollen and awkward above her ribs, affecting even her throat.

'Can we go and buy them?' Emma forgot her censoriousness.

'No, it's too late to go into town.' She saw their eager faces, said weakly. 'There's a puppet show at Kingsley House.'

'Oh, a puppet show!' Mark was immediately won over.

'That's babyish,' his sister said.

'And a display of Victorian dolls as well.' She looked with dislike at this child of hers.

'Mrs Blackley is going to take us but I'll have been there *first*. And could we have ices and make it a real treat?' She didn't answer, only shepherded them into the car.

Driving through Kinglsey Heath the terrible depression lifted a little. It was trim, even in winter, and the wide curves planned by Jake, the green spaces, gave it an airiness. Rogersgate, the town centre, named after Jolyon Roger, was busy with shoppers. The pool with the fountain had been emptied for winter and a large Christmas tree set up in its place. Lights were already twinkling on it, and two women from the enterprising Community Centre were standing near it with collecting boxes.

The Trust had already contributed generously to Kingsley Home, the nearby centre for handicapped children, at Tricia's instigation. She'd been deeply moved when she'd made a duty round as member of its committee. She should be thankful, she'd told herself, to have two healthy children. Today it didn't matter, nothing mattered.

Inside, Kingsley House was crowded with mothers and children. Emma and Mark quickly bounded away from her in the direction of the arrows, leaving her standing in the hall. She looked at the black and white tiled floor, the heavy panelling, remembered the opening ceremony that blustery day in July, Jake helping her through her first public occasion. A shaft of pain crucified her. She remembered the ray of sunlight from the glass-domed ceiling, bringing out the deep blue of his eyes.

They hadn't been blue in the London restaurant; they'd been dark, like his face, a dark cloud of misery. Nothing to my misery, she thought, then and now. 'Jake, my darling, my only true love . . .' She saw a woman's curious eyes on her. Did she look strange, standing there? 'Jake, you were my rod and staff, you led me into quiet waters . . .' Had she said that aloud? She turned away, words running through her brain, wanting to be said. 'You comforted me through the dark days of Roger's illness, you were my life . . .'

The misery was too much to bear. If she stood here much longer she'd draw attention to herself, a thin girl with big eyes, hands clutched at her side . . . she walked into the adjoining room. There was an air of neglect, a faded Edwardian aura. Her feet led her to the show-case where Cock Robin's little tragedy had been enshrined. 'I said the dove, I'll mourn for my love . . .'

She turned away, grimacing with agony. 'You look fulfilled,' he'd said that day. 'I was never fulfilled until I met you, Jake.' The words seemed to be torn from her heart. 'You completed me.' She descended into such a pit of despair that she jumped and shuddered when she heard the children's voices.

'Mummy, Mummy! It's finished. It's all over.'

'Is it?' She came back, focused on those two beings who were her property, hers and Roger's. 'Oh, is it . . . ? Would you like to see Cock Robin while you're here?'

'Oh, that!' Emma said, glancing at the show-case. 'That's for children.'

She went away with them, leaving her past behind.

*　　*　　*

302

Supper-time was usually easy at Howard's View. It was a good house for a family, spacious, warm, the kitchen had been a complete success. The children were amenable and went to bed cheerfully, giving her extra hugs because of their unexpected outing.

She wasn't surprised when Roger appeared in the bedroom, after his shower, his bare skinny legs showing under his bath-robe, the shy expectant look on his face like a child sidling up to be petted. She was already in bed, pretending to read a Company report. 'The shares have gone up again,' he said. 'Good, isn't it?'

'Yes, good.'

He took off his robe, giving her time to have a look, and climbed in beside her. His body was cool and he smelled of soap, toothpaste and his latest bath oil, like a chemist's shop. 'With you and Jake Russell at the head of things we can't go wrong. You know he's been married for some time?'

'Yes.'

'He kept it very quiet. So did you. Put out your light, darling. It hurts my eyes.' He didn't like his love-making to be illuminated.

He started. It only reminded her of what she'd lost. When he rolled off her in his fibrillating way she buried her face in the pillow and wept.

'What's wrong?' he asked.

'I'm terribly tired. I'm sorry. It was nice. I shouldn't do this to you.' She was lying in a pool of scalding tears. Her misery was great.

'You don't have to apologise,' he said. 'I know why you're weeping.' He turned away from her, and when she touched his shoulder, he shrugged away her hand.

*   *   *

It was her mother who saved her sanity.

On Christmas of that year Tricia gave the usual family party at Howard's View, inviting her parents, Roger's mother and the Wilkes' next door. Madge had become a friend by habit more than anything else, yet she and Tricia exchanged no deep confidences. Their lives were different. Madge found domestic life and children completely satisfying and had no envy in her. 'But, goodness, she's dull,' Tricia would think after one of their coffee sessions which fortunately could only occur on Sundays or holidays.

She went white-faced and stern about the Christmas preparations, only relaxing into a false gaiety when she felt the children's eyes or Roger's on her. The continual ache in her heart was so physical that sometimes at night she would lay her hands on the place, thinking she could feel some growth.

As usual, her preparations were meticulous, the table setting artistic, the food plentiful and perfect. Aided by wine the family party had its usual jollity, Mary Newton slightly giggly, Madge and Rab good-naturedly bickering, the children hysterical with over-indulgence, her mother calm, her father more long-winded than ever, she and Roger polite with too many endearments sprinkled in their conversation.

When it was all over Tricia went to bed with a headache as bad as she'd ever had, a feeling that her head would burst open and reveal this awful, clawing agony which was with her day and night. Fortunately Roger slept peacefully, snoring on his back, the happy victim of too much wine and food.

In the morning she was surprised to get a telephone call from her mother. 'Have you cleared up all that mess?'

'Yes. There's the dishwasher. And I'd done all the pots and pans and the serving-dishes as they were emptied . . .'

'I know how efficient you are. I'd like you to come over this morning and see me, Tricia.'

'See you? Is there anything wrong?'

'Not with me. Leave the children with Madge Wilkes. I don't want them jumping around when I'm trying to talk.'

'Roger is on holiday. Had you forgotten? Where's father?'

'He always has a Boxing Day game of golf with Bob Pritchard. Right. I'll see you in half-an-hour.'

Tricia swallowed two Codis, asked Roger to keep an eye on the children, got out the car and left, puzzled. Her mother wasn't in the habit of interfering in her life. She'd probably want some donation from the Trust for one of her numerous charities. She wasn't one to let the grass grow under her feet, and from early days she had resented the disturbance of public holidays, religious festivals or otherwise.

She had coffee ready in the sitting-room where Tricia had spent so much of her childhood. Nothing in it had changed, even to the arrangement of dried flowers on the bureau. 'If I went in for this ridiculous flower arranging,' she'd said once, 'I'd never get anything else done.'

'Hello,' she said when Tricia came in. 'Well, you don't look any better this morning than you did last night. Sit down.' She poured coffee. 'That's strong, as you like it. No milk.'

'Thanks, Mother.' She smiled dryly. 'Christmas is wearing for the housewife, as Madge Wilkes would be the first to say. And I don't get as much time as she does for preparation beforehand.'

'Well, you chose to work.'

'What's this?' She sipped her coffee. 'Are you getting at me about something?'

'No, I'm sorry. I should be more polite. It's dealing with the Deprived. I tend to cut through their ramblings . . .'

'You haven't given me a chance to ramble, and I'm not deprived.'

'Aren't you?'

'What?'

'Deprived.'

'I don't know what you mean.' The ache which had been subdued by the pain killers set up again, sickeningly. She was in no fit state to cope with this unmotherly woman who suddenly saw her as a 'case' to be dealt with.

'You should have seen your face last night. For a girl with everything, beautiful house, husband and family, interesting work, you looked . . . deprived. I'm used to it in other people, Tricia. It took me a little longer to see it in you. It wasn't until Gillian dropped a hint . . .'

'What has she been saying?' Her cheeks burned with anger.

'Now, don't get at Gillian. She didn't say anything she was aware of. I put two and two together. It's my job, just as you have yours. You get an extra sense. It's Jake Russell, isn't it?'

She got up and walked to the window. Movement was necessary. This heart of hers would break, fly in fragments over

305

her mother's worn Axminster, bits of it would have to be picked out from between the dried flowers. 'He's married now. It's all over.'

'So you did have an affair with him?'

She kept looking out of the window, said, almost absently. 'I never called it that to myself. I loved him.' She turned. 'There, it's said, Mother. I loved him, love him. Your bull-dozing tactics have worked. Aren't you happy?' Her eyes were dry and hot.

'Come and sit down, there's a good girl.' When she went back to her chair she found her mother had placed a small glass of brandy beside her coffee cup. 'Drink that. I'm a great believer in spirits at the proper time. They take the edge off.'

'If I'd thought that, I'd be an alcoholic by this time.' She lifted the glass and drank from it. The glow certainly did something for her, the pain was less.

'I'd heard he'd got married. Have you met his wife?'

'You see . . .' she raised her face to her mother, 'it's Crystel. Crystel whom I knew in Paris. Crystel . . .' Her voice broke.

'You poor thing. I'm sorry.'

'Don't say that, don't. I'll weep again. I've wept and wept till there's none of me left.' The brandy was helping. Her mother was the last person she thought of confiding in, and yet the most obvious. She could keep a secret. She took another sip. 'I can tell you. I should have thought of talking to you before but you're always so busy. So am I. I loved him. Maybe I loved him too much, more than he loved me. I began to hope . . .' She breathed deeply, quiveringly, 'But for Crystel Romaine, who belonged to my past, to step into my present life . . . and take Jake from me . . . it's the difficulty of accepting it. I wake up and tell myself it's a bad dream. How banal can you get . . .'

'But they must have met through you.' Oh, practical mother.

'Yes, that's true. I wanted, in a way, to . . . show him off at first. I gave up the idea when we became lovers, no long before that. He did once call on her, passing through, and then nothing until recently. Once I showed him her picture . . . oh, what's the use of talking about it.'

'Talk about it.'

'She wouldn't consider me, at least, not much. I had a husband, after all. And she wouldn't realise just how much Jake meant to me. They were married in Paris, I think. She'd gone there to work. I don't know why. Maybe to make a clean break with her lover. She's a logical girl, Crystel.'

'Are they going to live in England?'

'She's already here. They'll do what suits them. They're both that kind of person. They go in a straight line for what they want.'

'You haven't seen Jake since then?'

'No. He's been at the Latham office once or twice and asked to see me, but I told Gillian to say I was busy. I couldn't bear it. Maybe that's what gave her the idea about Jake and me . . . oh, what does it matter, the practicalities. I've lost him. I'm without hope for the future.' She stared dry-eyed at the carpet. Part of the design had gone where her father's feet had worn it. It was his chair. She was surprised the tears weren't rushing down her face as they'd done so often recently, unexpectedly, when she'd been dictating and she'd said to Gillian, 'Excuse me, must go to the loo . . .' It must be something to do with the atmosphere in the room, or her mother's business-like approach. She listened to the silence. Her mother wasn't given to making unnecessary movements. She could hear the wall clock in the hall ticking away in the silence. It had been one of her duties to wind it every Sunday. Was it her mother or her father who did it now?

'Everybody has a future.' She heard the precise voice.

'If they're alive. What are you going to do with yours?'

She shrugged. 'Go on from day to day. Work. Work hard. I'm thankful to God for the Trust, I'll look after the children, look after Roger . . .' There was another long silence. It would have been helpful if her mother had even clattered her coffee-spoon. When she spoke it was without emotion.

'I'm surprised at what you say, Tricia. I should have imagined this undoubtedly sad experience would have made a difference to you. I presume you were ready to leave Roger if Jake had asked you?'

'Oh, yes. I would have jumped at the chance. I'd overcome all my scruples. There's nothing like love for that.'

307

'Not now?'

'Leave Roger? What's the point?'

'There's your character, for one thing, your personality. Living with Roger hasn't done it much good as far as I can see. You wouldn't have fallen in love with Jake in the first place if Roger had been all you wanted. I'm surprised you want to sacrifice yourself over him. Let it be for something really useful, like my deprived children, someone who really needs you. Roger doesn't.'

She was shocked. 'I'm surprised at you. You to say that! He depends on me, I spin the world for him every morning and he jumps on.'

'He depends on his mother. He could live with her because he's never really grown away from her, and as for the other thing, there are always women. Frankly, I don't know why you didn't make a red light district in your Eternal City,' this was her joke name for Kingsley Heath, 'for people like Roger. It seems to me it's the only thing you haven't thought of, you who pride yourself on being so forward-looking.'

'Mother, you're outrageous!' She had to smile. 'All this do-gooding's making you eccentric. Are you trying to shock me? Are you really advising me to leave Roger?'

'I'm not advising. I'm pointing out that things haven't changed because Jake Russell has married Crystel. Roger doesn't *do* anything for you. You're not even thirty yet. Are you going to go on nannying him for the next thirty years?'

'What about the children?'

'You could share them. They grow up. They'll be away from you before you know it.'

'And my house?'

'It isn't your house. It's his and yours. Ask him where he'd rather be if you weren't in it.'

She shook her head in amazement. Was this a new technique of her mother's, learned at some of those courses she was always attending? Shock tactics? 'I never thought of leaving Roger for *no* reason.'

'You have every reason if you look at it honestly. You married the wrong man.'

'With your approval and encouragement.'

'That was your father. I only supported him at the time, wrongly, I see now. We didn't know how Roger was going to turn out. Well, I had an idea, but your father wouldn't listen. Nor would you, if you look back.'

'The Church was to blame for that. I didn't believe in living in sin.'

'We're both to blame there. Or the Church.'

'You mean, you aren't a believer any more?'

'I mean I'm a believer in practical Christianity, not in dogma. I believe in following the dictates of my own conscience.'

Tricia looked at her. 'You're the limit, Mother.' She said it in admiration. 'You've upset the apple-cart with a vengeance.'

'That's all I wanted to do. I wanted to stop you pining, which you're doing, over Jake. All that energy could be used in making sense of your own life. It hasn't gone away because Jake has. Believe me, Tricia, you have to work for your happiness. I found mine in what I did outside the home, not in it.'

'You stayed with father, though.'

'Yes, I know. You may well follow my example. You're more like me than you think.'

She got up. She smiled uncertainly at her mother. 'I think you're a nutter. You've cured my headache. But my heartache's still there.'

'Ah, yes, that'll take a long time to go.' She rose and came towards Tricia, put her hands on her shoulders and kissed her, awkwardly. 'I'm no good at this,' she said, 'that's another of my failures.'

'Oh, Mummy . . .' With the embarrassment, the tears came. 'I'll get out before I make a fool of myself.' She blundered out of the room, feeling like the schoolgirl who had lived in it ten years or more ago.

CHAPTER THIRTY
1979

IT WAS towards the end of March, before Tricia made her first move in following her mother's advice. She began to show a more active interest in Kingsley Home for Spastics. The Community Centre at Kingsley Heath had adopted the inmates, and more and more Tricia was drawn into organising outings and parties for them. It was too trite a panacea for the grief she still felt over Jake, but it was part of a kind of 'balancing' which went on in her mind. Mark and Emma were 'advantaged', and the spastics were 'deprived' . . . she was beginning at times to adopt her mother's jargon.

She had also to make some kind of penance for the hatred she felt for Crystel. She couldn't rid herself of the thought of her beauty, the beauty which Jake was now enjoying, and she suffered torments of jealousy which sometimes made her ill and waspish.

A month or so later she was appointed as Governor of the Kingsley Home which meant paying weekly visits. Sometimes she took Mark and Emma with her, hoping it would be a two-way benefit. After a week of doing 'funny walks' at home, they made friends in a way she couldn't emulate. Children *were*. Adults had preconceived ideas. Even to be actuated by the idea of breaking down the barrier between the fit and the unfit was to intellectualise the situation and spoil its spontaneity. Emma and Mark taught her a lot.

But the real reason for opening her heart to something else other than her preoccupation with Jake was the letter she received from Jan Sirica.

'Dear Tricia,' it said, *'No doubt you'll be surprised to hear from me. It's been so long — longer than I know or can bear*

to count . . .'

'I've had a letter from Crystel telling me she's married to a friend of yours, more than a friend, and how distressed she is about it. It's ironic, she says, that after all those years something like this should at the same time bring you together and drive you apart. She never doubts that she did the right thing in marrying Jake Russell . . . well, being Crystel she wouldn't . . . but it grieves her deeply to have made you unhappy.

'She says her husband has tried to see you, and she's written to me in the hope that I can intercede for her. She's tried to write to you, tore up the letters. It's a 'fait accompli', she says. How can she hope for forgiveness, far less your blessing.

'What can I say to help in this situation? Maybe the only thing is to tell you what's been happening to me. It's taken me practically a year to write any sort of letter. I've thought of suicide, many times . . .

'Last August my son Clay, my dearly beloved son Clay, fell from our seventh floor apartment and was killed. In Harlem, New York, US of A. That's a joke. There, it's written. I have to stare at the words because as I write them they still don't make sense. But I can bear the truth for fairly long stretches now, and I'm in one of those phases now. And was when I got Crystel's letter.

'George and I were quarrelling which wasn't unusual. Wait till you're in a hot August night in New York. And it happened, God knows why. You can imagine how it's gone round and round in my mind until I'm driven crazy. No, I promised myself I'd write calmly.

'There are several possibilities why . . . I'd made up a kind of punch . . . no, you couldn't think of Clay drunk, could you? Then . . . our key-rings. Clay stole mine out of my bag and when I found him playing with it I threw it over the balcony. "My precious key-ring," I said. But where is my precious Clay? Oh, God, see how my mind goes on and on and on . . . George said I gave Clay my problem.

'There was this girl, Ruth, in George's office. At first I kind of made her up, but, oh, she's real all right, and to hurt George, although I didn't honestly at that time think there was

*anything in it I said, "Well, it's a great damn pity Clay wasn't
yours and hers instead of mine . . ." something like that. No,
it was like that. Clay would hear me. And she's black. Could
it have been that? I keep on asking and asking . . .*

'Well conjectures are useless, which is a trite thing to say
but you can't imagine how useful clichés are in times like these
when it's impossible to express your thoughts in ordinary everyday
words.

'It — Clay, falling over the rails of our balcony on the
seventh floor in Harlem — finished George and me. I went
into some kind of hysterical illness. I kept on reproaching him,
that it wouldn't have happened if he hadn't been late and
spoiled the special meal, if we hadn't been living where we
were living, if only he'd taken Clay to Bear Mountain . . . you
see, I had to find someone to blame. You do see that, don't
you?

'My mother came to New York and wanted me to go back
to Cedars, but by this time Rony had taken me to her
apartment because I couldn't stand living any more with George
and I believe she and Momma fought over the body. I was as
dead as Clay. Well, Rony won and I'm glad she did, in
retrospect. If I'd gone back to my mother that would have
really finished me . . . I'd have been back in my childhood
for ever.

'It's been difficult, which is the understatement of the year . . .
another cliché. George came to see me often but I never
wanted him after Clay died. It was as if my love for George
went with Clay's body over the railings of that balcony. He
told me he was seeing Ruth. Well, he needed some comfort
and I wasn't giving him any. In the beginning I honestly think
I thought up Ruth, drew her in the dust with a stick. I come
back to this, time and time again as an awful warning to other
women, I guess. It's not affecting me any more. What was
between George and me is finished. But sometimes I can't get
away from the feeling that in the beginning Ruth was something
I blew life into with my suspicions, and Lo, as they say in the
Bible, she was there. I told him to go to her, and he went.
She's black. Did I say that? She'll be better for him than I
ever was, the rich white girl who was always throwing his*

poverty and his blackness in his teeth. Rony put it straight to me one night, and that was the beginning of my beginning to crawl out of my black pit . . . there, another cliché.

' "Stop crucifying yourself," she said, "and everybody else with you. Clay's dead. George has left you because you didn't want him. It couldn't have been such a great thing if it was only Clay who was holding you together. Oh, sure, you had something going for George at the beginning, hot pants, but the truth of it is you loved Clay more than George. That was why he left you. He couldn't do a thing for you. It was nothing to do with him being black, well, not too much. Ettie's the one, (that's Momma), who couldn't take it. You wanted a child to love because you were deprived yourself, we both were. Well, I've got my scars too . . . You were mad for dolls as a kid, George was the first man who came along so you decided you'd have a golliwog child, a Black Sambo . . ." I have to tell you, Tricia, I did have a Black Sambo when I was a kid, with blue trousers and a polka dot tie and a red waistcoat . . .

'I'd been mad at her all the time she was talking, but when she said that I laughed myself silly and then I started to weep. You won't ever have wept tears like mine, even over this Jake Russell. It was like a sluice opening, like the Niagara Falls, it was like a great, healing river . . . more clichés.

'Well, I got an apartment of my own . . . I'm in the way in Rony's because of her kind of life, but she helped me set it up and get this job I'm in, a kindergarten. I like it, oh, I like it, but I think I hug the children too much. I'm crazy for Clay at times, for the feel of him, his sharp bones, his smooth skin . . . not for George, that's all gone. Sometimes Carol, she's the Principal, tells me not to make favourites, but I keep looking for Clay amongst the children, I see a fuzz like his, or a boy who slips about in the eel-like way he had, or has big brown eyes, and the way he copied George in everything. Rony made me accept an allowance from Momma so that I'd eat good food or something stupid like that. An anorexic would have looked healthy beside me. She said it would make Momma feel better, and you shouldn't heap guilt on to people . . .

313

'Well, my God, I've let myself run on. What has all this to do with your problem? I think it's even written in a kind of boastful way, or at least that's what got me started writing. "So you think you've suffered, huh? Well, get a load of this!"

'But deeper than that, I think, I hope, is the feeling that the three of us had something going for us. Maybe it's just this. I threw away our key-ring in a fit of anger and George and Clay got it back for me. I can't get Clay back, but you can let Crystel and her man off the hook. My goodness, you're not down and out. A husband and two children. I bet neither of them will ever fall over a seventh floor balcony in Harlem, New York, US of A. I bet the nearest they'll ever get to that is watching Batman . . .

'That's cheap. Forgive me, Tricia. Sometimes I want to hurt and hurt . . . that's what makes me pick out one of the boys in the kindergarten and hug him against me to help me get rid of that grudge against the world, against everybody. That's what makes me look at that key-ring sometimes, that clover-leaf, and remember you and Crystel, the three of us . . .'

CHAPTER THIRTY-ONE

THE director of the Kingsley Home for Spastics on the old Latham Road was a worn youngish man of thirty-two, Mervyn Davies, not typically Welsh since his colouring was sandy and he had a thin face with a high-bridged nose. But he had strong broad shoulders which came in useful for handling some of his patients, a thing she'd seen him doing many times.

They called him Merv, and the brighter ones tried to imitate how he spoke. He didn't say, 'Look you,' but 'Hang on there', with a Welsh lilt which became more pronounced when he shouted at someone making their ataxic way along the corridor. He liked being imitated. 'It's the quiet ones who worry me most,' he said to Tricia, 'the ones who are as twisted inside as their limbs.'

He gave them elocution lessons himself, being a great believer in breathing techniques, and read them lots of modern poetry. He claimed that the Mersey Sound had done more for his lot than all the sociologists tied up together and rolled through the Mersey Tunnel.

He didn't approve of Drama Therapy, saying that anything with capital letters frightened him, but he made them sit at tables and order imaginary beer or coffee, and put their crutches down quietly so as not be a nuisance. 'It's *your* handicap,' he told them, 'so you've got to learn to deal with it, not get in other people's hair.'

They disagreed on nearly everything. She thought girls who could hardly walk shouldn't be allowed great platform soles to impede them further, and he told her she had no soul. And when she said Rogersgate was much nearer than Latham for the chairpushers, he smiled. He had a wicked smile at times, not showing his teeth, his mouth curving like a clown's.

'I'm willing to try again. I know the last time wasn't a huge success at our Centre. Three got twisted ankles and we had to send for the ambulance, one wet the floor and two others were discovered in the cleaner's cupboard trying to have it off.'

'You want everything tidy. They want reality, even if it's in a broom cupboard. Latham High Street on a Saturday morning with the market on's a reality. The pintable booth in School Lane's a reality. Likewise the public urinal in Wellington Square. There's no one better at recognising true from false than a sub-normal.'

Once she had made some oblique reference to her life not always being as rosy as he seemed to think, the way people who are suffering like to do, letting a little piece escape in the hope they'll titillate the listener to ask for more.

'Don't give me any hard luck story,' he said. 'I'm a bad listener to women with straight legs.' She was stung.

'You flatter yourself. You're the last one I'd confide in.'

'So you've something to confide,' he said with his wicked closed smile.

'Nothing that I'd ever tell you.' She disliked him very much at times, thought he was brash and rude, or crude, and when she heard that he was divorced it didn't alter her opinion, rather it confirmed her belief that nobody would want to live with him.

*   *   *

It was July now. Howard's View had never looked lovelier with its lawn sloping down to the lake as if it had been there for years. The flowering shrubs, the azaleas and the almond blossom were over, but Roger paid attention to rotation, and now the buddleias and the clematis and most of all the roses were in full flower. He even knew which rose faded best.

At breakfast one Sunday morning she read an article in the paper which affected her deeply. Roger was immersed in a gardening magazine.

'This situation with the Vietnamese Boat People has crept up on me. There's an article here about Bidong Island. One gets so

316

involved in one's own affairs.' She meant Jake. Grief after a time became selfish, restrictive. It didn't make any difference knowing that.

'It's been on the news. It's because they're ethnic Chinese, isn't it?'

'This article makes terrible reading . . . a twenty-year old girl raped so many times that she wanted only to die . . .' 'Is this rape,' she'd said, the softness of the carpet under her. 'It isn't rape if you're willing . . .' She felt ashamed of the memory, not that it had happened, but that the two situations were so different. 'It's the children who've lost their parents . . . that's the worst part of it.'

'Yes, it's sad.' He didn't sound too sad, at least not about the Vietnamese boat people as he looked over the sunlit garden. They were sitting in the patio dining-room where long ago she'd stood with Jake.

She became self-righteous to dowse the memory. 'Every country will have to take their share. What if Mark and Emma were living on a stinking island with no parents to take care of them, starving because the fish had become too polluted from all the corpses . . .'

'I know it's Sunday but don't preach, please.' The face he turned up to her from the magazine was peevish. 'You're becoming like your mother.'

He'd said this before, but this time it infuriated her. 'Do you think so?' She folded the paper. 'Well, that makes two of us.'

'What do you mean by that?'

'You're the spitting image of yours.'

'Is that such a bad thing? At least she minds her own business which is more than you can say of yours.'

She blew out her breath. 'What are we quarrelling about? I don't have the energy for it on a day like this. We were talking about the Boat People. All I'm saying is that Latham ought to take some responsibility for them.'

'Well, leave it to the authorities to decide. Who wants to talk about unpleasant things when the sun's shining. I'm going to see how the pond's doing . . .' he'd lately made and stocked a pool with aquatic plants and fish. She was irritated by his absorption.

'I wish you wouldn't run away when I want to discuss

something. I thought we might offer one of the houses in Kingsley Heath to a Vietnamese family. There's an empty one in Linnet Drive.'

'But that's ridiculous! I could sell it for at least twenty thousand.'

'Our shares have trebled in yesterday's report. We can surely afford that.'

There was a flush on his cheekbones. 'You've to think of the people who'd live beside them. You and Russell between you didn't leave me with much of a job, but I've made more of this one than I've been given credit for, selecting the right people . . .'

'The right people!' Her anger flared at the mention of Jake's name. 'The Boat People are the right people! They *need* it. They're homeless. It's you who have to face reality.' She remembered Mervyn Davies using the same phrase.

'Reality!' He bent forward, clutching the table with his hands, his mouth quivering. 'I had that once, reality! Oh, you never talk about it but I haven't forgotten. That terrible time when we were quarrelling, lunging towards me . . . pushing him away, my hands on his chest . . .'

'You said . . .' she had to steady her voice, 'that he was like a tree struck by lightning . . .'

'As he fell!' He shouted at her. 'I've had to live with the fact that I might have murdered my father!'

'Oh, no . . .' The dark doubts, buried for so long, were there. 'He had a heart attack. Roger . . .'

He met her eyes. She had to look away from the fear in them. Then she heard him mutter. 'I mean morally . . . that's it,' his voice strengthened. 'Morally.' He nodded. 'You've no idea what I suffered. You were too busy, always wrapped up in your work. The drugs helped but it's up to me mostly. I can't let my mind dwell on unhappy, unpleasant things. That's how I've got to live. That's why I like this garden. It gives me peace. Mother understands.'

'So do I.'

'You were on the outside. You don't know how I felt, how a hunted animal feels . . .' She'd listened often, through long nights, cradled him in her arms, never getting to the root of it.

'I've watched you getting well. That's what an outsider sees.

318

You're well now, Roger. I think you should face it, everything to do with your father's death, take it out and face it, talk about it to me. If you don't it'll only recur in your dreams.'

'I take a sleeping pill. I went back and told the psychiatrist about my dreams. He says I can take a pill every night, for ever, if I like. They're not addictive. I know myself now. I can't take a lot of worry or excitement. I couldn't live the life you do, rushing here and there. And now that Jake Russell's gone, I don't feel . . . menaced.' He looked at her, expressionless. 'I've put it out of my head. I'm glad he's gone away all the same.'

That was it. She felt despair now and for the the future. The door was closed against her. But was there any necessity to stay in a glass bubble with him? Her mother called Kingsley Heath The Eternal City. Mervyn laughed at its rarefied atmosphere. Was there an element of the contrived in it which didn't exist in Latham, a small town which had grown up without planning? An Ideal Place. Like a dream . . . she remembered driving through the Heath with Jake and thinking that. And that you might organise the exterior but never what went on underneath . . .

*   *   *

The boy kept falling as he tried to climb up the wall-bars. Tricia, watching, thought she was expected to show the same patience. At last he got to the fourth rung and hung on grimacing and waving his arms like a gibbon before he fell off. 'Smashing,' Mervyn said. 'That'll do for today, Tim.' He picked himself up and shambled off.

'I call him the Incredible Hulk.'

'Not to his face.'

'He takes it as a compliment. I've promised him a teeshirt with the gent on it when he climbs six rungs. There isn't a meeting today.'

'I know. I wanted to have a talk with you.'

'Step into my parlour as the spider said to the fly. We'll have some tea.'

They walked through the small engineering shop where the brighter boys and girls were making radio components. 'Hi, Merv!' The faces turned. 'Got your girl-friend, then?' Giggling and nudging.

When they sat down in his room he said, 'They lust after you. It's a problem in an institution.'

'What do you want me to do? Lend myself out once a week?'

'Would you really?' The smile was wicked. The door opened and one of the girls came in with a tray.

'Oh, thank you,' Tricia said, 'how lovely. Thank you very much.'

'Try carrying that tray steadier the next time, Maureen. This is a hell of a mess.'

'Someone nudged me.'

'Passing the buck as usual. Do we *pour* these biscuits?' The girl giggled and went clumping out, her legs and arms going in different directions.

'D'you always speak in that polite way?' Tricia took her cup and saucer from him.

'Nearly alway unless I'm in a bad temper and then they get the edge of my tongue. Anything's better than the Lady Bountiful bit you give them. "Oh, thank you, how lovely, thank you very much, you poor sodding cripple." '

'I hope I didn't sound like that.' She reddened.

'I hope I didn't sound like that' He mimicked her. 'Do you ever listen to yourself? You may communicate to your minions that way in your fancy office but you can't do it here. You haven't enough compassion. You haven't suffered enough.'

She tried to keep calm. 'Well, well you being the arbiter. But don't worry. I'm not going to offload on you. I'm here about the Boat People. I went to the Town Council today but they weren't too keen to discuss it yet. They hate people to jump the gun before they go through their endless red tape.'

He looked at her over the edge of his cup, said slowly, pedantically, ' "What possible grounds can there be, moral, political, historical or ethnic for the admission to this country of large numbers of those people, since we have no connections with them and no obligations?" ' He drew back in pretended fright. 'Hey, have you seen your eyes when you're angry?

320

They're beautiful enough when you're calm, but just now, wow!'

She got up. 'I'm going.'

'Sit down, fool. Don't you recognise a quote when you hear it?'

'Oh, him!' She sat down. 'Mervyn, I'd like to offer them a house in Kingsley Heath. You're on the town council. Would you raise the matter with them, soon? It's there, empty. I've persuaded Roger not to sell it to a "nice" family, and I've asked the London office if I can go ahead. They're willing to furnish it.' She had written a letter addressed to the chairman, and had received a reply with Jake's signature.

'I'm beginning to believe in capitalism after all. It's a good idea. I like it. Was it just honest-to-God concern for your neighbour, or further compensation?'

'I don't know why you get at me. Something must have turned you sour. I might ask you in return why you're doing the job you're doing.'

'It's the new form of analysis. You should try it.'

'Who doesn't compensate? It's a fact of life.'

'Give your reason then for compensating.'

She smiled at him. 'There were once three girls who met in Paris.' She fished in her handbag and brought out her key-ring. 'We each had one of those. It was our symbol, our badge of unity. We were going to change the world.'

'Sucker.' He sipped his coffee. She noticed his eyes, how warm they were. Unlike Jake's their brown colour was apparent since he had precious few eyelashes to hide them.

'The American girl lost her child and was left with this.' The silver clover-leaf caught the light. 'I've been lucky. I've got Mark and Emma.'

'And the other one?'

'Crystel? She's still got hers. And my lover.'

'And you still think you've been lucky?'

'Yes, in a way. I'm beginning to see what Jean Paul meant . . .'

'Who the hell's Jean Paul?'

'There's a lot you don't know about me, isn't there?' She put the key-ring back in her bag. 'I've decided to ask Jan, that's the American one, to come for a visit. She loves children.'

'And Crystel? Funny name.'

'She's French. No, not her. I'm not wearing a halo yet.'

He grinned, then burst out laughing. 'That's the first really honest thing I've heard you say.' He shook his finger at her, still grinning, 'you just hang on there.'

'I'll do that thing.' She felt suddenly light-hearted. 'So you'll see about the Vietnamese family for me? Tell them there's a house waiting and everything?'

'I'll be glad to,' he said.

CHAPTER THIRTY-TWO

HE had no name to begin with, nor mother; she had died, partly of a miscarriage but mostly of a broken heart. The woman called him some unintelligible Indo-Chinese diminutive, but Merv, who had arranged it all, christened him 'Wing'. His arm had been broken when he was beaten up by the Malaysian thugs and it had set badly. 'Like a broken wing,' he'd said to Tricia, looking embarrassed for the first time since she'd known him. Peter Jobley said it could be set again and put right.

* * *

Jan came for a visit around this time. When Tricia saw the skinny, dark-haired girl stepping off the train at Latham Station, her first impression was that she hadn't changed. Certainly her skirt length hadn't. And her knees were still bony. Her hands fluttered as she spoke to the porter, pointing to her luggage.

'Jan!' She called, and went running along the platform to meet her. It was only when Jan turned to face her that she saw the difference. Her youth had gone. The skin which had had a delicate blue tinge round the temples was a dirty yellow. There was some kind of rash. Her eyes were lifeless, and there were brown, deep half-circles scored underneath them. The black hair was drawn back unbecomingly in a plait. They hugged each other, talking incoherently at first.

'You haven't changed a bit,' Tricia said. 'I should have known you anywhere.'

'*You* have.' She stood back to look. 'You've got it together. You look like the front cover of *Fashionwear*. Like a career woman.'

'I'm the same underneath.' She laughed. 'Jan, I can't tell you how lovely it is to see you. It brings the past back.'

'It couldn't. It's gone. Did you bring your kids?'

'No, they're at home with Roger. I thought . . .'

'You thought it might upset me? It wouldn't. I see kids all the time. You don't have to apologise for yours.'

'I know, but I wanted you to myself.' She's brittle, she thought. In the car she said, mostly because after the first burst they were finding conversation difficult, 'Remember I told you in my letter there was a Vietnamese family living in one of our Estate houses?'

'Yes. Say, is this it? It's kind of neat, and nice. But miniature. Narrow roads.'

'No, this is Latham, but we're not far away. We'll be there in a few minutes. There's a child, without parents, who's come with them. He's called Wing.'

'You mean he isn't anybody else's?'

'Yes, his parents are dead. He'll probably be up for adoption.' She didn't say she was thinking of adopting him herself. She hadn't discussed it with Roger, but she'd lain awake in bed thinking of it. Knowing Mervyn had made her examine her motives. She'd have to be sure she wasn't thinking of adopting the child as compensation for a hurt.

'I came round to thinking about it but they don't like one-parent families. Nor anyone replacing a dead child with a live one, to make up.' (Nor a dead love affair.)

'You'll have to get married,' she said, 'then it would be all right.'

'Fat chance.' Jan looked out of the car window. 'Why all the fences? Is it to keep the neighbourhood dogs out?' Her voice was hard and bright.

'And the neighbourhood childen. I don't have to tell you the English are mad about gardens.'

'I never believed that but now I do. Will you look at them, the colour, and the green lawns . . . but so small compared with Cedars.'

'Snob!' She laughed.

'You always said that. It isn't snobbish to state a fact in US of A . . . why am I saying that for godssakes?' A spasm of pain crossed her face. 'But it isn't at all. If we say the longest bridge in the world is the Verrazano-Narrows in New York city it's because it *is*. Is that a duckpond or a lake? It's like out of Hans Andersen.'

'A lake. That's our house along there, the split level one.'

'That's sensational, Tricia. Like you, somehow, organised. You should see where I live in New York, a walk-up apartment, dingy brownstone. But I don't want to go back to Cedars now. I think I must have only wanted it for Clay . . .'

'Here we are,' Tricia said, driving in. 'Roger's the gardener. I'm too busy for gardens.'

'Shouldn't you be working today?'

'No, this is a very special day.' She drew up at the front door. 'There are Mark and Emma. They're dying to meet you.' The children were on the steps. Roger was standing behind them. They were grouped like a small reception committee. Tricia got out. So did Jan.

'Hi!' she said in a loud voice. Mark and Emma wriggled but were speechless. Roger came forward and shook hands. He was smiling his sweet, diffident smile. 'The famous Jan,' he said.

'Am I like what you thought?'

'Yes, I think so. Tricia had me genned up.'

'I'm not the beauty of the trio. That's Crystel.'

'You'll do for me,' he said, making Tricia lift her eyebrows.

'Come inside, Jan,' she said, putting her arm round the girl's shoulders. She could feel her shoulder-blades sticking through the thin dress. 'Mark and Emma are struck dumb by your beauty anyhow. What's happened to your tongues, you two?'

'Emma said she would have feathers in her hair,' Mark said, giggling, 'and she'd say, "How".'

'Well, she said "Hi!" That's near enough.'

'I was only teasing him.' Emma took Jan's hand. 'I know that's the Red Indians. Mrs Blackley was telling us all about them and we had to learn "Hiawatha." Do you know it?'

'Yes, I do, but I never get around to reading it. Could you say it for me sometime?'

'I'll do it now.'

'She's always doing it,' Mark said. 'She thinks she's clever because it's a long poem, but we're getting one much longer about they went to sea in a sieve they did in a . . .'

'Later,' Tricia said, 'Jan's dying for a cup of tea.' Roger was behind them with her suitcases.

'Maybe you'd prefer a drink, Jan, would you?' They had reached the sitting-room. Jan immediately went to the window. 'A real picture window. It's like a water-colour, my goodness! Yes, thanks, Roger,' she turned to smile at him, 'I could use a Scotch right now. I always feel woozy when I've been flying.'

'Right. I'll put those in your room first.'

When he'd gone Jan said, 'He's nice. Gentle.'

'I think he's fallen for you. I'm glad you like him. He needs to be liked.'

'Who doesn't? And your kids are really something, both like you. You must have the dominant genes.'

'Gosh, I hope not.' she felt uneasy, compensated, 'Jan, it's perfect to see you. I never thought you'd come when I asked you. I'm absolutely thrilled.' My Lady Bountiful bit, she thought, hearing the gush, but she couldn't say it all again.

'I'm beginning to live again. You wrote just about the right time. Rony urged me to come. She's been wonderful, Rony. She saved my life. I'm in danger of relying too much on her. It's time I stood on my own feet.' Tricia looked at the girl. Her skin was permanently marked by those deep scores under her eyes. Tears would collect there like in the bed of a river. And the line on the right-hand side of her mouth was even deeper. Her face made her seem about forty, until you looked at the immature body.

'I'm going to see that you have a good time while you're here,' she said. 'We'll have fun just the way we used to in Paris. I'll phone the office and say I shan't be in for a few days.'

Roger had come in while she was speaking. He was carrying a tray of drinks. 'That's a great offer, Jan,' he said, 'she wouldn't do that for everybody.

* * *

326

It was like the old times. Tricia put her whole mind to the task of making Jan happy. Her few days' leave from the office lengthened to a week, but she kept in touch with Gillian and found for the first time in her life that she was able to delegate. She knew she'd make it up when she went back, that she was capable of tremendous bursts of energy.

Surprisingly Roger helped her to entertain Jan, taking them out to dinner at night, planning expeditions and walks in the countryside. There seemed to be a bond between the two which had been there from the first meeting, and as Jan bloomed so did he. He was closer to being the attractive young man Tricia had married.

One afternoon Tricia took her to walk on the old Latham pack road above the town. 'You can see Kingsley Heath from here,' she said. The land fell away in a series of gentle folds, and further away they could see, before the shallow cup which contained the town, the neat red roofs of the Heath with the Victorian block of grey in the centre which was Kingsley House.

'Is that your empire?' Jan said, pointing.

'No, I helped, of course, but Jake Russell was the brains behind it.' She could say his name in the open air with the bird-song as a background.

'Crystel's husband?'

'Yes,' she said, trying to keep the bitterness out of her voice.

'You still can't take it?'

'What makes you say that?'

'Unhappy people can always spot it in others.'

'I try but . . . he was the love of my life.' The words came out in a rush.

'Clay was the love of *my* life. I didn't give enough to George.'

'I didn't give enough to Roger. I'll admit it. I'm bitter. It'll pass. I know that too.'

'That's the first step. She's so happy, Tricia. That's one of us at least. She's written to me a lot, I think to try and cheer me up, wonderful letters, but the happiness shows through. She misses her village.'

'St Henri.' The ache started up again.

'Her parents were a little disappointed she wasn't married there.'

'She always said she was a peasant at heart.'

'Some peasant. Such beauty, such elegance! She came to see me in Paris. She tells me about her clothes in her letters. It isn't boastfulness, I think it's to help me, to get me interested, in anything . . . I remember her saying she'd bought a raincoat in Paris while she was working there, lined with red fox. It was a wedding present from Jake, but can you imagine it, red fox next your skin. There's a sumptuous quality about Crystel . . .'

'Yes. The elegance of a . . .' she wanted to say courtesan . . . 'Frenchwoman.'

'She travelled to England alone . . . Jake had to dash back because of business.' Tricia had a vivid picture of beautiful, luscious Crystel in her fox-lined coat with her beautiful head, getting up to leave the aeroplane, smiling, men rushing to lift down her bag, hostesses smiling, 'She shall have music wherever she goes . . .' 'She's exotic and yet sensible,' Jan was saying. 'Always got her priorities right . . .'

'Would you have George back?'

'No, it's dead. Besides he wouldn't want to come back. He's got his priorities right too. He has Ruth, maybe a new family for all I know.'

Tricia put her arm around her. She saw the set profile, the air of fatigue which was always there, a fatigue of the spirit. 'Mervyn Davies, the man who came to dinner last night, is taking us to visit the Vietnamese family tomorrow. He thought you might like to see the little boy he told you about.' 'Love's the answer for an illness of the soul,' he'd said to Tricia in the hall. 'Why do so many people keep pets?'

'He's quite something, that man. An original. Do you like him?'

'I can't help liking him although he can be intensely irritating. But he's good.' She tightened her arm. 'Jan, I'm sure you'll be happy again some day.'

'How can I without my son?' It was said in an even tone, far more poignant than tears.

* * *

Wing was in a sand-pit with the other Vietnamese children when Mervyn drove them up to the house in Linnet Drive. He was crying, his fists stuck in his eyes.

'He's being bullied,' Mervyn said, as they walked towards them. 'The other ones want to throw him out the nest because he isn't family.'

Tricia and Jan stood watching the boy. He stopped crying but didn't move — the absolute stillness which is rarely seen in a European child. Like a child who has to keep alive by his senses, Tricia thought. Then, as if aware he was being watched, he looked up. 'I'll take him,' she thought . . . 'he's crying out for someone.' The round face, the dark almond eyes, the fringe across his brow make him look doll-like, a brown bundle ready to be picked up.

'He's got a bang,' Jan said. Something in her voice, perhaps the American intonation,. made the child look directly at her, a recognition in his eyes.

'See if he'll let you pick him up, Jan,' Mervyn said. He tapped Tricia's arm, and they walked down the path together to the gate and stopped there. 'She needs to be melted inside,' he said, 'children are much better at it than adults.'

'Maybe it'll upset her, remind her of Clay.'

'It's good if it does.'

'I was saying something like that to Roger the other day,' she said. They leant with their elbows on the gate. 'He had a terrible experience a few years ago. A violent quarrel with his father. Sometimes he thinks . . . he may have murdered him. It was before you came.'

'I'm glad you told me.' He spoke levelly, as if to help her, knowing it had cost her a lot to confide in him.

'I suddenly wanted to. Inviting Jan here has been like a catharsis.'

He said casually. 'Are you going to ask the other one, Crystel?'

She didn't speak for a minute or two, looked over the gate to the lake. 'Is that a duck-pond or a lake?' Jan had asked. There was nothing like an objective viewpoint.

'No,' she said, 'Jan can visit her.'

'Isn't there a different quality to your hating now?'

'Like what?'

'Isn't it beginning to get a bit mechanical? Don't you feel the depth has gone out of it?'

She bit upon her hurt like an aching tooth, to test it. It was still there, but there was no intensity in it. 'You could be right, but I hate it, not hating. I feel cheated. I thought it was bound to go on for ever.'

'What a masochist you are.' He turned round and smiled at her, then looked back up the garden. 'See what I see.'

Tricia turned with him, her arms along the gate. Jan was in the sandpit with the little boy. She was building a careful castle, patting it with the spade, and Wing was busy filling his bucket. She pointed to the castle and he lifted the bucket and emptied the sand on top of it, banging it down. The castle sank into a shapeless mound. They went through it again. Jan patted carefully with the spade, shaping the castle into its former glory. She touched his arm and held up her finger admonishingly, someone used to getting obedience. She stuck a twig with a leaf on top of the castle. Tricia heard her say. 'It's a flag. Flag . . . for you, Wing.' She looked up, saw them watching her, waved.

'I'm not going to adopt Wing,' Tricia said. Her eyes were stinging with tears. She turned towards Mervyn, not caring if he noticed. 'It would be wrong. Jan can't have him, I know, but there will be another way. I'm inclined to like neat solutions to everything . . . that's my failing. It's taking me a long time to realise there are no neat solutions.'

'Just wait and see?'

'Yes, that's it. Just wait and see.' His eyes held hers. They were full and tender, as if all the wisdom of the world was there, and the kindness.

CHAPTER THIRTY-THREE

WING became a fairly constant visitor at the house, and was soon dressed by Jan in a variety of American tee-shirts with distinctive lettering across his small chest. The only thing Tricia drew the line at was him teaching Emma and Mark to stuff their food into their mouths with their hands.

Once, when he was staying overnight, Roger said at dinner to Jan. 'I wish you could have him for good. He loves you.'

'I'd have to be domiciled here for a start.'

'That's a pity.'

She smiled. The deep scores under her eyes would never go, but her skin had a healthier bloom. 'I'm about ready to go home now. I've a job waiting. You've both been so good to me. I'll never forget it.'

'We'll miss you,' Roger said. His face had that special sweetness he seemed to keep for her.

That evening, when he was burning leaves in the garden, the two girls sat at the window watching him. There was a poignant, autumnal feel to the end of the day. Soon winter would be here, Tricia thought, she'd be back to her usual routine, work, caring for Roger and the children . . . thank God for work.

'You get on well with Roger, Jan,' she said. 'He'll miss you as much as I will.'

'I'll miss him. He's gentle.'

'You've said that before. What you see as his virtue, I see as his failing.'

'You haven't lived with the other type of man. I was crazy about George at first, he was always exciting, but when we were living in New York he could be . . . violent. Oh, I know most of it was my fault. He felt frustrated, life was hard, I was so wrapped up in my own misery that I didn't help him. But when you've known a man like that you prefer quieter paths.'

Quieter paths, she thought. What would it have been like living with Jake, both strong-minded, opinionated, driving, forceful. It wouldn't have been quiet. But the joy . . . I could take the violence if I had the joy . . .

Jan said. 'Anyhow we've got a bit of what we wanted. You've got your career, but not the man you wanted. And I've got for the first time, hope. Crystel never made demands. Do you still think of Jake as yours?'

'Not so . . . vehemently.' She smiled. 'I try not to think about it.'

'But you still want him?'

'I loved him, I love him . . . but I'm not so sure now that I want him.' She'd be honest. 'Roger will never be able to give me what I got from Jake.'

'Poor Roger. So gentle and loving . . .' She looked up. 'God knows I don't expect you to love Crystel. I understand. I still hate George for being the cause of Clay's death, or so I tell myself to keep myself sane, but since I came here . . .' she laughed, 'the hating has become as meaningful as eating hominy grits every morning. Don't you begin to feel the same?'

They didn't understand. She imagined what she'd imagined a thousand times, Crystel and Jake together as *they* had been together. She imagined she felt the great surge of feeling which no one else had ever stirred in her. But did she? She looked at the calm grey lake, gauze-like with the mist. The quiet sadness of the evening made any turbulence of the body difficult to imagine. There was no violence in autumn.

'You have to discount jealousy,' Jan said. 'And sex. I'm working on those two now.' Their eyes met, frankly. Tricia turned away.

She saw Roger's bent back as he stirred his bonfire near the lake, the blue wisp of smoke rising from the damp leaves. Soon it would burst into flames. Would she ever feel again that great burst of joy she'd known with Jake? She heard Jan's quiet voice. 'It's beginning to go, isn't it?'

'What?'

'The depth.'

She looked at her, saw the thin face, the face of someone who'd been permanently damaged by life. 'Yes, but . . . I don't want my love to die.'

'Everything has to die . . . look at Roger. Hasn't he a patient back? George had an impatient back. He strode forth into the world every morning with his fists up. Every black man has to be like that. Roger turns away, not wanting to be involved, that's his stance too. The only one who has none is Mervyn.'

'He's a cynic.'

'No, he's a realist. He says he could live without his spastics. That's what makes him able to help them. What is Jake?'

'Supremely confident, I *guess*.' She smiled and got up. 'Excuse me.'

She went into the narrow hall and opened the shagreen-covered book of telephone numbers. Jake, or more likely his secretary, had sent a change of address card when they'd moved into their new London home. She dialled the Putney number, and before she'd prepared what she was going to say she heard Crystel's voice, unmistakable, only the French said 'Allo' like that. She was trembling. She knew her voice was too staccato, too sharp.

'It's Tricia, Crystel, Tricia Newton.' She didn't give her time to answer. 'This must be a surprise to you. I'm phoning because Jan Sirica is with me and . . .' She stopped, wanting air in her lungs.

'Tricia? But you go so quickly. I am confused. I can hardly . . . Jan with you? In your house? But I thought she was in New York . . .'

'She came on a visit. We ought to have let you know. She's going back next week.' She swallowed. 'I thought you might like to see her?'

'*Might?* You always joke, Tricia.' The richness of the voice, the little break. 'I would like very much to see her. Would she . . . come here?'

'No, I want the three of us to meet in my house, here in Latham.' How brusque, how autocratic. 'It's been . . . difficult for me, Crystel . . . you know why. But Jan's going off soon, and I thought, we were such good friends, and I know she was waiting for me to do this. Could you come?'

'I could come. I want to come.'

'It would be like old times.' She laughed, excited. 'Now that I'm actually talking to you I wonder why I've waited for so long.'

'I understood . . . we understood so well. But underneath, we were good friends, close friends.'

'Yes, it's there, isn't it? I discovered that when Jan came. Three girls . . .'

'In Paris together . . .'

'Jean Paul . . .'

'Unbreakable. I so often think of you. And Jan. I grieve for Jan.'

'I think it's getting better. Now, I'll give you directions, Frenchie.' Suddenly it was all easy, as it had been in Paris. 'I bet you've never been in our part of the world. It's a bit complicated from London. Jake knows it . . .' She stopped, took a deep breath. 'Bring him. He knows the way like the back of his hand. He would be company for Roger.' There was a pause at the other end. 'Crystel?'

'I'm here. It's most noble.'

'No, it's sensible. We're grown up now. Mature. Knocked about a bit.' She had to speak fast because it wasn't that easy. 'Could you come this weekend? I know it's terribly short notice but Jan leaves next week.'

'I can hardly wait. Jake's in Sweden but he'll be back tonight. The moment he puts his key in the lock I'll tell him.'

'Give him time to get in.' Reaction was setting in. She heard her voice tremble. 'If Jake . . . agrees . . . we'll expect you both for lunch on Saturday.' He'd come. She knew that. There was a certain lack of subtlety in him as in most self-confident people. It was the first time she'd criticised him to herself.

'Oh, *merci mille fois*, Tricia. Wild boars wouldn't keep me away.'

'*A tout à l'heure*.' When she replaced the receiver her whole body was shaking. She told herself it was with laughter. She stood in the dark hall for a few minutes to recover.

When she went back into the sitting-room it was quite dark and Jan hadn't switched on any lights. Outside the bonfire was strong now with great tongues of flame, and its glow touched

Tricia's pieces of quartz, a silver photograph frame, her Meissen cup and saucer. 'They're both coming,' she said, and flopped down on the settee.

Jan looked up. 'Who?'

'Crystel and Jake. This weekend.'

'Oh, Tricia!' Tears were pouring down the girl's face. 'For godssakes, will you look at me? Was it difficult?'

'Only marginally more so than childbirth. She was delicious, Crystel, you know what she's like. Wild boars . . . charisma over the phone. She's dying to see you.'

* * *

The meeting was easy and natural and wonderful. Jake and Roger melted away on a tour of the garden and the three girls were free to laugh, to weep, in Jan's case, to exclaim, and of all things to admire each other's clothes. Crystel was extravagant in her praise of Jan's shift and Tricia's denim skirt and shirt, she herself was wearing a silver-grey suit which would not have disgraced Ascot. Tricia told her so and she took the remark seriously.

'I knew I was over-dressed. I admire so much your casual style, and American cottons,' this with a glorious smile at Jan, 'are *sensationnel*.'

Jan laughed. 'This is for crazy! We meet after all those years and talk about clothes.'

'So. Underneath I'm saying how much I love you both and how grateful I am to Tricia for making it possible to meet. Women discussing clothes make of it an alternative language.' 'It's better here . . .' Jake had said in the restaurant, 'It keeps it civilised.' He and Crystel were made for each other. She accepted it for the first time.

'There's a whole weekend to talk in,' she said, 'about Paris, and that night . . .' She stopped. Jan had known far greater trauma. So had she in her own way. She laughed. 'And compare key-rings.'

'I exchanged mine for Clay.' The deep scores under Jan's

335

eyes were like rivers. 'Oh, for godssakes,' she said, waving her hands, 'here I am, spoiling it already.'

'You can't,' Crystel said, 'that is the point of friendship.' Her hair glowed in its richness. There's an added lushness, Tricia thought, comparing her with Jan, as if Jake fed her on milk and honey. It wouldn't have suited me. She felt wise for a second, as if she could hold the past, present and the future in her grasp.

CHAPTER THIRTY-FOUR

TRICIA had gathered them all in the garden for a photograph before Jake and Crystel left. It was Jake who had suggested it, telling everyone what a fine photographer she was. He seemed to want to praise her every virtue. It was the only chink in his armour.

'Chat amongst yourselves,' she said. 'I have a problem here. The light's changed.'

'Need any help?' Jake asked. Roger and Mervyn were talking together, or rather Roger was telling Mervyn about his long-term plans for the garden and Mervyn was listening. He'd looked in to say good-bye.

'No, thanks, when you want something done, do it yourself. I'm sure old Jolyon Roger had a word for it.' She got out her light-meter which she still used with her old Leica, held it up.

It had been a good weekend, and not as traumatic as she'd imagined, thinking of Jake. He was leaner, darker than she remembered, but his self-confidence sat surely on him, ready to carry him through more difficult situations than the present one, meeting a discarded lover. She recognised that her love for him was still there, but it had an autumnal feel, like the weather. Would it be dead by the winter?

They'd had a chance to talk together this morning when Crystel and Jan were indoors and Roger had taken the children in the car to fetch Wing. She was pleased with herself. Her home had supported her, and the happiness of having Jan and Crystel there.

'Crystel's in the seventh heaven,' he'd said. 'It was generous of you to include me. I thought I could best show my appreciation by accepting.'

'It took me longer than it should.'

'No hard feelings?' His eyes were travelling critically over the tawny clumps of chrysanthemums, the vivid asters, the willow tree which was beginning to lose its leaves. He would have employed a landscape gardener.

'Mine were all soft,' she'd said. 'I'm working to make them hard again.'

'Don't overdo it. It's the contrasts in your nature which make you so very special.' And then looking directly at her, turning on his charm, 'We had some good times, hadn't we?'

'Yes, we had.' Like that time on the white shag-pile in her bedroom. She still stepped over the place where they'd lain. 'It's in the past now. And meeting Crystel again has been marvellous. If I had to lose you it couldn't have been to anyone I loved more.'

He'd been touched, had taken her hand. 'I owe you a lot. More than I can ever say without saying the wrong thing.' There was the quick smile which broadened his face.

'That you met Crystel through me?'

'You're needle-sharp. We're both very happy. Right for each other. The only drawback is that she doesn't know as much about the Trust as you do.' He'd laughed. 'I've been dying to ask you since I came . . . what did you think of this year's report?'

She'd laughed with him, pleased that it was so easy. 'You've increased the pension arrangements. Don't tell me you're thinking of retiring with Crystel to south-west France?'

'No, she loves London. Although St Henri is where her heart is.' His face had softened, then livened again. 'We're on the crest of a wave, Tricia. Going public was the best thing we did. After that initial set-back the shares have been very satisfactory. God, I've missed you to talk about things! I've got several big deals pending. Nottingham is only the beginning. You really must come up to London soon . . . what are you laughing at, woman?'

'Nothing, well, us. We always did mix business with pleasure. Oh, and by the way, I see you've included the under thirty-fives in the new emolument scheme, you cunning devil.'

'The chairman deserves the best,' he'd said. His look, she thought, was affectionate and admiring. 'You're a success story,

my dear. There's a great future ahead for you in the Trust . . .'
(my dear, now, not 'my darling'). 'I've got a lot of ideas
brewing . . . we really must get together . . .' He'd stopped.
'You're laughing at me.'

'No, not really.' He didn't know her as well as he thought . . .

*   *   *

'Ready!' she called. 'Arrange yourselves casually, and prepare
to look pleasant. Roger and Jake at the back . . . where's
Mervyn? You're out of the picture. Get back there, you're
needed for balance. Now, Crystel in front. Could you group
Mark and Emma becomingly around you, Crystel? That's it.
Lovely. You sit on that stool, Jan. Wing's too heavy for you.
We don't have difficulty in keeping *him* quiet. Our two are like
jumping beans.'

'Jumping beans, jumping beans!' Mark clowned.

'Stop that! Roger, could you come nearer Jan so that you
could keep your hand on Mark's shoulder, not to look too like
a policeman, I want you to smile like a fond father.'

She adjusted the focus. This kind of weather with the mist
hanging over the lake made it difficult, but if it came out
impressionistic, so much the better. That was life . . . emerging
from the mist for a while, fading back into it. She hadn't taken
her mother's advice about Roger . . . funny that coming into
her mind at this moment. There was no rush. Her options were
as wide open as the shutter.

'Say cheese!' she called.

*   *   *

It was a failure as a photograph. Jan had her head turned and
she and Roger were gazing at each other, Crystel was leaning
against Jake, crushing her hair, Mark and Emma were blurred
because they'd moved at the last minute. The only two who

were looking straight at the camera were Wing and Mervyn. Wing with awed fascination, Mervyn with an intentness and a kind of beauty in his face . . .

She'd take another one in another ten years.

THE END

A WORLD FULL OF STRANGERS
by Cynthia Freeman

The story of a family you'll never forget! A rich, dramatic saga of passion and love, of sin and retribution, spanning three generations of family life — from the ghettos of New York to the glittering hills of San Francisco . . .

DAVID, who destroyed his past to live a life of power and glory.

KATIE, who lived with her past, whose roots and memories were too deep for her ever to be able to forget.

MARK, their son, who had the courage to struggle towards the sacred heritage his father had denied him.

MAGGIE, the successful and glamorous woman David wanted because she was everything Katie was not.

0 552 11775 7   £2.50

THE COMPANY OF WOMEN
by Mary Gordon

'Intelligent, humorous, humane . . . an exceptional achievement'

The Observer

Felicitas Taylor had been raised by her widowed mother and three closest friends under the all-pervading influence of Father Cyprian, a fiercely independent Catholic priest. But his guidance was of little help when she finally gained independence. In a desperate search for love and acceptance from her peers, she became the object of a brutal and far-reaching lesson in seduction and betrayal. Only then could Felicitas find her true self and her place in the world.

'Immensely satisfying'

The Times

'Only sleep and hunger interrupted my reading . . . it was completely gripping from beginning to end'

The Spectator

0 552 12001 4   £1.75

MISTRAL'S DAUGHTER
by Judith Krantz

Maggy, Teddy and Fauve — they were three generations of magnificent red-haired beauties born to scandal, bred to success, bound to a single extraordinary man — Julien Mistral, the painter, the genius, the lover whose passions had seared them all.

From the '20s Paris of Chanel, Colette, Picasso and Matisse to New York's sizzling new modelling agencies of the '50s, to the model wars of the '70s, *Mistral's Daughter* captures the explosive glamour of life at the top of the worlds of art and high fashion. Judith Krantz has given us a glittering international tale as unforgettable as *Scruples,* as spellbinding as *Princess Daisy.*

0 552 12392 7   £2.95

PRINCESS DAISY
by Judith Krantz

She was born Princess Marguerite Alexandrovna
Valensky. But everyone called her Daisy. She
was a blonde beauty living in a world of aristocrats
and countless wealth. Her father was a prince, a
Russian nobleman. Her mother was an American
movie goddess. Men desired her. Women envied
her. Daisy's life was a fairytale filled with parties
and balls, priceless jewels, money and love. Then,
suddenly, the fairytale ended. And Princess Daisy
had to start again, with nothing. Except the secret
she guarded from the day she was born.

0 552 11660 2   £2.95

GOLDEN HILL
by Shirley Lord

Set on the exotic island paradise of Trinidad, *Golden Hill* tells the story of three families whose destinies interweave to shape the history of the island. It is a passionate story of love and hate, lust and greed, malice and envy in which the members of the three families struggle and clash violently against the background of the depression, World War II, and the island's fight for independence.

'*Golden Hill* is indeed golden and glorious. I don't know when I've enjoyed a novel as much. It is insanely romantic and at the same time historically fascinating. It is as sensuous as a Caribbean night and the characters are memorable'
    David Brown, co-producer of *Jaws*

0 552 12346 3   £2.50

THE WATERSHED
by Erin Pizzey

'One of those unputdownable novels, to rank in that respect beside *Scruples*, *Princess Daisy* or *Lace*'

Cosmopolitan

'As a romantic saga it has a great deal more to say about human relationships than most of the big glossy bestsellers that are foisted on us'

Over 21

Rachel was an only child. Motherless. Fatherless. The unwanted result of an illicit sexual relationship. Rescued and brought up by her two maiden aunts, she grew to love and trust the world. But she was to enter womanhood, unprepared and naive . . . She marries Charles, a handsome, aspiring journalist and their marriage seems destined for success . . . until one morning, after a passionate night of love, he confesses his deception. Rachel's world is shattered. She has reached a turning point in her life — her own particular watershed.

Erin Pizzey, courageous and outspoken fighter for women's rights, draws on a profound understanding of life and love to give us a picture of the many and varied emotions of today's woman. From sexual initiation to love and marriage. The thrills and pangs of promiscuity. Adultery. Lesbianism. The intense pain of betrayal. But always the pursuit of a blissful, enduring love . . .

'Written by a woman whose understanding of human nature is rooted in painful reality'

Cosmopolitan

0 552 12462 1 £2.50

CHASING RAINBOWS
by Esther Sager

A DAZZLING STORY OF LOVE, ENDURING COURAGE AND SOARING TRIUMPH!

As small girls, the two sisters had been inseparable. Warm-hearted Libby, adored by her silver-blonde younger sister, Winna. Then a childhood accident changed her life forever . . .

But as she grew into a beautiful young woman, Libby taught herself to overcome the physical disadvantages of her handicap. Then she met Adam — cynical, disillusioned and heir to the Bainbridge millions. Just as Libby was beginning to accept his love, Winna walked back into their lives . . . And Libby found that searching for love was just like *Chasing Rainbows* . . .

0 552 11981 4 £1.75

THE DEBUTANTES
by June Flaum Singer

They are the golden girls. A quartet of blue-blooded beauties whose names and faces fill the society pages. Poor little rich girls whose glamorous exploits make international headlines — but whose tortured private lives are the hidden price of fame:

Chrissy, survivor of a notorious custody battle between her mother and her grandmother, with a fatal weakness for all the wrong men . . .

Maeve, daughter of the celebrated Padraic, and Daddy's little girl in every sense . .

Sara, whose father could hide his Jewish origins from the world, but couldn't hide his taste for lechery from his blackmailing daughter . . .

Marlena, Sara's poor cousin from the South, swept into a world of affluence she couldn't quite handle . . .

0 552 12118 5 £2.50

SISTERS AND STRANGERS
by Helen Van Slyke

Three sisters return home to celebrate their parents' Golden Wedding Anniversary. Thirty years have passed since they were together.

Alice pines to find the son she has not seen since he was born . . .

Frances returns home famous, sophisticated, rich — and jaded . . .

Barbara has wasted her youth as the mistress of a famous congressman. Will he reject her to avoid a scandal?

Within days, the lives of all the sisters will change dramatically . . .

0 552 11321 2   £1.95

A SELECTED LIST OF TITLES AVAILABLE FROM CORGI BOOKS

While every effort is made to keep prices low, it is sometimes necessary to increase prices at short notice. Corgi Books reserve the right to show new retail prices on covers which may differ from those previously advertised in the text or elsewhere.

The prices shown below were correct at the time of going to press.

ORDER FORM

All these books are available at your book shop or newsagent, or can be ordered direct from the publisher. Just tick the titles you want and fill in the form below.

CORGI BOOKS, Cash Sales Department, P.O. Box 11, Falmouth, Cornwall.

Please send cheque or postal order, no currency.

Please allow cost of book(s) plus the following for postage and packing:

U.K. Customers — Allow 55p for the first book, 22p for the second book and 14p for each additional book ordered, to a maximum charge of £1.75.

B.F.P.O. and Eire — Allow 55p for the first book, 22p for the second book plus 14p per copy for the next seven books, thereafter 8p per book.

Overseas Customers — Allow £1.00 for the first book and 25p per copy for each additional book.

NAME (Block Letters) ....

ADDRESS ....

....